ECHOES OF TIME

The Dream

We passionately long that there may be another life in which we shall be similar to what we are here below.

Marcel Proust
Remembrance of Things Past

ECHOES OF TIME

ISBN-13: 978-0-9801510-3-9
ISBN-10: 0-9801510-3-1
Library of Congress Control Number: 2008911282
Printed in the United States of America
Editor: Carole Glickfeld
Design: Steve Montiglio
Author Photograph: Robert E. Castillo

Tigress Publishing
4742 42nd Avenue SW #551
Seattle, Washington 98116-4553
www.tigresspublishing.com

Acknowledgments

A special thanks to Kristen Morris of Tigress Publishing without whose constant and invaluable aid and advice this book could never have emerged from my computer, to Carole L. Glickfeld, the best editor a writer could have, and to Steve Montiglio for his incredible artistic talents on the layout and cover design.

Above all, it must be said that this book would never come to pass if not for the unflagging encouragement and support of my friends and family and I am deeply grateful for their patience and devotion.

TABLE OF CONTENTS

PROLOGUE

During the sixteenth, seventeenth and eighteenth centuries, the Caribbean was the center of some of the richest maritime trade in the world. But the voyage to and from the New World was a hazardous undertaking. Thousands of ships were lost at sea.

Treasure from the New World was of great importance to Spain and other European nations because it provided nearly 95% of the precious metals upon which their monetary systems were based.

At the beginning of the eighteenth century, Spain experienced the traumas of change in her ruling dynasty. The last Hapsburg to occupy the Spanish throne, Charles II, died in 1700. The following year, Philip of Anjou, the grandson of King Louis XIV of France, succeeded to the Spanish throne. A war of succession ensued among Austria, England and Holland.

In 1708, the Spanish war of succession ended with the French Bourbon becoming King of Spain. The monarchy desperately required an immediate injection of funds. For six long years Spain had suspended shipments of gold, silver and other valuables from her colonies in order to prevent their capture or destruction by enemy fleets. Now an armada of seventeen Spanish ships loaded with gold bars, disks, coins, silver ingots, emeralds and other precious stones was ready to embark for Spain.

The *Capitana San José,* a 64-gun flagship, carried the bulk of the treasure. The remainder was placed in the fleet's other heavily armed ships, the 64-gun *Armiranta San Martin* and the 44-gun *Galléon Gobierno.* Late in May of 1708, the fleet departed from the Panamanian port of Portobelo. The Spanish admiral was aware that the British navy lurked in the Caribbean looking for him. "*The sea is wide*" was his parting comment.

The British were closer than he thought. Six nautical miles

away from Little Brew or Pequeña Barú (today named Rosario Islands), northwest of Cartagena, four heavily armed British ships awaited him: the 70-gun *H.M.S. Expedition,* the 60-gun *H.M.S. Kingston,* the 50-gun *H.M.S. Portland,* and the fire ship *H.M.S. Vulture.*

The Spanish Armada arrived in the vicinity of the Rosario Islands late in the evening of May 27, 1708. Rather than risk a nighttime passage through Boca Chica, the narrow southern entrance to Cartagena, they anchored off the Baru Peninsula to say evening prayers. This delay allowed the British to sight the Spanish fleet around noon the next day. Immediately, they made sail to intercept and engage the Spaniards.

Realizing they could not reach the port of Cartagena, the Spanish fleet sailed west towards the British. The two were within a mere mile of each other as they maneuvered in light winds. Around 16:30 hours the battle began, raging well into the night. Heavily out-gunned, the Spanish suffered catastrophically.

At 19:30 the British Commander, Charles Wagner, prepared to board the *San José,* which had taken at least 250 cannon balls in her hull and rigging. But before his ship could reach the *San José,* she suddenly blew up, showering the crew of the *Expedition* with slivers of wood, and quickly sank. Only eleven crewmembers of the *San José* survived. The *Gobierno* fought on. But on May 29, following a bloody battle with the *Expedition,* the Spanish *galléon* surrendered its three hundred men and yielded its treasure of gold bullion and silver bars into British hands.

The *San José* carried the single most valuable cargo ever shipped from the New World, with an estimated value that ranges from $3.5 to $10 billion in today's dollars. It lay lost and out of reach for 300 years at the bottom of the Caribbean off the coast of Colombia. Her manifest survives in the Archive of Indies in Seville, its history shrouded in mystery.

"I must go down to the seas again, to the lonely sea and the sky.
And all I ask is a tall ship and a star to steer her by."

John Masefield (1878-1967)
(English Poet Laureate, 1930-1967)

AT nine o'clock in the morning a silvery flash of airplanes circled Madrid's Barajas International airport waiting to land. The great roar of planes as they took off drowned out conversation and rattled the windows of the passenger terminal.

A tall, broad-shouldered man, hidden behind a grey raincoat and felt hat, made his way through the crowd and walked up to the large plate glass window that overlooked the runway. He was followed by a round-bellied priest with a plum-like face and crooked yellow teeth. Eyeglasses with one chipped lens rested on the tip of his nose

Both looked attentively at an electronic screen. Lufthansa Flight LH4262 from Frankfurt flashed on the screen. Simultaneously loudspeakers announced its arrival.

The two men hurried to the passengers' exit door, each holding a color photograph of a light-haired man about forty, with lively eyes and a resolute expression. They were careful to stay out of sight as they watched the traveling salesmen, tourists, couples on their honeymoon and monks walk toward the terminal, until the stream trickled down to a few passengers. A young Moroccan couple, the wife cradling a girl, the husband dragging a suitcase, passed between them. Both men were silent.

The priest frowned, and when he spoke with a faint East

European accent, his voice was choked. "There is no sign of our man."

His cohort snapped, "What is the problem? There are still passengers on the tarmac." A smile came and went.

The priest gave him a cold look, and his lips trembled. Wiping his brow with a handkerchief, the tall, broad-shouldered man gazed down on the priest and smiled again with one side of his face; the other was almost immobile because of his broad scar.

The Iberia Boeing 707 flight from Kennedy Airport was gliding out of the stacked-up traffic pattern. It had been a long flight, and Robert Hamilton was exhausted but elated.

In the terminal, the arrival of Flight IB6250 flashed on the screen. Robert carried very little luggage, and he was quickly ushered through Customs. He walked rapidly, a garment bag and his suit jacket slung over his shoulder, the breeze lifting his blue necktie. The automatic glass doors slid back as he passed through into the meeting hall.

"Look. Our man from Frankfurt just came out. Follow him and don't lose him," the broad-shouldered man said to the priest. The priest glanced at the photograph, then to the man going through the door. He was tall, with the most handsome smile and ocean blue eyes; his lean, muscular body reflected someone who kept himself in prime physical condition.

Robert snaked across the crowded hall and progressed into the prematurely hot, moist and sticky air of Madrid. Behind him, the priest limped slightly. Robert stopped a moment, then headed for the first cab in the line of taxis. He noticed the priest staring at him for some reason with impassive eyes. Robert climbed into the back of the smoke-filled taxicab and announced his destination. The driver lowered his tabloid newspaper and pulled away from the curb.

The highway was not crowded, and they made good time until they reached the traffic-choked streets of Madrid. Robert looked as his watch. It was eleven o'clock in the morning. Finally, they drove down the tree-lined avenue and a few minutes later pulled into the forecourt of the Hotel Balboa.

The porter took Robert's luggage as he climbed out of the cab. A young man burst out from the hotel lobby and onto the street, nearly knocking Robert down. He was chased by a man who was older but looked equally as agile.

Seconds later, when the older man was practically on his heels, the younger man turned. There was a quick flash as sunlight glanced off the knife before the older man plunged it into the younger man's chest. Staggering, the young man collapsed to the ground.

Robert froze. His limbs would not obey him. He had drawn breath to shout just as a passenger climbed out of another cab and stepped in front of the victim. It was none other than the priest he had seen an hour before at the airport! The priest knelt in front of the man lying in a heap, blood spurting like a fountain from the middle of his chest.

Robert looked around. In the confusion the man with the knife had disappeared. A crowd gathered around, talking, shouting, exclaiming; the priest seemed at a loss and kept repeating: "What a misfortune! Good Lord, what a misfortune!"

Hearing the approaching howl of police sirens, Robert moved wearily away, shaken, but too jet-lagged to register the reality of this bizarre event. There was nothing he could do. And there was the porter, waving to Robert from the lobby of the Balboa. Robert entered the hotel.

Standing behind the counter, the concierge gave him a troubled look. After registering, Robert walked up the wide staircase, took the elevator and got out on the third floor. At the far end of a whitewashed, low-ceilinged corridor, he unlocked a wooden door. A single steel-frame bed with an old mattress and a ragged red blanket stood in the room. The only light came from one small window behind a table. With the lights switched on, he saw unframed posters of El Greco paintings hung on stucco walls, a night table with a jug of water and two glasses, and a modern telephone. Robert lowered his suitcase next to the wall behind the bed, his face wet with perspiration, his body ragged with fatigue. He pushed the window open and looked down on the unfamiliar street below. The rising spire of a Catholic church towered over nearby rooftops. He listened for sirens, but could hear no street noise. The whole hideous incident might never have happened. Perhaps it hadn't happened. Perhaps he was just over tired. Fatigue spread through him. He sank into the bed, closed his eyes and slept at once.

One thousand miles to the northeast, in Frankfurt, Germany, Adolf Fritz paced his office at the headquarters of Pharma Frankfuter. He glanced at his watch impatiently when the phone on the desk rang. Fritz reached for it. A woman's voice said, "I have Berthold Beitz from Madrid on the line."

"Hello, Mr. Fritz," the voice boomed over the phone.

"What took you so long? I have better things to do than stand around waiting for your call. What's going on with Müller and Wenninger?"

"Wenninger arrived in Madrid two days ago and checked into the Balboa Hotel. This morning I tracked Müller from the airport to the same hotel. Our men searched Wenninger's room, but Wenninger's son surprised them while they were at it. Apparently things went out of control and the kid had to be eliminated. The police escorted Wenninger himself to the station; we dared not follow. He hasn't yet returned to the hotel. We seized some papers but nothing of significance. Müller must have the important ones. By the way, he's registered under the name of Robert Hamilton."

Fritz fought to keep his voice calm. "Are you certain he is Müller?"

"Yes, Mr. Fritz, I checked his face against the photograph. The hotel clerk confirmed that when Müller registered he put Seville as his next destination. When the clerk asked what he was going to do there, Müller responded that he was doing research at the Archive of the Indies. So there's no question about it. Besides, he's in Wenninger's hotel, as I said."

"Listen to me very carefully, Beitz," said Fritz. "I want you to go to the Balboa immediately and stand watch outside to make certain that you don't lose track of him. You are not to go inside. If he leaves the hotel, trail him at a distance and stay out of sight. Is that clear? Keep me posted at least once a day."

"*Ja wohl.*" Beitz replaced the receiver.

Robert awakened to the distant sound of church bells. He glanced at the clock. He bathed, changed and half an hour later stepped outside onto the pavement. Only a small brown stain on the curb gave any clue to what had happened hours before. People strolled by; a pedestrian shouted for a taxi.

He walked through light rain along the unhurried streets of Madrid, the first European city he had ever visited. Like New York, it was a national melting pot. Seven o'clock was apparently the time to go shopping in the large stores around Calle de Alcala. People crowded around small craftsmen, and fashionable shops lined the streets.

From the Plaza Mayor, a great square in the heart of Madrid, he walked toward the Calle Segovia near San Joseph's church. The Café Galeón was crowded with people sitting at little tables with half empty cups of coffee. Blond, sunburned Germans, Scandinavians, and Frenchman with shirts open at the neck smoked, gestured, and talked with endless enthusiasm. In the back of the café was a dark, spacious dining room with only a few customers.

As Robert ordered his dinner, a bespectacled man entered the room, swollen belly first. He was all ungainly limbs, with a plum-like face, and short, grizzled hair. His pallid face had the wrinkled toughness of bleached leather. He reminded Robert of a drill sergeant.

As the man sat down at a corner table, Robert recognized him. The priest! The one with the crooked yellow teeth. The man he had last seen bending over the bleeding youth! But he was not wearing the cassock. In street clothes, he looked like a stevedore just up from the docks. But for the hard glitter of his eyes and a familiar limp, Robert might have not recognized him.

The priest ordered a Jerez with an odd accent. Was he an East European and if so, what was he doing here in Madrid? Once, when their eyes met, the priest smiled crookedly at him and dove into his food with gusto. At the next table, two Mediterranean men sat, drinking sherry, speaking in low, intimate tones.

After paying his bill, Robert walked towards his hotel. Around him the darkness hugged the streets and an ominous stillness enveloped Madrid. A few blocks before he arrived at the Balboa, something or somebody was moving about in the dark close enough that Robert could feel the cold air sliding down his skin. He heard steps again, coming up behind him. He turned sharply. One of the Mediterranean men from the restaurant was behind him in the distance. Robert took a deep breath. What was going on?

He turned abruptly into an alley and increased his pace. A low voice murmured in the shadows: "Müller! Müller!" He looked around; a silhouette was closing in on him, running swiftly. Robert sprinted away, heart pumping, breathing heavily. He glanced back but saw nothing but darkness. All was silence behind him. In front, the street lamps, traffic, inebriated pedestrians··· His pursuer had disappeared.

THE next morning at La Atocha, the beautiful train station that raises its magnificent iron framework arches over an inner tropical garden, Robert bought a ticket for the next train to Seville. He had only a few minutes. He ran to his gate and jumped onto the AVE, a high-speed train as it began to roll. From his window seat he saw few people. The train passed a row of semi-detached houses and buildings, entered a tunnel, and after a minute in complete darkness, shot wonderfully into an open meadow with grazing cows and hundreds of olive trees. Robert was enchanted by the scenery of roses, dahlias and lilies that crowded the tiny gardens of the stationmasters, the old villages and the flat central plateau of the Castilian *meseta*. After a few minutes, he could see the soft silhouette of the Sierra Morena mountain range, which floated beneath the clouds.

At the snack bar, he ordered a bottle of wine, and asked for the *tapas* menu. The waiter was just serving wine and bread when a group of French tourists filled the car. A few minutes later a middle-aged man came in, walked directly to Robert's table and asked if Robert minded sharing the table with him, since there were no more tables available. Robert nodded hesitantly. The man's close-set, blue eyes were hard and wary, but his manner was cordial. His receding gray hair and toothbrush mustache gave him the look of a traveling salesman. After a minute of small talk, he abruptly asked Robert if he was in the pharmaceutical industry. Robert frowned. "No, my business is in education."

The stranger held out his hand and introduced himself as Gustav Halder from Düsseldorf. Then he reached into his pocket, pulled out a brown envelope, and said, "You know, I have material here that would be very useful to you in your work." He hesitated before handing Robert the envelope. "I'll tell you about an incident that occurred only the other day and I can vouch for its truth. An industrialist went to Madrid to investigate a story for his company, and he decided to bring his older son along. He had some very important documents with him, which he kept in a dispatch case. They were very important, indeed. A day or two after he arrived, he stayed in his room to recover from a cold. The chambermaid entered his room at noon, and offered him a drink 'compliments of the house.' He fell deeply asleep shortly afterwards. While he slept, two men entered the room to search for the dispatch case, but the industrialist's young son showed up. When he saw the intruders, he ran. One of the intruders overtook him and stabbed him to death." Halder finished and looked at Robert directly. "Dramatic, isn't it?"

"Is that what happened the other day?"

"Yesterday, as a matter of fact," Halder responded. "There's just one thing I think you ought to know before I leave, Mr. Müller, and don't forget it. If you do well, you'll get no thanks from Leverkusen, and if you get into trouble you'll get no help. Does that suit you?"

"You are talking to the wrong man," Robert replied.

"I wish you good afternoon and *bon voyage*." Halder rose.

As soon as the train came to a stop, Halder hurried to the exit door. Through the window, Robert saw him on the station platform before he disappeared from view.

Robert paid for his meal and returned to his compartment. A man occupied the window seat, perspiring heavily. Robert sat down slowly. "When are we due to arrive in Seville?" the man asked as the train gathered speed. "At 2:30, the next and last station," Robert said. His heart thumped as he recognized one of the two Mediterranean men he had seen at the Galeón Café. Sitting beside the stranger, he kept all his attention on the stiff and lightweight sealed envelope in his pocket.

THE Hotel Taberna Del Alabardero in Zaragoza Street stood in the heart of Seville's commercial and community center, only a few feet away from the cathedral and within walking distance from the Plaza de Toros and the Guadalquivir River. The assistant manager escorted Robert to his room. "Each of the rooms has its own name," he told Robert, bowing politely. "Yours is the Cordoba. I trust that will be satisfactory."

Robert walked over to the window, which afforded a view of the Guadalquivir. "This will be fine, thank you."

He sat down on his bed, trying to still the racing of his heart. He took the envelope from his jacket pocket and opened it. It contained a sheet of white paper without letterhead. The words screamed up at him:

"Mr. Müller, you have had a brilliant career with your company. We know that you love your wife Elsa and your son Helmut and want them safe in Essen. We do not want anything to happen to you or to your family. Please convey this message to your Board of Directors: Keep out of the rainforest."

Robert stared at the letter. What on earth was going on? Was he in danger? Was this threat to Müller directed to him by mistake? He did not want to be responsible for the fate of the Müller family, but how could he prevent it? Should he leave town early the next morning and continue his intended trip to Bangkok without seeing Seville? But if he left the next day without seeing the Archive he would never forgive himself.

After a sleepless night he rose at dawn and ran water for a bath. The water was just short of scalding hot and he gradually let himself down into it. He remained there in deep meditation, then came to a decision and reached forward to pull the plug. He would solve the mystery, unravel the enigma. He had sought adventure and adventure had landed in his lap. He would continue around the world after he had cleared up this confusion. He did not want to be responsible for any harm that might come to Mr. Müller's family. He'd stay in Seville until those shadows reappeared, and he would confront them.

As a historian, Robert knew that Seville, Spain's fourth largest city and the capital of Andalucia, had a long and noble past. Conquered by the Romans, it had given the world two great emperors, Trojan and Hadrian. The Moors had held Seville, lying on the banks of the Guadalquivir, for more than five hundred years. Their architectural influence was everywhere evident, in its minarets, fountains, the great Alcazar and gardens that stood amid Renaissance, Mediterranean and Baroque architecture. The monuments of Seville lived side by side with a profusion of dynamic, modern structures.

He extracted a map and a note from his briefcase, put them in his pocket and left the hotel. He was caressed by the soft fragrance of the spring wind. His path took him past whitewashed houses, bright with bougainvillea, ocher-colored palaces with baroque facades, courtyards and mini-patios wreathed with trembling lattice-works of grapevines and jasmine bushes. He followed an empty road toward Sierpes Street to find St. Joseph's Chapel. Gradually the light fog, which had hung over the city, grew denser. After a quarter of an hour he realized that he no longer knew where he was. Suddenly everything looked alike. He wandered, peering at the doorways and street signs until a small wind sprang up and the fog began to lift and roll like a noiseless, ghostly sea. A curious Gregorian chant threaded the stillness, without direction, without source. The street was empty except for him. The sound came again, higher now. The fog parted and he saw a baroque chapel before him. Next to it stood a two-story brick house with stone relief, horseshoe-shaped in the Mudejar style, from the seventeenth century. At the top of the door he read: *20 Calle Sierpes*. He knocked.

A small woman in her fifties, with dark hair and a black dress, opened the door. The scent of orange blossom and jasmine impregnated Robert's senses like a cloud.

"*Señor*?"

"Good afternoon. My name is Robert Hamilton. May I speak with Father Pedro?"

"Do you have an appointment?"

"Yes. Mrs. Pilar de la Escasura from the Archive of the Indies arranged it."

The dark woman led Robert to a patio with a stone fountain in its center and neat rows of flowerpots. Soon, a young man came and bowed politely. "Mr. Hamilton, I am Guillermo Olano, Father Pedro's assistant. He'll be with you in a few minutes. Please come into his study."

The study was Spartan clean with a stone floor, brick walls, low beams, and a long, old, wooden table surrounded by seventeenth century leather armchairs with faded designs. Above a fireplace was a three-quarter-life-size painting of Christ. A huge wrought iron candelabrum hung overhead. A very large tapestry, depicting Charles V in the Escorial beside the Empress Isabel and Queen Leonora of Portugal, covered one of the whitewashed walls.

"I understand you are a historian," said a pleasant voice from the door behind him. Father Pedro was a sturdy, broad-shouldered fellow. He had a ruddy complexion, which neither the heat of southern Spain nor his age had affected. His hair was gray and thick, turning to white, with a trace of brown. He was in good health. His blue eyes twinkled. Robert guessed he was over seventy and in good health, like a well-fed, rubicund monk in an Old Dutch painting. His monastic life had given him an air of peace and calm.

"Father Pedro, thank you for seeing me. I understand from Mrs. Escasura that you are a well respected and eminent historian. My academic specialty is comparative literature and history. I've spent eighteen years teaching history in a private college."

"Yes, Mr. Hamilton, I know from Pilar that you are very interested in the eighteenth century. She and I were colleagues at the Archive of Indies." Father Pedro looked at Robert intently. "Let's sit down near the fireplace. May I offer you a *vino de pasas* produced in this region?"

"Yes, it would be lovely."

An old woman appeared. "Yes, Father."

"Two glasses." Father Pedro smiled at Robert. "First, I want you to know that I welcome you to my home because you are a historian and because Pilar asked me to assist you in your research."

"I know that the Archive of the Indies is the necessary starting point for any serious worker in Spanish colonial history. That's why I am here."

The old woman brought the wine on a tray. Father Pedro cleared his throat. "Tell me a little about yourself, Mr. Hamilton. When I saw you, you reminded me of a handsome American movie actor whose name escapes me."

"Thank you for the compliment." Robert shrugged. "But I am only a history professor."

It was easy to talk to this kind, attentive man, and before long, Robert heard the details of his life spilling from his own lips. He told Father Pedro about his boyhood in a small New England town, his love for the sea, his protected life at Harvard, his academic life as a historian, and the terrible boating accident that had robbed him of his beloved wife and son.

"And now?" Father Pedro prodded gently. "You are, perhaps, eager to escape from the confines of a calm and ordered life with its inescapable associations of tragedy. Do you wish to throw yourself into new lands, new ideas, and new associations?"

"Yes. That and a longstanding interest I wish to indulge. I want to spend a few weeks learning more about the Spanish *galleóns* that transported treasures from the Americas to Spain. I became fascinated when I learned that one of the most important sectors of the Castilian economy was that of the Indies trade. I'm intrigued to think that many of the treasures bound to Spain lie at the bottom of the sea." He sipped his drink before continuing. I took a two-year sabbatical leave from teaching to do research in Spain and to see the world, which I know only through books and movies. Asia and the Pacific of Joseph Conrad and Somerset Maugham have always fascinated me—romantics and soldiers of fortune, rebel souls with a mysterious past, artists in search of paradise—and here I am, Father Pedro, telling you about my past and my dreams and we've only met. But I feel you understand me."

Father Pedro clapped his hands together. "We have many things in common. We have each traveled extensively through our readings, we like history and from what I can see, you are a man who could become a friend. May I call you Robert?"

"Of course, I would be honored."

"If I were you, Robert, I would remain in Seville three or four weeks so that you can do your research and at the same time see the city and study a little of its history. If you came by train you may have seen the banks of the Guadalquivir River lined with cotton and rice fields, orange groves, stud farms, and bull ranches. This is a land with a proud seafaring history. The career of Christopher Columbus can be traced right to here, from the monastery at La Rábida. Their friars pleaded his cause with Queen Isabella, to Palos, where he set sail on his epic voyage of 1492. Our shores and rivers echo with the names of maritime adventurers like Ferdinand Magellan and Sir Francis Drake.

For more than two centuries, Spain's trade with the New World centered on Seville. Treasures from the Americas flowed into her coffers. Seville hosted Expo '92, to observe the five hundredth anniversary of Columbus' discovery. Next week the *Sevillanos*, clad in Flamenco costumes, will take to the streets to participate in the greatest parade of the year, the *Feria de Abril*. There will be bullfighting, fireworks displays, and all-night singing and dancing of *Sevillanos* in the *casetas* of the fairgrounds."

A bell rang softly in the distance. Father Pedro put down his wine glass and rose. "Please excuse me, but time has passed very quickly and I have to go to evening prayers. I shall be very pleased to meet with you again tomorrow and the following day to talk history, our favorite subject, and to have your observations of our beautiful city."

"That would suit me very well if it suits you, Father Pedro," Robert replied.

"I will ask Mr. Olano, my assistant, to show you my house and the monastery, if you have the time."

The monastery consisted of a simple, four-sided group of stone buildings around a cloister dominated by St. Joseph's Chapel. There were thirty monks, praying in the chapel and living in the cloisters. Father Pedro's house was part of the complex of buildings, with an independent entrance from the street and with a back door that opened to a high-walled garden.

"Father Pedro has put in his time at the monastery and is very much respected, appreciated, and venerated," Mr. Olano told Robert. "He worked as a director for three years and as curator of the Archive of the Indies for three decades. Before that he was a historian, teacher, and author of history books." The young man escorted Robert to the door. "Take the opportunity of seeing Seville, but I need to warn you about crime. We have high unemployment and we're close to the drug trafficking ports. Don't think you're safe on a crowded street. Be careful. Have a pleasant evening."

Robert walked in the direction of his hotel through dense air heavy with moisture. Again the many courtyards, alleyways, secluded streets and hidden corners threatened to disorient him. In a garden he came upon a woman sitting on a bench of Moorish tiles, like those in the gardens of the Alcazar, working at some embroidery in the dimness of the evening. She looked up quickly, evidently taken aback to see a stranger, and gave Robert an inquiring stare. He bowed, smiled, and was gratified to see her features soften.

ROBERT learned from the desk clerk of the hotel that one week before his arrival Seville had celebrated Holy Week, when the vivacity and color of the city were at their most intense, when the lacerated Christ and bejeweled weeping Virgins of the city's twenty-four parishes were paraded through the street on floats borne by barefoot penitents.

The next day, Robert left his hotel at 9 a.m. and walked towards the Archive of the Indies. *Sevillanos* clad in Flamenco costumes had started celebrating the *Feria de Abril*, the greatest parade of the year. It was the last morning of the bullfights and thirty thousand visitors had swarmed into the city from all over the world. Tourists packed cafés and hotels to watch the noisy, colorful parades and listen to the music of the marching bands. Astride prancing steeds, men wore broad-brimmed hats and *Andalusian* riding gear, their women riding sidesaddle behind them in long flouncy dresses. Flowing through the streets, the procession looked like a river of rainbows. Exploding firecrackers running along poles and wires added to the impression that Seville was a town gone mad.

Robert approached a man and in his best Spanish asked for directions to the Archive. To his surprise the man was American and answered in English. Swaying slightly, he apologized for being drunk. The previous night there had been fireworks and all-night dancing by the *Sevillanos*. From midnight until morning many visitors stayed awake, drinking and singing and making love, too excited to sleep. The April fair was an immense show of sensuality, bright and multicolored. It permeated the sense of smell with the fragrance of double carnations, the stranger told Robert; it satisfied the palate with wine, sherry, ham, and seafood or paella; it cheered the ear with the beat of the guitar; it seduced like the smoothness of a woman's skin in the spring. Delighted, Robert decided to find his own way to the Archive.

As the day wore on, the sun became a hot furnace beating on Robert's shoulders, baking the earth, the sky a deep, cloudless blue. Filled with a sense of contentment and even anticipation, caught from the joyous celebration that seem to surround him, he walked down the ancient cobbled streets with little on his mind but the beauty of the day, the country, and the Spanish people. As he passed a café in the *Plaza de la Alianza*, he noticed a tanned girl in a light spring dress with a red, patent leather belt around her waist. She stood resting one hand on a round table, and in the other she held a straw hat. She wore stockings and fine, buckled white shoes with high heels. She was talking to a man seated behind her in the café. Robert stopped. She was a lovely girl with delicate features, slender legs, and a wonderful figure. There was a European elegance about her; the way she stood, the way she carried her head, the graceful lift of her hand. She had magnificent green eyes and a complexion that he could only call peach-like. Because she was talking with her partner, she did not notice him and he had time to recover and walk into the café.

He sat down in a corner near the girl, and was about to order coffee when he suddenly caught a glimpse of her partner's face. It was the German, Halder! The man he had met on the train! Robert's mouth went dry. With a sinking feeling in his stomach he found himself back in the street walking faster and faster, fighting a desire to run for his life. He told himself that no one was looking for him, that Halder had not seen him. But such argument was useless. He could not get over it. The horror of that dangerous man with that beautiful girl pursued him through the street. That they were even on speaking terms was an abomination, a shadow on the beauty of the day, and even worse, a mockery of what was pure and beautiful.

It was 6 p.m. He had been out all afternoon. Robert passed through the bar-lounge of his hotel crowded with fashionable people. Their exuberant conversation almost drowned out the strident din of a jazz orchestra. When he asked for his key at the front desk, the porter told him that a young man had been asking for him. A Mr. Guillermo Olano. Just then, the young man came to him with outstretched hands, seized Robert's hand and shook it warmly.

"How nice to see you again, Mr. Hamilton!" He was well dressed with a blue blazer with gold buttons and gray flannel trousers. "Father Pedro sent me to tell you he would like to meet at the same time on Thursday rather than tomorrow, because of an unexpected matter. He asked me to tell you that, if you'd like, I can be your guide at the Archive of the Indies. "

"I'd be delighted. Won't you have a glass of Jerez with me?" At a corner table of the elegant patio Guillermo told Robert that he had been born in Colombia to a Spanish mother and a Colombian father. While attending a college associated with St. Joseph's Seminary, he was working as an assistant to Father Pedro. Soon, Guillermo looked at his watch and said he had to go.

Robert thanked him for his visit and his offer to be his guide. "See you tomorrow, then. Good night."

The next morning they met in front of the thick stone walls of the Archive of the Indies beside Seville's cathedral with its graceful Giralda tower, not far from the Guadalquivir River. They climbed a wide, pink marble staircase to the office of Mrs. Pilar de la Escasura in the Reference Department.

Robert thanked her for her help in putting him in contact with Father Pedro. She gave Robert a temporary researcher's card and directed him to the Reading Room, which had seats for thirty researchers at ornate tables. Except for the faint whisper of turned pages and occasional cough, the room was silent. Out in the corridor, Guillermo told Robert that the Archive of the Indies was one of the world's most important repositories. It contained the story of Castile's prodigious expansion into America and its four hundred years of Colonial rule. Robert knew it was vast but he marveled that forty thousand bundles of carefully preserved and guarded documents, fifty million pages, awaited the researcher.

At home he had read up on the Archive, and knew it was set up in 1784 when the King ordered the transfer of literally countless wrapped bundles of yellowed papers, called *legajo*s, from the Simancas archive to Seville in the old Bureau of Trade Building. Although most of Simancas's *legajos* were moved, some were left behind at the former repository.

"During his extensive research throughout Spain, Father Pedro discovered nearly a thousand bundles still at Simancas, many with erroneous titles," Guillermo said.

"Father Pedro told me one day," Guillermo continued, "that if a team of a hundred researchers spent their whole lives searching through the more than 250,000 large *legajos* in the Archives of Indies, he doubted they could locate all the important documents. The majority are not catalogued, and about twenty percent of those shipped from Simancas in 1784 have never been opened."

"Is it difficult to read the old language?" asked Robert.

Guillermo's face lit up. "During my first year with Father Pedro I became fairly acquainted with the Archive's organization and made considerable headway on my dissertation. The language of the Spanish documents has not changed significantly since colonial times. Anyone fluent in modern Spanish can, by adding some older words to his vocabulary, understand the language of sixteenth, seventeenth and eighteen-century documents. But the scripts and the age of the documents offer serious barriers."

"When I asked Father Pedro about the history of Spanish

galleóns, he seemed very interested," remarked Robert.

"As a director, he spent years in search of lost eighteenth century Spanish *galleóns*, in which I believe he is now the foremost expert." Guillermo smiled. "If you befriend Father Pedro, perhaps you could persuade him to talk to you on the subject, Mr. Hamilton. Many people have tried to get information concerning this, but Father refuses. I believe he does not trust the inquirers."

Their tour went on until midday, when Robert invited him to continue their conversation at a restaurant. Guillermo led him to Enrique Becerro. "The food here is simple but very good."

After ordering salmon, Guillermo told him that some of the pages display chains of joined, rounded letters called *procesal,* which look like a frieze of Arabic characters above the arched doorways of a mosque. "Only a practiced reader can pick Spanish words out of the endless curves of that writing," he said. "Other writing is Gothic in appearance, while countless pages feature an illegible curved scrawl. And there are scores of archaic abbreviation."

When they had finished eating, Guillermo returned to the seminary. Robert walked directly to the Reading Room to research the *conquistadores*. He wanted to find out who made up the handful of sailors and soldiers who had carved out an empire for Charles V, upon which the sun never set. Shortly after asking for the material on the conquerors of gold, the *portero* dropped a packet tied with a faded light khaki ribbon on the table. It seemed to Robert that it took hours to untie the ribbon, which was knotted through a hole in the upper left corner of the documents. When the bundle finally lay open, Robert scanned the pages. The documents were written by hand on linen paper with ink made from oak galls. Time and the elements had stained and faded some of them. The ink had bled through from the opposite page, forcing Robert to try to follow a sentence through a tangle of crossed words.

The effort was worthwhile because the documents were rich in detail. Robert read for almost two hours about members of good families who had cut loose from their moorings; career officers, including some who had been cashiered, functionaries, guilty of minor indiscretions, noblemen with debts, poets and adventures—it was a motley crew. Honest peasants rubbed shoulders with convicts. The majority were either Estremadurans or Andalusians. The event that greatly impressed Robert was the fall of Granada.

At 3 p.m. Robert looked up. At the next table sat the beautiful girl he had seen the day before in the café! She was bent over her reading, unaware that he was staring at her. Except for the archivist on duty, they were alone in the room. Robert hardly dared to breathe. When the *portero* came and spoke to her in a low voice, Robert could not hear what he said, but he heard her low, educated English voice reply, "Tell him that I will see him in ten minutes." She continued to read. Robert could not go back to his work; he could barely take his eyes off her. A growing need to speak to her robbed him of concentration. Oddly enough, the place gave him a sense of intimacy, and when he was about to risk breaking the silence, he felt his dry throat constrict, choking on the words he couldn't say. She stood up, collected her material, and without a glance in his direction, returned the material to the *portero* and left the Reading Room.

On the table where the girl had been sitting Robert noticed a beautiful, expensive gold pen with the letters A.L. engraved on it. With the pen in his hand, he raced down the pink marble staircase, until he saw the girl in the white dress coming towards him. She looked at him appreciatively. "Thank you for retrieving it. It's only a pen but it has a sentimental value." Her eyes, intense green, froze him to the spot.

"I had a feeling it might be important. It's very lovely," Robert managed. She smiled quickly and turned away. All he wanted was to look at her. And the pleasure in looking at her, simply looking at her, was rather like the pleasure of a boy looking across a classroom at a girl who has no idea he is watching her. His eyes followed her until she left the building.

All the way back to his hotel he berated himself for his stiff schoolboy awkwardness. He would never forgive himself for not starting a meaningful conversation. It would serve him right if he never saw her again.

CANDLES in ancient candlesticks cast evocative shadows on the ceiling and walls of the study. Father Pedro and Robert sat on either side of the stone fireplace, a mahogany table between them. On Father Pedro's side were documents, books and ancient maps beside a jug of wine and two glasses.

"I suggested changing our meeting because I thought it wise for you to visit the Archive before we met again, and also to give me time to prepare some material for you." Father Pedro seemed pleased with his little plan, "The other day you indicated, Robert, interest in the history of eighteenth century Spain and in shipwrecks lost in the Western Hemisphere."

"That's right."

"Here is a very relevant article in the *London Sunday Times*."

Robert took the paper.

A secret salvage operation to recover the cargo of the Spanish galleón San José, worth US 3.75 billion at today's valuation, has been assembled on the Caribbean island of Baru, near the Colombian port of Cartagena.

In Cartagena, it is believed that certain officials of an international firm have an interest in the venture. On Friday the president of the firm (who asked not to be named) emphatically denied that they had anything to do with the operation.

There is nothing mysterious about the San José. Her manifest, now in the marine Archive in Seville, shows her to have been bound for Spain in 1708 carrying 116 steel chests of Colombian emeralds and thirty million gold coins, in addition to a very valuable cargo consigned "secretly" to the King of Spain, Charles II—the most valuable cargo ever shipped from the New World.

Her cargo was common knowledge even before she sailed. A British task force commanded by Rear Admiral Charles Wager, flying his flag on the 70-gun H.M.S. Expedition, accompanied by the gunship Kingston, commanded by Captain Timothy Bridges, and the 50-gun ship Portland, commanded by Captain Edward Windsor, was sent to capture her.

Wager engaged the San José and her seven escorts, but a lucky shot hit the galléon's magazine and she exploded. The rest of the Spanish fleet escaped because neither Bridges nor Windsor "pressed their action," as Wager ordered.

Both officers were subsequently court-martialed and dismissed. Wager's consolation prize was a frigate full of cocoa beans.

"It is a remarkable story," mused Father Pedro. "During the past few years I have researched this topic. It all began when at the Archive we started receiving inquiries from various governmental agencies in Colombia, as well as from international companies."

"I confess that I am fascinated," Robert said.

Father Pedro hunched forward, his wine glass cupped lightly in his fingertips. He looked down as if engrossed in his thoughts. "This is the first time I have been prepared to share my research, but I feel we can help each other unlock the secret of the *San José's* cargo."

"You honor me with your trust and hospitality," Robert replied.

Father Pedro gave him a description of the context. At the beginning of the sixteenth century the main flow of Spain's wealth had been silver from Mexico. Then Pizarro and his *conquistadores* conquered Peru. The great incentive for expansion was the search for precious metals. After the *conquistadores* stripped the temples and tombs of the Indians, they sought the source of the treasure in the fertile valleys, the desert coastlands, the mountain ranges, and the jungles, opening areas they would otherwise avoid. The Spanish discovered a veritable mountain of silver at Potosi in present-day Bolivia, which produced enormous amounts of precious metal for Spain for half a century. They also discovered other mines of gold, silver, and mercury in the New World, and poured immense wealth back into Europe, right up to the nineteen century. To transport all these riches back to Europe, the Spaniards depended on the Spanish treasure fleets.

Father Pedro said, "The conquest of America opened up enormous economic possibilities. From the end of the sixteenth century, Spain received from its colonies large quantities of precious metals, jewels, dye wood, tobacco, and animal pelts, to say nothing of spices, vanilla, cocoa, and indigo. For over three hundred years, *galleóns* of the Spanish kings continuously plied the Atlantic Ocean and the Caribbean Sea, carrying needed European products to America and returning with Peruvian and Colombian gold.

"During the reign of Philip V, Spain was still a mighty European power, enriched by its American possessions, but it was on the verge of decline. She was at war with England, Spain's competitor in the colonies and on the seas. Military events were critical in Europe as well as the New World, where the British were winning many battles. This point in history is where our story begins.

"The Spanish treasury could not well bear the strain of the war, so Charles II dispatched the *galleón San José* to go to Cartagena in the Viceroyalty of New Granada, in what is present-day Colombia, and bring back the most valuable cargo of treasure ever assembled from the New World. It carried not only gold, silver, jewels, and precious Indian historical objects, but also a cargo that could change the lives of the human race: the *Materia Medicinal*—a compilation of all the herbal lore and medicinal secrets of the Amerindian population, meticulously researched and compiled by the Spanish explorers under the supervision of a physician, Don Francisco de Mendoza. To better understand the significance of this event to eighteenth century Spain and the world today, one must know something about its history."

Father Pedro told Robert that during a fair held annually at Portobelo, the Spaniards exchanged European goods for silver, which was transported from Peru to Panama by the South Sea Fleet. Gold and tobacco came aboard in Cartagena, copper and indigo at Havana.

He emphasized that Spain's economy was almost totally dependent on these shipments from the New World. Since Spain manufactured nothing that was needed by other countries, the wealth she received from her New World colonies merely passed into the economies of other European nations that sold their goods to Spain.

Taking advantage of their increasing control of the sea, the English initiated an offensive against Spain, attacking the treasure-laden *galleóns* from the New World, interrupting Spanish commerce with the colonies. The ultimate success or failure of these long voyages depended on how many ships were sunk throughout the Indies, claiming lives and treasures.

Robert thanked Father Pedro for illuminating the context in which the treasure came to be loaded onto the *San José*.

As agreed, three weeks later, Father Pedro appeared with Guillermo at the Reading Room. Robert was seated at one of the ornate research tables. He suggested they move to his office, which they did, after Robert returned the material he had been reading to the *portero*. There, he reported on his progress.

"At first I had great difficulty with the documents, but now I can understand the language of the seventeenth and eighteenth centuries more accurately. Buried among the fleet papers was the amount of cargo lost in the 1708 shipwrecks. The *San José* was the flagship of a Spanish treasure fleet. It carried twenty two million pesos when it was blown up."

"Am I correct that the waters were quite deep?" Guillermo asked.

"Yes, six hundred feet," Robert answered. He told them about a packet of letters he'd discovered from Don Francisco de

Mendoza, the medical doctor to the King of Spain.

"In one letter he notified the King of a medicinal treasure arriving in Portobelo. In another he wrote to a friend about his impending marriage with a Peruvian girl. I'd like to learn more but I did not envision my dream of adventure confining me to the Archive."

"Journeys take us to unexpected destinations," Father Pedro answered.

Months later, Robert was still hard at work in his study, silent but for the ticking of a clock. Robert wrote to Jack Sanger that he would like to postpone their planned trip to the South Pacific for a while, explaining how he had become engulfed in Don Francisco's past.

After writing his letter to Jack, Robert stared into the red heart of the fire and then paced, remembering the past when he had cried himself to sleep for not being able to sail in the blue, deep sea.

I have read so much history in my life. I have done so much hard work. I am still a year short of forty—my grip will fix now upon the world of adventure.

He stared again into the fire. Its red lights illuminated a stubborn strength in his face for one flickering moment then vanished again. The promise of his new world was so bright and interesting, seemed so full of meaning and opportunity, that the charm of his present academic life was by comparison too gentle and remote.

Reflections of his past fluttered briefly in Robert's consciousness, as he labored at the Archive: the wonder of how he transversed the journey from a toddler looking at picture books of the sea to being on the cusp of a major adventure. His mind again went to his childhood.

ONE summer morning, when Robert was nine, he started out before daybreak equipped with his father's binoculars, a fishing pole over his shoulder and hooks and baits in his canvas bag. His German shepherd, Drake, followed.

Soon he entered a wooded area and shortly after, he was on the ridge of a mountain. On one side, the horizon was brightening, and in the pale light of dawn, below him, aided by his binoculars, he saw a sailing boat at a distance. He fixed his eyes on the vessel, taking in the schooner's hull, spars, sails and the rigging, dreaming of the thrill of sailing a boat of his own one day.

Meanwhile, the warmer air had melted the frost, and drifts of fog floated around him, until the sun appeared. The vastness of the blue sky and the ocean, the height of the cliffs as they fell away below him, the sudden burst of day, filled him with euphoria. He could now barely see the graceful vessel as it sailed away; above the line of the horizon he discerned a pale reflection—like the sparkle of a little wave on the surface of the ocean that soon disappeared from view.

Robert and his dog made their way down to the waters of New England's blue, deep ocean. Suffused with joy at the certainty of catching a fish, Robert baited his hook for action, rolled back his sleeves, cast his line and began to dream of his future adventures on oceans of the world. It was three hours before he was jolted from his reverie by what was to be his only catch of the day.

The tide was about halfway out. The beach was deserted, smooth and firm. He undressed to his shorts, and walked across the smooth sand, warm under his bare feet. Out beyond where the headlands almost meet to form the harbor, there was a white line of breakers and the open sea. He waded out. The water was cold.

A short while later he lay on the beach to dry and closed his eyes until he was aware of the lapping of a few waves as a boat went by. He saw his dog a short distance away and called him back. Then they climbed up the rocky trail towards home with his single catch. This was his first experience at the sea unaccompanied by an adult.

His love for the sea, however, began when he was a toddler with his father on the beach looking at a picture book of sailing ships, then picturing these same ships on the ocean before him. A serious little boy, he had learned to talk at a very early age. His aunt would describe him as "old-fashioned," and "wise beyond his years." At the age of seven, he was permitted an amount of initiative that children scarcely attain. His mother had died when he was two, and he was under the less vigilant and authoritative care of his aunt. His father was an engineer, a stern, MIT graduate, who gave him little attention and expected great things. For all his brightness Robert found life a little gray and dull.

One day, uncharacteristically, he decided to miss school and found himself outside the Virtual Maritime Museum in the nearby town. He spent hours admiring the early sailing ships and the images rendered by the artists who traveled with Captain Cook and Captain Valdez and Galiano. He admired models of the powerful fleets used by the Vikings, Greeks and the Romans for communication, battle and trade. In one gallery he discovered paddle wheels and propellers, frigates and submarines.

After the Museum closed for the day and the door swung shut behind him, Robert did not notice the early evening lights, the traffic on the street; he was oblivious to the gravitational pull of the discipline and obedience at home that followed the school day. He forgot all hesitation and fear, forgot discretion, and forgot all intimate realities of his life. He had become an elated and wonder-happy little boy enrapt in another, warmer world, permeated with the possibilities of great adventure.

With his hands in his pockets, and making an infantile attempt to whistle, he strolled right along the familiar zigzag road; the evening light, reflected by the golden foliage of the trees, was of an unreal transparency. He arrived at his home, a large two-story wooden house, its slate roof dark with age. Trees cast still shadows like intricate black lace upon the wall. He opened the unlocked door with a gust of emotion. He went gently across the creaking boards of a narrow corridor that separated the entrance hall from the parlor. Near the casement window in her wicker chair, his aunt was mending a blouse spread out on her knees. She raised her head. Not daring to break her silence, Robert cast furtive glances at her grave, pale face and dreamy eyes, until she looked at him scornfully. "Where have you been, young man? Your father is very angry."

He started to explain but fell silent when his father's hand, jolted his shoulders. A brief flash of panic appeared in Robert's unfailingly calm eyes. Later there was a gap in Robert's memory as to his father's reaction at first—but he vividly remembered his somber aunt looking up and coming towards him. He had tried to share with them the joy he had felt after his visit to the museum but they would hear none of it. As punishment for his truancy he was not allowed out of the house for two weeks, except to attend school.

When afterwards he tried again to explain, his aunt punished him for his wicked persistence. No one would listen to him talk about adventures of the sea. Even his book with color pictures of boats was taken away from him for a time—because he was "too imaginative." And his stories were driven back upon himself. He whispered them to his pillow at night. In the following months he said nothing. He was afraid of being banished from the kitchen. Some time later, he noticed that the adults tolerated his presence more readily. Robert seemed, at the age of fourteen, to have won the right to be present at their late-night conversation—on condition that he remain invisible. He was thrilled by this change, and the last thing he wanted to do was to jeopardize such a privilege.

There was one friend other than the dog who would listen to his dreams and encourage his reverie, the curator of the Maritime Museum. Although Robert did not dare to play truant from school again, he spent every spare moment he had at the museum learning all he could about the seafarer's life. He seemed to have a natural affinity for the sea. It was Richard Brand, the curator, who, as Robert grew older, gave him a copy of Conrad's *Lord Jim*, which fired his imagination with vivid and romantic pictures of adventure.

The youthful Lord Jim was everything Robert idolized in life. He read with wild abandon; he saw himself saving people from sinking ships, cutting away the mast in a hurricane, swimming through surf with a line, or as a lonely castaway, barefoot and half-naked, walking on uncovered reefs in search of shellfish to stave off starvation. And when Jim died in Conrad's final pages, all the great adventures in the world passed from him to Robert.

In his teens he read everything about Spanish history that his school library possessed. He immersed himself in the much vaster shelves of his town library. He sought to complement the broad outlines of the museum with a systematic study, progressing from one century to another, from Marco Polo, Vasco Da Gama, Christopher Columbus, Amerigo Vespucci and Ferdinand Magellan, to Henry Hudson, James Cook, George Vancouver, and Sir Francis Drake.

At the bottom of his heart, however, he was waiting for something to happen. Like shipwrecked sailors, he turned with anxiety upon the solitude of his young life, seeking from afar some white sail in the mists of the horizon. He did not know what this chance would be, what wind would bring him, towards what shore it would drive him. But each morning, as he awoke, he hoped it would arrive that day; he listened to every sound and every vessel coming from the deep blue sea.

After graduating from high school and with the first warm weather, when the apple-trees began to blossom, Robert was no longer content wandering through the caverns of an ancient library; he wanted to travel to some of the islands of the Caribbean. He departed for the Dominican Republic—the portion of the island that Columbus called *La Española* when he discovered it in 1492. Robert was ecstatic over the beauty of its majestic mountains and its history—he visited Santo Domingo, the oldest city of the New World, founded by Columbus's brother, and admired the Gothic-Renaissance cathedral and a Renaissance palace where the conquistadors of Spain's golden age were entertained: Diego Velasquez de Leon, who settled Cuba; Hernando Cortez, conqueror of Mexico as well as Balboa, Pizarro and many others.

One afternoon he met Sofia. Robert had asked her for directions to the waterfront. She was a Dominican girl about his age, from a village nearby. Sofia inspected Robert, scrutinized his light-colored shirt wide open at the neck, started to walk away and then turned towards Robert and in a low voice said, "Here, come with me, I will show you something on the port! Come on, you won't be sorry..."

Robert followed her warily.

They walked beside the port with its enormous cranes and corrugated iron warehouses, and into a broad wasteland littered with old barges and rotten trunks. Sofia jumped from one boat to another and Robert followed. There was an abandoned landing stage and several pontoon bridges that yielded buoyantly beneath their feet. Following her, Robert had not noticed the moment when they left dry land for this floating island of abandoned craft. They held on to a broken handrail, leaped into a kind of junk, stepped over its side and slipped on the wet timber of a raft.

They finally found themselves in a channel that had steep banks covered in flowering alder trees. Its surface, from one shore to the other, was hidden under the hulks of ancient vessels packed close together, side-by-side, in fantastic disorder.

They settled on the thwart of a barge that bore traces of fire. The afternoon was warm, misty. The smell of the water mingled with the emanations from the alder trees. From time to time, a vessel that they could see passing in the distance in the sea sent a series of lazy waves into the channel. They could hear the grating of a cable, the lapping of water under a pontoon, the lisping of the reeds.

They went down the ladder and Sofia kneeled on the bottom of the barge and tugged Robert by the sleeve to make him do the same. It was only then that Robert noticed the two portholes on the bottom near the floor. Their panes were made of clear plastic. Without leaving her porthole, Sofia gestured with her hand, inviting Robert to imitate her. Robert glued himself to the other porthole.

Beneath the surprisingly clear waters Robert saw submerged the remains of a wooden hull shrouded by coral. Scattered in the debris he spotted what appeared to be old bottles.

The next morning they returned to the site with diving masks, and in the first dive they retrieved a bottle and an ironstone plate. On the next, they picked up two earthenware jugs. On another dive, they spied in the debris what appeared to be a tiny porcelain jar with a lid. When they started to climb up to the barge aided by a rope, they heard the footsteps, the click of heels on the wet clay of the bank, then a metallic hammering above them on the deck of the barge and already muffled voices reaching them from the bow.

Sofia gave Robert a confused glance.

"Swim slowly to the bank. I'll try to rescue the objects," whispered Robert.

At the other side of the barge, Robert pulled himself up with a rope and climbed to the deck. He spotted two soldiers bending over a rail, looking down into the water. Robert's legs gave way and he dropped to the floor. Lying flat on the surface like a lizard, Robert moved toward his treasure. One of the soldiers now was facing him; Robert's heart, pressed against the rusty deck, seemed to make the whole barge vibrate.

"Julio, come with me; maybe they are downstairs," commanded the shorter soldier.

Sliding on the floor, Robert reached his treasure and jumped into the water with the bag on his back.

Reaching the bank, he saw Sofia waiting for him, her eyes already filling with tears.

It was a great day in Robert's life. On that July evening he had, for the first time in his life, his first real friend of his own age and his first treasure.

At the end of the summer, Robert returned home like a young explorer with a thousand and one discoveries of the ocean in his luggage—from the treasure he had retrieved from the bottom of the sea, crustaceans, starfish, and shells of all kinds, to Spanish dictionaries and grammar, Spanish history books, and Spanish novels of adventure. In the autumn and particularly during the winter, he turned himself into a fanatic of erudition, an archivist obsessively gleaning all possible information about the countries whose mysteries he had only managed to plumb on his summer excursion.

Robert attended Harvard because of his interest in history. Friendships with the people then in residence bloomed during the very first week. Afterwards he discovered that Richard Brand, the former curator of the Maritime Museum, who had administered tests for scholarships, had told people to look out for Jack Sanger and Robert Hamilton. Sanger was a freshman like Robert, also studying history, and a minor scholar. He and Robert had rooms in Child Hall. Sanger was immediately struck by the books Robert had on his shelf.

"You are the first person I have ever met who has heard of Draper's *Intellectual Development of Europe*."

At the end of their first half hour together they became lifelong friends.

After graduation, Robert taught history at a New England college and Sanger became a foreign correspondent, his job involving the usual upheavals, small wars and work a day mayhem, which he wrote about to Robert. Every so often, however, Robert's mail included a pleasant surprise. He could spot Jack Sanger's letter from across the room: the address was written in urgent printed characters, with the no-nonsense, slightly askew strokes of a man who has struck gold and is racing to catch the last burro to Eureka. The envelope seemed to twitch and quiver from the energy within.

Many years later, a letter arrived announcing that Jack was building a vessel in Thailand and wanted Robert to sail with him in six months to the South Pacific—he knew that Robert had lost his wife in an accident two years before, was still a seeker, a dreamer, and that he was always on the lookout for adventure.

Robert responded with enthusiasm. He indicated that he would be in Bangkok in six months after traveling to Spain to visit the Archive of the Indies in Seville.

PART TWO

Under the sea where the mysteries are,
The sunken ships with pirate's treasures
and bodies never to be seen again.
Under the sea where the predators wait,
Where the corals move and the fishes play.
Under the sea where the divers go
to explore the sea beds and reefs.
Under the sea looks so quiet from above
but it's alive with the mysteries of the deep.

Ann Louisa

A typically Moorish city, with narrow, winding streets surrounded by ancient walls, Cordoba sat on the southern slopes of the Sierra Cordoba, on the right bank of the river Guadalquivir. A Moorish bridge on Roman bases connected Cordoba with its suburb across the river. At the south end of the bridge stood a stone mansion where many generations of Mendozas had been born, lived and died. A large, well-kept garden surrounded the mansion, which was set back on top of a hill overlooking the river. The hills behind the house were planted with olive and orange groves.

Francisco de Mendoza drew his first wailing breath on 12 June 1670. The knowledge of his aristocratic family's wealth and importance came to Francisco gradually as he grew older, and with it, the burden of responsibility.

His father, a marine engineer, passed on to his son his love of nature, his gift of craftsmanship and artistic sense, his refusal to admit defeat when confronted by problems and, most important, his love for adventure. Francisco grew up listening to countless stories of adventure in the New World, told by friends of the family after returning from the Americas.

From his mother's side he inherited love for humanity. At the age of nineteen Francisco asked his teacher how it was possible that Hernando Cortez had started off with fewer than five hundred men, yet conquered the Aztec Empire with a population of millions. How could such a tiny handful prevail? All the explanations seemed inadequate. The extraordinary story of Pizarro's conquest of the Inca Empire was only part of a larger puzzle. Relatively few Spaniards had ever crossed the ocean to the New World, yet they succeeded in impressing their culture on an enormously larger number of native peoples. The inherent strength of European civilization, in addition to undeniable technical superiority, did not seem to him an adequate explanation. Why, for instance, did the old religions of Mexico and Peru disappear so utterly? Why did villagers not remain loyal to deities and rituals that had brought fertility to their fields from the beginning of time? The exhortation of Christian missionaries and the intrinsic appeal of the Christian faith and worship seemed an insufficient explanation.

A casual remark by one of Francisco's teachers during a history class suggested an answer. When the Aztecs drove Cortez and his men out of Mexico City, killing many of them, Smallpox was raging in the city. The man who had organized the assault on the Spaniards was among those who died on that *noche triste*. The paralyzing effect of a lethal epidemic went far to explain why the Aztecs did not pursue the defeated and demoralized Spaniards, which gave them time and opportunity to rest and regroup, gather Indian allies, set siege to the city, and so achieve their eventual victory.

The lopsided impact of an infection disease that killed only Indians and left Spaniards unharmed, offered Francisco a key to understanding the ease of the Spanish conquest of the Americas, not only militarily, but culturally as well. But the hypothesis swiftly raised other questions: How and when did the Spaniard acquire the immunity to the diseases that destroyed the Amerindians? Why did the natives have no diseases of their own with which to mow down the invading Spaniards?

In his twentieth year, Francisco's younger brother fell victim to a plague that ravaged northern Spain with ferocity. This untimely death and the lack of well-defined quarantine regulations decided Francisco on a career in medicine.

In 1694, Francisco graduated at the top of his class from the University of Zaragoza with a degree in medicine. With his father's help he obtained a commission from the Navy to join a Spanish scientific expedition and sail to Mexico.

After his arrival in Vera Cruz he traveled to the interior of the country, taking note of everything he saw, even how they prepared their food. The Indians soaked the kernels of maize in a lime solution, which broke down some of the particles in a way that allowed human digestion to synthesize substances that were otherwise absent. Without such a treatment, a diet of maize led to a nutritional deficiency known as pellagra, which was often seriously debilitating to the European populations, but Indians escaped pellagra by soaking the maize and by supplementing their diet with beans.

After three years in Mexico, Don Francisco published his observations in Spain. This attracted the attention of the new Spanish king, Charles II, who told him, "I am looking for the right man to form and head a commission and to travel to the New World. Green medicines have been for centuries the domain of native healers and shamans. Now I want to bring that to Spain. The rain forests of New Granada, Peru, and New Spain have long been symbols of mystery and power. It is rumored that they hold the key to eternal youth and health. We must uncover this mystery."

Don Francisco told the King, "An Aztec friend of mine spoke of an ancient book of cures by Martin de la Cruz, an Aztec physician. Another Indian, Juan Badiano, translated the book from Aztec Nahuatl into Latin. An Aztec priest, Namexi Patli, allowed me to study it. This book is called the *Badianus manuscript*. The illustrated book revealed great sophistication in the use of drugs and the treatment of disease among the native people of the New World."

The King told Don Francisco of a letter that he had received from a physician attached to one of the Spanish galleóns. A third of the men had fallen sick within four or five days of arriving in Peru. Spanish medicines had been of little help. Some of the Indians offered green medicines. The day after the men drank a juice made from plants, they rallied, regained their strength and were able to go back to work.

"I have commanded our best universities, our army, navy geographers and map-making experts to help select the best men to accompany you on this expedition, which must remain secret, take possession of the *Badianus manuscript.* In addition, collect any information compiled by the Indians, and all you can about the green medicines already compiled by our Franciscan, Dominican, and Augustinian missionaries in the New World."

Don Francisco knew the magnitude of the task. There were many Indian tribes, speaking a multitude of languages and living on a huge, uncharted continent. But this knowledge could have a decisive impact on eradicating disease and it would certainly change the course of history.

The King designated Don Pedro de Aróstegui to immediately initiate the construction of the *galleóns San José* and *San Joaquin* in the Mapil shipyard, near San Sebastián. Among the general principles of these sailing men-of-war: the hull was made longer, so that the keel became about three times the beam of the previous vessels instead of two-and-a-half times or less, while the number of heavy guns between decks was increased until they ran in one or two tiers for the full length of the broadside.

In the following year the construction of the *galleóns* was completed, but due to the war between Spain and England, they were unable to depart.

Finally on the 10th of March 1706, six vessels of the *Tierra Firme* fleet sailed from Cádiz, bound for the New World under the command of Don José Fernández de Santillán (Conde de Casa Alegre), accompanied by his nephew, Don Diego, whose fleet comprised sixteen merchant vessels. Of the thousand men on board the *San José*, twenty belonged to Don Francisco's expedition, which also included nine officers and thirty musketeers. In addition the company had three drummers and a standard bearer. The ships carried supplies for the Colonies and would return to Seville before winter with gold, precious metals and other treasures from New Granada.

Forty days later the *galleóns* sailed through the narrow Bocachica pass into the fine, ten-kilometer harbor at Cartagena—a lucky break in wartime. Casa Alegre began informing himself about enemy movements in the vicinity. This time, Spain's principal enemies in the Caribbean were English and Dutch rather than French. On average fifteen percent of the crew traveling to the Americas perished due to epidemics, mostly caused by lice, via rats and roaches. The crew suffered the scarcity and contamination of water. Hygiene was calamitous. Bathing with water was not the custom, since it was considered unhealthy, especially by the lower classes, such as sailors and the ordinary crew.

The theologian Juan Bautista de la Salle recommended in his manual:

"*It is convenient in the morning to rub your face with a white linen to clean it, and if necessary with saliva, since it is worse to do it with water due to the susceptibility of the skin to the cold winter and the heat of the summer. It is also recommended to comb your hair at least once a week, since it deters the growth of louse.*"

Therefore, Don Francisco was determined with the support of Conde de Casa Alegre, to set about raising the health standards for the newly constructed *galleóns*, in order to avoid the costly mistakes of the past.

When the *San José* and the rest of the *Tierra Firme* fleet arrived in Cartagena, the Conde of Casa Alegre thanked Don Francisco.

"Because of your insistence on protecting the potable water, the usual epidemics were controlled. Thank you in the name of the King."

"Thank you, Sir," said Don Francisco.

"Oddly enough, a few days ago, I was making a rough estimate of the whole, and I dare say I've come pretty near it. From the year 1659, when I went to sea as a lad of fifteen, until today, I have walked on the decks of thirty ships, ranging from *galléons* to caravels and this is the first time that nobody of the crew became ill."

The hot, tropical sun beat mercilessly on the stones of the walled city and the series of forts protecting the approaches from the sea. Although it was already the siesta hour, Cartagena was in no mood for sleeping. The arrival of six *galleóns* was a cause for celebration. The vivid colors of flags that flew from San Sebastián Fort were repeated in the long pennants and flags waving from the masts and sterns of the fleet below. People thronged on the narrow cobblestone streets and stone quays at the harbor's edge. Dozens of boats flew back and forth between the quays and the great ship unloading the crew and cargo.

The fleet remained in Cartagena, waiting for the Peruvian *Virrey* to organize the Feria de Portobelo, the trade fair, and for the arrival to the treasures from Peru that included gold and silver cobs, over a hundred chests of emeralds, and the personal wealth of the Viceroy of Peru. Those treasures were to be reloaded on the *galléon San José*.

Finally on the 19th of December, 1707, the merchant ships from Lima departed via Panama. The fleet departed Cartagena on the 2nd of February arriving in Portobelo on the 10th of the same month.

For three weeks Don Francisco stayed in Cartagena, organizing his men and planning the expedition. He heard from local Spanish officials rumors of fantastic wealth hidden beyond the Andes, in the mysterious interior of the continent. Somewhere in the Chibcha Kingdom of Tunja lay a land so rich in gold that its king covered himself with the precious dust once a year to bathe in a sacred lake. This king was called "the gilded man," or *El Dorado*. In addition to his fabulous riches in gold, *El Dorado* was also rumored to possess an important manuscript on medicines, or green gold. More than one man had searched for *El Dorado*, but thus far neither the king nor his fabulous kingdom had been found.

Don Francisco learned of gold mines worked by Indians and Africans throughout the northwestern region of New Granada, many of them slaves. But some were able to retain a percentage of the gold they found, and so buy their freedom and set up on their own as prospectors. They could become owners of slave gangs themselves and lead lives of luxury even greater than that of the Spanish royal officials. Indeed, Don Francisco saw several elegantly attired black ladies walking the narrow streets of Cartagena with their pastel parasols, broad-brimmed plumed hats, and expensive silk dresses in resplendent colors. And he saw black men wearing brocaded waistcoats, ruffled shirts, and silk pantaloons far finer than anything he possessed. The New World, he reflected, seemed to be a place where dreams came true.

At last, the day of departure neared. Don Francisco's team was ready: native Indians, black Africans, a Franciscan priest who knew the native peoples of the region, a train of donkeys laden with provisions, ten horses and an eager *mestizo* boy, Julio, who had run away from home to join the expedition.

The day before the expedition set out, they celebrated mass in the newly constructed church of San Pedro Claver to pray for success. Candles blazed at the altar. The priest moved about in a cloud of incense and candlelight, surrounded by altar boys in red cassocks and white surplices, one of them swinging the smoking censer. One by one the members of the expedition approached the altar to receive Holy Communion. The priest raised the golden monstrance and blessed Don Francisco and his exploration team.

That evening, as he walked around Cartagena for the last time, Don Francisco was surprised to find how much he regretted leaving this beautiful city. The enclosed plaza paved with cobblestones; the narrow streets partly shaded by wide, overhanging balconies of ornately carved wood, painted white and hung with flowers, which ran along the upper stories of the houses; the intense brilliance of the sun and the corresponding vivid, blue shadows it threw; the excitement on the faces of the people — all this would cause him to miss this place in coming months even more than he missed the Cordoba of his boyhood. For this was the starting point of the rest of his life.

FROM Cartagena they rode and hiked southeast across New Granada's coastal plain to the Magdalena River. There they abandoned their horses and donkeys and transferred their supplies into five large dugouts with palm-thatched cabins in the sterns. Each dugout was large enough to seat four Spaniards and an Indian servant, an Indian pilot, and four Indian rowers, and to hold scientific instruments, plant presses, books, guns and provisions, such as live chickens, eggs, plantains, cassava, cocoa, brandy, and oranges. The Spaniards sat in chairs under the shade of the palm roof while the Indians labored at the oars.

Within a few days they found themselves swallowed up by an endless rain forest. The overabundance of exotic plants and animal life and the sights, sounds, and smells had an almost hallucinatory effect on the Spaniards. They saw a profusion of vegetation, wildlife and insects; everything seemed to feed on everything else, and as they listened to the Indians' tales of jaguars, anacondas, monstrous crocodiles, vampire bats, voracious piranhas, and cannibal tribes, the Spaniards realized that in New Granada men, too, were part of the food chain.

The jungle through which they passed was ancient and virtually impenetrable. Only occasionally did they see the smoke of Indian campfires. Crocodiles, parrots, and monkeys were their constant companions. After a month, the Spaniards began to feel that they had passed out of the eighteenth century and were rowing backward through time, into the prehistoric jungle.

The river swelled and picked up speed in the direction opposite to their travel. Late in the afternoon, thick clouds hung over the tops of distant mountains, a cold wind picked up, and within minutes the temperature dropped several degrees. The Indians continued to battle a strong current fed by constant thunderstorms. Don Francisco, the priest, and many of the Spaniards devoted themselves to collecting plants and tropical fruits along the banks of the river.

Weeks later, they reached the tiny village of Honda at the shores of the Magdalena. They headed west towards the Chibcha Kingdom of Tunja, and the fabled El Dorado. Tunja was 2,600 meters higher than Honda, on a plateau surrounded by the Andes Mountains. The road to Tunja often amounted to little more than steep steps leading ever upward, sometimes no more than half a meter wide, between natural rock walls and through an amazing array of plant life. Don Francisco kept careful records of the changes in vegetation, which occurred with the changes in altitude.

The Andes offered constantly varying weather, monolithic geologic formations that seemed to erupt from bedrock, eroded tracts, exploding waterways, lush plateaus, and vegetation that shifted constantly from emerald green to coffee brown. Clouds coagulated along the mountain peaks in immovable clumps against the sky.

The expedition climbed hard for several days reaching a canyon rim at an altitude of two thousand meters. A solitary, gray eagle hovered at eye level. From the peak of the canyon they glimpsed an Indian town in the breathtaking valley below, but it took four hours to reach. The Indians welcomed them to the village of Cascada and offered them food and shelter. For three months they remained, collecting plants and specimens.

Through Julio, the young *mestizo* who served as an interpreter, the Spaniards found that the village people looked to the plants and animals of the tropical forest for their medicinal needs. The Indians had a great variety of medicinal drugs, stimulants, narcotics, and hallucinogens, all provided by the tropical forest. Don Francisco counted at least 1,300 plant species used for medicines. He thought he had never seen a more charming place than the village of Cascada. High mountains surrounded the fertile valley. A river divided the village in half. On one of the mountain slopes bordering the valley stood the gray ruins of a Chibcha temple. Don Francisco made the climb one day. At the top he encountered a stocky man who held a tube to his lips. Inside the tube was a fine, rust-colored powder.

"The powder is a narcotic ground from the dried leaves of a plant cultivated by the Yukuna Indians," young Julio told Don Francisco. The Indian took a deep breath, inhaling the powder. Tobacco, Julio explained, was among the mildest of narcotic plants of the native cultures. The Indians called it *yem* or *mulu*. They took it for recreation, believing that many of the tropical drug plants contained spirits that would put them in touch with the divinities who ruled heaven and earth.

Don Francisco asked where he could find El Dorado. The Indian answered seriously: "So many gold-crazed Spaniards roaming through the country in quest of El Dorado, we cannot let them find our gold, because they will take it to Spain. But you who are interested in medicinal plants, which are good for all of us, may be teachable." He advised Don Francisco to start in the Kingdom of Tunja, which he did.

Don Francisco's expedition climbed the canyon wall and crossed a snow-covered pass. Some of the Indians offered the Spaniards coca leaves for chewing to help fight altitude sickness. An Indian woman offered Don Francisco chunks of *llipta* lime, which could be chewed together with the leaves as a solvent for tiny amounts of cocaine. Through Julio, Don Francisco asked her for directions to El Dorado. She pointed straight up into the air and shrieked in laughter.

Black clouds clustered along the canyon rim. Don Francisco's team made camp on the only flat place they could find: the trail itself. Condors sailed above them; below them drifted a sea of cotton-topped clouds, which obliterated the Indian village. A few days later the team hiked down out of winter into spring, walking through a chorus of yellow daisies and blue medallions. Indians took them to the beginning of a trail they said would eventually lead them to a Dominican mission. Asked whether they knew where El Dorado was, the Indians shrugged and continued to apply their face paint. The Spaniards asked whether the Indians knew of a shaman. They only shrugged again. This was a new experience for the Spaniards. In the hinterlands of New Granada they had always found the Indians to be exceedingly hospitable.

In search of the Catholic mission, Don Francisco's party traveled farther into the Andes Mountains to a vast stretch of plateaus and higher peaks, which stood watch over the entire Boyaca province. Now the explorers ascended into a different terrain, a harrowing landscape of cloud-enshrouded peaks and timeless mountain valleys of narrow paths winding above dizzying cliffs and icy mountain lakes. Here they found the ghostly overgrown ruins of the ancient Chibcha Kingdom. Finally, after many months, they walked through a valley in the pouring rain, over sharp bamboo shoots, to find the San Antonio Mission, which had been granted jurisdiction over the lowland tribes.

Built of whitewashed stone, now discolored and stained, its thick-paned windows were covered with iron bars. A low-walled garden sat between the front of the mission and the dusty trail. They could see red roof tiles shining in the sun against the pale sky. To the right was a chapel with a bell tower. The picture, thought Don Francisco, had the faded elegance of an old Renaissance painting.

The travelers approached eagerly, because they had been

some months without proper food and shelter. Even so, living conditions at the mission were Spartan. Five Dominican priests slept fully dressed on pallets of straw covered with rough woolen sheets. Each priest had his own tiny cell, furnished only with the pallet and a straight-backed wooden chair. Instead of a washstand, a small earthen jug and basin stood in a corner on the floor.

The Reverend Father Luis, the head of the mission, greeted the explorers. He was a tall man with a lean, weather-beaten face and white, even teeth. He offered them wine and good food, and talked about the mission and its accomplishments. He explained that for humanitarian reasons the natives had to be protected from exploitation. Don Francisco interpreted this to mean that the Indians were converted into childlike charges and transformed into a submissive, industrious workforce that made the mission's plantation highly profitable.

Don Francisco explained to Father Luis that in the name of the King of Spain, he and his explorers were searching for insight into the source of healing power and how magic, religion, medical plants, and medicine all fit together. "When the King offered me the opportunity to come to New Granada, I took it. My botanical studies awakened in me a desire to see the rain forest. I want to meet native practitioners and shamans and understand why there is such a low level of Indian disease and great biological vulnerability of the Amerindians."

Father Luis replied that the natives believed that humans were connected to their Creator through the elemental cord of the branch, the stem, or the vine and that the Sun created hallucinogenic snuff powder in his navel, but the daughter of the Sun found it. "Thus it became available to men—a vegetable substance acquired directly from the gods, and so came the Indians' food, their houses, and their medicines: from roots and bark, flesh and feathers, earth and the rivers. "Father Luis explained how he approached his major mission, spreading Christianity, by incorporating it into the native culture. The Dominican priests learned Indian languages and had produced a lexicon and grammar of native tongues. "We have too few missionaries to reach the remote villages and an immense numbers of Indians who have to be converted and sustained in their faith. We travel from village to village to celebrate mass and administer the sacraments. We teach the Indians new farming methods and new tools, introduce different crop varieties. We have built aqueducts and irrigation systems to bring arid land under cultivation.

Then Father Luis showed how he made the leap to understanding the value of native practices:

"While one of our priests was building an irrigation system he fell down a steep slope, splintered his leg, and wrenched his knee. One of our Indians mentioned that his father was a *curandero,* or healer, so we took our injured priest to his hut. The *curandero* said that he had learned many healing traditions from the *brujos,* or local witches. Hoping that it could do no harm, we consented to let our priest try a little *brujeria* healing. The old Indian and his son mixed some powdered leaves with tallow from the fat of a guinea pig and applied the mixture directly to the broken leg. The old Indian greased the knee with more of the tallow while his son built a small fire in the middle of the floor. The old man massaged the knee lightly for a few minutes and threw a handful of herbs on the embers of the fire, along with some green leaves. That filled the hut with a pungent aromatic vapor. The old Indian combined the burned leaves with tallow and applied the mixture to our priest's knee. Finally, he wrapped the knee in rags.

"At the beginning, all of us in the mission thought these actions nothing more than hocus-pocus, but in weeks our priest was walking with the help of a cane. Then we carefully noted the plants they used. This began our interest in healing plants. Let me take you to our 'green paradise,' as we call our experimental herbarium."

There were hundreds of medicinal plants and many questions. What part of the plant did they use? And what illness did they want to cure? Did they mix it with hot water? And how long was it boiled? How often taken or applied? He would ask for the Chibcha word for it and say it back. The Indian laughed and corrected him without being asked. They told him, the more you talk about it, the more you'll remember. He had to be careful with names. There could be one name for a part of the plant, and then another when that part was actually used for something.

Don Francisco remained at the San Antonio Mission for a few months, learning from the priests, the Indians, and the rain forest.

When they left the Mission of San Antonio, they divided into two parties and planned to meet again in Honda in two tears. One group traveled to Cumana on the little Venice coast, to the Casiquiare River, which links the Rio Negro, a tributary of the Amazon, to the Orinoco. Don Francisco's team went southwest, and not until they reached the plateau that cradled Santa Fe de Bogotá, did they feel the relief of a cool breeze. From there they traveled farther into the Andean mountains, coming to the Quindio pass to Cartago, then headed south to the breathtaking Cauca Valley, Here they stayed for a month, collecting plants from the slopes of Purace, a nearby volcano. As the rainy season began, they climbed back into the mountains. In the torrential downpour, flash floods and mudslides were a constant threat. The cold, barren desert plateau surrounding the city of Pasto presented an otherworldly appearance. Sleet and snow, driven by high winds, raked the plateau, and low clouds mixed with volcanic fumes formed a drifting fog that alternately obscured and revealed strange vistas.

From Quito the seat of a *Real Audiencia* they climbed Mount Chimborazo, the highest of the volcanoes around Quito, and then continued south to Cajamarca, an ancient Incan city. On this part of the journey they followed a road constructed under the Incan Empire of Tawantinsuyu, which had the City of Cuzco as its capital, in the central highlands of Peru.

FROM a mountain pass Don Francisco looked down upon Cajamarca, lying silently in a lush valley amid the high Andes. Originally, he had not intended to stop here, but in Cuzco he had received an urgent message from the Corrigidor of Cajamarca, Don Manuel Goméz. Apparently a smallpox epidemic was raging among the native people, and Don Manuel, hearing of his expedition and its purpose, begged him to come to Cajamarca to see what he could do. Not wanting to delay the search for the *Badianus manuscript,* Don Francisco had divided his team yet again and sent a small group back to Cartagena, and then to Mexico, to obtain it. Eventually, he hoped to rendezvous with the team in Cartagena.

His remaining group now consisted of only twelve men, but that could not be helped. He could not ignore a direct plea for assistance. They climbed down to the valley through canyons flanked by walls of rock. The city of Cajamarca had been built around the town square, the *Plaza de Armas*, a design reflecting the conquest culture of Spain, symbolizing central authority and power. The most important residents by birth, race, and occupation lived close to the *Plaza de Armas*, in the most prominent houses. The town was filled with trees, shrubs and ornamental flowerbeds and was flanked by baroque churches and two-story houses with colonial balconies.

Don Manuel Goméz sat in his office surrounded by four

curacas who stood with a stiffly formal attitude beside his desk. He explained that they were members of the best native families, and helped him mediate between the natives and the Spaniards, municipal officials, rural priests, landowners, as well as the *mestizos* subordinates. "Frankly, I don't know how I could run my office without them." The four *curacas* smiled broadly. "They will offer you any assistance you may need." He pleaded that an epidemic of a disease that they had never confronted before was raging and they needed Don Francisco's help.

Don Francisco stressed the need for calm. "Is there someone with a medical background who can help me examine the sick?"

Don Manuel indicated that his daughter had just returned from studying medicine in Seville and had worked with the Indians in Peru to find cures with herbs. "My wife who passed away was a *mestiza*, and her mother always used medicinal plants to cure the family." He invited Don Francisco to his house for dinner that evening to meet his daughter.

At the *Corregidor*'s residence, the most prominent house on the main plaza, Don Francisco was received by a striking young woman with shiny black hair swept up in a bun, a flawless olive complexion, and cat-gray, intelligent eyes. She wore an Incan necklace, a short-sleeved white blouse and a black, gracefully flared skirt.

She gazed at Don Francisco for a moment and greeted him warmly. "Welcome, Don Francisco. My father is attending to some matters, but will be with us shortly. He has told me a great deal about you. Please come in. I'll show you the garden."

She led him to a second door washed in pale green. A servant pulled a cord, the large door swung open, and they walked through a courtyard and into an enchanting garden. Enclosed on three sides by walls as high as the house whose old red brick, softened by time, supported a veritable carpet of roses, it filled the evening air with wanton, scented luxuriance. Palm trees rose high above them, while dark orange trees flowered lasciviously bright in the falling dusk.

They wandered about, listening to the singing of deep-throated birds high up in the trees. "It is very kind of you to show me your garden. I am infinitely grateful," Don Francisco murmured. The glorious blend of scents, or perhaps the girl at his side, had an intoxicating effect on him and he barely trusted his voice.

"It was built by Don Luis Montejo a century ago. He was the first member of my family to come to America."

"Tell me about him," Don Francisco suggested, hoping the tale might be a long one.

"For a young man from San Sebastián, who likes to read and write and who had gone to Madrid and graduated from a prestigious university, there were only two careers. One was the law, which bored him; the other was the priesthood, which intrigued him, despite a near-perfect absence of faith. The Dominicans, as well as the Franciscans and the Augustinians, wooed him. But he said no, finally, to the lot. He told his uncle in a letter, and I quote:

"'I would fail as a lawyer for I dislike the courts. I would not suit the church because I have always been more than susceptible to women and they to me.' Instead he boarded a *galleón* bound for Nueva Granada and succeeded in establishing a gold mining operation."

They climbed wide stone stairs to the parlor, a spacious room decorated with sober elegance. Light, paneled walls contrasted with dark tile floors. Don Manuel, in a black cape, stood in front of a large fireplace, his hands in his pockets. The light from the fire behind him made him look tall and very dark, very elegant, very different from the way he had looked behind his desk at his office that morning.

"Well now, Isabel," he said, smiling, "I don't need to introduce you to Don Francisco. You've been showing him the garden, I see—your special place." He stepped forward and held out his hand to Don Francisco. "Welcome to our home."

They sat before the fire and chatted amiably, but Don Francisco found even such an innocuous social duty a trial to his concentration. His gaze kept returning to Isabel. She flushed and turned away.

"You are very fortunate," Don Francisco blurted, "to have such a beautiful and intelligent daughter."

"Isabel has grown up," Don Manuel said serenely, glancing from one to the other. "She is my only child. I have groomed her to become a doctor. I always wanted to be a doctor when I was a boy. For the most part women have been excluded from the official practice of medicine, but Isabel's grandmother certainly has her own herbal treatments, especially for exclusively female needs, being a descendant of an Incan chief. Her grandfather is a Spaniard from Barcelona, a very strong-minded medical doctor. My mother-in-law is an advocate of spontaneous healing and 'earthly goods,' the green medicines..

"The wife of a Viceroy contracted malaria and came to my father-in-law for a cure. He was considering bleeding his patient's ill humor, but was open-minded enough to try a treatment recommended by his wife. It is known in Peru as *quina* bark. The Viceroy's wife's fever abated after she drank a brew made from the bark."

"You must excuse me, Don Francisco," Isabel said quickly, rising, her handsome face still awash with color, "but I have to make sure things are going all right in the kitchen. I will return shortly."

Don Francisco's eyes followed her to the door and even beyond.

Don Manuel coughed lightly. "As I was saying, from Isabel's earliest childhood, her grandmother has been the most important and influential figure in her life. Isabel's mother died when she was three. Due to my duties I have not devoted as much time to my daughter as I would have wished."

Soon Isabel returned and beckoned them to dinner, taking Don Francisco's arm to guide him.

They walked across a court lined by the tall windows of the house, past a magnolia tree that reached almost to the roof, through a huge entrance hall across a cool stone floor. They entered the most beautiful room Don Francisco had seen since he left Spain, with a high ceiling and several large windows. Moonlight shone through the glass panes. Twenty people might have dined comfortably there, but now it contained only a small round table, so that the three sat intimately close. Solid gold dishes sat on an immense mahogany sideboard below a fine painting by a Spanish master. Over the mantelpiece hung a three-quarter length portrait of Queen Isabel, *La Católica*, as a girl with a little gold crown on her small, prim head.

A corpulent *mestizo* served dinner. Don Francisco had the impression that Don Manuel enjoyed, in his well-bred way, the sensation of ignoring the pomp in which he lived. They might have been dining in one of the great houses of Spain; it was a ceremony they performed, sumptuous without ostentation, and it was saved from a thrilling absurdity only because it was in Spanish tradition. But a thought struck Don Francisco, when he realized that on the other side of the wall was a restless, turbulent population, sick and hungry, who suffered at the hands of the colonists and their *curacas,* the *Corregidores* and the local priests, who found ways to gain control of native lands and labor. Don Francisco's antagonism eased when he recalled that Don Manuel, the *Corregidor*, had married a *mestiza.*

Servants brought in a silver tray with wine for the men and limeade for Isabel. She clutched the glass in her hand and looked at Don Francisco. He was deeply tanned, his hair and mustache dark and his eyes alive. Around him everything shone: the dining table, the silver trays and gilt frames of paintings on the wall. She could not look away, even when his beautiful eyes lifted to hers. He reached into his pocket and drew out a paper. "This document was given to me by the King of Spain, entrusting me to deliver to him a compendium of medicinal plants. I would like to ask your father's permission for your help in this important task, after we have done what we can against the smallpox."

Isabel paused to catch her breath. "If···if father gives his consent, I would like nothing more than to work with—that is, to cure the native people of smallpox, malaria, measles, typhus, influenza and anything else that ails them." She stopped abruptly and lowered her gaze. "As for creating a compendium of cures, why, I think it may be the greatest contribution to medicine a doctor could make." She gazed imploringly at her father.

Don Manuel studied them both for a long moment. His daughter was flushed, his guest pale. "Dear Isabel, you know that your happiness is the must important thing to me and that at the same time, we are compelled to help our population. But we must give it a careful consideration. You are still very young and idealistic."

"I am four and twenty," Isabel cried, "and this is my calling!"

He turned to Don Francisco and continued sternly, "Your mission is of the greatest interest to me. As for Isabel's accompanying you, I must give this thought. Allow me some time."

Isabel dropped her eyes obediently and Don Francisco inclined his head. "Of course, Don Manuel. The matter is entirely in your hands."

Then the conversation turned to many subjects. Don Francisco told them of his life in Spain, his university days, and his future plans. "It is almost two years since we came to the New World, and the situation in Spain has changed drastically with the death of King Charles II. But the Viceroy has informed me that the new King, Philip, has ordered our mission to continue and has pledged the Crown's full support."

Too soon for Isabel, the door opened and the butler entered bearing a very heavy silver salver. How quickly the time had passed!

"I always have a glass of Jerez after dinner," Don Manuel said to his guest, "and in case you have acquired a taste for the local drinks, I can offer you one."

"I will have a Jerez," Don Francisco replied. He leaned back in his chair, holding out the glass of deep red liquid with both hands in order to bring out the aroma. The table had been cleared, and only a bowl of roses stood between Don Francisco and his hosts.

The servants lit new candles and left the room.

Don Manuel's eyes rested on the portrait of Queen Isabel. "I wonder," he said at last, "how life will change with the new King and what opportunities Isabel will have for her medical practice."

Don Francisco glanced at him quickly. "I suppose it is inevitable that the *mestizos* and the colony-born Spaniards will become more independent of us, the Europeans. No doubt the native peasantry will one day start a rebellion. As for Isabel, I think she will become a very successful doctor."

Isabel flashed him a quick smile, which reduced Don Francisco to speechlessness.

Don Manuel rose and extended his hand. "Don Francisco, I have a hacienda not far from here. Why don't you and Isabel go there on Saturday morning, and I will meet you in the afternoon for lunch? You will have time to talk with Isabel and give her a clearer idea of what you propose to do."

"You are very kind," Don Francisco replied earnestly, "so kind that I'll never be able to repay you. I shall never forget this evening.

When he left the *Corregidor's* house, Don Francisco walked through the empty streets toward the tavern where he and his Spanish companions had taken rooms, seeing only Isabel's face before him, such a lovely young girl with such intelligent eyes. He sighed aloud, unaware he'd made a sound.

In his candlelit drawing room, Don Manuel sat silently on the couch. Isabel walked up to him and kissed him on the brow. "Father, if you don't want me to go with him I will stay. Before today, my desire was never to leave you, never to part from you as long as we live."

Don Manuel drew her down beside him, taking her hand between his own. "Beyond any doubt I want you to be happy and to grow in your profession. I know your heart. You must realize that it is difficult for me to give my sanction because of the risks involved." He squeezed her hand. "My dear, we hardly know this man."

"I know him," Isabel whispered, looking down at their clasped hands. “I think I have always known him.”

Don Manuel squeezed her hand again. “Well, my dear, spend Saturday with him. Talk about anything you like. If, after that, you wish to accompany him on his mission, I will not stand in your way.”

“Oh, Father!” She slipped her arms around his neck. “You are gracious, indeed! Thank you for such faith in me! I promise you, you will not regret it.”

Deep into the night she lay abed, fully awake and thinking. Where had it come from, this passionate, unreasonable desire to uproot her life and accompany a strange Spaniard on his mission? When had this overpowering feeling begun? She knew the answer. It had begun the moment Don Francisco entered her private garden.

ON Saturday, four figures neared the tavern. One was a short man with a hunchback who gave the impression of being very powerful. His features were Indian, his nose very large, and his eyes brown and lustrous. He was running, pulling a white Arabian horse by the reins. Behind him rode a slim man in his forties with a short mustache, wearing an Indian poncho and a black hat. Two women followed on horseback, one of them old, the other young.

Don Francisco saw them from his balcony and ran down to open the door. There was Isabel on her black horse, wearing a beautiful blue dress and white hat. Their eyes met. Her lips parted, she drew in a little quick breath, and for an instant looked startled, as if she were falling from the horse. Then she regained control and dismounted, dropping into Don Francisco's light embrace. He backed away as she turned, and bowed low. "Doña Isabel."

She smiled. "Let me introduce my companions. Rosa has been with us for many years as housekeeper. She is practically a member of the family. El Chato," she introduced the hunchback, "is the steward of our haciendas. He also has been with us for a long time. And Antonio takes care of our horses."

"Won't you come inside for a moment?" Don Francisco asked. "I will send for refreshments."

"Thank you," Isabel responded, "but we should start out as soon as possible before the road gets crowded." Don Francisco bowed again, and mounted the Arabian.

The sun shone hot in a cloudless sky. The road was very dusty, for many people bound for the annual fair were riding or walking along. There was no shelter anywhere from the sun. Many people pulled cows and goats; others drove donkeys. Don Francisco and his companions rode slowly.

By the time they were near the main road, which led both to the fair and to Don Manuel's hacienda, La Ramada, the crowds had swelled. A crush of men and cattle close to the palings trampled the edge of roadside cornfields. At an intersection of roads the crowd turned to the left and Don Francisco and his companions turned to the right into an open track and headed uphill through the woods.

From the top of a hill they could see the undulating land of the Ramada, which extended as far as the eye could reach—a mosaic of little square wheat-fields, maize-plots, grass-land and barley crops, with here and there the blue smoke from native huts. On the other side of the hill was a magnificent view of the meadows, like a pastoral from the brush of Giorione. They saw sheep grazing and sleek cattle and horses, but they could only hear the voice of the wind.

All that vast land belonged to Don Manuel Goméz. In the distance was a large white house. Rosa and Antonio were some distance behind them. Spiky green bromeliads grew on the red-tiled roof; part of the house was almost hidden by foliage. As they approached, they found the ground around it, with its grand old trees, was tended like a garden. They rode into the yard, dismounted, and looped the reins over a rail.

Don Francisco and Isabel strolled into the garden and sat down on a bench overlooking the green hills below. Beyond the hills they could see the silvery waters of a large lake. The plowing season had just begun and farmers bent over foot plows of heavy wood. To the right were llamas and alpacas grazing on the lower slopes of the chilled snow peaks of the Andean mountains.

"I must thank your father for his wonderful invitation to spend the day at La Ramada."

"Last night after you left we had a long conversation. When I went to bed I lay awake thinking about Father's agreeable reaction to your proposal. For the first hour I was so happy, but as the night wore on I was wracked by the thought of leaving him alone. It will be very difficult for him without me. I am the only person left who is close to him." Don Francisco's warm, comforting eyes fastened on hers and Isabel plunged breathlessly on.

"When I left to study in Spain, he was counting the minutes for me to return. He does not like to be alone. He was inseparable from my mother, and when she died, I was all he had in his life. Last evening when I bid him good night, I saw the fear of my going away in his eyes."

"I can understand. It is completely natural for a father to feel the way he does," Don Francisco said softly.

"You don't like being alone?"

"No," he murmured. "Do you?"

Isabel rose suddenly, staring hard into the shining distance. "But I seldom feel alone. Most of the time I have friends around me, either my grandmother, or Father, or Rosa or El Chato when I am at home in Cajamarca. And here in La Ramada, the valley," she said, "has in it all that the heart could desire—sweet water, pasture, an even climate, slopes of rich brown soil with tangles of a shrub that bear an excellent fruit, and on one side great hanging forests of pine that hold the avalanches high."

Don Francisco contemplated the panorama—far overhead, on three sides, vast cliffs of gray-green rock were capped by cliffs of ice; but the glacier stream came not to them, but flowed away by the farther slopes, and only then huge ice masses fell on the valley side.

"How is the weather here?" Don Francisco asked.

"In this valley it neither rains nor snows, but the abundant sprigs give a rich green pasture, that irrigation spreads over throughout the valley."

"You know people who live in the mountains?"

"No, I mean the landforms." She smiled and took his arm, guiding him down one of the garden walks. "Do you know that they have spirits and different personalities?"

"I never thought of them as people."

"Oh, but they are very much like people! Each has a personality that is unique in its shape, height, and color. The energy that flows through that prominence is transmitted to human spirits who visit her. Do you see the tallest one in front of us? Her name is Atahuallpa. She is a friend I respect very much. When I feel uncertain I go to her. There is a waterfall in Capac where I go for cleansing and transformation. I call her 'Meditation,' because she soothes and calms my spirit. When I was debating with myself if I should become a medical doctor, I spent many hours at the falls and when I left, the uncertainty was gone. But I visit her only on important occasions."

"I can see that your friend Capac has a mysterious appearance. Tell me about the others. Are they friends also?"

"Can you see Cuyuchi?" Isabel asked. "That is my fun friend. She is always there for me when I feel happy. She is not too tall and she is easy to reach. Many falling leaves cover the base and I sit and slide down, then when I reach the bottom I land in her arms, which are made of mounds of dry leaves. And my other friend Ninan, to the left of Cuyuchi, has an intricate network of footpaths and tracks, like the mazes in your European gardens, with trees forming high walls. They are real teasers. At the moment when I think I am completely lost in its labyrinth, I find the way."

"Your willingness to enter into the unknown enables you to face uncertainty with remarkable courage," observed Don Francisco.

Isabel colored prettily. "Well, Don Francisco, now tell me about your friends."

"I had one friend — a lady friend — who guided me much

as your mountains guided you. I was infatuated with her for a while. I told her that I loved her — I thought I did — but she said I shouldn't squander words. She told me that one day I would meet the woman I love, and I should save the words until then."

He glanced quickly at Isabel and then looked away—suddenly silent.

"I wish that my life were not so complicated," Isabel said slowly.

"You seem able to deal with any kind of complication."

"I am not European; I am not Indian, but a species midway between Indian and Spanish. This is the big dilemma of my culture. I am a mixture of master and servant, conqueror and conquered, colonizer and slave, a mixture that in the *mestizo* is as much cultural as racial. There is this conflict in me — I carry in my blood the culture of domination and bastardy."

"Mixed blood can be of great value. It gives you a different perspective."

"My grandmother not only gave me my Inca blood but, more than that, my love for medicine. My father sent me to study European medicine in Madrid. Even my education is an amalgam."

"Were you impressed by European medicine?"

"From the very beginning, I found that in Europe they concentrated on the chemistry of the body but disregarded the notion that the mind, body, and spirit are integral and inseparable. One day I attended a lecture given by Thomas Sydenham, the so-called English Hippocrates. He was the only person who talked about a connection between the body and the mind."

"But we in Europe have made great advances and have made a serious attempt to throw off the superstitions inherited from the past."

"But all that research has not contributed much to the practical treatment of the sick. Don't Europeans view the mind and body separately; don't they treat the human body as a machine, a thing that works without any intelligence of its own?"

"I didn't know there was another way."

"Oh yes, indeed. The Inca way."

"I am learning quite a lot from you, Isabel. There are very few women anywhere with open-mindedness like yours."

Isabel's gray eyes twinkled, the edge of a smile playing on her face. It was such a complex face, he thought, and so expressive, with her eyes startlingly wide apart, her eyebrows arching with the radiating lips.

"And I am sure I have a great deal to learn from you, Don Francisco," she responded shyly, lowering her gaze.

"Tell me about how the Incas practice medicine."

Her glowing look stopped his breath.

"You will be sorry. When I start talking about medicine it is difficult for me to stop."

He bowed politely. "You underestimate the beauty of your speech."

Isabel flushed. "I am afraid I might test your patience. But you asked for it. When the Spaniards explored Peru, they were surprised to discover the high standard of medicine in the Inca kingdom. In his report to the King of Spain, Francisco Pizarro wrote that it would not be necessary to send European doctors to the Inca Empire. The hygienic conditions of Cuzco were far superior, he said to those in contemporary towns of Spain; steam and sweat baths served for the treatment of rheumatism; a great number of medicines were stored ready for use in the pharmacies. There is no collection of medicines in any other civilization that contains quite so many narcotic and intoxicating drugs as that of my people, the Incas. My grandmother told me of these 'magic' drugs, which were used to induce states of trance."

"Yes," Don Francisco said, "I remember learning at university that the skill of Incan physicians appears to have been as extensive as that of the ancient Egyptians."

"There were specialists for eyes, teeth, phlebotomy, intestinal and bladder complaints. And as surgeons who treated wounds by sewing them up with human hair, set broken bones, made a fixation device for fractures, and carried out caesarean sections. Dietary prescriptions and physical exercise for ailments were widespread. Hospitals were available for clinical treatment. My father's countrymen had no inkling of this when they overthrew Atahuallpa in Cajamarca. They described it as 'magic' and destroyed all evidence of a civilization, even the royal library of pictograms written on scraped bark. Don Francisco," Isabel continued warmly, "the destruction was so thorough that only a meager relic of medical science practiced by my ancestors survived. Most of what we know now about my ancestors' medicine comes from people like my grandmother."

"I would love to meet your grandmother. Would it be possible?"

"Certainly! Maybe we can go to her house tomorrow morning."

Arriving at La Ramada two hours later, Don Manuel found Isabel and Don Francisco still talking in the garden. She suggested he show Don Francisco the stables.

"How are you two getting along?" he asked, kissing his daughter's cheek.

"Perfectly," she whispered.

Isabel hurried to the kitchen, where the cook and Rosa had no need of her assistance, but from there she could watch the approach to the stables without being seen. How tall he was, she mused, and how darkly handsome! Were there other men on earth with his graceful manners, his ease of conversation, and his interest in healing? Behind her back, Rosa and the cook smiled knowingly at one another.

During lunch on the terrace Don Manuel asked Don Francisco why he had decided to travel to the New World instead of practicing medicine in Spain.

"Most of the treatments I learned in five years at the University of Zaragoza did not get to the root of the disease and to the promotion of healing, but rather suppressed those processes or merely counteracted visible symptoms. I knew that if I were sick I would not want to be treated the way I had been taught to treat others, unless the only alternative was death. That made me uncomfortable about treating others. I have always believed that the primary function of doctors should be to teach people how not to get sick in the first place, as your Incan ancestors did. Teaching prevention should be primary; treatment of existing disease, secondary."

"Here the doctors are few and far between," Isabel interjected eagerly. "Our people rely on folk medicines, especially the herbal recipes used by our ancestors. Many of our doctors can do little more than set a broken bone, deliver a baby, or comfort the family until the patient gets better or dies. Typhus, diphtheria, smallpox, pneumonia, and other ills brought by the Spaniards cannot be cured, since our people have no natural defenses for western diseases. When I came back from Spain, medicine was more art than science."

Isabel continued, "A doctor educated in Madrid told me that it was nonsense to believe that there are different diseases. In his view, there is only one. He called it 'irregular arterial action' caused by excess excitability of the blood vessels,' in other words, high blood pressure, which could be fixed easily by bleeding. Many patients are being bled into unconsciousness or even death. Do you remember Father, when Grandmother talked about the importance of meditating when a person is sick? Spontaneous healing can be triggered by mental events. I think." Isabel grew emphatic. "The mind can suppress the ability of the body to resist disease and can unbalance the nervous system, leading to disturbances in digestion, circulation, and all other internal functions."

"You may be right," Don Francisco replied, warmed by her enthusiasm.

"During my travels in Mexico and Nueva Granada, I met many healers who believe that the primary causes of health and illness are not physical but spiritual. They direct their attention to an invisible world, beyond the world of the senses. In this realm they search for reasons for illness and ways to cure it. Some believe in spirit causes of illness, others in the ability of deceased ancestors to affect one's life and health, others believe in possession by spirits, and still others in the possibility of psychic attack by malevolent shamans."

"Yes!" Isabel cried. "All that is true, very true as my grandmother says···"

Don Manuel sighed inwardly as he listened to them and watched their glowing faces. He was a spectator now, and powerless to do anything beyond observe their headlong dive into the maelstrom. Yesterday, had he acted quickly —before dinner—he might have prevented it and kept her near him, safely ashore. But now it was too late. Oblivious of time, they talked and gazed and ached and talked some more, drifting away from him, moment by moment, toward that powerful vortex of joy and desire, from which there was no return. He looked out the tall window at the still, dark night and remembered with perfect clarity and a stab at his heart, the buoyant intoxication of his own youth, the vivid yearning and exultant hope of paradise in a woman's arms. He struggled against tears. The ferocity of his pain surprised him. But it was all too late. Isabel was gone. She would never be his again.

In the stillness of the evening, when the minutes dripped from the clock, Isabel, her father and Don Francisco had lost any notion of the passing of time. They remained on the terrace. They were still conversing eagerly as the blazing sun set over the lake in an explosion of color.

THE silence was absolute. The sun was just rising, and mist lay on the mountains above the ancient village of Chan-Chan. Crowding a hilltop amid slopes shingled with stone houses and terraces was the ancestral home of the Callawayas, medicine men to the Incas and their descendants. At the end of a dirt road, from a dimly lit passage of the court, an old and proud woman emerged, wearing a hand-woven garment and sandals. Don Francisco was struck by the serenity of her face. He stopped to allow Isabel to precede him.

"My child, I was thinking of you a few minutes ago," the woman said, her arms outstretched.

"Grandmother, I am so happy to see you. How are you?"

"I am fine, my child." She turned to Don Francisco. "You've come with a young man."

"Yes, Grandmother, this is Don Francisco, a medical doctor from Spain. I told him all about you and he was very eager to meet you."

"It is a great pleasure to meet you." Don Francisco bowed.

"Isabel's friends are my friends," replied the woman, looking him over sharply. "Please come inside." The woman turned in through the tall trapezoidal entrance to her house. The faintness of her voice implied physical weakness, but her serene bearing implied strength. She was, Don Francisco thought, the last feeble echo of a sound made long ago. Her forehead, now wrinkled, bore the stamp of adversity, and she had the curious coloring of black hair gone white, as if she had in reality strewn ashes upon her head. But there was an unquenchable flame in her, which no ashes could dim.

A broad ray of light fell into the center of a small room, with few and simple furnishings. In one corner was a back-strap loom with the beginning of a fine fabric.

Isabel embraced the old woman. "Grandmother, Don Francisco has come to our country to learn our ways of healing. I told him that perhaps you could introduce him to our ancestors' ways."

Her eyes fixed upon Isabel and then upon Don Francisco, the old woman recounted, "One hundred and fifty years ago, the Supreme Inca, Huayna Capac, my ancestor, ruled a vast empire. He was venerated by his people and enjoyed every luxury. Under his rule, amputations were performed and artificial limbs were made to end in a hollow wooden cylinder, in order to accommodate the stump. My ancestors removed tumors and performed operations with knives of copper and bronze instruments."

"Grandmother, tell Don Francisco about the festivals of health."

Don Francisco leaned back in his chair and listen attentively to the old lady.

"Once a year, a big festival of health took place. All houses and dwellings were thoroughly cleaned. Old people like me, who could not work, performed what services we could and the state was responsible for our keep. The state also looked after the lame, crippled, and deformed citizens, who were forbidden to marry. They took forceful measures to prevent the misuse of medicines and also to discourage drug misuse."

"Grandmother, we were talking with Don Francisco about the relation of the body and the spirit in the process of healing. Tell us what you believe."

"The cause of an illness can be found in the sins of the

patient. Illnesses are caused by spirits, empowered by a shaman or through a person's own mistakes. Remedies are either herbal or emanate from beyond—a world that a shaman enters with the help of vision-inducing plants."

The old woman rose and slowly made her way to an old chest in the corner. One by one, she lifted out old worn and fragile books, browned with age and covered in a spidery scrawl.

They sat on the floor together and looked at the pages that depicted events of everyday life of a time long past. Impressive and realistic drawings showed tumors, a diposis as a result of glandular disturbances, leprosy, syphilitic symptoms, paralysis of the facial nerves, oraya fever, and disfigurements caused by leishmaniasis of the skin and mucous membranes, among many other pictures of the human condition. The old woman told them this was only a third of a collection of books once possessed by Emperor Atahualpa, her ancestor.

Don Francisco realized immediately that the books contained a wealth of information on medicinal plants and cures that complemented and surpassed in many ways, his findings of the secret lore of the Amerindians.

"Grandmother, Don Francisco and I are planning to go to Cunyaca to help cure the sick. Father is afraid that if the smallpox is not controlled it will spread throughout Cajamarca."

"This strange disease has come upon our people and has made many very sick. Many are seeking some charm or antidote against this plague—people believe that sins are the real cause and must lie in the negligence of the Spaniards, to set up Christian temples so soon after they enter our country.

"When the Spaniards brought this disease to our land," the old woman whispered, "some of our medicinal men attempted to prevent it by placing the dried crust of skin lesions in the noses of susceptible persons, in the hope of producing a mild form of the disease. Sometimes it worked. But sometimes it led to death. And the treated persons served as sources of infection for those who had previously escaped the disease. So they gave it up. There is no cure for smallpox. Only prevention—stay far away."

The old lady stood up, holding the books in her arms. "Remember, Isabel, that when I die I want you to have these treasures, all that is left from our ancestors."

Don Francisco stood up and said, "Please let me help. I will put them back in the chest for you."

After a long pause, the old woman nodded sadly. "I may as well give you the books, Isabel. I am very old. I don't have many years left to live. I know you will take good care of them."

"Grandmother, you always protected me, taught me the secrets of life and again today you are giving me the last treasures you possess. I love you and I always will," Isabel said with tears in her eyes.

Isabel opened the door and bid good-bye to her grandmother. Outside, the setting sun cast a delicate, copper glow over trees, grass and mountains, all that they could see. Night loitered close behind, waiting to engulf that shining world in darkness. Isabel's eyes filled with heavy tears that slowly, one by one, rolled down her cheeks. She knew in the bottom of her heart, as her grandmother knew, that it was the last time they would see one another. In the stillness of the night she and Don Francisco returned to Cajamarca.

The doorbell jangled faintly. With a candle and a volume of prayers in hand, Father Tomas frowned at his clock. It was after eight at night. What in Christ's name now? he wondered crossly. He'd only just returned from his evening prayers and was minutes away from bed.

The bell rang again.

The priest was tempted to ignore it; if it was important, let them come back in the daytime.

Another ring, longer and more demanding reverberated in his ears.

He quickly walked through the darkened courtyard; he slid

back the iron bolt and pulled open a heavy door. Framed in the narrow gateway, looking drawn and anxious in the dim light of the moon, stood Don Manuel.

"*Corregidor!* What brings you here at this late hour? Come in, please."

Don Manuel strode through the gate. "I must speak with you, Father Tomas!"

For the twenty years Father Tomas had known him, he never had been so agitated. The trouble, whatever it was, must be serious to have brought the *Corregidor* to him in such a state. Father Tomas led him inside and gestured to his most comfortable chair. "How can I help you, *Corregidor*?"

"It's about Isabel," Don Manuel said slowly.

"Yes?"

"Recently she met a young Spanish doctor, who came to this country leading an expedition commissioned by the King. He is collecting and compiling the herbal lore, and medicinal secrets of our native people. I brought him here. Father, I asked him to help us contain the smallpox epidemic in Cunyaca."

"Yes?" Father Tomas prompted after a long silence. "That sounds like a good idea."

"Now he wants Isabel to accompany him."

"He could hardly find anyone better qualified."

"Not only to Cunyaca. He asked her to accompany him on the rest of his expedition."

"Then, where is the problem? Surely it is better to have two doctors."

"He doesn't want her for her skill. He's in love with her."

Father Tomas said nothing, but watched the *Corregidor* twist his hands together.

"It is a very dangerous mission; she could die from smallpox. I have known this man for a very short time. Isabel is so idealistic and enthusiastic, and so innocent about men. Oh. God, what a troublesome mess! After all, she is my only daughter and I love her more than I love myself."

"*Corregidor*, perhaps I could have a talk with her and convince her to change her mind."

"No, Father Tomas, I already gave her my consent."

"You did? That was brave and gracious of you."

"If I did not, she would resent me for the rest of her life. I don't want that between us. But I cannot let her go alone. The reason I came here was to ask you to accompany Isabel, and keep her safe. This man's intentions may be honorable — I believe they are — but no one is completely impervious to temptation. Will you do this for me? Father Tomas?"

"You want me to leave the church and be Isabel's chaperone?" the priest asked nervously.

"No, I am not asking you to leave the church, but to take the church with you, to the poor people who are dying every day in Cunyaca. Bring them the comfort of the last rites, and take care of my Isabel."

Father Tomas squirmed unhappily in his chair. His whole life — the little world he had made for himself — to be overturned by a foreigner he had never seen! But Don Manuel's grave, dark eyes commanded him. "I will accompany Isabel," Father Tomas said reluctantly.

Don Manuel heaved a sigh of relief. "For an instant when I saw your expression, I thought you were going to deny me."

Father Tomas laughed cautiously. "I have not your courage, *Corregidor*. But let's drink to your daughter's happiness." He brought over a jug of red wine and two glasses.

"I need one just now. And so do you, for your new adventure, Father," said Don Manuel, clicking glasses. "By the way, you will not go alone. This afternoon I asked El Chato to accompany Isabel as well. You should have seen the expression on his face."

LEANING against the old laurel tree, in the middle of the square, Don Francisco felt his leather satchel give under the weight of his shoulders. Julio, with his permanent big smile, squatted beside him, holding the reins of the horses and sharing the still gentle heat of the newly risen sun.

As Don Manuel approached with a priest behind him, he was holding his daughter's hand. The old man's solemn face and sad piercing eyes struck Don Francisco who expressed thanks for the horses.

"Good morning, Don Francisco. I want Isabel to ride on a horse that she is familiar with," Don Manuel said and introduced Father Tomas.

"He will accompany you. He may be valuable to you as an interpreter, but the real reason I asked him—" He paused and met the young man's eyes. "Father Tomas has known Isabel all his life. I have also asked my steward, El Chato, to join your party. You will find him a very faithful servant."

Don Francisco bowed low. "I would be honored to have anyone you've recommended in my expedition, Don Manuel. I am sure they will be of great comfort to Isabel."

Looking at her now, it dawned on Don Francisco what made her seem so different. She was wearing the everyday clothing of a countrywoman: the long- sleeved white blouse, buttoned to the neck, and the long black skirt held at the waist with a sash. He'd never seen her in these native clothes, never imagined her in them. Her thick hair was pinned back carelessly. Never had he seen her more natural, or more beautiful.

Don Francisco fumbled in his satchel for his plans. As all gathered around, he pointed to areas of his proposed travel on the map. "I expect that by horseback we will take from three to four weeks to arrive at Cunyaca."

"What then? Do you think you will be able to cure the disease?" asked the priest.

"Prevention by means of isolation is all we can do. We must educate the native population. Therefore we will remain in Cunyaca until we are able to isolate the sick from the healthy people — and thus contain the disease in areas of the city. Naturally we must be very careful in not contracting these terrible diseases ourselves."

"Where are we going after we complete our mission there?" inquired Father Tomas.

"Northwest towards Ucayali, according to the legends and true believers, an ancient underground temple stores medicinal manuscripts. There are also reports of rare artifacts, handcrafted and sculpted, along with jade and gold, and precious gemstones. Our main concern is the manuscripts."

"Yes! I heard many times about the temple from some of the older people in town but it has always remained a mystery," said Don Manuel.

"After Ucayali, we will travel northwest towards the Amazon Basin, and north to Honda, in Nueva Granada, where we will rendezvous with our team coming from Venezuela."

Don Manuel said nothing more, but only watched as Don Francisco awkwardly mounted his white horse.

The conversation left Don Manuel sad and confused. Nothing Don Francisco could have done or said would make it less painful or more reassuring of his daughter's safety.

Soaked by a constant drizzle, the long line of horses, donkeys and men slogged through a moss-blanketed forest, down into a deep ravine, and up into the mountains, following a winding ancient stone road. Don Francisco's clothes were so wet, it was impossible to tell where his sweat ended and the damp from the rain began. It had been a hard departure from Cajamarca. He had never seen a grown man so close to tears as Don Manuel Goméz, as he bid farewell to his Isabel. Even now, eight days out, Don Francisco's heart twisted at the recollection. There they had stood in the hot morning sun in the open square, his expeditionary team ready to leave, the prayers said, the blessing given, the horses stamping, impatient to be off to a great adventure. Isabel embraced her father, whispered in his ear and kissed his cheek. Father Tomas—what a wise decision that had been, to provide Isabel with a reliable chaperone; it was a weight off everyone's mind — tried to gently urge Isabel away. But Don Manuel could not let her go. He held her in his arms, saying nothing, all his words spent. His lined, tormented face, so stern and wise, crumpled like old paper under the strain. It was El Chato who finally put an end to it. The *Corregidor's* steward — loaned to the expedition at the last moment, probably as another protector for Isabel — had plucked at Don Manuel's sleeve until he dropped his arms and released his daughter. But he did not move as they started off. Don Francisco took the last glance at Don Manuel as they found their way out of town; he was a lonely figure standing in the middle of the square, shoulders thrown back, watching them disappear. He had promised Don Manuel he would see his daughter safe and happy again. He hoped it was a promise he could keep.

Within hours of their departure, they came upon the valley and the green fields of Cunyaca. Here in the high sierra resided the sick, most of which spoke Quechua, the tongue of the Incan Empire. Don Francisco sent Julio ahead to alert the village headman of their approach, but the boy returned and reported he was unable to find anyone of authority. Slowly the expedition rode into town. They found it empty but for an occasional pockmarked youngster and mangy dog idling in the dust. They passed a burial place choked with graves. The stench of decay seeped up through fetid pools of water. In one hut they found the mother of the Mayor of the town. Her emaciated skin lay loose on her bones as she wasted away from the disease that had already killed the rest of her family.

"My body will be buried," the old Indian woman whispered. "I am lucky because in other families, their bodies will stay where they died. Their families are afraid to claim them, afraid that they will get sick if they transport the dead."

"Mother," Isabel said, taking her hand, "we are here to help you."

The old woman closed her eyes. "You are too late."

That was only a taste of things to come. No age was spared, no palace, no hut. People collapsed in the streets, as if struck by lightning. They sank paralyzed to the ground before the Incan altars. The empty streets were filled only with the stench of the corpses littering the ground. Civil life had ceased; the only people left in the squares were a few corpse bearers.

Don Francisco, Isabel, and their medical team set about separating the healthy from the sick, the living from the dead. The healthy were taken into the mountains; the sick were moved to high ground to be cleaned and fed. The dead were buried in mass graves, and the city was burned. They worked for more than nine months until they were able to contain the epidemic. From time to time it flared up again, in isolated areas, here or there, but its virulence was broken. All articles that were suspected of contamination from a smallpox patient were thoroughly disinfected by heat before they came in contact with unprotected persons. They educated people in how to take care of their families and combined theoretical and practical instructions at the sick bed. In those nine months of arduous work, Don Francisco and Isabel grew into a close-knit and effective team.

Late in the evening before their departure from Cunyaca, Don

Francisco sat outside his tent, recording the events of the day in his diary and reflecting on the past months with Isabel. The rain had stopped, and the night was black. The silence of the night was interrupted by the voice of Father Tomas. "Good evening. Where is Isabel?"

Don Francisco recognized the priest by the dim light of a candle. "She was very tired and retired to her tent."

Father Tomas sat on a log, at some distance. "We have passed through some very terrible experiences in the past months," he began. "Isabel has been your constant companion in moments of tragedy, as well as in moments of danger."

"She has a very rare strength of character."

Father Tomas smiled. "Come, Francisco. There is no need to be so circumspect with me. I know you admire her."

Francisco closed his diary and laid it on the ground. "Yes, I do. But it is more than that; she has changed my life. Never have I seen things so clearly. It is as if my senses had become attuned to every resonance in her voice, every scent of her hair; I see her beauty in the smallest things — in the quivering of a blade of grass, in the humming of a bee, in the breathing of the wind, in the intoxicating fragrance of an orchid, in the warm pounding of the rain. You might say she has become my world."

"I am very glad that you feel that way," he said softly. Father Tomas leaned forward. "Last night she confessed to me that she loves you very dearly. I am only a priest, and I am by no means an expert in love, but I think I know Isabel pretty well. This is love that has grown in the months you have been together. And yet you have not confessed your feelings to each other."

"Oh, Father, but we have, in the touch of our hands, in our heedfulness for one another, in the unspoken excitement when we meet, in what we don't say, and what we don't do."

Father Tomas rose and came forward. He dropped a hand on Don Francisco's shoulder. "Thank you for opening your heart to me, Francisco. I think you should tell Isabel the way you feel. Now. Good night."

In the heat of the still night, Don Francisco gazed up at the gleaming stars and opened his diary and wrote:

Our mission will continue tomorrow. The quest for green medicines brought Isabel to my side. The rain forest is a symbol of mystery and power, a sacred link between humans and nature and Isabel is the link of my universe.

I take flight. Beneath me the world waits, pregnant with benefaction.

The rain forest, mysterious, powerful, offers me my future, a spark that a blossom to flame — my Isabel, my sweet love.

EARLY in the afternoon of November 9, 1706, John Churchill, Duke of Marlborough, was at lunch in Blenheim Palace, his expansive country home in Oxfordshire, when he was interrupted by a summons from Queen Anne. As military strategist, tactician, statesman and diplomat Churchill had no parallel. No victory in the long history of European conflict had been more decisive than Marlborough's at Blenheim, three years before. His extraordinary gift for combining land and sea power successfully in waging a war with Spain and France made him one of the most valued men in England.

When the Duke entered the royal palace the following afternoon, he found Queen Anne in conference with a dozen men: Doctor Nehemiah Grew, the founder of the sanitary movement; J. P. Frank, head of the Westminster Hospital; John Coakley Lettson, founder of the general dispensary; Jacob Benignus Winslow from Odense; Alexander Munro from Edinborough; Francise Javier de Balmis, the man who introduced vaccination into Central and South America; and military strategists and men from the war department.

John Churchill learned that the Crown's agents in Spain had reported that a scientific expedition had been sent to New Granada and Peru several years earlier to bring back information on medicinal herbs that had been widely successful in treating and preventing disease among the native population, and even among their European conquerors. Nehemiah Grew urgently advised the Queen to take possession of the *Materia Medicinal*. Such a manuscript was worth its weight in gold. If even half the Englishmen who died each year could be saved, the production of the nation's mills would triple, the economy would grow by leaps and bounds—England might easily become the most powerful nation on earth.

Queen Anne's gaze traveled over the eager faces of her counselors and came to rest on the Duke of Marborough's stern visage."What do you think, my Lord? Can it be done?"

Marborough inclined his head. "Who is leading the expedition?"

Queen Anne consulted the report at her elbow. "A young Spanish physician. Don Francisco de Mendoza."

John Churchill smiled. "Let him compile the information. Once he has it, we will take it from him."

A steady, day-long drizzle drenched the expeditionary team, as their horses carried them higher up an ancient Inca mountain path, beneath a cliff. The fierce cold of the Andes reduced everyone to silence. Men and animals moved with a ponderous gait.

Isabel caught her first distant glimpse of Ucayali, through the leaden clouds in the gray morning light, a thousand feet above the plain. Relief warmed her freezing body. The expedition burst into cheers. It was almost two months since they had left Cunyaca, and provisions were getting scarce.

In Ucayali the streets were almost empty. A few Indians, mostly women, squatted before baskets of fruit and woven goods for sale. A few Spaniards strolled in the arcades along the margins of the plaza, while a pack of llamas, heads held high, pointed ears gaily decked with streamers of colored wool, and little bells of copper and silver, strutted proudly over the cobbles behind their *mestizo* master.

The wind had risen, and swaying branches cast restless shadows over the people's faces.

Candles blazed at the altar, but the rest of the church was dimly lit. Don Francisco and Isabel knelt down before Christ on the cross.

As they walked along the marketplace, where sacks brimming

with amulets — bits of metals, plants, and animal parts — were displayed, the team stopped and gathered to watch an old blind healer, in a cap and cloak, work his magic. With herbs and charms he sought to restore vigor and dispel fear in an old, fragile woman. They all listened intently to the shaman. Julio waited until the healer had finished, and then approached him. "We are trying to find the lost temple of Cinfan."

The old man shrugged. "I am a Callawaya, my ancestors served as medicine men to the Incas and I practice the ancient herbal arts. I cure fever, I prevent crop failure, and I ensure the earth's bounty." He turned away to continue his mumbled prayers.

Julio spoke up. "It is very important for us to find the temple. Please help us!"

The shaman looked up. "What do you want from the temple?"

"We only want the knowledge of healing," Don Francisco interjected. "Not gold, not fame."

"No? Are you not flesh and blood?"

"I am a physician. So is my companion. We are on a journey to collect the ancient wisdom of healing. To us, that is a treasure more valuable than any gold."

The empty eyes gazed at Don Francisco as though they could see into his soul. "How do I know this is true?"

"You have my word."

The old man sat perfectly still. Finally, he nodded. "What has been foretold has come to pass. Meet me here in the square tomorrow morning. My son Curva will take you to find what you seek. But tell no one else the way. And touch nothing."

Afterwards, the Spaniards were greeted with friendly curiosity by the town's inhabitants, who told them tales of an underground temple sheathed in precious metals and a mysterious God that protected all things of health and beauty. This was the fabulous lost temple of Cinfan. Don Francisco tried to quell the expedition's excitement.

He knew that similar reports had already led them to nothing more exciting than a few slabs of ancient masonry. Yet, such disappointments had not deflected him from his overriding purpose: to find the lost temple of Cinfan, known in legends to be the center of Incan medicinal knowledge.

The next morning they met the old man and his son who led them on three hours of arduous trekking, out of the soggy reed-covered ground of the dense Amazon rain forest. Not a single man had spoken even in a whisper since they entered the jungle, and in order not to lose sight of one another, they walked in single file a few feet apart. Their guide Curva was a grown man, but he moved as gracefully as a boy through the almost impenetrable growth.

Curva led them to an improvised bridge of long, spindly tree trunks, lashed together with vines that stretched precariously across rocks in the rushing Ucayali River. A single misstep and a man could fall in. On the opposite bank the team mounted a steep trail, grasping vines to ascend the slippery rocks, and keeping anxious eyes out for poisonous snakes.

They rounded a promontory and suddenly were confronted with the walls of a ruined entrance of fine Inca stone. Curva stopped. "Cinfan," he said. He bowed to Don Francisco, then bent and whispered in Julio's ear a curse against those who dared trespass on the temple or steal from the gods. After straightening, he turned back and disappeared in the densely forested jungle.

For a while the sun moved slowly across the blue sky. Isabel was silent. It was like an impossible dream come true. Isabel found herself struggling to resist holding Don Francisco's hand and to tell him that they should confess their love.

During the past months she had hidden her emotions, guarding against the pain that comes with rejection, and then the silence was interrupted by Don Francisco. "This is a winding road leading up to the temple, and very steep and narrow and dangerous. May I hold your hand?" Isabel found herself blushing, looking at Don Francisco and holding his hand. He took her in his arms and kissed her. It was nothing Isabel had ever experienced before. She trembled in his arms, and she thought: *Thank you, God. Oh, thank you.*

The clouds hung oppressively low in the sky, the shades of the evening drew down, darkening the stone doors that led to the temple. Alone and awestruck, they approached in eerie silence, Don Francisco and Isabel leading the way. The entrance was hard to see at first, for it was partly covered with trees and moss, the growth of centuries, and shadowed by bamboo thickets and tangled vines. The grotesque beast carved in the stone door seemed poised to leap out at them.

After a brief struggle they pried the door open.

The dim light that filtered in illuminated the uppermost flight of dizzying stairs descending into total darkness.

One of the men refused to enter. The others trembled at the prospect of entering a total blackness, deep under the earth. They lit torches and followed Don Francisco and Isabel down the stairs leading to the temple.

For more than half an hour, their arduous descent proceeded slowly. In half darkness and descending at such a depth, the physical effort was considerable. None had energy to spare for talk. It was difficult to breathe the centuries-old musty air.

Dozen of tombs were encrusted in the walls of the stairwell, containing mummies with knees drawn up their chest, and wrapped in a netlike material. At the bottom of the stairs, torchlight glittered off gold and silver. The men stood mute, blinking at the sight before them.

All four walls of the temple were covered from top to bottom with plates and slabs of gold. Over the high altar hung the image of the Sun on a gold plate, twice the thickness of the rest of the wall plate. The face of the God was round with beams and flames of fire. On both sides of the Sun's image were the bodies of the dead kings, children of the Sun, embalmed so that they appeared to be alive. The main gates to the great hall were lined with plates of gold.

They walked in awe from hall to hall. One was devoted to the Moon, another to the planet Venus, another dedicated to the Rainbow. All were decorated throughout with gold.

In another section of the temple they found the remains of young women buried with an array of objects indicating that they were priestesses. Don Francisco speculated they had not died naturally, but had been sacrificed to the Sun God.

"We must not take any treasure from this temple except medicinal knowledge," Don Francisco whispered to the staring faces of his men.

Their only answer was a deathly stillness.

Finally they entered a very large room that depicted on its four walls, the medicinal knowledge they sought. There were many skulls with a large rectangular piece missing. Don Francisco and Isabel were fascinated. Never had they seen such precision in removing bone from a skull.

Depicted on the walls were hundreds of medical practices and treatments as well as lists of medicinal herbs and their uses. The virtues of the juices and resins of special trees were also described.

Don Francisco and Isabel sat on the floor to organize all the bits and pieces of information. Then they assigned various tasks to their men, enabling them to do the work of many months in less than two weeks.

The food and water rations in the cave where they stayed were cut to bare necessity. Don Francisco saw greed and fear in some of the men's faces.

The first night they pitched their tents inside the cave and tried to sleep, but managed only a few hours—the maddening, persistent rasping sound of some kind of monster worked on them, until they could take it no longer. Don Francisco scrambled out of the mosquito net and grabbed a torch in one hand and a bush knife in the other.

Watching Don Francisco confront the source of the noise, one of the men implored Father Tomas, "Father, if I don't get out of this cave alive, please give this ring to my wife."

The torch light revealed a large snake with its body rolled around the skull of a Mochica Indian, emanating from a moss-covered, stone slab. Speechless at the ugly scene, Don Francisco used a knife and stabbed it several times through the serpent's body.

The men gathered around the immobile reptile. Don Francisco appointed two men to dig around the slab; after excavating for few meters, one of the spades struck what sounded like, and was soon revealed to be, a perfectly preserved wooden box. Once all the dark-looking earth was removed and piled on each side of the rectangular pit, Don Francisco saw a large coffin like box, its cover badly warped.

It was Don Francisco himself, awkwardly straddling the hole, his shoes caked with mud, who bent down and pulled at the top of the box. It gave way without effort, having disintegrated long ago. As the board slowly lifted, the inside revealed Incan skulls and bronze trepanning instruments—knife, tweezers, chisels, hammer, scalpel, and needle. An engraved stone depicted an operation of a man suffering speech impairment from a brain lesion, using a tourniquet around his head, Inca-style to stop bleeding. They also found a ceramic jug depicting a doctor straddling his patient, while performing a skull operation.

Early the next morning, Don Francisco, Isabel and their men, having recorded all the information they could, covered the site and replaced the slab.

"We cannot continue staying in this temple too much longer, we need to go out," said one of the men.

Don Francisco ordered his men to camp outside the temple at night, even if it meant a loss of time and effort, but it was important for their morale and health.

Isabel noticed that Julio was very quiet and nervous most of the time; his perennial smile had departed his lips. She expressed her anxiety to Francisco, but he dismissed her concerns.

On the third day, Julio approached Isabel with his hand in his pocket. "I am going out of the temple; I will wait for you outside, until you all decide to leave this place."

"Is anything wrong, Julio, are you afraid?"

"No, I am not." But Isabel could see his tears emerging. There was something so touching and earnest about Julio, she thought. "Why don't you tell me what's wrong?"

"I can't," he responded with almost terror in his eyes, as he pulled out his hand from his trousers' pocket.

Isabel put her handkerchief gently into his hand, and for a moment the two sat together in silence.

"I'll tell you one thing," said Julio at last. "I'm afraid of the Gods."

"You should not fear God—God is all wisdom, all goodness, and has the power to punish or forgive the sinner in just manner."

Julio put Isabel's handkerchief into her hand and said no more.

Oppressed as they were by the foul smell, the darkness, the temptation of the gold in the temple that could not be theirs, they were also pressed by the limitation of time they were given in which to gather information, knowing that there would be no other opportunity to return to the site, to fill in any gaps. The team worked as many hours as their bodies would allow. It was hard to keep the men's spirits up when things went wrong.

There was no longer raw panic, merely an ardent desire to leave the temple as quickly as possible.

"I have only a half-glass of water and a morsel of bread in the entire morning," said El Chato to an Indian.

"Why don't you pray for water to your God? I am also thirsty!" exclaimed the Indian.

"Hey, look at that water spring," one of the men screamed.

Other men nearby thought he was having hallucinations or had lost his mind. Then Don Francisco looked with his good eyes and saw it too. El Chato nudged Father Pedro next to him and asked if he could also see the spring.

"Yes. It is a miracle! God is with us."

"Oh God, give me water," El Chato said but in prayer.

As they were ready to depart the last day with the medicinal treasure, one of the men tried to remove a gold artifact from the temple. A time-bitten skeleton tumbled down, with a bony hand, holding a small golden figure. Beside the rib cage of the skeleton was a rust-eaten breastplate, and the skull was still encased in a Spanish helmet. Everyone was stunned by the grotesque figure. Suddenly they heard a thunderous roar, and the ground began to undulate as if some monster were shaking the earth.

Julio's eyes closed and he fainted. Father Tomas caught him in his arms, before Julio reached the ground, and they ran for their lives. All the others ran after the priest, blessing themselves in darkness on the steep stairs leading to the outside. There was a long tumultuous shouting sound like the voices of a thousand demons. Their impetuous fury nearly lifted everybody from their feet. Upon recovering from their shock in the safety of the outside, the team found no sign of recent rain. Julio opened his eyes to a serene sky resplendent with stars.

The trail out of Ucayali heading toward majestic peaks grew steeper and narrower as it rose. The expedition was headed west into the rain forest. They walked beneath a thick canopy formed by giant trees. Light filtered patchily through the canopy, weaving patterns on the forest floor of gloomy green. The sides of the wettest branches turned into hanging gardens of orchids, bromeliads and ferns. The wind buffeted a small monkey; butterflies glided effortlessly through the darkness. The silence was broken high above the ground by packs of monkeys; their dry, mousy smell lingered for a long time in the air. As Don Francisco and Isabel passed, they heard a rush and whiz over their heads. Isabel kept perfectly still and caught sight of one of the monkeys sitting immovable in a tree. She discovered that the whole forest around her was alive with monkeys, perched like fruit on the branches.

At the mercy of insects, they struggled from one thick undergrowth to the next, fighting the feeling of panic that rose, as their feet sank out of sight into the fetid black swamp water. With each step, the earth beneath them seemed like the sea. Finally they reached solid ground and decided to make camp. Everyone needed a rest.

The sunlight was still bright but slanting and filtering through the green leaves of the forest when they broke dry branches to build a fire so they could boil potatoes and corn for broth.

"Where is Julio?" Father Tomas asked El Chato. "Wasn't he behind you?"

"I last saw him two hours ago. He was holding a long bamboo pole probing the ground. He was going to try to find a better way to cross the muddy swamp. I thought he would arrive before us."

Father Tomas looked down at El Chato. "But he's not here!"

"You saw him disappear two hours ago and you did not say a word?" Don Francisco cried.

"*Señor*!" El Chato replied, sweating. "I was too busy to see what happened! I was in constant fear of slipping down into the bottomless mire or ending up in the digestive tract of one of those wild animals — I am sorry for my weakness." He hung his head.

"I'd better go and look for him. I will go part of the way, to see if I can find him. Otherwise I'll return for help."

"We'll go with you," responded Isabel.

"No, you'd better wait here. Julio could arrive any time, and you need to rest, we have a long day ahead of us."

Isabel watched Don Francisco walk along the open track until he disappeared among the trees.

He looked in all directions upon fields of muddy soil and high grass waving in the wind. Francisco tested the depth of the mud with his pole, and then waded across, soaking his clothes to the waist. With each step the mud released his foot with a loud squishing noise. With each step he disappeared farther into the green horizon.

The rest of the team waited anxiously. Time crawled by.

"Oh! Where is Don Francisco?" cried Isabel, wringing her hands. He's had plenty of time to return! What's happened to him?"

"I am sure he will be here soon," Father Tomas responded gently.

Two hours elapsed, and the afternoon turned golden.

"I can't bear it another minute." Isabel jumped up and grabbed a pole. "I'm going to look for him!"

"Let's cross the swamp and then form into parties, along different paths," Father Tomas suggested.

"Don Francisco may have found Julio injured," El Chato observed. "That might have delayed his return."

Skirting the muddy, thick grass that stretched into the far distance, they reached the other side of the swamp and scattered through the dense undergrowth. They spread out into a half-circle, moving along within a few paces of one another. Isabel pressed purposely forward up the path, with set lips and fixed eyes. Father Tomas walked closely behind her, reassuring her that everything was going to be all right.

The ground rose, the trees closed in on them, the undergrowth became thicker. They pushed their way through the encroaching bushes. Suddenly El Chato uttered a great shout of dismay, and every one in the line halted, then hurried forward.

Isabel turned towards the cry, trailed by the weary priest. Thrusting through thorn-branches she came out into a clearing. Julio lay on his back, his brown, slender shoulders flattened to the ground and his arms spread wide. Isabel knelt beside him and turned him over. A feathered arrow protruded from his rib cage. Julio's lips were drawn back from his teeth in a frozen smile. Isabel looked for any sign of life, while the men hovered anxiously around her, tense and silent. As she examined his inert body, a ceremonial knife fell from the pocket of his trousers.

"I know it came from the high altar!" exclaimed El Chato.

"It was wrong to take it from the temple, but he is so young," murmured Isabel.

Another cry sounded from the bushes not far away. At once the silence changed into noise and motion. Isabel and the men tore through the bushes to where Don Francisco lay on the wet ground. She rushed to his side, falling on her knees, pressing gentle fingers to his throat, laying her ear on his chest.

"Oh, my God," she choked, "you are still alive!"

She examined his body with care and clinical efficiency. An arrow had pierced the surface of his arm without penetrating deeply. Blood oozed from a wound in his left upper arm, but she could find no other injury.

Father Tomas bent down to her. "Is he going to live?"

"I don't know. It is difficult to determine if it is a poisonous arrow, and if it is to predict its effects. Native poisons are very different, some potent, some not. *Curare* can produce weakness, paralysis or death. We must find an antidote called *Mulo* by the natives. It will help revive the paralyzed muscles." She described the plant. "It reaches the height of a man, and the green leaves may reach the length of my arm, and tend to be thick, broadly ovate."

"How can we help you, Doña?" asked the priest.

She asked to have the men carry Don Francisco to a more comfortable place.

El Chato and the priest lifted the paralyzed man. From time to time, they had to lay him down and rest, but Isabel didn't let them stop till they reached a small hill.

Then El Chato and the Indians went to search for the green antidote that could save Don Francisco's life, disappearing into the woods like shadows in the night.

Throughout the solitary hours of the night, Julio's body lay inert while the priest stood motionless looking up towards the heavens.

A short distance away, her head reclined upon Don Francisco's dormant chest, Isabel lay limp, waiting for the first sign of recovery. Shortly before sunrise, El Chato appeared. He held up a fistful of green stuff.

"Doña Isabel! We found it, I think! Is this the plant?"

Isabel examined the plant. "Yes, yes. Oh, thank you. El Chato! Now! I must prepare the antidote."

Higher up the hillside on a narrow natural terrace, Father Tomas marked out the place for Julio's grave and men began to dig. The ground was moist but light, and they made a deep pit to prevent wild beasts from reaching the body. Gradually the diggers sank to their shoulders, and by mid-morning El Chato, the shortest of the gang, had almost disappeared into the depths of the grave.

They carried the once agile body of the Indian boy to the gravesite, his face concealed by the cloth. As his body was placed in the grave, and covered with moist earth, Isabel raised her head from Don Francisco's chest and dried her eyes with the back of her hand. She joined the burial ceremony. She had applied the antidote and after many hours of waiting for the results, she was sick at heart, struck by the horrible thought that soon they would be burying her adored companion's body, too. Turning to gaze at Don Francisco one last time she heard one of the Indians screaming, "Don Francisco opened his eyes!"

Isabel's breath stopped. She ran toward her beloved. "Francisco! Francisco! You are alive!"

The mourners abandoned their burial activities.

"Let Doña Isabel be alone with Don Francisco and then we continue,." said Father Tomas.

Don Francisco regarded Isabel with wondering eyes, as if unsure what he saw was real or part of a dream, outside his control.

Isabel raised his head gently and cradled it against her breast. In a tender voice she said, "You are really alive, Francisco, you have returned, you are with us."

His lips moved stiffly. "Why are you weeping?"

After a long silence she responded, "I have never wept this way before, and I have never wept because of pain or annoyance, but always from joy." As she wept, her liquid eyes shone brilliantly. "You had an accident but now you are all right. So long as you live, I can be happy again."

They looked at each other for a long time, seeing each other clearly, with new eyes, and speaking to each other without needing words.

An hour later, Don Francisco fully recovered from his paralysis. Isabel told him of Julio's death, and how close he had come to sharing the same fate.

Late in the afternoon the burial continued and Father Tomas presided over the Catholic funeral service, even though Julio was never fully catechized and always spoke of the God of the white people as if He were not his own. He was buried with Father Tomas's silver crucifix and the ceremonial knife from the temple of Cinfan in his arms.

One evening, after another long and suffocating day, searching for a place to camp, they clambered down a trail, past tumbling mountain creeks, to the valley floor and the gentle slope of the Napo River.

While the men were pitching goat-hair tents and stringing their hammocks above the boggy ground, Isabel walked to the riverbank, poured a bucket of water on her head, took her shoes off and sat down at the edge, swinging her legs so her feet just dangled in the water. She shook her wet hair and began to sing an Indian melody. Suddenly she stopped. She could scarcely believe her eyes. A tiger stood at the edge of the jungle, less than ten meters from her. She rose slowly, moving cautiously, and made her way down to the camp. Once she stumbled and fell against the muddy bank, and panic struck, but the tiger had disappeared into the darkness of the jungle. As she struggled to stand up, she felt Don Francisco's strong arms lift her off the ground.

"Are you hurt, Isabel? What happened?"

"I think I've twisted my ankle."

"Slide your arm around my neck."

He lifted her with ease and carried her back to camp. She

looked up at him shyly, scalded by the intensity of his nearness. His arms were like iron, yet his body moved softly against hers.

"How did it happen?" he asked roughly.

"I went to the stream to wash my hair. I saw a tiger—"

"A tiger!"

"With huge, green eyes— a magnificent beast—but I stumbled on the bank."

"No wonder." Thunder rumbled in the distance. His arms tightened around her. "I'll have the fire built up tonight and post a watch."

"Oh, Francisco, I'm sure he's gone by now."

He carried her into the tent and bent over her with professional attention. "It appears to be only a sprain. Shall I dress it for you?"

Isabel laughed. "Thank you, Doctor, but that I can do myself. You'd better see to the gear. I think we're going to have a storm."

As he reached the curtain of the tent, rain fell suddenly in a thunderous roar, forming a second curtain, solid and glittering. He paused, glancing back at Isabel, disheveled and breathless in her hammock.

"Go on," she whispered. Still, he waited, poised, then with a sudden jerk hauled himself through the curtain and disappeared from view. Isabel shut her eyes and exhaled.

The next morning, under a blue sky and with a cool breeze coming off the river, Isabel rose slowly from her hammock and limped cautiously back to the riverbank. A solitary orchid grew on the surface of a half-drowned musty tree trunk, a bright jewel of the jungle. The petals were light blue, its back and wings streaked with red. She had never seen such a perfect shade of blue. She reached out and touched the delicate flower.

Don Francisco's gaze had followed her from the moment she left her tent. He rose without knowing it. His feet followed the path she had taken of her own will, moving as silently through the undergrowth as any jungle animal. He stood watching her with the orchid in her hand. She was so perfectly still, so perfectly exquisite, a glowing personification of the flower's beauty.

Isabel lifted the orchid to her nose and drew a slow breath, her eyes closing. Francisco took her shoulders from behind, bent and kissed her neck. "My darling Isabel."

She gasped and turned to him. "Francisco!"

He kissed her before she could say more. They embraced, gazing at one another with grave excitement.

"I have loved you from the first moment I saw you. Marry me, Isabel. We're meant for one another."

She breathed. "I have known it from the same moment. I love you more than life, Francisco. We must write to Father, to ask for his blessing."

"I will do it now — I will send one of the natives to Cajamarca. Oh, sweet woman, how long I have waited for this moment!"

And I!' she returned, leaning into him. "Don't let me go. Don't ever let me go."

"Isabel, I yearn for the moment when we will be husband and wife. But I cannot wait until we return to Cajamarca. It could be a year, even more. If your father gives his consent, let us marry as soon as we arrive in Cartagena. There is a beautiful church there."

"Yes." Her hand gripped his more tightly. "I shall write to Father and ask him to meet us there."

He took her in his arms, and kissed her. "Isabel, Isabel, all night long, I held you in my arms, in my dreams."

She rested her face against his chest. "Soon, my love. Be patient."

"Would you marry me, Isabel, if your father refused my suit?"

"My dearest Francisco, of course I would. I love no one but you. And never will. My father will consent."

Hiking their way through the jungle, they discovered hundreds of species of trees, climbers and creepers, in addition to a huge array of parasites and herbs. With wonder, Don Francisco told his companions, "Those trees are more than one hundred meters high." They saw hundreds of species of birds and species of mammals, together with scores of reptiles, uncounted insects swarming over the greenery. "It looks like Nature gone mad," said one of Don Francisco's Spanish men. As Manuel spoke, he swung a machete to cut a tree branch and suffered a deep gash on his arm. With Manuel wondering whether he would bleed to death or die from infection, a local Indian who the Spaniards had befriended ran into the jungle, returned with some dark red tree sap, and had Manuel drink it. The bleeding stopped within minutes. In a short time the wound healed rapidly, without a scar.

They traveled by canoe along treacherous river feeding the mighty Amazon and then the Amazon itself, so wide it looked more like a sea than a river. The water did not flow, but eased its way through the forest as if responding to a distant call.

They spent days fighting the currents, mosquitoes and heat. They arrived in Leticia, an odd little settlement, cut off from the world. For a week they stayed there, studying the vegetation, collecting information and replenishing supplies. From Leticia they passed through jungles, over plains and across mountains before they reached Miraflores. From there, the precious cargo was transported by mules through the lush tropical forest, corn fields, and valleys, and high rugged terrain along the Vaupes, Guviare and Magdalena rivers and their tributaries, until they reached Honda. There they met the two other expeditionary teams, which already had arrived from Mexico and Venezuela only a few weeks before.

"We must spend the next few weeks cataloging our findings," Don Francisco told his people. He described a host of plants that the Indians used to prevent tooth decay, painlessly extract teeth, dissolve kidney stones, heal burns, and cure and prevent scores of other maladies. All in all, Francisco was very pleased. They had been able to assemble and classify nearly 3,500 medicinal herb species to treat hundreds of common ailments. Complemented by the acquisition of the *Badianus manuscript* from Mexico and the book from Isabel's grandmother, the native art of healing had been documented in great detail, with drawings of two thousand plants, and more than four thousand recipes.

"I think it will be the greatest collection of ancient medicinal wisdom ever assembled," Isabel said with pride.

The wealth of their findings from Peru, Nueva Granada and Mexico was written on parchment made from sheepskin. They carefully wrapped the documents and secured them by cords, then rolled them up and put them in glass bottles, sealing the narrow necks with wax and silver. The bottles were put into mahogany barrels and packed with sawdust. The barrels were then sealed with tar and strapped with metal.

Don Francisco arranged for the expeditionary team to transport the precious cargo from Honda north to Portobelo via the Cauca and Atrato rivers, until they reached the Gulf of Uraba, and then overland to Panama. In Portobelo the *Materia Medicinal* would be put aboard the *Galléon San José*, which would receive the treasures bound for Spain. Before leaving for Seville, the *San José* would call at Cartagena.

Francisco planned to travel with Isabel straight to Cartagena, to celebrate their wedding in that beautiful city before continuing on.

On the morning of the expedition's departure for Portobelo, Francisco was at breakfast when he heard a quick step upon the staircase, followed by a loud knock at the door. Father Tomas burst into the room, out of breath, and clutching a much-folded paper in his hand, which he thrust toward him.

Don Francisco read a tersely worded warning, from the Governor of Cartagena: He was not to come to Cartagena, but to leave Honda for Portobelo with his men, as soon as possible. Through Spanish intelligence they had learned that twenty Englishmen were already in Honda, looking for Don Francisco. A hundred mulattos from Jamaica supported them.

"Why do they want *me*?" Don Francisco cried.

"They have orders from England to confiscate the *Materia Medicinal* and transport it to London! Hurry, Don Francisco, hurry, I beg you! We must leave at once! They are already in the vicinity!"

"BUT I can't leave without Isabel. She must come with me."

"It will be too dangerous for her. And there is no time. We must leave now."

"But I have to inform her of what is happening. I must!"

"Write her a note if you wish, and I will deliver it to her once you are safely away. I will take Isabel to Cartagena; you can meet her there, when the *galleón* stops on its way to Spain. But in the name of God, Don Francisco, a short note only. You must leave immediately for Portobelo! Those mulattos are searching the village now!"

As his companions hastily packed his belongings, Don Francisco composed his letter to Isabel.

My dearest:

Forgive me for not keeping our appointment this morning, but I have just learned from the Governor that the Crown of England has sent a team to seize our precious manuscript and vast samples. They are searching the town for me.

I must depart immediately for Portobelo and see the Materia Medicinal safe aboard the San José. Go to Cartagena de Indias with Father Tomas and El Chato. You will be safe if you are not with me.

I will meet you there. We will marry before we depart for Spain. Be brave, my love. I love you, and God be with us always.

Francisco.

He sealed the letter and handed it to the priest. Someone thumped on the front door. Francisco fled.

Captain Robert Clive pushed his way into the house followed by four large men. "That fat priest was seen leaving the house. You, Johnson, and you, Woods, search every room."

A sound came from the end of the corridor, behind a door. The men loaded their muskets.

"Open it!" ordered Clive. Two men sidled up to the door and threw it open. The room was empty. One of the officers raced to a gate beyond and wrestled excitedly with the latch.

"Where does that lead?" Clive growled.

His men took up places on either side of the sliding barrier and yanked it open. "To the cellar." There was no one inside, but clothing littered the floor. "There's your answer!" Behind a chair was the mouth of a tunnel that led to the garden.

Two men in priest's robes stepped into the sunlit street. "Where shall we go?" Father Tomas asked Don Francisco.

"I don't know of any temporary place to hide until the cargo is loaded onto a boat. Is there a tavern nearby? Or a church?"

"Yes, a church in Calle Real, not too far from the river."

The streets were empty and the city was overcast and quiet. They walked along Calle Real, across Plaza de Dios and then over the river into the old town.

"What's going on?" Don Francisco wondered. "Where is everyone?"

"Probably they're sitting in their homes, afraid to venture outside because of the foreigners."

The church was empty. Through the stillness they heard a rattling of a wagon. A horse came galloping towards them. Restive, shying at the shadows, its wild eyes and distended nostrils gave it a ghostly look in the pale light. The driver was pulling on the reins. The horse reared. Foam flew from its mouth.

"Father," the driver exclaimed, "I was looking for you. We need a priest. My mother is dying. Please come give her the Last Rites."

"All right, all right, son, calm yourself," Don Francisco said, looking the wagon over. "If you will take me to the port, Father Tomas will go with you to see your mother. And after that, you will take him back to the center of town. He has an important message to deliver."

It was already seven o'clock in the evening and Isabel had not left her room. She had spent the whole day in feverish agitation, worrying about Francisco's absence, about her father and his reaction to her letter. Would he be in Cartagena when she and Francisco arrived? There were a thousand details to take care of before their wedding, but uppermost in her mind was how to dress in the next hour, when she was to accompany Don Francisco to a dinner hosted by the Mayor of Honda. She hummed a breathless, excited melody as she brushed and braided her hair. Someone knocked at the door. A male voice in the vestibule said, "Is *Señor*ita Isabel at home?"

A man's steps sounded in the corridor. Isabel gazed into the mirror, but she did not see herself. It was Father Tomas' voice.

She rose hastily and went out to meet him. "Father Tomas! What is amiss?"

"My child, it has been a trying day. There are Englishmen in town determined to take possession of the treasure. But do not fear, he is all right. Don Francisco asked me to give you this letter."

With perplexity on her pale face, and trembling hands, Isabel opened the letter and stood transfixed. Father Tomas anxiously watched her but could detect no tears, no outward signs of any emotion at all. But the letter dropped from Isabel's frozen fingers and floated slowly to the floor.

DEEP into the night, under the cover of darkness, Don Francisco's men loaded the precious cargo aboard a ship, headed down the hazardous Magdalena and Atrato rivers, toward the gulf of Uraba. At Pito it was off-loaded onto mules, carried to El Real de Santa Maria, and then placed aboard a flat-bottomed barge for the final stage of the trip.

When they arrived in Portobelo, the yearly fair was in full swing. The fair usually lasted an entire month, but this year the urgent need for the treasure in Spain cut its duration to less than a week. Due to the war with England, no treasure had been sent from South America to Spain in six years.

Soon after Don Francisco arrived in Portobelo, seventeen ships arrived from Spain to receive the *Materia Medicinal* and tons of gold and silver from the inland mines of Potosi.

Don Francisco watched as a great part of the Peruvian treasure, along with all the precious information he and his team had gathered over the past eight years, was loaded into the *San José*, commanded by Captain Bellanueva, a 64- gun flagship that was part of the Spanish Flotilla. Don Francisco could hardly comprehend the enormity of the treasure: gold bars, silver ingots, gold and silver coins, gold chains, gold disks, emeralds, rings, brooches, religious medallions, reliquaries, with an estimated value of over seven million pesos, and the *Materia Medicinal* carefully sealed in barrels.

Since only three ships were heavily armed, they received the remaining treasure. The *Almiranta San Martin*, 64-guns; the *galleón Govierno*, 44-guns; and an unidentified *Urca*, commanded by Captain Francisco Nieto, all in the Spanish Flotilla that was part of the Armada.

On the 28th of May, 1708, the flotilla departed from Portobelo. Due to light winds it did not reach Islas de Baru until June 8. Early in the afternoon, leaning over the taffrail, Don Francisco detected a squadron of four ships cruising off the coast of Nueva Granada and immediately went to the Captain Bellanueva's own cabin and reported what he had seen. By the time the captain went on deck, the four ships had disappeared from view.

The men posted at the rigging could not confirm the apparition.

Don Francisco paced the deck with an unquiet and tremulous step, scanning the horizon, until he heard the alarmed voices of the men at the rigging, announcing the detection of four British ships. Two of the men rushed to inform Captain Bellanueva. Moments later, the entire crew was in a state of alarm. The British obviously had sighted the Spanish Flotilla, and were making sail to intercept and engage them.

Captain Bellanueva ordered his crew to spread more sail. Only several leagues away, was the safe port of Cartagena, but the winds were light, progress was slow, and the British had the weather on their side.

As evening drew on, it became clear that the Spanish Flotilla would not reach port in time. The Captain ordered his men to engage the British ships. The Spanish Flotilla formed a line of battle with the *galleón Govierno* in the lead, the *galleón San José* in the middle of the line and the *Almiranta San Martin* taking up the rear. The remaining fourteen ships were positioned about equally between the three large *galleóns*.

The battle ensued, lasting well into the night. Although Don Francisco and Captain Villanueva were almost instantly aware of the British attack on the *San José*, a few leagues ahead in the starboard column, in the darkness and confusion, they could not make out exactly what had happened or how many ships had been hit.

Commodore Charles Wages, Captain of the British Expedition, engaged the *San José* in the small hours of the morning and mauled her severely. Of the 250 cannon balls smashing into her hull and rigging, one finally struck the powder magazine. The *San José* exploded and quickly sank. The explosion was so forceful that the lower gun ports of the Expedition were flooded by a wave of water. Don Francisco's first thoughts were for the safety of his painstaking haul of gathered documents: Had they been blown to bits? Then, as the cold water closed over his head, he thought, *Oh God! We are going down!*

WHEN Isabel arrived in Cartagena she was struck at once by the view of the city at sunset, its gray walls and red-tiled roofs. The houses were built with thick walls of stone and brick around open courts in the Moorish style, and their iron-barred doors and windows gave the impression of being a part of the fortification.

She climbed the hills until she could see the wide expanse of ocean. Soon, she would see the *galleóns* sailing towards Cartagena, with Don Francisco aboard.

In her hand she clutched a letter from her father. Don Manuel had received the news of her engagement with enthusiastic approval. His letter expressed his affection and trusting love for the couple, and better yet, he was on his way to Cartagena to attend the wedding in person. Isabel's step was buoyant. In less than one week she would be reunited with Francisco and with her father.

The next day, she and Father Tomas went to order her wedding dress.

Father Tomas hugged her paternally when he saw her draped in satin and lace. "Child, you're going to make a beautiful bride."

Isabel laughed aloud. Day and night she smiled. She could not keep her happiness from showing on her face. They made their way through the crowded streets, to the order of the Lady of Mount Carmel monastery, outside the center of Cartagena, where through Father Tomas's intervention, she had been given temporary lodging. As the priest bid her good night, he said, "Tomorrow we are going to the Church of Pedro Claver to see to the arrangements. Are you nervous?"

"I am excited."

In her room, she looked at herself in the mirror, "Francisco, my love, I am ready for you. Please hurry."

That night, full of anticipation, she lay for a long time in her bed, with her eyes fixed on space. Her mind was flooded with thoughts of seeing Francisco again.

At daybreak, she was awakened by the ringing of the bells of the Church of St. Teresa, high in the Turbaco hills. She always enjoyed waking up slowly, languorously stretching like a kitten. She kept her eyes closed, recalling from the near past her memories of Francisco before and after he had asked her to marry him.

She had just donned a white dress and was slipping her bare feet into shoes, when there was a knock at her door. She opened it.

The Mother Superior gazed at her. "My child, a gentleman wishes to see you."

"Father Tomas?"

"No, somebody else."

She hurried to the entrance hall.

A tall, pale man was at the door. "Good morning, *Señor*ita Goméz. I am Luis Zapata, the Governor's envoy. I come in his name to ask you to accompany me to his office. He has some news for you, and he wants to convey it personally."

As *Señor* Zapata and Isabel entered the palace compound, crowds of agitated people were shouting and screaming; frantic police ran about. "What happened?" Isabel asked. But the pale man turned paler and did not answer.

The Governor's house was of green brick, with wrought iron

balconies, and guard towers at each corner. It was a hot, wet day, and as far as the eye could see, columns of heat waves rose like *galléons* in formation.

The Governor, Don Miguel Augusto de Villanueva, was in a panic. He was a small, mustached man, and his whole body shook as he talked and paced. "We need to set up an inquiry with all of the crew of the *San Martin.* The French frigate's Captain, Andres Chonlu, and his people are nothing more than spies. How could I have believed them?"

Seeing Isabel, the Governor stopped and bowed politely and asked her to follow him to his private suite. Her heart thudded painfully against her ribs and her limbs moved heavily. Something was very wrong.

The Governor greeted her with warmth. "*Señor*ita Goméz, unfortunately I have some disturbing news. I didn't inform you sooner, because only this morning, we were able to obtain a report of the incident. The British attacked the Spanish Flotilla coming from Portobelo. The *San Martin* was the only *galleón* to reach Cartagena. The human casualties aboard the other *galleóns* were very high."

Isabel fought to keep tears from her eyes. "Was no one saved? Did they all die?"

"I am afraid I don't yet have all the details."

Isabel moved clumsily towards the door unable to feel her feet. "Please, let me know as soon as you receive news of Don Francisco."

Father Tomas entered the room. "Isabel! I just received word," he began excitedly.

"Tomas! Tomas! He is gone!" Isabel cried.

"No, child, not so hasty. People are saying that some of the crew from the *San José* was picked up by passing vessels."

Señor Zapata hurried in. "Governor, we have more news." He thrust a thin parchment into the Governor's hands.

Isabel's head began to whirl. Father Tomas took her arm to steady her.

"Have a seat, *Señor*ita," the Governor said. "Zapata, read it aloud."

Preliminary Finding on the Spanish Flotilla Tragedy

This report dated June 20th, 1708 was compiled and prepared by the investigative panel that included: Captain General of the Armada of Indies, Count of Casa Alegre; Joseph Fernandez de Santilla and five other ranking officers representing the Crown.

This report is based on testimony from the survivors who reached Cartagena as well as from officials in Cartagena and Portobelo.

Isabel could barely absorb the details.

At 17:30 on the 8th of June, a few leagues from the port of Cartagena, the Spanish Flotilla engaged in battle with English warships. Soon after, the San José exploded and sank.

The Expedition then engaged the Govierno, the San Martin and the French privateer Urca. The remainder of the Spanish Flotilla scattered when the San José sank. Within hours, the San Martin broke off from the engagement and slipped northward into the darkness, managing to reach the safety of Cartagena.

Isabel's eyes narrowed and her face turn cold, she was shaking.

The Govierno sustained sufficient damage to her rudder to render her helpless. Unable to defend herself or run for the cover of darkness, she surrendered to the Expedition at about 02:00 the following morning. During the succeeding two days the Kingston and the Portland pursued the San Martin, but the galléon reached Boca Chica before the English mustered enough courage to engage her.

The outcome of the British and Spanish engagement was the loss of the Govierno and the personal belongings of the passengers who were returning home; and the San José with nearly all the passengers and crew, about nine hundred people and the loss of the valuable cargo, including a secret treasure called Materia Medicinal. There are differing accounts of the fate of the survivors from the San José.

Isabel tried to control her feelings, she didn't know if she should cry or scream.

On June 9, 1708, the Expedition anchored close to Rosario Islands and disembarked all Spanish prisoners captured from the Govierno and five survivors from the San José who witnessed the capture of a few other survivors. There were contradictory statements as to the number of these prisoners.

In the name of the Investigative Panel

Count of Casa Alegre

As Father Tomas finished reading, Isabel uttered a sharp cry, shook with noiseless, convulsive sobs, and fainted.

She woke up in her room at the monastery. She did not rise from bed. She did not eat, speak or sleep.

The next morning the Reverend Mother entered Isabel's room with a firm step. Isabel lay on the bed with her face hidden in her hands. She had not stirred from the position in which the Reverend Mother had left her the night before.

"Come, come, my child, you must have hope."

Trembling with despair, Isabel wept. "I cannot. I cannot. All is lost! Please leave me alone, please let me stay here."

"You can stay with us as long as you wish."

During the following week the sisters tried to console Isabel, tried to give her hope. Isabel had difficulty sleeping. She could not move. It was as though all her senses had been paralyzed for so long that she was unable to take in what happened. She stared at her feet for hours at a time and rarely responded when anyone spoke to her. She seemed to live in a distant world where neither voices nor visions could impinge on her dream-like state.

When Don Manuel arrived in Cartagena he was shocked to find his daughter so thin and pale, so immobile. He determined to take her home, but she refused, reviving from her melancholy just long enough to adamantly reject his overtures of consolation.

Don Manuel was distraught over his daughter's unhappiness. He had always admired her courageous behavior. He felt helpless. He remembered how much solace she had once found in church. "Talk to the priest," he begged. "Perhaps he can help you."

But Isabel would have nothing to do with God. She stayed

in her room at the convent, alone for hours and days. Every day when her father returned to see her she was seated in the same chair, staring at the walls, waiting for news from Don Francisco. For three months, Don Manuel visited his daughter daily, prayed for her, begged her to come home with him. But Isabel refused. Nothing he could say or do would convince her to abandon Cartagena. At the end of three months, he sadly said good-bye, paid the good sisters for her upkeep and left her in their care.

One evening Isabel had a long talk with the Reverend Mother. "Why do people join convents?" Isabel asked.

"Most of them come to dedicate themselves to God. But some come because they have no hope. We give them hope. Others join us because they feel they have no reason to live. We show them that God is the reason. Some come because they are running away. Yet others seek us out because they feel estranged and want to belong."

As time passed, the intellectual aspects of the Catholic Church stirred Isabel. She read St. Augustine's Confessions, the writings of St. Francis of Assisi and of St. Teresa, the founder of Carmelites Descalzas. Isabel watched the nuns as they prayed or walked shoeless through the halls, sensing in them an almost overpowering serenity. She envied the joy they seemed to radiate. To Isabel, the convent seemed a house of love.

One day she went to see the Mother Prioress. "Could you help me to join the convent in Seville?"

"Why in Seville, my child?"

"Seville was the city where Don Francisco and I were planning to live after our wedding."

Four months later, she arrived in Seville. Seven weeks later, she took her vows.

Our Lady of Mount Carmel Monastery was a medieval fortress dropped into the heart of Seville. But the city had little effect on the Carmelite sisters who lived in complete isolation, rooted in the sixteenth century.

Even the priest who visited them six mornings a week was unsure of their number and the range of their ages. They remained hidden to visitors, communicating only through a barrel-shaped, revolving wooden cabinet called a turn, first used in the Middle Ages to pass goods into monasteries without violating the cloister.

To enter the turn room in the Seville cloister was to step back in time. Parishioners bearing handwritten pleas for prayers or bags with food that the nuns depended on for their meals were taken through the gates into an anteroom, then into a tiny parlor. They placed items for the nuns inside a polished oak barrel half submerged in the bricks, and like a secret revolving bookcase, the barrel was spun around so that a sister in a room on the other side could take the contents. Above the turn was a hand-lettered sign, "In the House of God, Talk to Him or Do Not Say Anything." They believed that only by shutting out the world could they be completely devoted to their sole mission: prayer.

The living conditions of the convent were Spartan. The nuns slept fully dressed on pallets of straw, covered with rough woolen sheets. Isabel had her own tiny cell, furnished with a pallet and a straight-backed wooden chair. There was no washstand. The winter cold struck like a knife, and chill, pale light filtered in through barred windows from an inside court. A small earthen jug and basin stood in the corner on the floor. No nun was ever permitted to enter the cell of another. There was no recreation of any kind — only work and prayer. The nuns rotated their kind of work every two weeks. There were work areas for bookbinding, weaving and making cookies and bread. Isabel began making candies to sell to the public. Inside, the nuns kept up their prayers undisturbed.

They usually rose before 5:30 to say the morning portion of the Divine Office, which was intended to make the entire day holy. They attended Mass at 6:30 and received communion through a small gold door in the chapel wall. Then they spent the rest of the day in nearly complete silence, responding to letters, doing chores, but mostly praying — together or alone in their cells. Yet the inmates lived in an ecstasy such as they had never known in the outside world. Here Isabel renounced physical love, freedom of choice and ownership of possessions, but in giving up those things she also renounced greed and competition. The pressures and temptations of the material world vanished.

FROM the end of June 1708 until August 1711, Don Francisco was forced to conform to the inflexible rules of his captors. All inmates had to go to meals, and no talking was permitted in the lines. But what the jailers could not do was take Isabel from his mind.

The Reading Jail was a forbidding, vast, two-story building with heavily barred windows. There were turrets at each of its four corners and the English flag flew over the door. A tall, muscular man with a twitch in his eyes frantically climbed the stairs leading to the warden's office. He was drenched from the driving rain as he stepped inside to announce, "The Spaniard and another prisoner escaped from his cell!"

The warden glared in disbelief. "How could that happen?"

"When I entered the guard room to relieve Morton, I found him gagged and tied up, lying on the floor."

"That idiot Morton!"

"He told me that an Irish prisoner was going to be executed this morning and a priest was called to give him the last rites. Morton escorted the priest to the man's cell, but before he could open the door the priest hit him with a heavy metal cross. When I found him, his clothes had been taken, as well as the keys of the cells."

"What time was this?"

"The priest arrived at five in the morning, according to Morton. I found him at six-thirty and immediately sounded the alarm. A contingent of soldiers is looking for the escapees. Morton was taken to the infirmary. As soon as I sounded the alarm I came to report to you."

Rubbing their cold hands together and blinking in the sudden glare of the candlelights, Don Francisco and his rescuer stepped out gratefully from the boat that had brought them back to Spain. Don Francisco was taken to a sick ward in his hometown of Cordoba. He had lost some four stone in weight and was in wretched condition.

Before he fell into an exhausted sleep in the clean-smelling bed, Don Francisco felt a great sense of peace settle over him. Safe in his country that he had given up for lost, and with the prospect of seeing Isabel again, the physical pain in his body evaporated; the world seemed transformed and mellowed. During the last year of his harsh imprisonment he had rarely allowed himself to think of Isabel or his home in Spain, or of the family and friends he had left behind. They had seemed remote and unreal, belonging to a past life, but suddenly he found himself dreaming of Isabel again and her image was immediately before him, intensely present and comforting.

As weeks passed and Don Francisco slowly regained his strength, he was invited to Madrid, where he was received as a hero. The King asked Don Francisco if he was willing to accompany a team of shipwreck experts to locate and salvage the *San José*'s cargo. Preparations were underway, and in eight months a rescue ship would leave for the Island of Baru off the coast of Cartagena. The team would include a surveyor, divers and other experts. Don Francisco's help might be crucial. Eight months, the King assured him, would give Don Francisco sufficient time to recuperate from three years in the English prison.

"One thing I must request from the Crown," Don Francisco

replied, bowing. "I need your help in locating a medical doctor from Peru. The last time I saw Doña Isabel she was traveling to Cartagena to wait for me. It is essential that I find her. We were—we are going—to be married."

The King promised Don Francisco he would find the woman for him in return for Don Francisco's pledge to help locate the wreck of the *San José*.

During the next eight months Don Francisco and a group of the King's men with the help of the authorities in Nueva Granada searched everywhere for Isabel, but in futility. One day, when he returned home, Don Francisco found a little thin man with a long, sallow face and a weak chin. He did not give his name, but bowed quickly and spoke in a low voice. "Don Francisco, we have traced Doña Isabel to a convent in Seville. She became a nun." He bowed again and walked away.

Don Francisco could not believe she was in Seville, so close to him. He could not believe she had entered a convent. That she was found was the best news that he ever had received, but that he could lose her to God was unthinkable. "I must get out of here and travel to Seville at once," he thought. That night, his heart was screaming. "No, I must keep calm and write to her first and wait for her reply."

He sat in his room trying to compose a letter. Exhausted with the vain effort, he fell asleep in the chair. At four in the morning, he went back to the desk and wrote:

My darling Isabel,

I know this letter is going to astonish you. Yes, I am alive and living in Spain!

God knows I do not have the right to call you darling, after the terrible thing I have done, leaving you alone in Honda for a treasure that now is at the bottom of the sea. But I promise to make it up to you if it takes me a lifetime. I want you to be my wife. My dearest, this is like the breaking of a dam. I don't know what to write down first but I owe you an explanation for not contacting you for more than three years.

When the San José went down I managed to stay afloat until the crew of the British Expedition picked me up from the cold water. A few days later, we anchored close to Rosario Islands and most of the Spanish survivors disembarked. But when they learned that I was a doctor they ordered me to remain on board and I was taken to Port Royal in Jamaica. Weeks later they put me on another ship bound for England. As soon as we landed I was transported to a prison in Reading. I was held there until last month when I was able to escape with the help of a Spanish agent who brought me back to Cordoba.

Life in prison was terrible. We were fed gruel and water once a day and we had to endure long and cruel interrogations almost weekly. The prison authorities dealt particularly harshly with foreigners. I almost lost all hope of getting out.

I know how hard it must have been for you all this years. But the most important thing is that we both are alive.

Since I left prison I have been searching for you constantly. Yesterday I found that you had entered the convent. God will understand if you leave the convent, my dearest love. That does not mean you will leave the Church. I am not trying to compete with God, but if this letter can make you half as happy as just knowing that you are alive makes me, then you belong in my arms. My Sweet, let me come to you. The world is before us; I will come to Seville as soon as I receive your reply. I must see you face to face. If you love me half as much as I love you, please write quickly to the above address.

Yours, Francisco

He read this letter over perhaps ten times, cutting a phrase here, inserting a sentence there, then copied it onto a fresh page. He sealed the letter and when the sun came up he arranged for it to be delivered to the convent in Seville. From that moment there was nothing left to do, but to wait.

The days passed so slowly that he felt he would go out of his mind. The nights seemed to drag on interminably. But finally, one afternoon, her letter came. He tore it open frantically.

My dear Francisco:

I hope this letter will not be as painful for you to read as it is for me to write. If your question is, did I love you, the answer is, yes, with all my heart, with all my soul. If the question is, do I love you now, the answer is, I love you as much as I can love a human being. There has not been a moment since our abrupt departure that I have not thought of you. If there is one memory I will always retain, it is the memory of you and the moments we spent together and the dreams that we dreamed. But time passes, my dear; events occur and people change. Do not ask me to choose between our earthly lives and Heaven, between Christ and mortality, between wonderful feelings of serenity, and earthly passion and desire, for I have made my choice. Some years ago—I have lost count—I took my vows. That means I wed God. Since then, God has been a perfect husband. I know that we wanted to save society with medicine. But that which saves society is not that which can be seen upon the surface of things. It is not the power of industry, or battles between galléons of war, or the genius in letters or art; it is what touches its depths in a silence called the "Silence of the Eternal God."

I loved you, dear Francisco, but I also fell in love with God. Please, if you still love me, do not try to contact me. God be with you forever,

Sister Isabel

Tears welled in Don Francisco's eyes. Her words seemed to fill the room and reverberate against the walls, growing louder and louder until they were screaming in his heart, a crashing of waves in the sea, deafening him, drowning him and Isabel, sucking them down deeper and deeper until he could not breathe any longer, and everything — earth, air, sky and sea — became dark and silent.

Meanwhile, Isabel, in her thick brown wool habit, shoeless, with a veil over her face, had gone to the Reverend Mother and with tears in her eyes, asked to be transferred to the monastery in Ronda, ten hours by wagon from Seville.

Two months later Don Francisco received a dispatch from the Royal Court.

At the time of our meeting with his Majesty the King, we informed you that there was a great anxiety all over Spain with the lost treasure aboard the Capitana San José. The Genovese bankers informed the King that unless the treasure is recovered, they would be unable to negotiate any further loans for him. Philip V fell into such a state of shock that he had to be confined to bed by the physicians. The King ordered that the salvage vessel leave in the next twenty days, to locate and salvage the treasure and the "Materia Medicinal" so vital to our country. Your presence, advice and support in locating the San José are crucial to our endeavor. We anticipate your attendance before his Majesty within the next two days.

Miguel Triana Buenaventura
Adviser to the Royal Court

On July 27, 1712, the sky was high and clear and the wind blew warm in Seville. The *Flota de Nueva España* commanded by Lt. General Manuel Goméz Rincon sailed down the Guadalquivir River for hundred kilometers before reaching the sea. Aboard the salvage ship *La Esperanza* Don Francisco look in the Seville landscape for the last time. His eyes glittered dully in his sunken face. He turned suddenly away and went to the galley for dinner.

Three months later the Royal Court received the news that the *Flota* had left Vera Cruz with Indian divers on the way to Baru Islands and the *San José*. In November heavy weather with gale winds struck the ships.

At first the fleet continued towards the Baru Islands, but as the day wore on, the wind rose to hurricane strength and the *galleóns* lost sight of each other amid towering, foam-whitened waves that lifted the ship's bow higher and higher, before dropping her into the oncoming sea. More immediate than the fear of storms was the nausea of seasickness. Sailors aboard *La Esperanza* crossed themselves. Waves and sky were crashing together. With storm winds blowing out of the north northeast at over sixty knots, as the ship pitched and rolled in waves whitened by the wind and pelted by the rain, thick foam blew across the surface of the sea in long streaks, sometimes flying whip-like into the air. The evening brought renewed hope when the wind lessened and the sea subsided.

Next morning the sky blackened, the winds rose, waves exploded high into the air, salt spray mixing with rain, and the wind drove it all with a furious whistle through bare rigging. The frantic sea crashed down on the quarterdeck, sweeping away men who were not lashed tight to a mast. A second wave struck squarely mid-ship. Every man was sent sprawling once more, and the fore-topmast came crashing down, though only one man was injured by it.

There was not a stauncher vessel afloat than *La Esperanza*. But no ship ever built could have weathered such an encounter. The timbers along the starboard side were so damaged that they were like needles in a basket. The crew tarred canvas under the hull in an attempt to seal off the openings; the crew pumped water, watch officers entered in, watch officers went out. It took four days and nights. "Sir," said a man with trembling voice, "we're sinking." The Lt. General Manuel Goméz Rincon said, "You've done all that men can do to save *La Esperanza.*"

Finally the overstrained whip staff and tiller splintered, leaving the ship helpless. At the mercy of wind and sea, the salvage ship swept onward, but the ferocity of the storm increased. The ship was deep in water across her waist. Those left aboard bound themselves to rails and stanchions. The reefed sails were gone, shredded, the halyards snapped like whips in tearing wind. The powerful waves began to break the vessel apart. In the next instant a wilderness of foam hurled across the ship, rushing over fore and aft, sweeping the entire deck from stem to stern. Don Francisco lifted his head, gasping, to discover that he, the chaplain and the cook, were alone on deck. Everyone else had gone overboard. Don Francisco asked the chaplain to hear his confession. He fell to his knees at the side of the priest and in front of Our Lady of Carmen, patroness of those who risk their lives upon the sea.

With a thunderous crack, the deck split, wrecked, tilted, and began to spin into the sea. Down they sank into a maelstrom, dark green with a silver rim of froth. The rim grew rapidly smaller—Don Francisco plunged madly within the grasp of the whirlpool, and amid the roaring, thundering tempest of the ocean, a brilliant light appeared, and he heard Isabel's clear voice coming from the dark sky. "*Francisco, come with me to the All Mighty Lord.*"

The winds dropped abruptly to absolute calm. The sky overhead glowed serene, cloudless and clear, the silence more deafening than the cacophony of the storm. Sister Isabel extended her hand from the blue firmament and Don Francisco took it, vanishing from the surface of the deep into *the silence of the eternal God.*

PART THREE

Once ago I loved the sea
And as I did, it loved me.
But I found another love for me,
And she became my bride to be.
We were as happy as can be,
Unlike my old love, the sea
She was meant for me.

Leo Convoy

IT would be another scorching day in Seville. That much was evident, even at 9 a.m. when Robert reached the Archive of the Indies that had been his home for many months, transformed and resolute. Before coming to Seville, Robert had considered those dedicated to the quest of sunken treasures, romantic fools chasing a handful of gold at the end of the rainbow. Father Pedro had opened his eyes to the world of medicinal plants and had awakened a deeper interest of the history of the Spanish Armada and sunken treasures, including the *galléon San José*.

Robert spent the morning ordering photocopies of original documents on shipwrecks, dealing exclusively with the New World. When he arrived in the afternoon to collect them, he was escorted to an empty conference room and told to wait. Five minutes later, a man in a dark suit entered and was also told to wait for copies of the documents he had ordered. He gave Robert a curt nod and sat in a chair facing him.

After a few minutes the stranger broke the silence. "I've seen you a few times in the reading room, are you involved in serious research?"

"Yes, I'm interested in the history of the Spanish Armada. How about you?"

"Well, I see we both have the same interest," the stranger replied, extending his hand. "My name is Dr. Wenninger."

"I'm Robert Hamilton, pleased to meet you. Are you a medical doctor?"

"No, Mr. Hamilton, I am a scientist."

"I'm a professor of history."

The attendant entered, bringing the reproductions of Robert's documents.

"A pleasure talking to you," Robert said.

"We should make an effort while we are in Seville to meet again for a drink and lively conversation," suggested Dr. Wenninger.

"I really would like to, but today's my last day in Seville."

"Where are you heading to, if I may I ask?"

"Ronda. I leave early tomorrow."

"What a coincidence! I am also planning to visit Ronda before I return home next week. I'll be staying at the Hotel Parador, and I'm planning to attend the bullfights. The season started early this week."

"Splendid!" Robert smiled. "We must see each other and go to the bullfights together."

That night, with the documents spread out on the bed, drinking Jerez as the warm, fragrant breeze rustled the papers before him. Robert reflected. He was approaching middle age—the fires of his youth might no longer flare so brightly, or last so long. But the moment had come to realize his dream — to hunt for the richest single Spanish *galléon* ever lost in the Western Hemisphere. The Archive of the Indies had whet his appetite. He also wanted to do more research at *El Museo Naval, El Museo Nacional, La Biblioteca Nacional, El Archivo Historico National* and *La Academia Real de Historia,* all in Madrid. He also planned to visit the British Museum, the Public Records Office, the Admiralty Archives and the National Maritime Museum in London. He would give himself six months, but before leaving Spain, there was one thing he absolutely *must* do — visit the monastery in Ronda, where Isabel had spent most of her life almost three hundred years ago. He carried with him an introduction from Father Pedro to Sister Teresa.

The monastery had barely changed in three hundred years. Concessions to modern times were few and grudging. The Carmelite nuns had electricity but appeared to use little of it. They had only recently abandoned wearing veils over their faces and using straw sack mattresses in their Spartan rooms, switching to thin foam rubber pads on flat boards, because straw was too difficult to maintain. But the sisters still wore thick brown wool habits in winter and summer as their predecessors did, and because their order was discalced, they always wore sandals.

Arriving at 9:30 a.m. for a prearranged appointment, Robert rang the main doorbell and identified himself through a voice speaker, and the electric lock of the door opened. A gentle voice behind a turn instructed him to pick up a key in the turn and open a door at the left of the entrance hall, so he could see the jeweled and golden hand of Santa Theresa de Jesús. Wondering at the incredible preservation of her hand since the sixteenth century, he returned to the front of the turn and was directed to return the key and pick up another key and open a door leading to the windowless reception room.

Behind a set of iron bar partitions, one behind the other, installed at the top of a two-foot-high solid wall, he saw the Reverend Mother, Prioress Maria de La Paz, a bright-faced woman in her sixties, cheerful and energetic. Her companion Sister Teresa Maria was perhaps ten years younger, far from beautiful, though her spirituality gave her an almost unearthly loveliness. She seemed always to be smiling inwardly, as though she carried some wonderful secret within herself. The sisters dressed identically. Robert introduced himself as a historian — they asked him to go to another turn that was embedded in a wall at his right to retrieve a jar with green tea and a plate with muffins that they wanted him to taste. The nuns produced muffins, fruitcakes, candies, and marmalade daily to be sold to the public.

Robert sat in front of the iron bars and talked about Isabel and Don Francisco, about the work he was doing, and they discussed the convent. The Carmelite diet was strictly vegetarian. The principal meal was taken at 11 a.m. and consisted of thin soup, a few vegetables, and occasionally a piece of fruit. They told Robert about the history of their monastery, including how the reliquary of Santa Teresa's hand was kept in Ronda until 1936, when they were forced to abandon their convent and take refuge in the old people's home near the Merced that was looked after by the Sisters of the Poor.

The Red Army knew that the Carmelite nuns kept the invaluable reliquary of Santa Teresa. The Communist Committee demanded it be handed over, and the Prioress did not have any other recourse but to let the reliquary fall into the hands of these non-believers. When the National Forces invaded Malaga, the hand was taken to Francisco Franco at his general quarters in Burgos. He kept the hand until the day he died. When The Caudillo died, his wife returned the hand to the Carmelite nuns in Ronda.

"The main reason I came to visit the convent is because after spending months at the Archive in Seville researching the *San José* — an eighteenth century *galléon* that was sunk by the English — I found a vivid description of the lives of two medical doctors, Don Francisco de Mendoza and Doña Isabel Goméz who became a Carmelite after the tragic death of her beloved Francisco."

"Yes, Mr. Hamilton, we are very familiar with her life — she was the founder of the St. Francisco hospital. She devoted a great part of her life curing the sick and she passed away here in this convent at the age of eighty-seven. Let us take you to the cell where she died. It is in an area where visitors are allowed to enter on special occasions. If you care to visit the hospital, perhaps you may obtain a book there about the hospital and its founder."

Early the following morning after returning from the hospital, Robert asked Julio the porter at his hotel, what he should see in Ronda. The Real Maestranza, the porter told him, the bullfighting ring. But there was so much else he shouldn't miss. Would he like a city tour? Julio could get his brother to cover for him, and for a few pesetas he would be delighted to show Robert the charm of Ronda.

"Ronda is the most beautiful city in Spain. Come with me to our bridge and you will realize the truth of what I am saying. Look over there where the sun sets in the evening. Can you see those blue peaks? Well, those are the Sierra de San Cristobal and the Sierra the Graza Lema.

"Do you see those two men taking photographs from the top of the hill?" Robert asked.

"They must be tourists."

"I saw them following us and taking pictures from a distance."

"Please, Mr. Hamilton, don't worry, they are O.K."

"I can see them running now towards the end of the bridge."

"See? They are gone now, Mr. Hamilton. Look to your left. That is the Sierra Perdiguera, where the road to Algeciras passes towards Gibraltar, the land of the smugglers and highwaymen, wounded hearts and lost hopes. There is nothing more beautiful than this gorge with its River Guadalevin at the bottom, clinging to its banks."

"What does Guadalevin mean?"

"Deep river."

They descended into the gorge and into the valley. From the distance Robert detected one of the men he had seen previously—with his binnacle peering at him. Without uttering a word they returned slowly to the hotel.

At six o'clock that evening, Robert entered Romero's restaurant in Virgen de la Paz, opposite the Real Maestranza — Ronda' s bullring. This hour was between siesta and dinner, and the restaurant was nearly deserted. The bartender, a jovial fellow, greeted him. "Welcome, what can I offer you?"

"I am waiting for a friend," Robert explained, "but I'll have a tinto, please."

He sat at the bar, where he could keep an eye on the door for Dr. Wenninger. They had agreed to meet for drinks and then go to the bullfight. The day had been uncommonly hot and humid, but the light evening breeze blew fresh and cool through the open door.

He thought about Hermann Wenninger as he sipped his tinto.

Wenninger had begun his career at Bayer AG's plant in Leverkusen thirty years ago as a junior chemist. But by his own account he was a workaholic. He had done well, risen through the ranks to become a member of the Board of Management of the diversified, international chemical and pharmaceutical complex. An interesting man, he enjoyed research and he liked bullfights.

Robert gazed at an oil painting of a young bullfighter who stared at him with direct, almost living eyes.

"Who's that?" asked Robert, pointing.

"Pedro Romero, for whom this restaurant is named."

"And who was Pedro Romero?"

The bartender grunted. "A master who killed six thousand bulls."

"That seems like a lot of bulls to me."

"My friend, don't you know that besides killing the six thousand bulls he killed them face-to-face? He was born in Ronda in 1755 and became a bullfighter at the early age of eight — I should have said that he was born a bullfighter."

"And who is this *torero*?" Robert asked, pointing to a faded photograph below the painting.

"He is Dominguin. He ate here four weeks before he was killed."

There were pictures of others on the walls: Orson Wells, Ernest Hemingway, Antonio Droonez, and other well-known personalities.

The bartender, eager to have an ear, came closer.

"Before the Maestranza was erected, the members used to have their entertainment and festivities on the parade ground. The ring was inaugurated in 1784, the widest ring in the world and it has nearly five thousand seats."

Robert nodded. "You don't say."

At that moment Dr. Wenninger came in. He was perspiring, his face unusually red and his shirt wet. It was obvious by his expression that he was in distress. "I'm sorry for being late, Robert."

"What's happened?" Robert asked.

"Let's order a drink first." He ordered a beer and for Robert a bottle of *Manzanilla*. "I wanted to talk to you alone," Wenninger said suddenly. "Let's move to that table at the corner."

"Why are you carrying that briefcase with you to the bullfight, Hermann?"

"It's a long story. I have a gut feeling that I can trust you, Robert; I hope you can help me." And lowering his voice Dr. Wenninger said, "You are interested in medicinal plants, so am I. That is the reason I am in Spain. What I am carrying here," he patted the briefcase, "has to do with the medicinal plants. I will give you the name of a person at Bayer in Leverkusen. If for any reason you cannot get in touch with me, contact him. He will know where I will be and perhaps can be of great help to you: Professor Hubertus Von Pierce."

"Hermann, what is this all about? Are you in danger of some kind?"

Wenninger was still sweating. "Robert, when I returned to the hotel, I found a man trying to force his way into the room. As soon as he saw me, he ran down the stairs. I chased him out of the hotel and then for about a block or two, but he was faster than I was and I lost him in the crowded streets. I'm sure that what he wanted is this dispatch case. Tomorrow I'll leave Ronda for Madrid, so let's enjoy the evening."

Robert looked into Wenninger's eyes and had the dreadful premonition that he was the father of the young man that on the day of his arrival to Madrid was savagely killed in front of the Balboa.

Robert's stomach tightened with every second that passed. "Hermann, please, what is going on?" he asked, disconcerted.

Wenninger fell into a long, deep silence and when Robert looked at his face in the dim light, he saw it was lined with tears. Without quite knowing what he was doing, Robert put his hand on Wenninger's shoulder. "Please open your heart to me and tell me what is happening; you can trust me and perhaps I could help you."

Their eyes met briefly.

"This dispatch case contains very important and critical papers for my company. Some people who want these papers have followed me ever since I left Madrid. They would do anything to get them. My heart is completely destroyed and still I refuse to believe that whoever wants to take procession of my dossier killed my innocent oldest son in Madrid."

"Oh! My God!" Robert gasped. What he had suspected was confirmed by Wenninger.

Robert caught Wenninger gazing at him with yearning and defeat.

"I'm not the best man for this job," Wenninger continued cryptically, but my boss, Helmut Müller, could not travel so he asked me to come to Spain for him." Wenninger paused. "How strange," he said, frowning. "He looks very much like you. You might be twins, except for the way you part your hair."

He glanced at his watch. "Time to go. It's nearly seven. I'll tell you the rest when we get inside."

Across the street, people were crowding the entrance to the ring. Young and old converged from different directions, some carrying cushions and others holding bottles of *Manzanilla.* As they moved slowly through the multitude, Robert noticed that Julio was among the fans — and at a closer glance he realized that he was in the company of the two men he'd seen earlier.

Something about Julio had bothered Robert, but it was not until now that he realized what it was.

The ring was already full with spectators. The brilliant sun threw half the arena on fire and ten thousand eyes fixed on the burning La Maestranza's earth, where the great contest would take place. The white-gold earth of the arena and the blood red hideaway enhances the excitement of the event.

Trumpets announced the start of the *corrida.* A grand entry procession of the *cuadrillas,* led by two mounted *alguaciles,* entered the ring. Proceeding on foot, the *matador* was followed by his *banderilleros* and mounted *picadores.* At the rear were the *chulos* driving a richly caparisoned *arrastre*-three-mule, removing the bull carcasses. The *matadores* were wearing short jackets, waistcoats and knee-length, skintight trousers of silk, richly embroidered in gold.

After the opening parade, the Mayor of Ronda threw down to the *alguaciles* the key to the bullpens. As the bull passed through the bullpen, *banderilleros*, one at a time, attracted the bull with the cape.

Robert leaned forward in his seat, shielding the sun from his eyes with his hand. The huge bull charged into the ring, and a *matado*r stepped out from behind a small wooden barrier at the side of the ring and teased the animal with the silken work cape in a very graceful manner.

'The *picador* will be next," Dr. Wenninger said excitedly.

The *picador* entered the arena, riding a horse covered with heavy padding. The bull lowered its head and charged. As it buried its horns in the horse's padding, the *picador* drove an eight-foot lance into the bull's shoulders.

While Robert was watching this absorbing spectacle, a man selling refreshments and candies passed in front of him. He was a short, thickset man with a clean-shaven face. He wore a white cap and a white jacket unbuttoned at the neck, which showed his hairy chest. He approached Wenninger and offered to sell him some beer. Dr. Wenninger declined. Then, he took off his uniform cap and revealed his shaven head. At that moment he looked at a man five meters away and the man nodded. Suddenly a terribly certainty hit Robert, the fact that the nodding man was one of the photographers he had seen that morning. Another realization swept over him: Julio was a few meters away from that man.

Robert's attention was half on the man, and half on the bullfight. The *matador* took a position below the mayor's box with the *montera* held aloft in his right hand, the *muleta* and *estoque* in his left. He formally requested permission to dedicate the *faena* to the owner of the restaurant, Pedro Romero, to whom he tossed his *montera.*

After the *matador* did everything possible with the bull to prove his complete mastery, he prepared for the kill.

"This is the brute strength of men over a color-blind bull," Wenninger breathed.

At that moment Robert recognized the clean-shaven head and face. He felt his lips quivering. An intense cold spread through his body, his voice stolen, his eyes fixed. Robert put it all together: It was the very same person that he had seen the first day when he arrived in Madrid, the same man who had run after Dr. Wenninger's son, armed with a knife in his hand, and who had killed him.

He was circling behind Dr. Wenninger. Robert cried, "Hermann! Look out!"

The crowd roared. The *matador* thrust forward the *muleta* with his left hand, while his right hand sunk the *estoque* between the bull's shoulder blades at the junction with the neck, a quick death without shedding any blood.

The crowd screamed with passion and admiration. All eyes trained on the ring, all eyes but Robert's. He felt paralyzed, incapable of acting or even thinking. He stared at the madness that was taking place, as the knife came down, again and again, into Wenninger's body.

Wenninger let out a terrible cry of pain, turned to Robert and fixed his eyes on him.

Robert's shout was lost amid a thousand others. He jumped up, but the clean-shaven man was possessed by an animal fury. Robert heard the snap of his teeth as he pushed the limp and bleeding body towards him, seized the briefcase and ran towards the arena while the *matador* circled the arena to the applause of the spectators.

Robert tried to hold Wenninger, but he stumbled into the lap of one of the spectators.

"The briefcase!" Wenninger gasped. "The briefcase!"

Robert saw the killer jump over the *barrera* and lose hold of the briefcase. The killer quickly tried to retrieve the case that was now on the other side of the *barrera* when he saw Robert rushing towards him. The killer hesitated and then continued to run towards the exit to the street.

Robert picked up the briefcase and brought it back to Wenninger, who looked at him with glazed eyes. "Good!" he gurgled with a half smile. "You saved it."

In the riot of noise, every gasping breath was like an echo. Then Robert noticed Wenninger's mouth dripping with blood. Half-open, it tried to form words with his lips. For a moment his face was almost normal, and then it collapsed suddenly into the strange face of the dead.

Robert noticed that the killer was already close to the main exit, and a *carabinero* guarding the entrance had been alerted and was running towards him.

The *matador* was being acclaimed; the crowd's attention was divided now, between the matador and the human chase: Robert saw the man who had nodded to the killer turn, run, and vanish from sight, as did Julio.

Spectators applauded. Some cried "*OLÈ*!" "*Excellente matador*!" "*Perfecto*!" But some were aware that something was wrong. People in the vicinity of Wenninger's body were screaming. At the same time, a shot rang out and the clean-shaven man running across the arena stumbled, and fell to the ground in a pool of blood.

At the exact moment that the bull's carcass was being dragged from the arena, two paramedics carried Dr. Wenninger's body on a stretcher. The screams, roars, cheers, and confusion of the crowd had died away, replaced by a stony, unhappy silence. Robert stood by Dr. Wenninger's corpse as it was lifted and transported to a waiting ambulance at the main entrance to the bullring. Two *carabineros* asked Robert if he knew the dead man. "I only met him a few hours ago," Robert responded. The briefcase felt suddenly heavy in his hand, but he knew Wenninger wanted him, not the police, to have it.

Robert forced his way out of the swarming bullring and went

down a narrow winding street, quickly arriving at his hotel. He packed up his belongings and twenty minutes later walked onto a platform to take the next train bound for Madrid.

He spent part of the night on the train reading the contents of the briefcase. He learned about the pharmaceutical industry and the world of international business, greed, deception and intrigue. The terror he had experienced hours before only grew as he read.

From a folder of newspaper clippings, he glanced at an article published a few weeks ago in the *Frankfurter Allegmeine* morning paper:

Sat./ban Frankfurt/Berlin 7 June. Five months ago, a young woman, Erika Switzer, was found dead in Wiesbaden, 70 kilometers from Frankfurt, hanging by a rope from the deck of a luxurious house. On one level the death was ruled a suicide. Was this a personal tragedy, the sad end to a troubled life?

On another level, Ms. Switzer's death, and the year leading up to it, provided an unusual insight into the life of a shadowy businessman now being sought by the authorities for extortion, antitrust violations, price-fixing, production of dangerous drugs and serving as a go-between for the food additive makers, the pharmaceutical industry and deep-sea treasure hunters.

The mysteries of Ms. Erika Switzer will not be solved any time soon. What does emerge from documents found in her mansion is an image of a man (who uses several names) as a brazen but wily con artist, a master puppeteer whose dealings span the globe. He acquired a reputation for mystery and as the one behind the deals arranged between the pharmaceutical companies and food additive markets, from Frankfurt, London, New York, Cartagena and Lima. He is accused of being the leader of a multi-billion illegal international pharmaceutical cartel.

In a rapid widening of the German Government's effort to crack the illegal international cartel, it is charged with price-fixing and contamination of food additives with toxic components.

During the investigation the Government discovered that the cartel was actively involved in a scheme to produce and distribute contaminated products that would produce adverse reactions and disease, in order to market the cures, creating billions of dollars in revenues.

The illegal food additives contaminated products such as breakfast cereals, hand cream, poultry, and orange juice.

More than three million people a year die in Europe, North and South America from adverse reactions to contaminated food additives.

"Greed, simple greed, replaced any sense of corporate decency or integrity," a representative of the Justice Department said. "This is shameful and criminal behavior that violates the very essence of a competitive, open and free market. We will not tolerate this terrible crime; we will hunt down the cartel's members, to the end of the world if necessary."

Robert was perplexed.

Late the next morning, Robert checked into the Balboa Hotel in Madrid. What Robert had read was a clear and imminent threat to the future of humanity. He knew that he had to take some action quickly and he could not let the *San José*'s treasure fall into the wrong hands.

He placed a call to Professor Hubertus Von Pierce in Leverkusen. Then, with Wenninger's papers in hand, Robert spent most of the afternoon talking with Berlin, London and New York.

The evening had grown sultry and heat was rising from the earth when Robert returned to his hotel from an early dinner.

The desk clerk handled him an envelope from Berlin.

On his way to the elevator Robert opened it and pulled a sheet torn from a fax machine. He read:

Dear Mr. Hamilton:

Today I received a call from Prof. Hubertus Von Pierce in Leverkusen. He explained to me the situation. I will be happy to help you as much as I can. Please contact me at your earliest convenience when you arrive in Berlin.

Sincerely, Christopher Beck

As the Boeing 727 lifted from the tarmac and climbed steeply, the morning sun, which minutes earlier had cleared the horizon, tinted the Spanish landscape soft red-gold. Two hours later the plane landed smoothly in Frankfurt. It was raining as Robert descended from the plane.

Twenty miles away, Adolf Fritz stood at the window of a skyscraper looking down from thirty-five floors above Romerberg Square. The chairman of the board of Pharma, Frankfuter GMBH, a multi-billion-dollar conglomerate of multi-national pharmaceutical companies, was a picture of the bourgeois gentleman in his luxurious office furnished with exotic wood, leather and chrome.

The door opened and Werner Bischoff entered and was ordered to sit. "I just returned from the I.G. Farben's chemical works people at the chemical apparatus fair. I saw a report on what happened in Spain."

Adolf Fritz glanced at the report:

Extremely Confidential. Dr. X has been promoted as planned. Mario tried to escape with Dr. X's briefcase but Müller recaptured it. Müller boarded Lufthansa flight 4379 bound for Frankfurt on Monday, 3rd.

Walter.

"You'd better go back to your fair with your friends," Fritz snapped.

As Bischoff walked toward the door, a bespectacled man in a gray suit peered in. "Mr. Fritz, may I interrupt?"

"Aren, you are the man I need," said Fritz, the ice in his voice starting to melt.

In his late fifties, with spectacles, Aren looked more like a professor at Heidelberg University than the chief operating officer and right-hand man of the Chairman of the world's largest pharmaceutical consortium. He fiddled with the tobacco in his omnipresent pipe as he waited for Adolf Fritz to speak.

"Bischoff just brought me a communiqué from Walter. Dr. X is out of the way as well as Mario. An associate of Dr. X's, Müller's trying to pass himself off as an American historian using the name of Robert Hamilton. He left Spain for Frankfurt on Monday."

"Has any action been taken?" asked Bechen.

"Bischoff had sufficient time to intercept Müller at the airport, if he'd acted as soon as the fax was sent. Dr. X, from Bayer, was staying with his son in Madrid. His son had to be 'promoted.' After the autopsy, the Ronda police released Dr. X's body to a Bayer representative. So I want you to do the following: First, contact Berthold Beitz at his brother's house in Werfen. Instruct Beitz to send a floral arrangement of red roses to Dr. X's wife with condolences from our group. The funeral will be held at Sankt Nicolaus Kirche and he will be buried at Leverkusen. It is important to let Müller attend the funeral, but he must be captured immediately afterwards and brought to our Frankfurt warehouse. Beitz should recognize Müller. He met him in a restaurant in Madrid."

Fritz continued. "Second, contact Gustav Halder and ask him to mobilize to Berlin. Have our people there check all major hotels, train stations and airports for Müller, alias Robert Hamilton. If they find him, seize him and keep him in our country house.

"As for you, Aren, I need you to do the same checking in

Frankfurt. At any cost, find Müller and the dispatch case."

"I will put some of our men to work on this case immediately," said Bechen.

Fritz stared at Bechen a long instant. "How do you intend to proceed?"

"Müller headed up the investigation team intruding into our medicinal plants business. His master plan allowed Dr. X to obtain our secret files in Spain. Why don't we go after his family first? His wife, Elsa, has a ten-year-old son. This would enable us to find his whereabouts more rapidly."

"I am fully aware of that," Fritz growled. "As I am aware that there *is* a man by the name of Robert Hamilton who teaches history at Bates College in Lewiston, Maine. According to his fellow teachers he is somewhere in the Far East. We don't know yet what the connection is between Müller and Hamilton, or why Müller is impersonating Hamilton. Beitz is completely convinced that the man he saw in Madrid is Müller. He checked with Bayer in Leverkusen and found that Müller left for Madrid the same day that Beitz's men detected the so-called Robert Hamilton at Madrid airport. Beitz is an extremely skilled and highly placed agent, knowledgeable in identification matters. He has a remarkable mind. I questioned him many times as to why Müller is impersonating Hamilton, and his answer is that Müller is the greatest fake and best actor of the decade.

"One more thing, Aren, please notify all the members of the board that tomorrow morning at 9:30 sharp we will hold a meeting on the *San José*."

At three p.m., Aren Bechen, seated at the conference table in his office, began to review a stack of minutes of meetings, memoranda, reports, computer printouts and well-guarded corporate secrets, such as company accounts, production figures, marketing analyses and, more important, the master plan for becoming the most powerful multinational conglomerate in the world. He would carefully summarize them at the meeting of the Board of Directors. It was almost 2 a.m. when Aren Bechen, absently stroking his meticulous gray moustache, was satisfied and rose.

A few hours later, Bechen entered the huge board room. The custom leather-covered table was designed to provide flexibility. Concealed microphones were built into the apron. The audio-visual system, based on rear screen projection, was directed toward a wall of black glass in which two panels of solar glass were backed by a black screen. Walnut-paneled acoustically treated walls were designed to insure confidentiality. The only touches of color were provided by three expensive French Impressionist paintings on one wall. On the other walls portraits of the founders of Pharma, Frankfuter GMBH, Doctor Mortimer Fritz and Raymond Fritz hung in a precise row.

Bechen prided himself on his good taste. He had been instrumental in selecting the decorators and working with them down to the last detail, just as he had spent an hour with his assistant working out the last details for the meeting.

At 9:30 a.m. sharp, the thirty members of the executive board, each one in a conservative, expensive suit, entered and sat in his designated chair.

Adolf Fritz, in a dark blue suit, was at the head of the table. "Good morning, gentlemen. Thank you for coming. We are pleased to report that 2000 was a successful year." He followed this opening with a summary of their financial condition. "Supporting sales were up despite the considerable turbulence in the currency markets. Productivity also increased again, and we substantially improved our growth potential with investment in research and capital expenditures totaling DM 10.5 billion···. One particularly satisfying aspect of 2000 was the operating results income after taxes amounted to DM 5.1 billion, well in excess of our target. We are, therefore, proposing to raise the dividend by DM 3 to 20 per share. However, in view of the economic risk and ever increasing tax burdens here, coupled with the expansion of our competition, nationally as well as abroad, it will not be easy to achieve the profitability of 1999. We will, therefore, rigorously continue reining in cost and implement a plan of action to enhance profitability and international competitiveness···.

"This strategy requires some risk. I want to make clear that only the people who are now present will know the full extent of our plans. As major stockholders, you are expected not to talk to anybody, including the members of your families." He paused and made eye contact with each of the thirty pairs of eyes. "To nobody," he repeated.

Aren Bechen stood in front of the projection screen.

"Gentlemen, to answer some of the questions you may be asking yourselves, I will briefly provide a foundation for understanding our master plan more completely.

"What do we look for when we consider foreign investments, given their complexity and multi-faceted nature? Why assume risks of expanding overseas? The answer: Total returns from our international and unconventional operations more than justify the risks. This statement may seem difficult to prove when I refer to the problems in our major markets, which I shall call Countries X and Y. They are as follows:

"Legislative inquiries have contributed to adverse press publicity.

"Suggested price controls have been seriously studied and some adopted.

"Legislation designed to remove drug patents has been introduced.

"The use of only generics has been advocated by some teaching universities.

"Country X proposes tighter control at federal and local levels. Their politicians have adroitly used the specter of out-of-control drug prices as the cause of rising costs for all medical care.

"And finally, legislation has been drafted that would dictate to the physician the type of drugs available for hospitalized patients.

"You too might ask, "Why get into that kind of a mess?"

"My reply, we are already up and operating, for Country Y is

Germany and Country X is the United States. So perhaps one answer as to why we go into Latin America and Asia is to get away from it all. By comparison, most of the developing countries' markets are simple. No restrictions, freedom of movement, nor is there a risk of being exposed when we operate in an unconventional manner⋯.

"Now. To the master plan. For some years we have followed a case that is pending in the Colombian courts in relation to the *San José*, a Spanish *galléon* that was sunk by the English in 1708, the richest ever lost in the Western hemisphere. The Colombian government invited international firms to present proposals for locating and recovering the *San José*'s treasure off the coast of Colombia. It includes gold, silver and very large amounts. But the real treasure we are after is the most complete collection ever assembled of drawings and descriptions of medicinal plants used by Indians in Colombia, Peru and Mexico. It is called the *Materia Medicinal.*

"Why, you may ask, would a booming, Twentieth Century pharmaceutical conglomerate be interested in such a quaint historical document? An international survey by our competition confirms that when it comes to health, a growing segment of the population in industrialized countries wants to return to nature. Natural remedies are more popular than ever before. This single document is thought to hold the key to millions of natural remedies⋯.

"We cannot take the chance that the competition will get hold of the *Materia Medicinal.* A man who we shall call Dr. X is working for Bayer Leverkusen on the same mission. He was spying on our operations and gathered vital confidential information in Spain. We believe that the information he gathered is in the hands of a man by the name of Müller, passing as a historian named Professor Robert Hamilton.

"Now, Gentlemen, I give you Dr. Otto Garthoff, head of research at our Berlin laboratories."

Dr. Otto Garthoff was an intense middle-aged man, rotund

and eager. He spoke briskly.

"Professor Klaus Weber and I have studied Dr. Francisco de Mendoza's most exciting report, drafted for the King of Spain in 1707. I will read to you a few paragraphs:

We have been experimenting with a collection of herbs that grow in the rain forest in a region called Huila in Nueva Granada. Two of these herbs are excellent food preservatives, keeping our food fresh for longer periods of time and also improving substantially its taste. We also feel healthier when we eat the foods. A full description of the plants will be sent to you with the rest of the Materia Medicinal.

When we try to use both plants in the same food we encounter a completely different effect. The herbs will render the food with more appealing taste but with negative effects — all the Indians and two Spaniards that consumed that food after one month experienced poor appetite, fatigue, headaches, renal colic, diarrhea and vomiting. In a few cases inflammation of the tongue and rashes also occurred.

The combination of these plants causes cyclical symptoms, first lasting for three or four days, then disappearing, then recurring after four or five weeks. On the advice of some natives, we experimented with a drug treatment derived from a plant also native to Huila's rain forest and found that all the people afflicted by the ailment recovered in less than twenty-four hours....

"Gentlemen," Dr. Garthoff continued, "if we take advantage of this opportunity, we will become the most powerful multinational conglomerate in the world. To achieve this goal, we will use all necessary resources to get the Colombian government to award the contract for the search and recovery of the sunken treasure to Ocean Reconnaissance Fleet. O. R. F. is a consortium of our group and an American company engaged in the quest of shipwrecked treasures. As might be expected, they are primarily interested in the gold and silver. Once we have in our hands the *Materia Medicinal*, we will send a team of scientists and explorers to determine the source of the food-preserving herbs. Our research laboratories in Berlin will develop a food preservative using Dr.

Mendoza's herbs in our food products division in Latin America. Our marketing departments will wage a massive publicity campaign···

"Gentlemen, if any of you have objections or questions, I will be happy to answer them. Thank you for your attention."

After a pause, Aren Bechen stood up. "I want to thank you, Dr. Garthoff, for your very astute presentation. We will recess for thirty minutes.

The door of the boardroom opened to admit three white-jacketed waiters with silver trays and Bavarian china, followed by pots of Colombian coffee. Fritz pulled Bechen and Garthoff aside and said, I trust you will not give any additional information to the board. You have already told them all they need to know."

Bechen and Garthoff exchanged glances. They nodded.

"But you will tell me two things: How are we going to expand in South America under the present German laws, and how did Halder got the original documents from the Archives?"

Bechen stroked his immaculate moustache and spoke mildly. "As I said, our returns from our international operations more than justify the risk. Halder went to the Archives himself and simply took them."

Fritz blinked without expression and turned to Gartoff. "Otto, tell me how we are going to secure the contract from the Colombian Government, and how do you really expect to make money selling a food preservative?"

Gartoff smiled nervously. "To obtain preferential treatment we will bribe the Colombian officials. It is done all the time. Compared to other countries, they are relatively cheap."

"As for the other question—" He paused and wiped a bead of sweat from his forehead. "When we succeed at marketing the preservative-enhanced products to the food industry, I propose we gradually introduce food using both preservatives in selected geographical areas. As soon as we receive reports that people are experiencing the symptoms, poor appetite, fatigue, headaches, and so on, we publish articles saying that an epidemic has begun and blaming poor sanitation and malnutrition. We will sell the other companies food with the mixed preservative, which will rapidly increase the outbreak of illness. The majority of the people affected by this food poisoning will never realize the source of their sickness. At that moment, we will launch a massive publicity campaign announcing that we have developed a miracle drug that cures the sickness in twenty-four hours."

"Brilliant!"

"Latin America is outside the jurisdiction of the FDA. Self-medication is so widespread there that it opens up a huge potential market. Tens of millions of human beings. Drugs can be bought there like chocolate bars—without prescriptions. We can entice pharmacists to arrange their stock to display our new drug conspicuously. Et cetera."

Fritz lit his usual fat cigar ever so slowly, sending a billow of smoke drifting to the ceiling. "Well, gentlemen," he said deliberately, "you will take all the risk. For I know nothing about this. If you manage to succeed—" He smiled slowly. "You will receive a handsome remuneration—a percentage of our increased profits. If you fail and get caught, you are on your own. Your usefulness is past." Fritz looked at his watch. "Time to reconvene the board meeting."

IN a small private meeting room of the Federal Crime Police Office, the Bundeskriminalamt BKA in Wiesbaden, a man paced, still reviewing the speech he would shortly make. In the adjacent office, Inspector Captain Hans Höfer carefully watched the man's movements, while he spoke on the telephone with Inspector Brune D'Anselme at Interpol headquarters in Paris. Capt. Höfer replaced the receiver and walked into the meeting room. "I am Inspector Höfer, can I help you?"

"They are going to kill me." the frantic man cried. "They are going to kill me because I'm a spy—please, you must know what has happened."

"Calm down," Capt. Höfer said, leading him to a chair. "Start by telling me your name."

The man identified himself as Paul Friedrich, a laboratory technician. He claimed to have stolen secrets from Pharma Frankfuter's headquarters in Frankfurt. So remarkable was his tale of industrial espionage, his connections with Dr. Wenninger in Leverkusen and Spain, that at the beginning, Capt. Höfer did not believe him—not even when Friedrich provided audio and videotapes.

Friedrich's story could not be true. How, for example, did a junior lab technician gain access to the confidential business plans of one of the country's largest pharmaceutical conglomerates?

Did Pharma Frankfuter, a very powerful organization, really permit itself to get involved in such questionable business practice as Friedrich alleged? Farber, Frankfuter, with Hoechst BASF and Bayer were the world's four largest chemical firms. Who was interested in getting access to those trade secrets? Was Friedrich the man who murdered Dr. Wenninger in Ronda or, was he, as he claimed, only working for the murderers?

Friedrich told Capt. Höfer that after the killing of Dr. Wenninger, he began to believe that he was being pursued by Pharma agents and would be safer in the hands of the German police. At the beginning he thought about going to the press with his story, but decided to contact the BKA to save his life.

His fear and undisguised anxiety finally convinced Höfer that he was telling the truth.

"Do you have a hiding place for the next few days, Mr. Friedrich?" Höfer asked.

"Yes, maybe my girlfriend's sister outside of Mainz, not far from the Rhine."

"Excellent. Take care. Next Monday I want you to call me at 10 a.m."

When Friedrich left the gray five-story building of the BKA, Capt. Höfer called his assistant. "Engel, I want you to follow Friedrich and dig up all you can about his past history."

"Paul." Olga leaned toward her lover across the small dining table. "Will you get to spend more nights with me now?"

Friedrich put down his fork and knife and glared. "Listen, Olga, that is nonsense. We're leaving early in the morning. I told you, I've been followed. We both could be in danger. We'll stay with your sister until the dust settles."

"But why? Who is following you?"

Silence reigned in the shabby untidy apartment for a few minutes.

Paul swallowed nervously and tossed off the rest of his wine.

"Well, Olga, you might as well know. It's like this. I stole some secrets from my company and I think they are going to kill me."

"How ridiculous!" Olga laughed. "Companies don't kill people!"

"Agents working for Pharma Frankfuter do."

"Sure they do. They have such important secrets to protect," she said.

"If you only knew," Paul said despairingly. "Their secrets are deadly."

"Why did you steal for them if they are so dangerous?"

"I should think it's obvious. I want a place that I can call my own."

"Darling," Olga crooned, suddenly affectionate; "I know you are doing it for me. But the DM 100,000 in our joint banking account does not justify your being killed. I want your happiness more than anything else."

Paul shrugged as if the words made him uncomfortable. "You'd never believe the crimes Pharma has committed in South America."

"Crimes? There you go again."

"Listen, Olga."

Paul lowered his voice to a whisper. "If you knew half of what I know now, others have a plan to use some three-hundred-year-old herbal medicine to create a monopoly by obtaining patents which will enable them to set prices without fear of being undercut. Indomort is promoted for arthritic disease, but it has a high incidence of side effects including gastrointestinal disturbances and it adversely affects the central nervous system. Not to mention multitudes of fatalities."

He recollected the reports of perforation and hemorrhage of the esophagus and small intestine and the deaths from hepatitis and jaundice. And then there was cyanadene, a painkiller that occasionally killed the patient who had the pain. Pharma was selling it throughout Latin America. Paul told Olga that they promoted cyanadene for trivial complaints for which safer drugs were available. "These are only a fraction of the dangerous drugs they sell in Latin American markets—they get away with it because regulations are minimal and self-medication is prevalent. Do you see, Olga?" Paul's face glistened gray with sweat. "They must be stopped!"

Olga stared disdainfully. "Oh yes. My dearest, I do see. I see clearly." She dug into the pig's knuckles with sauerkraut and mashed peas on her plate, finished her beer, and led Paul into the bedroom. They made love until Paul fell asleep, clutching at the plumpness of Olga's obese milk-colored body.

At dawn Olga dialed a number in a public telephone booth in Universitatstrasse. She listened impassively as the phone rang fifteen times.

Bechen growled, his voice sleepy. "Olga! What's up?"

"You were right, Aren. Our man is in the arms of God. Come get his body. I received confirmation of your deposit into the Zurich account. I expect an equal amount to be deposited today."

"Done. Destroy the paper with my telephone number. Do not contact me again. Leave for Australia within the next two days. You can pick up your ticket at the airport ticket counter. It's paid in advance."

"One more thing." For the first time Olga's voice wavered. "Please take good care of him. He's not very strong-minded. But he's an excellent lover."

Two hours later, three men with white jackets entered Olga' s apartment. Two carried the body of Paul Friedrich into an ambulance. A third man carried away a stack of papers and videotapes and departed in a black Mercedes.

AFTER traveling for five hours in the Frankfurt-Main train to Berlin, the *Deutsche Bahn,* Robert arrived at midnight at the Zoologischer Garden station. In the long and grueling day, he had made contact with Prof. Hubertus von Pierce, who traveled from Leverkusen to Frankfurt to meet him and provided substantial information on salvaging the *San José.*

Berlin was hot and humid. A black taxi slowed to a crawl and Robert hopped in. "Please take me to the Hotel Berliner Hof." From his room, Robert called Christoph Beck. Even though it was past midnight Beck answered the telephone at once.

"Mr. Hamilton, I was expecting your call. Please listen carefully to my instructions. Leave your hotel at 9:45 a.m. and walk to August Platz, ten minutes from your hotel. Turn right into Goethestrasse. My apartment is number seven. Ring the bell downstairs and I will open the automatic door. Take the elevator to the third floor."

Later that morning, Robert found the apartment and its owner equally bizarre and, at the same time, fascinating. The small, one-bedroom apartment with a tiny living room and kitchen was crammed with hundreds of items, all related to two subjects: bicycles and timepieces. There were racing and collapsible bicycles, bicycles that weighed from seven to thirty five pounds, models of bicycles, velocipedes, photographs, T-shirts, small models, big models, ashtrays, all with motifs of bicycles, wheels, rims, spokes, hubs, frames, and clocks and watches of all kinds, sizes and ages.

"Bicycles are my life, Beck a midget of a man, explained, "I was born on a bike and when I die, I will take my best bike with me. I sell them, fix them, rent them and ride them." Beck grinned. "I have pedaled an estimated forty thousand kilometers across Europe. Besides my computer, all that matters to me is traveling on my bike."

The round-faced, bearded man adjusted his glasses and said, "Well, Mr. Hamilton, now let's come back to my hobby. Computers. I report to Karl Schneider, an industrialist who serves as a liaison for an association of several pharmaceutical and chemical companies. I am the center of communication, between Bayer, Biologische Arbeitsgemenschaft, Berchin, Merck, Squibb, Union Carbide Deutschland, Hoechst, BASF, and ten other companies. I flick on my computer and I can check, for example, the price paid by our members for raw material compared with the price paid by local manufacturers for importing similar material. I communicate by computer with each of our members and the manufacturers of raw material so they can decide how big a rise in prices for raw material should be charged to local manufacturers of pharmaceutical products. We want to maintain a minimum difference of one hundred fifty percent in favor of our associated members so the locals cannot compete with us in their own markets. When the decision is made, I alert all shipping departments of our raw material members in Europe and the United States. Electronically, this takes about three minutes. Well. This is one example of what I do for the Association."

Beck rubbed his head, which was going bald. He spoke fluent, heavily accented English.

"A large drugstore in Argentina may stock a hundred thousand items, including cosmetics and sanitary articles. Every year members try to launch at least fifty new products. But new chemical compounds with therapeutic properties are not easily discovered. To make up for the deficiency of real new medicine, our members use Parisian haute couture methods: a new look is given to old products that are not selling well enough. New variations in concentration, size and form are created; combinations of two or more well-established medicines are introduced as a new product; finally, products are recommended for the largest possible number of symptoms. For example: One of our associated companies had been selling *Prostasol* for years to treat enlarged prostates. The company received another patent on the same compound used in the manufacturing of *Prostasol* and introduced it last year as *Baldpecin,* a pill to cure baldness. My job is to coordinate and inform our members by computer so they do not step on each other's toes."

A muffled ringing interrupted him and Beck reached under some bicycle magazines for his mobile telephone. "*Guten morgen, Herr Schneider, Ich verstehe, Ich verstehe.* Beck handed Robert the phone. "Herr Schneider."

Schneider's voice sounded deep and welcoming. "Good morning, Mr. Hamilton. I am glad you could come to Berlin. Are you busy this morning? Permit me to send my driver to bring you to my house outside of Berlin. Christoph will accompany you."

Robert looked puzzled as he replaced the receiver.

"Don't mind his manner," Christoph said, catching Robert's expression. "He is used to taking charge."

Forty minutes later they stepped into a dark blue Mercedes.

The car passed Siegessaule and turned. Christoph said, "Look, that is the Brandenburg Gate, the symbol of German unity since the division of Berlin." The car passed along the once magnificent boulevard Under Den Linden and headed south to Kopenick. The city gave way to farmland and then after to a small town with a castle. The car swerved to go up a long wooded hill to an enormous estate on the summit. They drove through a grand iron gate past a stone gatehouse, up a long driveway lined with majestic lime trees, and stopped in front of an imposing set of doors.

The chauffeur opened the car door. A man at the front door greeted Robert and Christoph. "*Guten morgen,* Mr. Hamilton. Mr. Schneider is waiting for you in the library."

The man ushered them through an enormous rotunda with a domed roof, over floors of dark Italian marble. The spacious library boasted a huge fireplace, a high-beamed ceiling and low, comfortable silk couches. The walls were lined with hardwood shelves containing hundreds of leather-bound books embossed in gold.

A very tall man rose from behind a huge mahogany desk.

"Welcome. I am Karl Schneider. Thank you for coming, Mr. Hamilton. It is good to see you, Christoph. I want to thank you for the report I received yesterday. First rate. Let's have a seat."

As Schneider walked toward the couches, Robert became more conscious of Schneider's height. He was at least six feet five inches tall.

"May I offer you something to drink?"

"A glass of white wine will suit me fine," Robert responded.

"And how about you, Christoph?"

"A beer for me, thank you." A few minutes later the butler appeared with the drinks.

"Well, Mr. Hamilton, I understand from Professor Von Pierce that we share an interest in the *San José*.

"Yes, indeed. My interest is so keen that I've cut short my trip around the world to rescue the *San José* pharmacopoeia. It's important for humanity that the *Materia Medicinal* not fall into the wrong hands."

"Whose hands are the right hands, Mr. Hamilton?"

"The secrets in the *Materia Medicinal* belong to the entire world, Mr. Schneider. Not to any one man or organization or nation."

"Ah." Schneider nodded. "I am glad to hear you say so. I thought perhaps you represented an American interest. But I think we think alike. Dr. Hermann Wenninger called me from

Ronda the day before he was assassinated and told me about you. To be frank, we needed to know about you and I asked Christoph to run a check on your background. You must understand our concern, Mr. Hamilton. In regard to the *Materia Medicinal,* there are powerful people who are interested only in possession for gain.

"However," he continued, "the report Christoph submitted was a very good one and I propose that we work together. I have money and connections in high places. You, from what I hear, have brains. How can I help you?"

Robert stared a moment before he recovered his composure. "That is a wonderful offer. Can you help me raise the *San José*? Even if you are familiar with some parts of this venture, let me summarize my plans. First off, I propose to recover the *Material Medicinal* at the time of the sinking, the ship was carrying the riches of Colombia, Peru and Chile back to Spain. And today the value of the cargo is conservatively estimated in excess of three billion dollars, not including the value of the *Materia Medicinal*, which is, of course, invaluable.

"I'd like to assemble a team of experienced professionals in sub-sea recovery, engineering, material science, ocean chemistry, marine biology, marine geology, corrosion, ocean physics, archaeology, administration, shop operations, computer science, international laws of the sea, maritime history and marketing—all to launch a salvage operation. Breakthroughs in modern technology have changed the hunt for sunken treasure from a dream to a commercially viable operation."

Robert continued. "Two years ago the Colombian government requested proposals through the governments of the United States, Canada, and nine European countries, for the recovery of the treasures. The ten-member Evaluation Committee awarded points for factors like survey-mapping, experience, personnel and a consortium's ability to finance the project. Subsequently, the Evaluation Committee found irregularities with the first-ranked Swedish proposal and invited the second-ranked American group to negotiate the contract. At that point, a group mostly owned by the Pharma Frankfuter Ocean Reconnaissance Fleet bought the rights of the contract from the Americans. But when ORF's financial package was reviewed by the committee, they found that ORF wanted a substantially more favorable percentage of the deal with the Republic of Colombia. In addition, the lack of importance they gave to the salvage and preservation of artifacts of historical value, and the provision that ORF would be the sole owner of the *Materia Medicinal*, convinced the committee to suspend negotiations. One week later the bid was declared void."

"What happened then?" Schneider asked.

"Well, ORF filed suit against the Colombian government, and the court of Barranquilla pronounced in favor of ORF. The Colombian government, suspicious of some irregularities, investigated the judge and appealed the decision. As yet the Supreme Court has made no decision, but the Court is expected to rule in favor of the government. ORF has apparently used intimidation, bribes and extortion to obtain the contract."

Schneider looked at Robert with interest through his gold-rimmed spectacles. "Mr. Hamilton, how do you propose to succeed with the Colombian government?"

"That is a good question, Mr. Schneider. Not unlike my salvage plan, I proposed to form a team with the best experts in the world, using state-of-the-art technology. I will give priority to preserving for posterity all artifacts with Hispanic cultural value. I would not break up the treasure, but conserve the entire archives in order to reveal the history of one moment in time. The entire project must be done in an archeologically sound manner to protect the environment."

"And how do you intent to finance the operation? Capital contribution?"

"The financing could require as much as ten million dollars. This is where I might need your help. Mr. Schneider! I have no contacts in the financial world."

"It's not too difficult to find investors," said Schneider.

"However, unscrupulous salvagers have frightened many potential investors away.

"The amount of gold bullion in bars, disks and bits is estimated to be of tremendous magnitude. The investor will receive many times his capital contribution. We will negotiate the percentage split between the Republic of Colombia and our consortium. And any kind of distribution shall be based upon valuation by independent professional appraisers.

"As for the *Materia Medicinal*, I believe that an international agency should be established under the United Nations umbrella, to work with the international community of pharmaceutical industries, to monitor and regulate the research and manufacture, distribution and pricing of the new drugs that will be derived from trees, plants, herbs, roots, extracts, gums, fruits and seeds."

"Well, Mr. Hamilton, an excellent proposal!" exclaimed Schneider. "Now I will tell you why I am interested. I am a member of the Board of Directors of Vereeniging Gold Mining Company. VGM's principal offices are in Pretoria. We're the largest producer of gold in the world. We own eighty percent of the mines in the famous gold-bearing Witwatersrand of South Africa. Therefore, we are very interested in maintaining the price stability of gold. We do not want that gold from the *San José* to flood the gold market. For us it could represent a loss of millions if the price drops.

"We all have our own independent interests in the venture. At the same time, we have a common interest, to ensure that the treasure does not fall into the wrong hands." Schneider rubbed his hands together and beamed at Robert. "So what do you need to start things rolling, Mr. Hamilton?"

"Support in obtaining venture capital."

"Mr. Hamilton, this is what I can do for you. Initially, we can make funds available to you for out-of-pocket and third party expenses. That will enable you to put the team in place and raise venture capital. We are not under any obligation to you and you are not under any obligation to us, if you wish to suspend relations before twelve months are over. If you are able to find investors, they will have to be approved by us."

"Christoph will introduce you to the pharmaceutical association and perhaps they will invest in this venture. How does this sound so far?"

"I am delighted, Mr. Schneider! It is a very fair proposal."

Schneider stood up. "Let's have a drink to seal the deal and then make arrangements for lunch."

They were having a brandy in the study when the butler came in. "I am sorry to disturb you, Mr. Schneider. Miss Leigh has arrived."

"Please bring her in," Schneider said. "Robert, I have a surprise for you. I asked a young lady whom I believe you met casually in Seville, to come over this afternoon."

Robert recognized Ann Leigh by the way she moved her shoulders as she entered the room. She was wearing a tailored suit that made her appear even taller. She had been with Gustav Halder at the café and in the Archives in Seville. What in the name of God was she doing here? The answer came to him: She worked for Pharma Frankfuter!

Schneider was frowning. "I see I have surprised you, Robert. Let me introduce Ann Leigh."

Ann smiled and extended her hand. "It is lovely to see you again, Mr. Hamilton."

Robert was thrown into confusion by the touch of her fingers. "I confess I am startled. I never expected to see you here in Germany. It is a pleasure for me, too."

Schneider was smiling again. "Let's move to the garden. It's too lovely a day to be inside."

The garden, perched like a swallow's nest high up on the hills overlooking a lake, was the perfect place for a good light lunch. Scents of roses and wild jasmine floated up from the terraces below.

Christoph took a chair near Robert. Christoph and Robert were in an expansive mood. "Let me enlighten you. When you saw Ann for the first time, she had taken a temporary summer job with Pharma Frankfuter. She wanted to practice her Spanish and German. She was sent to Seville to work under Gustav Halder and do research at the Archive. She found very important documents about medicinal plants and asked the Archive to make photocopies, which she gave to Halder. One night, quite by chance, she read a copy of a communiqué that Halder had sent to his boss in Madrid and became alarmed to find that Halder had stolen some of the original documents from the Archive. She was more shocked to discover that Halder wanted to get rid of Hermann Wenninger and Müller. So she resigned her job."

Ann continued the story. "I alerted Hermann Wenninger. He was in Seville at the time. I told him Halder was convinced that you were Müller, passing as Robert Hamilton. Of course, Dr. Wenninger knew your real identity, since the real Müller is his superior and recuperating from an operation in a Cologne hospital. Wenninger asked me to contact Karl, so I wrote to him from England. He offered me a job here in Berlin. I've been working here for the past two months."

"I see." Robert breathed, able to meet her eyes at last. They were beautiful eyes, wide, green and shadowed by dark lashes.

Ann colored faintly. "A good many people were shocked here in Germany when they read that Dr. Wenninger had met his death in such a dramatic way, and you also could have been killed," Her voice was gentle, sweet, a running counterpoint to the heady roses and wild jasmine. How could he ever have thought her an enemy?

The conversation turned, steered carefully by an observant Schneider.

Karl told them about his life in South Africa. Christoph talked about his involvement with the environmental groups and how he had organized the biggest bicycle rally in Berlin. Then Ann spoke about her life as a student in England. Lastly, Robert related a little of his life as a history professor in Maine.

When all trace of shyness had yielded to easy conversation, Christoph spoke.

"Robert, Karl and I asked Ann to come this afternoon to meet with you because we would like her to assist you in your venture. She speaks Spanish and German, which is a great asset. But what could be of even greater value to you is the information she gained while doing research for Halder? I've asked her, and she's willing to work with you. Karl will pay her a salary, but as things progress we will discuss the possibilities of a substantial financial incentive. How do you feel about this?"

"I cannot think of a better idea," Robert said excitedly.

"Well, in that case, I suggest you two meet in the next few days to structure your plans."

"An excellent idea, we can start this evening — or perhaps I am too hasty. Would tomorrow do?"

Ann gave a little smile, that delightful smile of hers that took his breath away. "Tomorrow would be fine, I am free all day."

"Would you like to suggest a place for lunch?"

"A convenient place for me would be in East Berlin," Ann said, "not too far from your hotel. I'm in a small flat overlooking Kollwitz Platz. Renting in East Berlin is much more affordable than West Berlin. We could meet at The Fernsehturm, the television tower, located on the south side of Alexanderplatz. It's a futuristic structure and offers a spectacular panoramic view of Berlin. Take the lift to the 'The Bull' at the top. I'll wait for you there. In fact, we could go to the tower restaurant and sit and watch the entire city go by below."

AT ten-thirty the following morning Robert came up from the S-Bahn into the windy expanse of Alexanderplatz. Gigantic blocks of architecture, which made a person appear tiny and lost, surrounded the famous square. Berlin was unseasonably warm for September, and he was sweating by the time he reached the television tower only a few blocks away. Ann had been right. From the top, he had a spectacular panoramic view of Berlin.

Robert looked down eagerly at the foot of the tower. A. L. was no longer simply an abstract set of initials in a golden pen; it was suddenly someone tangible, a flesh and blood person who set his heart racing. From his vantage point of five hundred feet above, he picked out Ann's figure in the distance, riding her bicycle toward the tower. Robert was in high spirits. All the pieces were finally falling into place. He watched Ann dismount as tourists fluttered by her into the tower's entrance. She moved her bicycle out of their path, just as a man drew near her. Something about him looked familiar to Robert. It was Halder! Two other men joined Halder and surrounded Ann. Robert's heart began to throb. What was going on? Could Schneider and Beck be wrong, after all? Was that lovely woman capable of such betrayal? He had trusted Ann, but now he could see one of the men looking up, pointing directly at him. He turned, and avoiding the elevators, ran down the stairs, there were thousands of stairs. He paused on a landing to catch his breath and listen for footsteps. If they thought he was Müller, they would kill him if they could. Even in public. Wenninger was testament to that. The dim stairs seemed wholly hostile, filled with invisible enemies wanting to strike at him. Karl, Christoph and Ann had tricked him into believing they were genuine. What else could explain Ann's conversation with Halder at the foot of the tower? But how was he to escape their notice? Surely, they'd be watching all the doors.

Suddenly, he heard footsteps echoing in the stairwell, men's voices in German calling from above and below, their voices echoing in all directions. Robert couldn't see them, but he heard their footfalls. Without warning, he felt a breath on his neck. He whirled. A man stood behind him, in uniform. Speaking German, then English. "Excuse me, Sir, have you seen my colleague?" He turned on his flashlight and Robert could see he was a maintenance man. "No, no, sorry," Robert mumbled, weak with relief.

He hurried down to the mezzanine and looked down from the balcony into the street. Ann had jumped on her bicycle and was being pursued by Halder and his men. As she looked back over her shoulder, Robert saw panic on her face. Halder grabbed the bicycle, and Ann fell, sending her briefcase flying. One of the men sprayed some substance into her face. Robert ran down the last set of stairs and into the street. Men in white jackets were hustling Ann's limp body into an ambulance, which suddenly materialized. Two men jumped into the back, and it sped away with a squeal of rubber on the pavement. Onlookers exclaimed that a young girl had been handcuffed and gagged with a piece of cloth. Someone had taken down the license plate number of the ambulance. Robert looked for a taxi or a police car to give chase, but without success, so he jumped onto Ann's bicycle, which had been lying on the ground and started after the ambulance.

The ambulance turned into Karl-Liebknechtstrasse, a main thoroughfare leading to Unter Den Linden in the direction of

West Berlin. The traffic was heavy, stop-and-go, and he had no trouble keeping the ambulance in sight. He looked in vain for the police. When he got to Mark Engels Platz, he was less than fifty meters behind the ambulance. Then the ambulance turned into Breitestrasse and sped away. By the time Robert reached the corner, the ambulance was gone. Robert found a telephone booth and called Christoph Beck.

Beck convinced Robert not to contact the city police. Beck would contact a friend at the provincial police who could put them in contact with Interpol. They were dealing, Beck said, with international criminals.

A late afternoon conference got underway in the office of Inspector Andrew Eames, in charge of the Interpol branch office in Berlin, located in a stone building at Platz Der Akademie. Seated in the Inspector's spacious office were Capt. Hans Höfer of the Bundeskriminalamt (BKA) and Inspector Bruno D'Anselme from the Interpol headquarters in Paris.

"Gentlemen, let me introduce you to Mr. Robert Hamilton and Mr. Christoph Beck. Mr. Hamilton has informed me that a young Englishwoman, Ann Leigh, was kidnapped this morning." He glanced down at his notes. "Two days ago, a Paul Friedrich visited B.K.A., claiming to be involved in industrial espionage and asking for protection. He, too, has since disappeared along with his girlfriend Olga. I've instituted a nationwide search. Odd as it may seem, gentlemen, there may be a connection between these two disappearances." He paused dramatically. "Friedrich had documentation that Pharma Frankfuter is involved in illegal operations, though we have not been able to prove or deny his allegations thus far. Gentlemen, Pharma as I'm sure you know, has friends in high places. Various members of the Board are related to some of the most aristocratic families in Germany. Therefore, without proof, we have to be very careful in making accusations. But we cannot ignore what evidence we have. Mr. Hamilton recognized one of the men who kidnapped Ann Leigh. His name is Gustaf Halder, and he is employed by Pharma Frankfuter."

Eames's brown eyes, behind rimless glasses, turned their cold stare on Robert. "Mr. Hamilton, I understand your concern in trying to find out the whereabouts of Ms. Leigh. I assure you I do realize this could be a matter of life and death. However, you must understand that until we have evidence that these crimes fall under our jurisdiction, our hands are tied. Until we have specific indication that the crimes are of international nature, Interpol is bound by international agreements not to participate officially. So, at present, this is a matter for the local police and the K.B.A. Good afternoon, gentlemen."

Late that evening Robert sat in Christopher's apartment debating what to do. "Isn't there a way to find Ann by ourselves, without having to wait for the police to solve the case?" he asked, passing a hand through his hair for the twentieth time. "They're slower than molasses in January."

"Certainly," Christoph replied, wondering at the expression. "But where do we start?"

"We have the license plate number of the ambulance. Can we find out in whose name the ambulance is registered?

"We can go to the Landpolizei," Christoph suggested. "Oh this gives me a good idea, Robert. As I told you, my passion for bicycles and computers is going to be useful."

"Christoph!" Robert cried, "I know you are a passionate man, but what does that have to do with finding Ann?"

"Let me demonstrate. Cyberspace has the potential to help us find Ann. With this modem, this computer and this program—" He clicked on the keyboard. "All insurance companies have access to the Landpolizei's Automobile section, the German equivalent of the Motor Vehicle Department. And, like many large corporations, Pharma Frankfuter has built their own private network to support data communications nationally and internationally. It has a gateway to the Internet and to T-on Line run by Deutsch Telekom.

"Pharma employs what it calls the Kerberos Authentication System to protect the identity of their users. The Kerberos protocol is designed in such a way that sensitive information is never passed over the network in clear text. However, the more network your traffic traverses, the greater the exposure to snooping. I guess you can call me a 'hacker-cracker,' after all," Christoph said. "I was thinking Ann's bicycle could also be a clue. Did you tell me that one of the kidnappers stopped her by holding the bar of the bicycle and before he kicked the back wheel? It's possible he left fingerprints on the bike. Why don't we find out?"

"Would you suggest we take the bicycle to the police?"

"No, I have a better idea. My good friend Hermann Vogel works for the federal intelligence service, the Bundesnachrichtendienst. They're based in Munich, but Hermann works in BND's branch office here in Berlin. Their lab handles firearms, blood toxicology, DNA, metallurgical, petrographic and spectrophotometric examinations. And the document section handles the entire range of evidence involved in forgeries, fraudulent checks, and documents, not to mention the electronics section that actually develops state-of-the art equipment..

"I've known Hermann since we were small and he belongs to my bicycle club. He called me a few weeks ago because he wants to buy a bike from me. I'll call him tonight and ask him to take Ann's bicycle for fingerprints and dirt tests. And I'll give him a bike as a present." Christoph's gaze rested in a determined way on his shoes, which were sadly in need of repair.

"Robert, I'll need a few days to navigate the Internet. It won't be wasted time. I promise you. Meantime, why don't you take one of my bicycles and this mobile; use it to keep in touch with me and to make whatever investigation you like!"

"Thank you, Christoph. Please call me as soon as you have some news. I won't sleep until I'm on the track of those men."

FORTY hours later, Robert paced restlessly in his hotel room muttering under his breath and ruffling his hair until it stuck out in wayward tufts all over his head. The telephone rang. He leaped for it. "Christoph?"

"Hello, Robert, I have excellent news. The ambulance is registered under the name of a corporation, Autovermietung Berliner. One of the owners is Ludwig Günter, who happens to be a Board member of Pharma Frankfuter. So now we have a definite link. The stumbling block is that Autovermietung Berliner is a leasing company. They lease trucks and ambulances to private companies and hospitals. A hospital here in Berlin had the ambulance under lease for one year. But a few days ago the hospital reported the vehicle stolen to the police."

"Then we have no clue yet of Ann's whereabouts?"

"Not yet. But wait one moment. I believe in America you call it a *chop shop*, where stolen vehicles are dismantled and the parts sold off. Chop shops can be found mostly in East Berlin. I made a comprehensive computer printout of them. I'll fax you the list and a map of the area. Take the bicycle and go to East Berlin. Go from shop to shop inquiring for the price of a part for a '90 Ford van and see if you can find the ambulance.

"What we hope is that the ambulance hasn't been completely

stripped yet. It's a 1999 Ford, 7.3-liter turbo diesel, manufactured in England and exported to Germany. It looks like an ordinary ambulance, but try firing a .44 Magnum at the vehicle—it handles bullets as blithely as Superman does. It was fortified to withstand attacks by shady characters with guns or crowbars in their hands and larceny, or worse, on their minds. The box is type II manufactured by Maschinenfabruk Augsbur-Norenber. Are you up for this, Robert? Can you do it?"

"Of course I can," Robert said.

Christoph said he would ask his nephew to accompany Robert to help him with the German language

Three hours later Robert found himself in the company of twenty-three-year-old Otto Barl, a red-haired, lanky lad with a good sense of humor, riding through Kreuzberg 36, in Otto's green Fiat. They cautiously made their way into the heart of Sustern, one of the most popular centers of the underground scene.

Their first step was a junkyard behind a two-story apartment building of smoky glass. Turkish children took turns holding water hoses and spraying each other behind a chain-link fence. On the junkyard side, a man was grilling meat and drinking at the entrance of a vacant lot on a dead-end street. What appeared to be German and Turkish men were busy dismantling vehicles.

Robert inquired if they had parts for a 1997 Ford van. They indicated that they didn't deal in foreign vehicles. While Robert was at the counter Otto looked around for the white ambulance, but it was not in sight. That afternoon and in the following days, they visited thirty-eight places along a canal, in small dead-end streets and cul-de-sacs. They found chop shops in small garages in residential areas. They worked from early morning until 7 or 8 p.m., then rode back to Robert's hotel for a drink, before retiring for the night.

On the fourth day, they went to a junkyard that carried foreign auto parts. A tree on the lot had been used to lift an engine of a vehicle by means of a chain over a strong branch. There were engine hoists, jacks of all kinds, air compressors, hand tools, welding torches. There were heaps of tires, floor carpeting, air bags, hoods, fenders, bumpers and grills, transmissions, chassis, and piles of license plates.

Otto called Robert's attention to a white van at the back of the immense yard. Robert went to the desk, while Otto took photographs of the white Ford. The motor and the hood were gone; the box of the ambulance had been lifted from the chassis and lay on the ground. Otto re-joined Robert and asked the man at the counter if they had parts for a 1997 Ford van, 7.3 liter. The man asked what kind of parts and Otto said, the steering wheel.

The man pointed to the white van. "Look and see if the one in that van is what you're looking for."

Inspecting the van thoroughly, they found duct tape on the floor as well as a gold pendant stuck in the doorframe, which Robert picked up and concealed in his breast pocket. They bought the steering wheel and the front floor mats made of a plastic lighter and stronger than bulletproof vests—the same material that was tucked like insulation behind the body panels and the back seats. In addition they took the carpeting and two holding bars that were screwed to the roof of the ambulance box. One hour later they arrived at Christoph's apartment building and proudly displayed their discoveries.

TWELVE-year-old Erik Biekenbaker held the string of a yellow, red and blue kite, when the warm wind suddenly veered and the kite began to descend. Despite his efforts the kite dove into a beautiful green field between John Foster Dulles Aller and Hans Der Kulturen Der Welt in front of the Spree River. The boy found it hanging from a tree branch at the bank of the river. As he reached up for it, the wind carried the kite into the water. Erik climbed out on a branch and poked the water with a long stick. After hearing a bubbling sound coming from below the surface of the turbid water, he saw the vague outline of a clothed form, a pale bloated face with dead eyes rising toward the surface. Erik screamed.

Within the hour policemen and homicide detectives arrived at the scene, joined by BKA officers and BND laboratory agents. Capt. Höfer of the BKA carefully pushed the hair away from the corpse's face. "Oh, my God, it's Friedrich!"

The body of Paul Friedrich was taken to the morgue of the BND for forensic investigation.

Three days later, at a meeting in his office at the BKS in Wiesbaden took place, with the head of Division II, Group D of Interpol, BND and the Landpolizei as well as BKS's top investigators and outside experts, Capt. Höfer said, "Gentlemen, as the report documents, the victim's cause of death was asphyxiation by strangulation. Friedrich was apparently killed shortly after he visited our office here. Now I would like to ask Hermann Vogel, a laboratory technician from the BND, to explain some important findings."

Vogel rose and spoke in a solemn manner. "I am here today because evidence our lab was examining for another case happened to yield evidence relevant to this one. We examined the steering wheel, handlebars and floor mats of an ambulance that was previously reported stolen and later found partially stripped in a chop shop in East Berlin. Hair on the floor mat was determined to have come from Paul Friedrich's head."

Capt. Höfer took the floor again. "Now, gentlemen, Inspector Andrew Eames from the branch office of Interpol in Berlin will relate his findings."

Inspector Eames came to the front of the conference table. "It is indeed a pleasure to have such experts gathered here today. Let me review a few facts about another case. Last week the BKA received a report that Ann Leigh, a young English woman, was taken hostage and forcibly dragged into an ambulance. Witnesses reported that when the victim struggled to free herself from the kidnappers, some chemical agent was sprayed in her face, and she was gagged with a piece of cloth. The bicycle that she was riding subsequently revealed fingerprints on the handlebar. Dirt from the ambulance floor mat and dirt from the scene of the kidnapping were analyzed and determined to have come from the same place. This, gentlemen, indicates a likely link between homicide and the kidnapping. "

"Inspector Eames," one of the detectives asked, "given this minimal amount of information, is Interpol going to intervene?"

Eames' eyes flashed. "Yes. We have already been in contact with Scotland Yard in London. They notified Ann Leigh's family in Princess Risborough, Buckinghamshire, of Ann's abduction. Her parents had already received a ransom letter, but instead of asking for money, it demanded that her mother travel to Berlin, and bring with her certain documents that Ann had obtained in Seville. Non-compliance, they threatened, would result in Ann's body floating in the Spree River. And this was before Friedrich body's was found there." He paused and looked around at the gathered men. "That is connection enough for me. The kidnapping now becomes an international matter."

"Thank you, my good friend." Inspector Fritz Hofmann from the Landpolizei, tall, mustached and cigar-smoking, addressed the meeting: "The state police have focused on three areas: first, the whereabouts of Olga Batzle, Paul Friedrich's girlfriend. She was seen on the day that Friedrich was murdered. We suspect she may have been murdered, too, and we are dragging the river. Second, the ownership of the ambulance. Since the same vehicle, the ambulance, was used to transport Miss Leigh and Mr. Friedrich's body, we are trying to ascertain when it was actually stolen. We were able to recover numerous parts from the chop shop and are currently testing these objects for evidence. We also analyzed dirt left inside the ambulance cab, such as soil left on the clutch pedal.

"We are questioning the staff of the rental company and of the hospital from whom the ambulance was allegedly stolen, besides gas station attendants, and self-service and road service people. We also interviewed those working for the chop shop, to ascertain who was driving the vehicle.

"Not least, we are investigating the allegation by Paul Frederic one day before his death that his former employer Pharma Frankfuter was after him to kill him. He had documentation to that effect, but that also disappeared with his body." Hoffman sat down.

"What we heard today is a summary of this investigation so far," said Capt. Höfer. "We are dealing with very dangerous criminals and must work swiftly. Remember that the murder of Dr. Wenninger in Spain was also motivated by the seizure of Spanish documents. The key to success is for all of us to coordinate our activities at all levels. How the informational items are handled and how the information system fits into the total activities of each of our organizations will eventually determine the effectiveness of the whole investigation. So, I would like to suggest that we form a coordination committee headed by Inspector Bruno D'Anselme, head of Interpol in Paris.

"Let me repeat. We must work very swiftly before we find Miss Leigh's body floating in the Spree and the valuable Spanish documents are permanently lost. "

EARLY the following morning Christoph Beck was still working on his computer. Every cell in his body longed for sleep. The early sunlight of a misty Berlin morning fell on his desk and illuminated a fat manila folder on top of an untidy clutter of paper. The file was labeled in crude, red crayon: *ANN*.

Christoph answered a knock on the door. "Hermann Vogel! What the devil are you doing here at this time?"

"Looking for you, of course."

"Aren't you supposed to be at BND?"

"I have important news, Christoph, I thought prudent to tell you in person."

Over coffee, Vogel gave Christoph a detailed account of the meeting in Capt. Hans Höfer's office the day before. "I was able to match the fingerprint from the ambulance steering wheel with those on file. I had a terrible time gaining access to the files. I've put my neck on the line, Christoph. You are one of my best friends, but this is the last time I will be able to help you with the investigation. I may already be suspected of snooping,"

"I'm indebted to you, Hermann. I really am. Any bicycle you want. Solid gold, if you like."

Vogel smiled. "All right. All right. Let me tell you what I found. There were eighty-two drivers with the name Bruno Ginter.

Using age, height, color of hair, weight, profession and address, I narrowed the list possible suspects to seven."

"That is wonderful!"

Vogel handed him a sheet of paper. "Good luck!"

Christoph gave the list to Robert and Otto Barl, when they showed up a few hours later. "You must find out which one belongs to the fingerprints on the steering wheel."

"This is great news, indeed, Christoph," Robert said eagerly.

He and Otto rode in Otto's small green Fiat to Rykestrasse. Otto jumped out of the car and went to a three-story, brick building. Robert waited in the car. The door buzzer sounded in Ginter's apartment. Mrs. Ginter opened the door and led Otto to the living room. "Bruno will be with you shortly."

A few minutes later when Bruno came out to the living room, Otto realized that this Mr. Ginter was not the man he was seeking for. He was blind in one eye.

The next stop was a semi-detached white house with a red tile roof. But this Mr. Ginter was away in South Africa, his wife informed Otto.

Five miles away Otto knocked at the door of an old stone house.

"I am sorry. Bruno is not in. He works at the clinic until nine o'clock."

They drove to Charlottenburg in West Berlin and spoke to another Bruno, asking "What type of work do you do?"

"I work for the air force as a mechanic. What do you want from me?"

As the mechanic closed the door in their face, Otto told Robert cheerfully, "We all need a few defeats. A certain humbling from time to time is good."

It was already five o'clock and the traffic in Berlin was intensifying. "Shall we call it a day or try the rest?" asked Otto.

"Let's try the rest, maybe they'll be home after five," Robert replied.

They drove towards Tempelhof near the Berlin airport to an isolated brick house in need of painting. The afternoon shadows had long since lengthened into evening and the night air was sultry and cloud-laden. Otto rang the bell but there was no response. He inquired next door and learned that Bruno Ginter no longer lived in that house, but that his parents lived a few houses up the street. They drove to the top of the hill. At that moment they spotted a car approaching them. A few seconds later the car stopped and a man got out and walked to the house they were looking for.

Robert nodded to Otto. "This must be our man."

"What do we do next?"

"Let's wait here until Ginter leaves his parents' house and then follow him home. We'll park near the corner."

Otto felt around in his knapsack and pulled out a peculiar looking device that Robert had never seen before.

"What on earth do you have there?" Robert asked.

"Oh, flashlights, screwdrivers and a 'jimmy' to open his car."

In the distance, they heard the rattling of a house door. A few moments later they saw Ginter climbed in his car and then take off at a fast speed. They followed him at a safe distance until he turned into an apartment complex and went down a garage ramp. Robert got out from the car and walked down the ramp while Otto parked on the street. Robert ran towards Ginter, who was at the elevator, but the door closed before he could get there. The elevator light climbed upward and stopped at the 10th floor. Robert walked back towards the ramp. Otto was waiting with the jimmy in hand.

Three minutes later they had in their hands Ginter's car registration and some envelopes addressed to him at 10-B Mainfeld 40 Berlin. They memorized the information, returned the documents to the glove compartment and left the garage.

They looked at each other for a few seconds. Otto grinned and Robert said, "We. Did. It. Now we know who his bosses are." And then the sobering thought: W*e have only nine days to find Ann.*

At dawn, they returned to Mainfeld 40 in two cars: Otto in his Fiat and Robert in Christoph's Mini. Robert parked on the street and Otto parked inside the garage.

An hour later Otto called Robert's mobile. "Robert, he is coming up."

A few minutes later, Robert detected Ginter's car climbing up the ramp and exiting into the street. Thirty seconds elapsed and Robert followed, communicating with Otto by telephone. "Otto, he is proceeding towards Invaliden Strasse. Now he turned east onto Rosenthaler Strasse. Heading —towards — Prenzlaueb." Robert struggled with the wheel in one hand and a map in the other.

"Robert, I am a few blocks from Prenzlaueb Avenue, I can see him now!" Otto exclaimed.

Ginter's car approached a complex of brick buildings, surrounded by pristine lawns. "It's the Chemische Fabrik Pharma Labotatorium. Another sign says, 'Restricted Do Not Enter.'"

It looked like a university rather than a factory, located in an isolated part of Berlin. Two uniformed policemen with guns guarded the main steel entrance. Ginter showed his security pass and was permitted to enter. "The world of well-guarded, corporate secrets," Robert commented over his mobile, "Ann might be there."

"They decided to keep this plant under surveillance, alternating hours."

There were long hours of anticipation while they lay in wait for any clue to help unravel the mystery. Vehicles went in, vehicles went out. Hour after hour passed. At 4:20, Otto called to say a blue panel delivery van had entered the compound.

"Is it marked?" Robert asked.

"'Istanbul Food Delivery,'" Otto replied.

"Otto, as soon as that blue van pulls out, we should follow it."

Half an hour later Robert and Otto followed the van in a southwesterly direction, winding through desolate streets until it stopped in front of an old large stone building, whose better days were long behind it. A sign on the door read "Istanbul Food and Catering." They parked their cars and entered. They asked a Turkish matron if they could talk with the driver of the van.

"That is my husband, Mustafa." She called out to him.

A man soon came out from the rear of the store. He was tall and balding with quick dark eyes and an olive complexion and munching a wad of rolled fish. "My name is Mustafa Koprulu. At your service,"

"To get right to the point, Mr. Kopruly, would you want to make some money by answering some questions?" Otto asked.

"Come into my office. I will order *ayran.* I just returned from Istanbul and my work is catching up with me."

When they were seated, Robert spoke to Otto, and Otto turned to Mustafa. "For a few minutes of your time we are willing to pay you 100 DM."

"Very good, gentlemen. I am at your command."

"They asked how long he had been delivering food to Chemische Fabrik."

"Since two days after I returned from Turkey. That must have been Tuesday one week ago."

Otto and Robert looked at each other. That was the very day that Ann was kidnapped.

"And to whom do you deliver the food? At what time? In what building?"

"I deliver twice a day, at noontime and at 6 p.m. Today was different. They wanted me to deliver only once at 6. I was a few minutes early."

"What do they order?"

"Sometimes fried meatballs, potato pancakes with apple sauce and often sausages. Usually the order is for two people. I deliver the food to a man in uniform that waits for me in front of a gray building without windows. He stopped and then, impulsively, told them the guard uses two keys to open the door.

"Mr. Koprulu, you are very kind. We are going to pay you 120 DM for your information. But you must promise not to talk to anyone about this."

"You have my word."

Robert leaned over and spoke to Otto. "Would you like to make ten times as much, helping us in another matter?" Otto asked the driver.

Koprulu played with his long mustache. "More than likely, but, it all depends."

"You will not regret it. I cannot explain all the details now, but it will be good for your pocket and good for your soul. Please give me your telephone number and I will call you tomorrow."

While leaving, they encountered Koprulu's wife, bringing three cups of cool *ayran,* or yogurt and water, with little Turkish cakes. She was a small woman, but active and wiry. Robert said to Otto, "Tomorrow talk to her. She is the person we must convince."

The light from Christoph's desk lamp fell over the dull surface of his desk, over the telephone, the computer, over Christoph's pale face. For two days he had hardly slept, organizing and rehearsing with Robert, Otto and Koprulu down to the last detail. During his food deliveries to Chemische Fabrik, and with the assistance of a cousin who had worked in the construction of the facility, Koprulu obtained detailed information about the complex that occupied more than forty acres, which included an administration building, an eight-story modern glass and brick structure dominating the site, the experimental laboratories, research center, manufacturing plants, genetic engineering and biotechnology labs, auxiliary service buildings and manufacturing plants. On a wall of Christoph's apartment was a computer printout of the names of the members of his bicycle club who had agreed to participate in the mission. Every movement was rehearsed. Mustafa Koprulu was as enthusiastic as a child at his first picnic. On the other side of the city, delicious odors rose from Mrs. Koprulu's kitchen. This would be another dinner to be delivered to the Chemische Fabrik.

IT was a lovely Sunday morning. The clouds dissolved into one another, revealing a blue firmament above. Only two guards stood in front of the solid steel entrance door at the Chemische Fabrik. Most of the guards who normally protected the industrial complex were away on holiday or had the weekend off. Five big cartons lay on the floor of the van. Koprulu flashed his security pass at the guards, as always. They waved him through as usual.

From the top of the hill above the plant, members of the bicycle club wheeled down in a bicycle rally, each member carrying a toy gun, a bicycle helmet and a mobile. When the two guards opened the gates to let the van pass, the contingent of bicycles forced their way into the compound, knocking the two guards down. Hundreds of bicycles converged around the isolated gray brick building. A uniformed man with a rifle stood at the door. In his left hand he had a ring full of keys. When he saw the hundreds of bicycles coming, he turned and ran towards a phone. At that moment, Otto, Robert and three members of the club emerged from the cartons and descended from the van. Robert overtook the uniformed man. Otto right behind him. Together they overpowered the guard and took away the keys and his rifle.

Koprulu guided them to the door of the isolated building where he usually delivered the food. Robert opened the door with two of the keys. As soon as they entered the building lobby, a man armed with a long pipe came toward them and shouted something. When the man lunged at them, Koprulu caught his forearm in a downward thrust and brought it down over his knee, hard. Robert heard a sound like a snap of a branch. There was a howl of pain and the pipe fell to the ground. The guard turned and ran toward a door, but they knocked him to the ground, and forced their way into the room beyond. It was windowless, lined from floor to ceiling with shelves filled with tubes, jars and bottles.

They pushed open a door labeled: "Genetic Engineering Department" and then a door labeled "Insecticide Production Unit." Glass-lined tanks hung suspended from the ceiling. No one else was there.

In a building extension were tablet compression rooms, where powders were formed into tablets and stamped with Pharma Frankfuter. They reached a door marked "Restricted—Do not enter." Robert and Otto walked through, followed by more than fifty cyclists. Stale air hung in layers, ammoniac and sweat: the stink of fear and despair omnipresent. They could see cages filled with dogs, monkeys, hamsters, white mice and cats. Many of the animals had repugnant-looking growths protruding and cascading over much of their bodies. Some had their scalps shaved and connected by wires to electrodes that had been implanted in their brains. Somebody screaming, "Otto! Robert! Over here!"

Robert raced down a long corridor toward the last room in the building to where a cyclist stood before a door marked "Restricted Area." Ann lay on a dirty mattress, blindfolded with duct tape and gagged with a piece of cloth, her hands and feet tied with ropes. Each of the ropes was fastened to a steel ring secured to the wall. In a corner of the room a tall man with a freckled face, a tonsure of bright blond hair, bled from his mouth and rose amidst a group of annoyed cyclists. Three other men were being led away with their hands tied behind their backs.

One of the cyclists took off Ann's gag while others untied

her feet and hands. At that moment Robert entered and gently, painstakingly, peeled off the duct tape. Ann stared up at him, blinking, unseeing. She lifted a hand to the raw skin on her forehead. "It will be all right, Ann," Robert murmured helplessly. "It will be all right. It's over." As her eyes grew accustomed to the half-light, Ann opened her mouth to say something, but no sound came out. She was pale and weak, and with blisters on her arms and legs and scratches on her face, but her beauty, her real beauty, was untouched. Robert tried to help her up, but Ann burst into tears. He lifted her and carried her in his arms towards the door.

At that moment two guards burst from nowhere. One struggled to snatch Ann from Robert's arms and, failing, grabbed Ann by the throat with both hands and began choking the life from her. Robert lost his balance, steadied, and in a single fluid motion kicked the man in the head. The brute staggered back a step, paused, gasping, and collapsed. By now Otto and a cyclist had wrestled the other man to the ground.

Robert lifted Ann in his arms again. "Let's get out of here."

ROBERT sat on a bench outside of the emergency unit of the Bismarck Hospital. Dr. Bechel came through the door and spoke to Robert, "Miss Leigh has had a traumatic experience. She exhibits many symptoms common in hostages. She is depressed, withdrawn, frightened of everything. Her excessive sweating and increased heartbeat coupled with dilated pupils and other signs of fear concern me. I am prescribing psychiatric therapy. Rest, good nutrition, and emotional support will help regain her mental balance. Youth is on her side. I expect a full recovery."

"When will I be able to see her, Doctor?"

"Not until tomorrow. Today we should let her sleep."

The next day, Ann sat up in bed, her blonde hair freshly brushed, her head propped up on a large pillow. When Robert entered, her eyes came suddenly alive and she tried to smile.

"How are you this morning?" He reached for her hand, careful not to disturb her I.V. tube.

"Better," she managed to utter.

"I'm so glad. So glad," he repeated, gazing at her.

His hand felt warm and comforting around hers. She glanced toward the chair. Robert pulled it up next to her bedside and sat down. "Ann." He leaned closer, scanning her face. "You'll be all right—completely well. Very soon!" The eagerness in his eyes delighted her. In spite of the cracked skin at the edge of her mouth, in spite of her throat, Ann smiled, and whispered, "Yes, Robert."

On a sunny afternoon three days later, Robert was again sitting in a chair looking at Ann. She lay sound asleep. The only sound was the ticking of the bedside clock.

She came out of her sleep slowly and opened her eyes. "Robert, are you here?" Her hand lifted her hair. "Oh! God, I must look terrible."

He laughed gently. "Hardly."

"I'm sorry I never made it to our first appointment. I was really looking forward to having lunch with you at the TV tower."

"We'll have that lunch as soon as you're up and out of here—any day now. You look great!"

A glow of red crept over her cheeks.

Dr. Bechel stepped into the room. "Well, well, Miss Leigh, I can see you're feeling much better. When Mr. Hamilton is here, you hardly need these pills."

Robert rose. "I'll be back in few minutes."

When he returned, Ann was checking herself in a mirror, comb in hand. "I look awful, I'm sorry you caught me in the act."

"I brought these roses for you."

"Oh Robert, They are beautiful. Did you rush downstairs to get them now? You shouldn't have! But thank you so much."

"I have something else for you," Robert said, sliding his hand into the inside pocket of his coat. "Is this golden pendant yours?"

"Yes! Wherever did you find it?" Her hand went automatically to her neck. "My father gave it to me when I graduated from college. You are full of wonderful surprises. I was thinking this morning that I must have lost it in the struggle. Thank you."

"I found it in the van."

"I am getting in the habit of leaving clues behind for you."

A nurse with a wheelchair pushed open Ann's door. "Good morning! The doctor thinks it would be good for you to get a little fresh air in the garden. Would you like to accompany us, Mr. Hamilton?"

"Certainly. May I push the wheelchair?"

Robert lifted Ann into his arms, and placed her gently in the chair. He released the brake on the wheelchair and wheeled Ann down the corridor, into the elevator. The nurse stood behind him as they rode down. The elevator opened into a small and well tended peaceful garden. Robert rolled the wheelchair to a green bench and locked the brakes of the chair.

"Please take care of Ms Leigh," the nurse said. "I'll be back in a short while."

They sat there in the warm sunlight, Ann breathing deeply, slowly getting back her energy.

"I felt so disgusted with myself, not being able to prevent your abduction," confessed Robert. "I saw you arrive with Halder at the TV tower and I thought for a moment that you were still working for them. Then I realized I was dead wrong, but by the time I made it to the base of the tower, you were already gone."

"Robert, you have done so much for me, I don't know how to thank you."

"I owe it to you. I was in part responsible for the abduction. Your ordeal must have been devastating. You were very courageous."

"It was difficult. But I think I grew up rapidly. When you confront death you learn to appreciate the smallest things in life. I could not believe I was actually going to die. Sometimes I felt as if I was in front of a big screen and I was not part of the act."

"Did you think your captors were planning to kill you?"

"They knew I had vital information on the *San José*. I thought their intention was to obtain the information and then kill me. I was interrogated many times, almost every day, but I never told them where I kept it.

"Before I left Seville, I went to meet Halder at his hotel. It was my daily routine to give him the research I had done at the Archive each day. As I walked into his office, I noticed some original documents from the Archive on his desk; he swiftly put them in his briefcase. I was shocked. He had stolen valuable historical documents. That confirmed my suspicion that I was working for the wrong people. I was going to confront him and resign on the spot, but I realized the danger. The phone rang and Halder took the call in the adjacent room.

"That's when I rushed to the briefcase and took some of the documents he'd stolen and put them in my handbag. When Halder returned he gave me instructions for the next day. I left his office and rushed to my hotel to check out. Three hours later I was boarding a plane for London. The first thing I did when I returned to England was instruct my lawyer to return the documents to the Spanish ambassador in London and notify the Archive of the Indies in Seville. The director informed my lawyer that the Archive would keep the document in a safe for the next three years before it would be available to researchers again.

"My lawyer told me the police tried to capture Halder, but he'd left Spain before they could."

"It is an extraordinary story. What did the documents contain?"

"Information about the treasure, but most important is the location of the *San José*. It gives the coordinates—latitude and longitude. I have several copies of the documents in different safe places but none in my house."

The nurse returned to take Ann to her room. "Well, you've had plenty of fresh air."

Robert looked at his watch. "You need a rest, I'll see you tomorrow."

The next day as Robert entered her room, Ann was propped up in bed, her green eyes lit up.

"Well, you must know by now that they're letting you out today."

"Yes, I feel wonderful! Robert. Karl and Christoph came to visit me last night after dinner. It was so nice of Karl to arrange for his private plane to fly us to England and for you to come with me. I am on top of the world!"

"I didn't want to tell you until you had fully recovered but news of your kidnapping has caused a major sensation. It's on

The *Suddeutsche Zeitung*, The *Berliner Kurier*, the *Tagesspiegel* and the *Morgenpost* this morning. Some are suggesting a possible involvement with Pharma Frankfuter. The *Neues Deutschland*'s article on the front page says that a full investigation by the German legal system, including the BKA, BND and Landpolizei, is being carried out. They wrote that it could become a political time bomb."

As Ann and Robert left the hospital, television crews tried to get into the lobby. The couple was forced to leave through the rear door, where a uniformed chauffeur driving Schneider's Mercedes waited to take them to the airport. At Tegel International, Schneider's pilot and copilot were on hand to greet them. They boarded Schneider's converted Boeing 727 and leaned back in their seats and relaxed. The plane flew over France in a thin mist of upper atmosphere, far too high for them to have a clear view of what lay beneath.

Hearing his name over the p.a. system, Robert went to the front of the plane, where the door to the cockpit was slightly ajar. The copilot pushed it open and handed him a phone. "There is a call for you."

"Robert, this is Karl. I trust you are comfortable. My people have been instructed to take good care of you. How is Ann?"

"Miraculously, she's recuperating very fast."

"Well, good news! I spoke to an old Balliol chum of mine, Michael Harley. He's chairman of McCone, Lodge and Cooley in London. Top-flight investment bankers, substantial connections in the City. They know the best people in Threadneedle Street. I told him about you and the *San José* venture and he will be able to help you raise financing, in the center of the City, at the corner of Cornhill and Grace Church is a six-story brown building. Call on him as soon as you arrive in London. He's expecting you. Please give my love to Ann."

Robert returned to his seat.

"You look as if you were on cloud nine," Ann said.

"That was Karl. He sends you his love. He's putting me in contact with a financier, and this could be the start of something big."

"Congratulations!"

"This calls for a celebration!"

The flight attendant filled a glass of Riesling and held it out to Ann and then filled one for Robert. Robert watched Ann as she drank. *How young she is,* he thought. *How young and innocent, how self-sufficient and lovable.*

"I told my parents a little bit about you," Ann said, "and that I planned to continue working with you. They don't want me to. You know how parents worry about their children! But if you still want me, I would love to —more than anything else!"

"Your support would be invaluable, but we don't know if the danger has passed. It probably hasn't."

"Would you stay with me in Princess Risborough?" Ann smiled at him. "I'm sure you could get along very well with my father. We could enjoy long uninterrupted conversations."

"It would be lovely, but I must decline your kind invitation. First, I'm sure your parents want you all to themselves after such an ordeal, and besides, I have to see the financier in London. But I could visit you next weekend."

"I would love to see you at home and discuss the *San José* venture in detail."

"It's a pity we never saw each other again in Seville after I returned your pen," Robert said.

"A few days after we met at the Archive I returned to England. I was very happy researching the *San José*. It's a pity I wasn't doing it for you instead of Halder." She asked how he became involved in historical research."

"Spanish history has always fascinated me—but my interest intensified when I started teaching. I found several books on shipwrecks that were extremely exciting. You know — *galleóns* intact with chests of treasures in their holds and skeletons at the wheel. I had decided to visit the Archive first and then travel around the world. The incident in Spain made me change course. "What would you like to do, really like to do, if you could choose?" Robert asked.

Ann laughed. "I imagine myself as happily married one day. I like doing this research. I would like to travel to exotic places. I like adventure. But my real goal in life is to contribute in a mindful way to the improvement of society. And what is *your* goal?"

"My goal now is to search, locate and salvage the *San José*."

"Let me help you!"

"I would like very much for you to be part of that dream, but you must give it some time to make sure that that is really what you want."

MCCONE Ludge and Cooley were located at 12 Grace Church, in a turn-of-the-century stone fortress that had been renovated years earlier into a graceful and elegant building. A gracious and efficient staff member awaited Robert in the reception area and he was ushered into a spacious office reminiscent of all traditional financial institutions, with extensive use of mahogany, a leather couch and panoramic window.

A staff assistant pointed out the view. "From the window you can see most of the City of London which can be crossed in thirty minutes. A majority of Britain's financial institutions are here. That square to your right? At the center of it are the Bank of England and the Lord Mayor's mansion house. The area includes insurance companies, the stock exchange, the commodity markets and nearly all the banks."

The door opened and Michael Harley entered his office just as his telephone began to ring. Harley picked up the telephone. "Karl, you called at the right time. Mr. Hamilton is already here." After a brief conversation the tall, good-looking, white-haired man turned to Robert. "Good morning, Karl sends his regards. Excuse me for being late. We talk too much, but I like Karl. I went to school with Karl first at Rugby and then at Oxford."

"I am very pleased to meet you. Mr. Harley. I know Karl

regards you as a very good friend."

"Your project sounds fascinating."

"I propose to recover gold, silver and priceless valuables — the *Materia Medicinal* from the *San José*. By today's standards, the cargo is conservatively estimated in excess of three billion US. I will need financing of at least ten million, to raise and recover her. I am looking to you to secure the financing."

Harley gazed at Robert thoughtfully. His fingertips drummed on the tabletop. "The investments need to be structured to minimize the risk for the investor while still allowing the undertaking to proceed in an orderly manner."

Robert sat up straight before he spoke. "Great advances in technology have changed the hunt for sunken treasures from a dream to a commercially viable. My plan is to put together a team of experienced experts in sub-sea recovery, as well as experts in fields such as archaeology and international maritime law."

Harley rose. "A project like this presents formidable financing challenges and risk. We will structure the investment." An assistant came into the office. "Mr. Edward Robinson has arrived."

"Robert, come and let me introduce you to my partners. They are waiting for us in the board room."

The six bankers in the board room all wore black suits with waistcoats, white shirts and conservative ties. A stocky, middle-aged woman with a pleasant face and a comfortable manner brought in a tray with coffee, tea and freshly baked pastries. Robert was introduced one by one to all the board members.

One of them introduced himself as Edward Robinson. In a rich voice, which resounded with confidence and determination, he got right to the point. "Mr. Hamilton, if you would be so kind as to provide us with a written proposal, we will be happy to consider it. Our first questions are: Is it economically feasible? Is it technically feasible? Is it politically feasible? We understand that Schneider is willing to invest up to twenty-five percent. This will considerably facilitate financing. We will work in the next two months on the means of financing, we will need from you the complete project scope."

"Thank you," Robert said, "I will be happy to present you with a full written description, but I'd like to give you some idea of the project scope now." The six bankers looked pleased.

Robert went into detail about his choice of Sir Ronald Harris, the renowned English wreck-hunter, who would assemble a team of experienced experts in sub-sea recovery, marine archaeology and specialists in sub-sea equipment manufacturing as well as scholarly authorities.

He described his intention to secure the approval and cooperation of the Colombian government. "We believe we possess documents that pinpoint the location of the *San José*, but it must be confirmed, then presented to the Colombian government before we could initiate the survey. After salvage, we would disperse the recovered artifacts and cargo as follows: Naturally, the division of the treasure will be made as per contract between our group and the Colombian government, following all Colombian and international laws. Second: The disbursement of treasures between our group and the investors will be as per agreement. Third: Marketing of film rights, books, articles, technology development will be shared with the investors as per prior agreement."

After Robert's oral presentation, the partners unanimously agreed to raise the capital, pending a formal written scope of work and proposal from Robert. One of them, Anthony Hunt, a sixty-year-old financier who roamed the world as consultant to international corporations across political and geographical boundaries, was known at McCone, Ludge and Cooley as the master of mergers and acquisitions. While everyone in the City and in the financial world tried to keep one step ahead of him, no one would lay odds on being able to do it. He gave Robert the names of some influential people who could help him put the venture together.

IT was almost one week since Robert and Ann arrived in England. Although they communicated by telephone, they had not seen each other for a while. But today, Ann was traveling to London to meet him. It was a beautiful October day, the sky was blue and the sunshine cast shadows on the elegant buildings of Regent Street. The popular shopping street was so crowded that people were carried along, rather than walking, from shop to shop. Robert arrived at Marylebone just as Ann's train pulled into the station. He recognized her agile and graceful figure among the passengers converging at the arriving hall. She wore black. Her chestnut hair gleamed red-bronze in the bright light, cut short and skillfully shaped to frame her fine-boned face, emphasizing her green eyes. He caught brief glimpses of her, as the crowd between them shifted. When he reached the platform she was gone. It took him a minute to find her near the door. "You look lovely, Ann."

"You always make me feel so good," she replied with a smile.

As they walked along Baker Street towards Hyde Park, he asked, "How about tea at Brown's?"

She laughed. "How did you know, Robert? It's my favorite place."

They strolled through the park along the Serpentine paths, and then through Mayfair with its eighteenth century streets and squares, beautiful old houses nestled among modern blocks of offices. Brown's Hotel with its lovely tearoom was the perfect place to be with Ann. They sat in the corner on comfortable red leather chairs and ordered high tea. He wanted to tell her how sophisticated she looked, but he could not. Almost helplessly, he said, "You cut your hair."

She smiled faintly. "I wanted to look different for you. I am very anxious to know how your meeting went with the financial people in the City."

"Very well. They'll begin approaching investors as soon as I give them my written proposal."

"That's great, Robert. And Sir Ronald Harris? When are you meeting him?"

"Last night after I spoke with you, he called me at my hotel and asked me if I could have dinner with him at his house tomorrow. I asked if I could bring you along. I hope it is all right with you."

"My father is a friend of Sir Ronald so I suppose it will be fine to accept." Her voice trailed away. The sound of the tearoom drifted between them. Ann was leaning back in her chair but, hidden by the tablecloth, her hands were clenched in her lap. "To tell you the truth," she said, "I was anxious to see you again."

Robert leaned toward her, his hand reaching for hers.

"I've been thinking it over and after consulting my parents; I've decided to accept your invitation to assist you in whatever way I can."

Robert lifted her hand to his lips. "You are wonderful, I am a lucky man."

On the table, the waiter placed a silver stand of small trays filled with scones and cream, slices of cakes and various breads, small jars of honey, jams and jellies, and a silver pot of tea. Ann poured. "It never occurred to me when I was in Seville that one day I would be having tea with you at Brown's."

When they finished, they moved to an intimate bar across the hall, where they talked for hours about her life in school, at

Cambridge and her studies of liberal arts, his days at Princeton, the *San José* venture, Seville, Berlin, Goya's exhibition at the Prado, books, La Chatte de Colette, impressionism, Sibelius symphonies, and the existence of God. The conversation ranged from the superfluous and trivial to the profound and the humorous. Hours passed as if they were only minutes. As the sky darkened beyond the window, the dimmed lights of the bar made the lights outside on the street more brilliant.

"I suppose I must return to Princess Risborough. The next train is at 9:10. It was a lovely evening. I learned a lot about you," she said. "There are probably thousands of things I've never told you, Robert."

The only sounds were the rattling of glasses and muffled conversation from the bartenders.

"All that matters is that you make me feel great. I can't believe that we were here for almost five hours. I feel as if I've known you for years."

They walked toward Piccadilly Street. A taxi stopped in front of them. "Robert, you don't have to take me to the station. After all, we're going in different directions. Thank you for the lovely evening."

"It was my pleasure." He kissed her cheek and held the door of the cab. "See you tomorrow."

THE gray evening of early fall descended upon London, and mild, warm air, a memory of summer, circulated in the streets. Robert and Ann drove past Regent's Park with its dreamy white terraces. They headed north toward Hampstead Heath, London's most famous open space, which had long been a fashionable place to live, especially for intellectuals and the artistic elite. It was hard for Robert to realize that this was only a few miles from the heart of London. The Heath spread itself over sandy hills and into secluded valleys. There were broad stretches of grass and gorse and trees.

Ann's Volvo took them to 16 Church Row, a street with a row of trees down the middle. "I used to have brunch on Sundays," Ann said, "with a girlfriend at the Spaniard's Inn, an old tavern near here."

The house with Doric columns and a long sweeping driveway set amid the green of many acres was one of the largest on the Heath. The Flemish tapestry in the entrance hall provided the backdrop for Chippendale candlestands. A large portrait of Sir Peter Harris was prominently displayed. The maidservant ushered them into the drawing room, adorned with a Bristol chandelier, a Charles II lacquered chinoiserie chest, an English mahogany breakfront and French Empire candlestands flanking a portrait by Thomas Hudson. The lacquered Queen Anne desk held a covered cup and inkstand of period English silver.

Robert and Ann sat in two Chippendale wing chairs on an antique Persian rug, awaiting Sir Ronald Harris. He looked exactly the way Schneider had described. In his early fifties, he was slightly thickset, but neither fat nor lean. He wore a brown tweed jacket and light trousers and a casual button-down- collar shirt without a tie. His clipped white beard covered his cheeks and left his chin and lips free. He stood absently by the door with his hands in his trouser pockets, watching Ann and Robert. Then he bowed.

They stood up and shook hands. "Come and sit down on this couch. Mr. Hamilton, how delightful to have you here with Ann. I am a good friend of her father's, even if I only see him occasionally. I met him many years ago at a rowing club. We used to canoe on the Cam at Cambridge."

"My father sends you his regards," said Ann. "When I was small my father kept a boat at Magdalene Bridge and we made trips past the Backs, the lawns sloping down to the riverside. We used to canoe to the bottom of Mill Lane and Silver Street. And we would walk across Jesus Green and over Midsummer Common to the college boathouses."

"You have an excellent memory, Ann. I remember you were very small," said Sir Ronald. "The venture that you are involved in is a very exciting one, Mr. Hamilton. May I call you Robert and you call me Ronald? It makes things less formal."

"Of course, please do," Robert said.

"As a historian, you would very much appreciate my belief," Sir Ronald said, "that divers and successful treasure hunters like me would rather make a contribution, even a small one, to archaeology than destroy shipwreck sites in a hurried, indiscriminate quest for gold and other treasures. Few professional underwater archaeologists have worked closely with amateurs on such excavations and been pleased with the results —but closer cooperation on a larger scale is still needed. When Karl told me about you, I became very interested in collaborating, because of your academic background and the amount of research you and Ann have already done."

"I value your expertise in oceanography, underwater exploration and archaeology. How did you get involved in treasure hunting?" Robert asked.

"Four exciting years I spent in the Caribbean, locating and excavating several old wrecks that yielded important artifacts and some treasure that made me anxious to locate other wrecks. Why spend weeks and months snorkeling and searching for wrecks, when all I had to do was to use information I had already accumulated from books and treasure charts? There are those who erroneously believe that only limited research is necessary to locate an old shipwreck. With today's fantastic underwater electronic location equipment, any wreck can be located if only its general location is known. I read the impressive research that you and Ann put together. I believe we are on the right track."

Sir Ronald ran his long fingers down between his collar and his neck and then let his white whiskers glide through his hand. He was gregarious in manner, and elegant. "I'm very sorry I've not offered you anything to drink," he said. "What would you like?"

They both asked for wine.

I have a Chardonnay grown in the Burgundy district of France or a Cabernet Sauvignon grown in Bordeaux."

"I will try the Chardonnay," Ann responded. Robert chose the Cabernet.

Sir Ronald rubbed his hands circumspectly. "Well, well, my dear chap. I will join you with the Cabernet."

Vivaldi's *Four Seasons* floated softly in the background during dinner. The music and the wine and the food mellowed everyone. It was not until after dinner in Sir Ronald's study that talk turned again to the *San José*. The study was a large room with French windows. The walls were adorned with memorabilia and sketches and drawings of *galleóns*, navigation charts and compasses.

A green table held a vase and a Cambodian dragon. Near Sir Ronald's chair stood the elongated visage on an Assyrian statue.

"Based on our conversations over the phone I have been assembling the team. As I mentioned before, there are too few qualified people working in the field. The average wreck diver has no one to record the archaeological data he has obtained. In our case, we have Douglas Lawrence, formerly at the University of South Florida. His special interest is in colonial Spanish trade and ceramics. He will be assisted by Eugene Taylor, one of the foremost history researchers in the world and author of many books on the subject. Sir Ronald reaffirmed his support, then spoke of John Reed, a former director of Advanced Systems and Oceanography, the world's largest underwater services company. Also, we'll have specialists supported by Seawrek, an oceanographic services company involved in deep water searches, survey and recovery operations.

"Fortunately, state-of-the-art technology in underwater survey equipment favors our efforts. A high resolution, dual beam, side-scan sonar unit will be the prime instrument used to survey the sea floor and locate the *San José*. A sub-bottom profile sonar system will run simultaneously with the side-scan sonar unit to monitor the depth of any observable bedrock underlying the sea floor sediment. Magnetic anomaly detection equipment may also be used when side-scan operations detect sea floor anomalies.

"A Differential Global Positioning System navigation system will fix the precise position of the survey vessel during all search activities. Underwater acoustic transponders can continually track the position of the instruments that is surveying the sea floor. Computer software will combine the DGPS position of the survey vessel with the relative position of the towed instruments. A very advanced unmanned, remotely operated vehicle will investigate sea floor anomalies, recorded during the side-scan sonar survey. A salvage vessel 150 to 270 feet long will be capable of maintaining a station over the wreck site, in moderately severe weather, via the use of a multiple anchoring array. After being properly outfitted in the United States, the salvage vessel will sail to Cartagena, Colombia, during the best 'weather window.' A local boat, twenty-five to forty-five feet in length, will transport personnel, equipment, food, et cetera, to and from the salvage vessel."

"I don't have to remind you that the cargo will be very delicate," Robert said.

"Indeed," Sir Ronald said, "as articles are retrieved, they will receive an initial cleaning, be photographed, weighed, carefully recorded. They'll be subjected to initial conservation and secured against loss, damage and physical degradation. We'll have the entire spectrum of equipment: tools for cleaning artifacts, conservation treatment tanks, chemicals, direct current power supplies, monitoring instruments, and secure storage facilities."

"How lucky we are to receive your support and guidance!" Robert said. "Many missions and much money have been expended by many groups over the last twenty years. Many deals have been struck and broken by all sides. Based on reports, none of them achieved a fair balance between commercial benefits and archeological preservation. This program would meet these goals."

"My primary motivation," Sir Ronald explained, "lies in the excitement of discovering a new wreck, finding new and unexpected artifacts, long-lost messages from the past that the ocean whispers. Running successful projects with large numbers of local divers and crew is also immensely satisfying." Sir Robert spoke eloquently on computerized mapping systems in conjunction with side-scan sonar. "We will take a nice picture of everything sticking out from the murky bottom," he said. "A magnetometer will detect iron and steel, even when they're buried well into the sand, to give the searchers a good idea of what's old and relatively new beneath the waves. Finally, a water blower, powered by the wash from the boat's propellers, will push away the sands while sending clearer surface water down to aid the scuba divers.

"Two years ago the Colombian government tendered contracts for the search for the *San José* to other groups. This search was unsuccessful. The target turned out to be a geological anomaly. As you and I agreed in our telephone conversation, this is an opportunity to establish a world-renowned initiative. It excites me to think that a substantial fund of moneys, derived from the recovery material, can be used for educational initiatives, scholarships, student loans, Colombian archaeological studies, excavations and preservations, et cetera, and to establish a museum in Cartagena to be kept as the heritage of the people of Colombia, and to share with the people of the world the legend and history of Spain. At the same time, it can provide revenue to the Colombian government.

"Given the time and cost required to sell recovered material and convert it into cash without bloating the world gold market, we need Schneider advice to develop a very careful plan for the disposal of the commercial value of the treasure.

"More important than the gold," Robert interjected, "it will be essential that the *Materia Medicinal* does not fall into the wrong hands. I propose that an international agency be established through the United Nations to monitor and supervise the use of this compendium, so that no one pharmaceutical company can monopolize production and use of the plants."

"This is an idea that we should present to all governments concerned, as well as to the United Nations," said Sir Ronald.

"I am all for it," Robert replied.

AT the St. George Hotel the next morning, Robert spoke to his eager face in the bathroom mirror. *You've come a long way, a long way, indeed. You are in the middle of a wonderful adventure, and you have met a lovely girl.*

Half an hour later, he walked spiritedly through Hyde Park, enjoying the softness of the grass and the fragrance in the air.

Ann was as smartly turned out as ever in a soft silk dress of blues and greens, with her light blue coat draped over her shoulders. They made their way through the crowded Kensington Road and then to a little street where they descended the stairs to a cellar. The original house dated from 1662 but was rebuilt when Albert, the maître d', waiter, manager and well-fed owner took over. With its wonderful leaded glass windows, original red tile floors from the old house, simple white walls and cheese bar at the base of the circular stairs, the cozy restaurant made Ann feel as if she was in a Parisian cellar. They sat in front of a candlelight wine bar, while they waited for a table. Albert ushered them to a very comfortable booth made from old port wine barrels and opened a bottle of wine. French torch songs played in the background; young couples rubbed noses as they conversed in whispers.

"I am glad that finally you are able to come to Princess Risborough for the week-end," Ann said. "My parents are eager to meet you."

"I'm looking forward to it."

"How is your hotel?" inquired Ann.

"Very pleasant, but I'm thinking of renting a flat for a few months."

"If you like, I can help you look for one. I have a friend in the property business."

While they ate, Ann and Robert made plans for the weekend and for the next week. He asked her about Princess Risborough and her favorite place in the Chilterns."

"When I was a small girl I walked with my parents along Ickneild Way to Monks Risborough and up the top of the hill to the eighty-foot white leaf cross. They believed it was cut into the side of a hill in the eleventh century by the Normans. Our house is called Creadle Dean in Cadsden Road. It is adjacent to Chequers, the country retreat of the prime ministers."

Albert poured their wine and served a Grand Marnier soufflé on lovely plates.

Robert gazed at Ann. "I also want to know you more and more."

"I know you have a past that you never want to forget." She smiled shyly

He lifted her hand and kissed it. "Ann, you're very human, warm and with a great intellect. That's a most unusual and delightful combination which pleases me. My wife and son died two years ago in a boating accident."

"Oh, Robert, it must have been terrible. Were you very much in love with your wife?"

"Yes, I was. But that life is past."

Silently, they touched their wine glasses, then turned to the soufflé.

The road to High Wycombe in Buckinghamshire wound past villages that had kept their traditional Chiltern character, with brick and flint houses leading up wide streets to a Norman church. Arable and dairy farming on the foothills and sheep rearing on the higher slopes went on much as they had done since Saxon times, when yeoman farmers settled there.

Cadsden Road ran through tall beeches, leading to a spacious Tudor cottage that sat on seven acres of lawns surrounded by apple and beech trees. The driveway to the house passed through rock gardens clad with heather and alpine plants. Ann rang the bell and her mother opened the door so promptly that Robert was startled.

"Mr. Hamilton, I am so pleased to meet you. Ann is always talking about you."

"I haven't an idea what the time is, but I know I'm fearfully late," said Ann.

"Mrs. Leigh," Robert said, "I want you to know how grateful I am to you and your husband for inviting me up for the weekend."

Ann's father came to meet them, and after a hearty handshake, they all entered the house. Mr. Leigh, tall, slender with the same fine features and well-rounded lips as Ann, guided them into the living room. Mrs. Leigh brought tea and scones.

"As we were arriving in Princess Risborough," Robert said, "we saw a group of hunters in front of a pub. They hunt in this area?"

"Yes," Mr. Leigh replied. "Nearby there is a forest. *Forest* has come to mean a densely wooded area, but originally it meant simply an area set aside for hunting by the king or powerful nobles. The Normans had some eighty such forests, and protected hunting rights with ferocious forest laws. Until the reign of Richard I, who was more interested in crusading than in hunting, a man could be blinded merely for disturbing the royal deer. You as a historian would be interested. The new forest is full of the fascinating oddities of history, most of them arising from long, drawn-out disputes between the monarchs, intent on preserving hunting rights, and the commoners living in the forest. In this area, hunting is still very much alive."

Ann's mother guided the conversation into urban small talk. Her delicate features, the aristocratic shortness of her upper lip, and the wealth of fair hair suggested her upper class background.

Afterwards, Ann showed Robert her room, then took him to the room where he would spend the next few days, spacious and airy with windows overlooking the garden. They went to the garden and climbed a hill overlooking the Chiltern valley, from which they saw sheep grazing. They sat beneath an immense Burnham beech tree and watched an exceptional sunset from atop the hill. Ann's face was so close to Robert's that her blonde hair fell over his shoulders.

"See the birds down there in the chestnut tree," she said.

"I see an ocean of birches and beeches on the horizon," said Robert. As he held her hand, radiance lit up her eyes. He took her in his arms, kissed her, holding her tightly to him. His lips took possession of hers. He felt her skin through the thin fabric of her dress. The sunset, dark red and green-blue, changed to a lighter golden red and orange, and set into twilight-colored foam. Suddenly Princess Risborough exploded into lights, an entire village of lights that appeared to mirror the stars above.

Ann straightened up and smoothed her hair. "Robert," she said, "we must go back. I am afraid of falling in love with you."

"I already have, with you," responded Robert, embracing her.

They walked down a path illuminated by the light of the moon, holding hands. The evening wind caressed their faces.

Back at the house, the magic of the sunset still held them in its thrall and they longed to be alone together. They declined Ann's parents' invitation to dinner and dined instead at Great Missenden and danced there.

"He says he's crazy about me," Ann whispered to her mother late that night. "And I'm crazy about him."

"Darling, isn't this all a bit premature? I know he appears to be a wonderful man, but don't rush into things."

"Good night, Mother. You shouldn't worry."

The next morning the sky above was a faint blue. A few clouds floated like sleeping white swans. It was nine o'clock when they entered the empty tennis courts.

"It's been a long time since I've played tennis," Ann said. "I'm sure you could help me improve my game."

They played in concentrated silence. *We're well matched,* Robert thought. *We're both hard, fast players.* But it was Ann who finally scored the winning point by making a cross-court drop shot beyond his reach.

"Wonderful game!" he said. "Congratulations!"

"The game was very even. I enjoyed playing with you, Robert."

They went for bicycle rides in the country, drove to Hambleden and walked through some of the most glorious valleys in the Chilterns. They took a narrow road from the village leading to Fingest, notable for its Norman church tower, and to Turville where a black-capped windmill stands on a high ridge. They spent every moment they possibly could together.

They talked over the telephone the next week, and soon were meeting every day in London. They walked in the park together or went to picture galleries. They had lunch in Soho, a bustling district of narrow, rather dowdy streets, famous for its foreign restaurants and shops. They walked through St. James Park; they went rowing in the Serpentine and rode horses on Rotten Row in Hyde Park. They looked for a flat in Belgravia, Kensington, Hampstead, and finally in Chelsea.

They strolled one afternoon in Cheyne Walk, a street separated from the embankment by a line of gardens, and found a row of fine, early eighteenth century homes, many with wrought iron fences and gates. They found themselves in front of a house with a board announcing a flat for rent. The shutters were closed and there was no sign that anyone lived there. They rang the bell and the door was opened by a man who led them into the house, which had been converted into four equal flats.

The flat had one bedroom, a spacious living room with large windows overlooking the river and a small kitchen and dining room. The living room had been furnished with back-to-back sofas, and corner chairs. Two sets of French doors opened out onto a verandah.

Without further ado, Robert signed a six-month lease. A few days later he moved in. It was like suddenly being plunged into a new life of excitement.

One evening, Ann knocked softly on the door. Robert opened it. She walked in with groceries in her arms and said, "Robert, let me fix you some dinner. We must celebrate your new flat and we've been eating out almost every night."

"You are wonderful. I will cook for you next time."

"I like very much cooking for you but I would also love trying your culinary creations."

The dining room table was festively set with a bottle of champagne and candlelight. The dinner turned out to be a banquet. It began with hors d'oeuvres followed by filet de sole au gratin and complemented by Brie cheese and fruit and coffee.

They ate heartily. They discussed the possibility of Ann accompanying Robert to South America. Robert left the dining table to go find a map. While he was searching for it in the bedroom, he heard the door behind him close. He turned to see Ann's face lit by a candle she carried, moving towards him. He wanted to go to her but held back. He let her come to him. She put the candle on a table and walked into his arms. She closed her eyes and let herself be engulfed in the heat that flowed from his touch. In a moment he was holding her to him, pressing her body along his, and turning her toward the bed. The candlelight glowed on the table a vivid orange-red and then flamed out.

"If it had not been for you, Robert, I might have lived and died and never known love."

By the end of the week Robert and Ann completed the project proposal and delivered it to Michael Harley. That evening, as they started through Regent's park, heavy raindrops beat warmly against their faces. He took her in his arms to protect her from the rain, aware of her wet skin through the fabric of her dress. The night-air felt soft and deep and pregnant with benefaction. They stood there, and they were rain and storm and water and earth.

The rain became a glistening silver curtain. The smell of the soil was strong and rich from the beautiful gardens—the bushes fragrant, a thousand blossoms open to the life-giving wet. Trees spread a thousand open arms and penetrated the soil with millions of probing roots. The magical rain embraced their desire like a sheet of falling stars. They walked through the gardens and then along the street toward Marylebone station as they had so many times that past week. On the platform, Robert kissed Ann goodbye.

She gazed at him with green eyes under long, dark lashes. "Thank you for everything." Her wet face, caressed by the silver rain, shone, cherubic as a child's.

"I will see you next Friday." He whispered, "I love you."

On the way back to his flat, he looked once again at the gardens in Regent's park. How desolate they now seemed, how flat and dull their colors! Of all their former beauty, only the memory remained.

FRIDAY morning, the noise of a vehicle in the street jolted Robert from sleep. As he opened his eyes, he saw the sun coming through the window. He got out of bed and went to the window. The grass was wet with dew and he saw the mailman walking towards the entrance door on the moist gravel path. A few minutes later, there was a knock at his door.

"Good morning, Sir. Express mail for you."

It was from McCone, Ludge and Cooley. The letter read:

Dear Mr. Hamilton:

We have been able to secure financing for the project. We have obtained commitments from six investors. Please contact us at your earliest convenience so we can review the details.

Sincerely yours, For McCone, Ludge and Cooley
Michael Harley, Senior Partner

Robert gave a shout. He could not have expected better news. He took the receiver and dialed Sir Ronald who was out. Robert left his telephone number.

As he brewed black tea for breakfast, Sir Ronald called back. "Is it you, Robert? Where on earth have you been the past two days?"

Robert explained the reason for his disappearance.

"Good old boy, she's quite a girl. Where are you now? I need to see you."

"I'm in my new flat."

"Wait there and I'll ring you, when I get close."

Robert poured a cup and added sugar, blew on it a few times and drank his tea. Soon, Sir Ronald drove his gray Bentley up in front, and to Robert's surprise, Karl Schneider pulled up behind him.

Both men got out of their cars. "To what do I owe the honor? I was not expecting you until next week," Robert said to Karl.

Karl laughed his barking laugh. "Surprise, surprise."

"I was able to free myself sooner; it's great to see both of you. Let's have lunch," suggested Karl. "I'm at the Ritz, not far from here."

"This is my party, old boy. I've already made reservations at my club in Pall Mall," Sir Ronald interrupted.

Robert went in Karl's Mercedes, which followed Sir Ronald's Bentley to the Hurlingham Club, a polo club with Doric columns. A true bastion of privilege, Robert thought, as he and Karl followed Sir Ronald through the vastness of the entrance hall and into a beautiful white and gold dining room. Sir Ronald walked firmly across the room to a table by the windows. The head steward placed large menus with leather covers at the left of each of them.

"The food is excellent here. Any of the pâté de champagne left, James?"

"Yes, Sir Ronald."

"Please, pâté for me, followed by lamb, beans and your excellent salad. What about you, old chaps?"

"I've a mania for really good smoked salmon," Karl said, "with salad and haricots verts."

"As for me," Robert said, "duck with turnips, asparagus with Hollandaise sauce."

Sir Ronald looked up at the steward. "Have you got all that, James?"

"Yes, Sir Ronald."

"How about some wine? I suggest the Mouton Rothschild 1979."

"Very well, Sir Ronald."

Karl Schneider opened a briefcase and pulled out some papers. "I wanted to talk with both of you, about something critical." He paused for a moment and looked at Robert. "Would you like to meet Herr Müller? His full name is Helmut Müller. He used to work with Bayer in Essen, but now is working as a consultant for Bayer at Leverkusen. He resides in Cologne with his wife Elsa and son. It is important for you two meet him, because he apparently knows the exact location of the *San José*.

Robert looked at Karl in disbelief. "This news couldn't be better. Looks like something out of a dream, I am very eager to meet Müller. How was this information obtained?"

"Partly from transcribed journals, ship's logs, personal correspondence and computer-enhanced analysis of the movements of the Spanish and British— prior to, during, and following the engagement. According to Bayer, they have the original ship's logs. How he got the information for Bayer we don't know. It will give us an opportunity to compare his information with what Ann obtained, specifically from the transcripts of the court martial proceeding for the captains of the British ships. Bayer agreed to meet with us, to negotiate the terms and conditions for the release of the information that Müller safeguards."

"I welcome this unique opportunity," said Robert.

"Good. But there is a problem. You must travel to Germany right away. Müller has accepted a consulting assignment in Australia and will be leaving next week. But more important, the political situation in Germany is becoming very complicated as a result of the Pharma Frankfuter scandal. Müller himself may be what you Americans call a 'hot item.' If we are to find him, we must move fast. We know that he lives in Cologne, and we had not been successful trying to obtain the information through Bayer."

"What do you suggest?"

"Robert, I know it is very short notice, but you and I must depart tonight for Dusseldorf. My plane will be waiting at the airport to fly us to Cologne. Sir Ronald, you can meet us in Cologne as soon as you can get away."

Sir Ronald smiled his agreement. "So be it. James, the Mouton Rothschild. Bring it straightaway, would you? Well, gentlemen, it looks like this project is going to fly. I've contacted Marine Explorations Company of California. They own the *Auguste Piccard*, the world's most versatile undersea vessel. Constructed in Switzerland in 1967, I believe, fully outfitted, with sensors, tools, including the unmanned underwater vehicle, or DART, it provides remote observation—equipped with sonar, television, still cameras, and excavation tools, retractable wheels, arms with steel fingers driven through fiber-optic cables."

"You bring us very good news," said Robert.

"Well, that is the good news. The bad news is that over the years the sub has been left to deteriorate and needs a complete overhaul."

"And what is the condition of the surface support ship?" asked Robert.

"The *Sealion*, as the vessel is called, is in better condition, but needs some repair. They are being kept at the Alabama Dry Docks in Mobile."

He asked Robert to contact a potential candidate for ship captain, Jack Swanson, who lived in Vancouver, Canada. "I suggest, Robert, try to evaluate the man not only for his capabilities as a sea captain but also for his personality."

"I hope he is willing and available."

"Robert tells me McCone has come up with most of the financing," said Karl to Sir Ronald. "We have Robert and Ann's research on the *San José*. So what's left?"

"The only thing left is to obtain the contract from the Colombian government, and to strike a deal with Bayer for the location of the *San José*."

"Well, apparently we have many things going for us. Now we have a long and arduous road," said Robert.

Later that night, Robert called Ann to inform her of his imminent departure and what had transpired. She was not happy, but she struggled to hide her feelings. "Wonderful news, Robert, but I am going to miss you terribly. Take care of yourself and remember that I love you and I need you."

"All this is happening so suddenly. I'll make it up to you. It's going to be hard without you," Robert said.

"If you want, I can fly to Cologne in a couple of days."

"Let me assess the situation. I'll call you tomorrow. I must go, but remember that I love you very much."

It was unseasonably warm for October when they landed at Trisdorf-Köln airport. The night traffic was light as they drove on the Autobahn to the center of Cologne, where the Excelsior Hotel stood on the most famous and elegant square in the city.

No sooner had Robert unpacked his clothes than Karl Schneider appeared at his door with news of a telephone call from Christoph in Berlin. He had been following the Pharma Frankfuter investigation daily, through the Deutsch Telekomang, the German telephone company and Internet access provider. The *Tagespiegel* had published details of the Pharma Frankfuter scandal. Using some of that information, he was able to access their gateways to snoop into their private data network. He had found that Gustav Halder traveled to Cologne, but so far Christoph had not been able to ascertain his whereabouts. The following morning, Müller himself was to call Karl to inform him of the time and location of their proposed meeting.

Five hundred miles from Robert and close to midnight, Ann was wondering if he had arrived safely in Cologne. She was debating if she should call him or wait for his call.

In his room, Robert thought of the wonderful autumn days with Ann in England. He reached for the telephone, and then pulled back his hand, realizing that it was close to midnight in England. Well, he thought, he would write an e-mail. He opened his laptop and composed a long, warm letter.

ROBERT followed Karl from the lobby of the hotel out into the streets of Cologne. Around them, screaming youngsters flew by on roller skates and pavement artists, used colored chalks to create beautiful scenes on Roncalli Platz. Passers-by stopped to admire them and toss a few coins in the shadow of the Cologne cathedral. Waiters in white jackets went in and out of cafés, onto terraces carrying food and drink.

At the tourist office and information center in Unter Fettenhennen, Karl followed the instructions he had received from an anonymous caller early in the morning. "Do you have a program for the Philharmonic Hall?" Karl asked. "What is the program for Friday?"

"Ludwig van Beethoven Piano Concerto Number One," the attendant replied.

Karl led Robert to a bookstore in Hohe Strasse, where he asked the clerk for a biography of Ludwig van Beethoven in the hardcover edition. Karl purchased it and the clerk gave him the book in a plastic bag with the name Hohe Book Store.

Bewildered, Robert followed Karl toward the river near the Hohenzoller Bridge, where Karl sat on a bench in Rheingarten and Robert sat beside him. Nearby were delightful rustic pubs and gourmet restaurants. Dozens of artists, young and old, displayed their paintings to tourists from England, France, Japan, and South America. A nondescript man sat at the opposite end of the bench, also carrying a bag from the Hohe Book Store.

"Excuse me," the man said suddenly, extending his bag to Karl, "I believe you left this on the counter."

Robert gasped. Karl stared at him blankly, accepted the bag, and opened it. It contained a Beethoven biography in hardcover, a small mobile and a note that read:

Dear Mr. Müller:

Please follow Otto, he is instructed to take you to the place of our meeting.

I am looking forward to meet you.

Karl handed the note to Robert and said, "Yes, this is mine. Thank you. Are you Otto?"

"Yes," the pot-bellied man answered. "You must stay here. In ninety minutes somebody will pick you up in a boat. Keep the mobile open for instructions, Mr. Hamilton." The man turned to Robert. "Follow me at a distance."

Robert followed several feet behind Otto, walking towards the Cologne cathedral. After doubling back on his own trail several times, Otto turned into the main entrance of the Wallraf-Richartz Museum. As the door opened, a uniformed guard operated a turnstile that admitted one visitor at a time.

Otto purchased a ticket and moved with the crowd into the large rotunda. Robert followed suit and stayed well behind him. Otto went through a side exit door, and then towards the cathedral's south entrance. A few seconds later, Robert ascended the steps leading to a 95-meter-high gallery. Robert admired the magnificent stained glass windows, the slender main nave leading to the choir, and the bell chamber with its bells. He labored for breath as he neared the top. Perspiration from his forehead dripped into his eyes. Finally, Otto opened a door and walked through an arch into a 360-degree observatory, offering a spectacular panoramic view of Cologne.

At the parapet wall, Otto approached him. "A breathtaking

climb," he said and handed Robert a handwritten note, then vanished.

The note read:

Do not leave, somebody will contact you in exactly ten minutes. Beethoven is the clue. Follow him.

What the hell am I doing here? Robert wondered sourly, but he waited.

A group of Japanese tourists overtook the observatory. A German who spoke in English held up a flag of a tour company. "The Cologne cathedral forms the center of the city and provides the measure for everything else. It is 144 meters long, 86 meters wide and its tall spires are 157 meters high. On August 15th, 1248, Archbishop Konrad of Hochstaden blessed the start of construction. The new Gothic style cathedral was planned to house the sepulcher of the three magi. During the Second World War the cathedral was severely damaged. It was not until 1956 that the cathedral could return to its intended purpose, in all its glory—"

At that moment a priest with a small audio cassette player sidled up to Robert. The vibrant movement of Beethoven Piano Concerto No. 1, C Major, Op. 15, wafted from the cassette. The priest walked alongside a ramp and entered an elevator. Robert followed.

Adolf Fritz flung open the door of Aren Becher's office, at the Pharma Frankfuter headquarters in Frankfurt am Main. Becher stared into the man's blue, eternally angry eyes.

"You and Berthold Beitz have been barking up the wrong tree for months. You assured me, Aren, that Beitz was extremely skilled and knowledgeable in identification matters. Well, you are dead wrong. You have confused Müller with an American named Robert Hamilton. Müller is the man who knows the secret of the *San José*. He has been living in Germany all this time. Now we find ourselves in a real mess. The government grows suspicious and we cannot wait until the political fires die down. We must get that information from Müller. Your blundering brought Robert

Hamilton into this affair, now he is interested in the *San José*. He is even spearheading a salvage operation! Karl Schneider, the South African gold mine magnate, is providing monetary support to the operation. Well, Aren, your response?"

Aren shrugged. "I have to admit that Beitz misguided us."

"Misguided *you*. You should not have relied so heavily on Beitz's judgment. He is not a very intelligent man and he is driven by his keen desire to please us. The damn fool is a good workhorse, we can use him, but we need to control his activities. The beauty of Beitz is that he is expendable." Adolf Fritz breathed deeply, trying to calm himself. He wiped his wet forehead with a handkerchief from his breast pocket. At the window overlooking the spacious square, he said:

"Listen, Aren, we cannot afford to fail now. We have placed an agent at the Excelsior Hotel in Cologne, where Schneider and Hamilton are staying. Nick is monitoring all their outgoing and incoming calls. Müller knows that he is being followed. Yesterday he asked Schneider to wait for a telephone call today at nine o'clock. At 8:45, we called Schneider and instructed him on how to proceed in order to meet Müller, which he followed to the dot. At 9 a.m. Schneider's telephone was busy talking with us, but Müller's call was transferred to a man working with Nick. This man has a great gift of imitating voices, and he was able to pass for Schneider. So, at this moment, Müller must be trying to pick up Schneider at a pier on the Rhine. The instructions I gave to Beitz were to let Schneider make the connection with Müller at the river. Then capture both of them alive. As for Robert Hamilton, our people have taken him already. We will extract from Müller all information pertaining to the location of the *San José*."

Fritz looked at his watch. "Aren, call Beitz on his mobile and tell him that this time the plan must not fail. Ask for the latest developments. And immediately call me at my office."

At 11:30 a.m. in front of the pier, Karl Schneider impatiently looked at his watch.. The river was dark and boats went by—bulky cargo boats carrying ore, grain and oil products both up and downstream on the river, along with pleasure boats, large vessels carrying tourists, and barges. Then a 45' pleasure boat docked at the pier. A few minutes later a man in his late teens came down off the boat and said, "My name is Helmut Müller. My father is inside. Are you Karl Schneider or Robert Hamilton?"

"I am Karl Schneider."

"Where is Mr. Hamilton?" the boy asked.

"I don't understand," Karl said. "He is supposed to be with your father, according to his instructions."

"But he is not aboard. Please come and talk to my father."

Helmut Müller senior was in his late forties, a six-foot-tall, athletic figure with pleasant and inquisitive hazel eyes, light brown hair. "Mr. Schneider, I presume? I am pleased to meet you at last."

Karl Schneider stared at him. Müller looked very much like Robert Hamilton. "Where is Robert. Hamilton?" he asked.

"According to your instructions we were supposed to pick up a Beethoven biography and come to this pier to wait for further instructions, so we did. A man named Otto asked me to wait here and gave me this note." Karl showed him the small sheet of paper.

"I've not given any such instructions. This is not my note! What is going on? This morning I told you both to meet me here at 11:30. I said nothing about Beethoven." The two men glared at one another. Müller's eyes narrowed. "Now that I think of it, that voice sounded very much like you, but as if you had a cold, yes... somehow hoarse. It sounded harsh."

"Oh! My God!" Schneider cried. "Robert Hamilton could be in great danger! We are both in danger. They will stop at nothing."

"Should we go to the police?"

The mobile that Otto had given to Schneider in the plastic bag rang. Schneider opened the bag and answered it. An inarticulate, husky voice with a German accent said, "Schneider, listen very carefully. Your mobile has been bugged. If you try to disable or destroy the telephone you will activate an explosive device. If when we call the mobile and we are unable to get in touch with you, Robert Hamilton will die. Any wrong move and you will find Hamilton riddled with bullets in the streets of Cologne. Now, tell Müller to take the boat to Bonn and wait to hear from us."

Schneider closed the mobile.

The perplexed Müller said, "What is going on?"

"They have Hamilton," Schneider said slowly. "We have been set up. They will kill him unless we comply with their demands. We must take the boat to Bonn and wait for instructions." Schneider pressed his index finger to his lips. Müller nodded. Taking a pen and a paper from his pocket, Schneider wrote:

The telephone is bugged. Do not say anything that can complicate the situation.

Müller passed it to his son.

At a hastily held meeting in Wiesbaden, the stunned members of the investigation team listened to tapes. By the end, everyone had a worried expression.

"Well, gentlemen, what you just heard is a conversation between Adolf Fritz and Aren Becher, and you may agree, very incriminating. I hope they will satisfy the prosecutor," said Inspector Hans Höfer. "The tape was recorded and provided to us by Werner Bischoff. He agreed to become an informer, in exchange for a prosecutor's grant of immunity."

"All the pieces have fallen into place," said Inspector Strenger from the Cologne police. "Adolf Fritz and Aren Becher have been at the center of the investigation and now we have the tape as evidence. Why don't we arrest them?"

Höfer regarded him with impatience. "We are investigating Pharma Frankfuter's illegal activities, as well as individual Directors of the Board. However, to arrest Fritz and Becher at this moment would be close to suicide. They are very powerful and with very strong connections in high places. Inspector Strenger, what actions will you take to find Hamilton, Schneider and their kidnappers?"

"On one thing we are all agreed. We are facing a very powerful and dangerous organization. So you can understand the complexity of the operation, Cologne is the third largest city in area, the fourth largest in population. Finding these people will be extremely difficult." Inspector Strenger folded his wrinkled hands and mulled. "Don't lean on me to solve the problem in one day, Hans, but we will search Cologne, leaving not one stone unturned. We have already mobilized."

They were interrupted by a call from Christoph Beck in Berlin. After a few minutes of listening to him, Inspector Höfer asked, "Who is he? How were they transmitted? And from where?"

Christoph responded from his cellular phone, "He is Helmut Müller's son. He was communicating from a computer in his father's boat. His father and Karl Schneider are on the deck and he is in the cabin. They are going down the Rhine towards Bonn."

"Excellent, Christoph. Please keep in contact with the boy and with us."

At a quarter past five the same day, there was a knock at the door of the manager's office at the Excelsior Hotel. Inspector Strenger, accompanied by two men dressed in civilian clothes, identified themselves as detectives from the Cologne police. The Inspector addressed the manager:

"We have gathered irrefutable evidence that a member of your staff has been working as an informer for a powerful organization under investigation. His first name is Nick."

"Nicholas Stager? He works in reception," the manager replied.

"Has Stager been working long for your hotel?" the Inspector asked.

"For several years, he was at our sister hotel in Frankfurt, but he only started working in this hotel last Friday."

"Bring him here."

The manager summoned him over the intercom.

A burly, bespectacled man in his late thirties backed through the door and put a pile of papers on the manager's desk. "Is that what you need, Mr. Getman?"

"That's fine, Nick, but the reason I called you is because this gentleman wants to talk to you."

"I am Inspector Strenger of the Cologne police. You must come with us to the station. If you cooperate, this won't take long."

The man paled, nodded and followed the inspector meekly.

The interrogation room at the police headquarters was as familiar to the inspector as a second home. He knew every grain in the big table, the way the spotlights hung from the ceiling. He noted every nuance and gesture of the men he interrogated. The Inspector, clearing his throat and politely covering his mouth with a fist, looked Nick in the eyes and said, "Listen, Nick. You look like a good fellow. We know more about your activities than you ever can suspect. So you might as well cooperate with us."

"I do not know what you are talking about, Inspector. Mind if I smoke a cigarette?"

"Go ahead; make yourself comfortable, it could be a long session. It all depends on your cooperation. Who hired you to monitor the telephone calls of Mr. Karl Schneider at the Excelsior Hotel?"

"I don't know what you are talking about, Inspector."

"How did you get mixed up with Pharma Frankfuter?"

Nick began to sweat. He avoided the Inspector's eyes. "I don't know what you are talking about, Inspector."

"Yes, you do." Inspector Strenger turned to the detective beside him. "He's yours, Oscar. Let me know how you fare." Detective Oscar Duisberg of the police department, with a bullet head, a thick neck, powerful shoulders and short, pumping legs, was a bulldog of a man. He continued the drilling for six hours. At one moment, Nick started to walk away and Detective Duisberg followed him across the room until the wall stopped Nick. He continued to speak to his back.

"Who is this man?" the detective asked him, yanking him around and handing him a photograph.

Finally, Nick began to shake. Then he began to weep. "Adolf Fritz. He threatened to fire me if I did not cooperate, and he offered me 2,000 DM for the information."

When the Inspector entered, he patted Nick on the back and said, "Nick, everything is going to be all right. You help us and we will help you."

Strenger signaled to Duisberg, who left the room. Inspector Strenger knew well that privacy was an essential psychological factor contributing to a successful interrogation..

In actuality, adjoining the interrogation room was an observation room, with a two-way mirror and a speaker, connected to a concealed microphone permitting the investigation team to hear as well as see what was happening.

"Nick, I know that you must be hungry. You have not eaten anything for many hours."

The inspector leaned back in his chair and lit a cigar. "Don't think Detective Duisberg has a heart of stone or is ill-natured. He sometimes wants to go to the root of things and forgets that the person he is investigating could be hungry. Would you like to eat, Nick?"

"Yes, Inspector. Please," Nick responded.

Strenger had food brought in, along with a bottle of soda. "I would like to ask you a few questions, but before I begin, do you know why you are here today?"

"As I told Duisberg, I don't know anything except that my company asked me to come to work at their hotel here in Cologne, and to keep close tabs on telephone calls made to and from a couple of rooms at the hotel, and monitor the two guests staying in those rooms. But I'm not sure what this is all about."

"One of those men, Robert Hamilton, has been kidnapped by your employer. Perhaps, murdered. That makes you an accessory to a very serious crime."

Trembling, Nick pushed the food away. He was sweating profusely. "Inspector, I told you all I know."

"You told us that you monitored the telephone calls from

Rooms 302 and 304. What did you do with that information?

"Inspector, they asked me to e-mail that information as soon as I received it, which I did. They did not give me their names, only the e-mail address. My instructions were also through e-mail. I had no idea they were... they meant to... kidnap anyone. You must believe me."

"Nick, I know times are hard. If you were paid for being an accomplice to the crime of kidnapping or murder, and you tell us all you know, and help us all you can, well, as far as I'm concerned, you can leave this room right now."

"Well, Inspector!" Nick vacillated. Wiping the sweat from his face with his sleeves he said, "I told you. I was asked to keep surveillance on Rooms 302 and 304."

"But you knew that they were planning to abduct Mr. Hamilton, didn't you? You see this file, Nick? This is an evidence case folder." The inspector flipped through the contents. "This file contains material of incriminating significance."

Nick wiped his eyes fiercely. "Fritz threatened to fire me if I didn't cooperate. He offered me 2,000 DM for the information. I needed the money because we're living with my in-laws and our married life is hell with meddling relatives. We wanted an apartment of our own. But I don't know anything else."

"Not according to our files," the inspector responded, looking down at empty sheets of paper. "Two men have disappeared. If you had anything to do with it, you should tell me that now."

"Two men? Inspector, I only know what I told you. Why don't you ask Adolf Fritz?"

"Who is working with Fritz? Give us their names."

"I don't know."

"If you only have a suspicion, I want you to tell me that, even though it may be wrong. I'll keep it confidential. Now, who do you think actually did the kidnapping?

"I don't know, Inspector," Nick said.

"Is there anyone you know well enough, who you feel is above suspicion and who could help us in the investigation?"

"Mr. Bischoff told me to keep my nose clean, but I didn't listen."

"Nick, do you know what happens to an accessory to kidnapping?"

"I wasn't involved."

"Are you willing to take a polygraph test?

"Yes. If··· necessary."

Inspector Strenger paused and calculated the level of fear in the quaking man before him. Who terrified him more, Fritz or the police?

"Why are your fingerprints on the note given to Hamilton by a man called Otto? Did you write that note? Do you know Otto?"

Nick began to weep openly. "Otto was supposed to give it to Hamilton. Did you find Hamilton?"

The inspector took a recorder from a desk drawer. "One, two, three, four," he counted into the microphone, adjusting the voice level. Then he leaned back in his chair and lit a cigar. Nick drank some water and began to talk. It was like the opening of a dam.

"Nick, you must understand that you have admitted complicity in this crime."

"I didn't help in the kidnapping. I was only an informer. I didn't know they were going to kidnap Mr. Hamilton."

"Give me the names of the people involved from the top down. First their titles then fill in their names." Strenger pushed one of the blank sheets of paper toward Nick.

Nick wrote the names. For three more hours he told the inspector everything he knew of the operations, except where Robert Hamilton was.

"We are dealing with an evil organization, aren't we!" the inspector exclaimed, taking off his reading glasses and setting them on the table wearily. He felt sorry for Nick, only a small pawn in the big game.

"All right. Adolf Fritz and his henchman, Aren Becher—they operate with the help of gangsters and underworld people. Those characters kidnapped a British girl in Berlin and now Robert

Hamilton. Five years ago, the König Group bought the Excelsior chain but actually... you see, it doesn't belong to the König Group. It belongs to Pharma Frankfuter," divulged Nick.

Strenger shut off the recorder. "You were an accomplice to a crime but you are willing to cooperate with the investigation. Your prison term could perhaps be substantially shortened, perhaps even dismissed. You wish the truth to be known in this matter, do you not?"

"Yes."

"Will you testify to the truth of what you've told in a court of law?"

Strenger turned the recorder back on. "Yes, Inspector," Nick answered. His face was wet with perspiration in the suffocating interrogation room, but for the first time he smiled at Inspector Strenger.

A bee was buzzing outside the open window. Ann followed it with her eyes. Very likely it had been attracted by the carnation. The bee circled around the desk lamp several times, and then buzzed through the window back to the sun. At her desk in her sunny spacious room, next to the library and the music room Ann had spent nearly all morning, daydreaming, conjuring up images of Robert. The breeze from the garden made the curtains flutter. Her heart was battered with excitement and premonition. Other bees were buzzing over wild flowers growing at one side of a well manicured lawn. Ann was melancholy. Robert had stolen her heart, her breath, and her sleep. She longed for news from him. Ann sighed and returned to her diary.

October 28 today is more than one week since R. departed for Germany. Only 1 e-mail the night he arrived in Cologne. Promised to call, but he never did. I'm very worried. Yesterday went with Mother to London. Not at all like the London I saw earlier in the season, when I was with R.

A knock came at her door. "Dear," her mother said, "there is a telephone call for you, from Germany."

Ann ran downstairs, past her. "Mother, it must be Robert!" she said over her shoulder. She lifted the receiver.

"Ann! This is Sir Ronald Harris calling from Cologne. I'm afraid

I have bad news for you. Last night I arrived at the Excelsior Hotel and found that Robert and Karl had not returned there since they left it last Wednesday. Today, I went to the police and learned that they have been investigating their disappearance. I was hoping you'd heard from him."

"Oh, my God! I can't believe it! No Sir Ronald. I haven't. Not since he reached Cologne, when he sent me an e-mail. What do you mean? Is he missing? Where can he be?"

"Listen, my dear, the police think we may be dealing with criminals. It is possible Robert and Karl have been kidnapped. I'll call you as soon as I have some news."

"Kidnapped!" Ann screamed, clutching the receiver. "But why? What's the point? Oh, Sir Ronald. Don't leave me here! Let me help look for him! Waiting here for news will drive me insane."

"If I had any idea at all how you might help, I'd certainly call on you," Sir Ronald said. "But for now, just take down my number and call me if you hear from Robert."

Ann replaced the receiver as though it had suddenly become very heavy. She staggered into the morning room and fell back in a chair. Her mother stood at the doorway in her nightgown. "You look as white as a sheet. Are you ill?"

"I don't know." She tried to take a breath and she couldn't. She tried to blink and couldn't. The moment felt surreal.

"Bad news?"

"Robert has been kidnapped. It cannot be true."

The two women exchanged a frantic look.

"Would tea help?"

Ann shook her head, suddenly weary. She walked upstairs and returned to her bedroom without closing the door. She sat on the edge of her bed, looking unseeing at the window.

The bee reappeared, but it was no longer buzzing around aimlessly. It flew toward a framed picture of Robert and sat on the rim. Her mobile rang. She lifted the mobile to her ear.

"Miss Leigh! This is Christoph Beck from Berlin. I've been

trying to reach Sir Ronald."

"Christoph, Robert disappeared from the Excelsior Hotel!"

"Yes, Ann, I know."

"Sir Ronald's been trying to reach you."

"My line's been busy. I was able to get a clue that can help the police."

"What is it?"

"I found out through the insurance records that Beitz's mother lives in Cologne. But before I inform the police, I'd like Sir Ronald to check the mother's address and her background. You know how the police can make a mess of it."

"Christoph, is Beitz involved in all this? Oh, that rascal! I want to help. Please give me all the information and I'll work with Sir Ronald. I will fly to Cologne tomorrow."

"You had better stay at home, Ann. This is very dangerous stuff."

"I'm well aware of the danger, "Ann replied stiffly. "But I'm also aware that if I don't do what is needed now, I'll regret it for the rest of my life. Please, Christoph! Robert spared no pains on my behalf when I was kidnapped, and I am going to do everything I can to find him. Please give me instructions and I will follow them explicitly. You will not regret it."

"I'll fax the information to a friend of mine in Cologne, Helmut Koening. He owns the Altstadt Hotel, close by the river in the old town. The address is Salzgasse D. 5000. You can trust Helmut one hundred percent." Christoph gave her a number to dial···

"I'll do it as soon as I hang up. And thank you for everything, Christoph!" She gave him Sir Ronald's number.

"I'll let Sir Ronald know. Take good care of yourself and good luck."

At the back of the house by the old stable, Ann found her dog, Spots, lying contentedly in the sun. She talked to her for a minute or two, stroking her head. Then she turned into the vegetable garden. "There you are, Dad."

"What a nice surprise, Ann! Come to help?"

"Dad, can I talk to you for a moment?"

He rose, trowel in hand, his brow furrowing at the tense expression on her face.

"Dad, I need your help. Robert is missing in Cologne. The police think he has been kidnapped, I want to help look for him, I *must,* so I'm leaving for Cologne tomorrow. I always come to you for advice, but this time I'm asking for your support and your blessing. My mind is already made up. You must help me persuade Mother."

"Come, let's sit on the grass."

She sat with her back against a broad chestnut tree. Her father sat in front of her and crossed his legs.

"I am in love," Ann said quietly. "And I want to help Robert before it's too late."

Her father took in her words, her expression of severe worry. At last he nodded. "When are you leaving? I will persuade your mother and we will take you to the airport."

Ann fell into his arms and kissed him. The sun was high and the trees cast dark, cool shadows on the afternoon. The birds were silent, but a hum of contented bees surrounded father and daughter as they walked slowly, holding hands, toward the house. Ann gave her father a long hug. "Thank you, Dad."

TWENTY-FOUR hours later, Ann checked into the Altstadt Hotel in Cologne. An express mail envelope from Christoph Beck was waiting for her at the registration desk. She ripped open the envelope as she walked towards her room. After closing the door behind her, she leaned against it, breathing erratically.

My God! What am I doing? She sat on the bed before a mirror and stared at her reflection, seeing herself only vaguely, as through a veil. *Ann, you must be strong.* She read.

Dear Ann:

I am sorry I could not accompany you, but I was happy beyond words to hear that you are willing to help. I want you to know that. Frau Bertha Weidfeldt is Beitz's mother. She remarried, to an art dealer, Claus Weidfeldt, a few years after Beitz's father died in a car accident. Mr. Weidfeldt is in his eighties and Bertha is running an antique shop called Antikensammlungen. I enclose a photograph of Beitz from a publication some years back.

This is the only lead I have at the moment. Try to locate Beitz in the best way you can but be careful. It could be dangerous. Let's keep each other fully informed. I spoke with Sir Ronald and he will contact you tomorrow.

Your friend,

Christoph.

She walked to the window and stared thoughtfully at the boats passing up and down the Rhine River.

After a shower, she dressed in a royal blue turtleneck sweater, matching pants and a single-breasted jacket. Satisfied that she looked like a casual tourist, she went downstairs to the small lunchroom. The solitary waiter brought her a wide-mouthed cup of thick black coffee. She broke off a piece of roll and buttered it sparingly. As she ate, she considered her four clues: *Antikensammlungen*, the name of the antique shop; the name of the antiquarian, *Bertha Weidfeldt*; an address and a photograph of Berthold Beitz. She took the photograph out of her coat and laid it on the white tablecloth beside her plate.

The snapshot was taken apparently at some kind of office gathering. A few people in the background were drinking wine in front of a big wine barrel. Beitz was a big man, with great broad shoulders; short, grizzled hair, and a large nose.

As evening fell, Ann descended the steps of the U-Bahn. A gust of warm air came up from the bowels of the underground. The train for Zulpicar Platz came along and by the time she arrived the darkness took her by surprise. She shivered lightly as she emerged into the street. The air was unusually chilly for late October. Slowly, she found her way along a winding road that traced the route of the original medieval city wall, then turned into a very narrow street with shops and houses with picturesque timber fronts, oriel windows and overhanging gables. Soon, she found the storefront she was looking for. The dark mahogany panels in the display windows gave the feeling of a shop one could not afford. Two windows displayed collections of coins, European and Near East antiquities, antique clocks, colored tea pots, Toby jugs, vases, plates. The shop gave the illusion of opulence, nicely matched to the pieces sold within. An elegant brass signboard read "Antikensammlungen sells at retail and to the trade, hours between 10 a.m. and 6 p.m." Through the glass door she could see a life-sized marble torso of a male. The small letters she could scarcely read, "Roman, circa 1AD."

Walking north along the uneven road, she found herself opposite a Brauhaus with a wood paneled façade, pondering whether to go in. It was just after 8 p.m. as she crossed the street. On the steps outside the pub sat an old man with a Tyrolean hat, his walking stick across his knee and a mug of beer in his hand.

Ann bid him good evening, then went up the steps into the pub, typically dim, smoky and smelling of beer.

"Hello, *Fraulein*." The corpulent man at the bar spoke as if he'd been expecting her. "Now, what is your pleasure?" They chatted as Ann sipped her first Kolsch, a famed local beer. "Your German is very good but you have an English accent."

"Yes, I am from England. I came to spend a few days in Germany." Ann sipped her drink and studied the room. The wooden bar stretched at least thirty feet the length of the building. She thought it must be the longest bar in Germany. It was crowded with people who seemed to be having an office party.

"Please call me Klaus," the barman said. "Anything to eat?"

"I'm Ann Leigh. I'd like to try a traditional Westphalian meal."

"How about pig's knuckles with sauerkraut?"

"That will be fine." The food, and the glass of red wine she drank with it, made the world seem a little less precarious. Klaus's affability had a calming effect, as well. She took a deep breath and plunged. "Herr Klaus, I am trying to find a good antique store. I would like to take something back to my father."

"There are a few antique shops in this area but I am afraid I cannot recommend one in particular. But I am sure that the Baron could help you. He was here a few minutes ago. I am confident he will return soon for another beer." He laughed at his own joke.

Ann excused herself to go to the ladies' room, threading her way through the celebratory crowd, people laughing, talking, singing, and raising their mugs in the air.

When she returned, she saw Klaus walking beside the man she had seen outside on the steps. The Baron hobbled into the bar with the help of his walking stick, an empty mug of beer in his other hand and a cigarette in the corner of his mouth. He was a big, energetic man with a mixture of blond but mostly white hair, and a red face.

"Allow me to present Baron von Bülow. Baron, Fraulein Leigh asked me where to find good antiques at a good price and I suggested that perhaps you could guide her," said Klaus.

The Baron bobbed his head sideways··· "I believe I can help you. Would you have a drink with me?"

"I will have another Kolsch. Thank you."

He paid for their drinks and Klaus carried them to a dark wooden table on the far side of the room. The Baron toasted her health and drank.

Ann sipped her beer. "My father collects antiques and I am looking for a good buy." The Baron suit's was well worn and rather formal, his bearing authoritative but kind, his eyes quick and intelligent. She wondered if he was a professor.

He lit a cigarette. "Tell me, Miss, what kind of antiques you have in mind."

"Ancient Chinese art, perhaps middle Chou period, or Shan dynasty, possibly a jade piece or a bronze figure. My father collects mostly from the middle Chou period, Shan and T'ang period, eighth century. I know wonderful collections exist in Germany."

She could see that he was surprised by the extent of her knowledge and charmed. However, she exhausted all she had learned in two semesters of her art history and her part- time job at the London Museum.

"I am so pleased that some young people still appreciate art," the Baron commented. "How much are you willing to spend?"

"That all depends, but perhaps not more than 20,000 DM."

The Baron named three antique shops in another section of the city.

Ann paused. "Are you familiar with an antique store located a few blocks from here? Antikensammlugen?"

"Oh yes, I used to deal with them frequently. But not anymore."

"Why not?"

"A very long story. Probably you would not be interested."

"Oh, but I am," Ann urged. "Please."

The baron's quick eyes scanned her face "Very well, I am prepared to tell you my story, if you are prepared to listen. I was born in a castle in Weimar, East Germany. My father, Baron Karl von Bülow, owned a very large castle. He and his father collected many works of art. When the Second World War started, I was sent to live in Heidelberg with my grandmother where I went to school. I was too small to go into the army. I was only sixteen in 1945. When the Russians occupied East Germany, my mother and two sisters moved to Heidelberg, bringing with them a large number of works of art, which were hidden in my grandmother's house. My father had died during the War, we lost all the money we had and we struggled to survive. All of our possessions were in East Germany. So my mother started to sell off our art collections, mostly to Americans. That allowed me to go to university to study history and art.

"Courageous Heidelberg citizens succeeded at the last moment in handing the city over unscathed to the American military command. The university was re-opened and I was one of the first students to attend. Afterwards I became a professor at Heidelberg University. Throughout the years, my mother and sisters sold off our artwork, and I was the one who negotiated the sales. For many years, through Herr Beitz, an art dealer. He was an honorable man, but when he died in a car accident a few years later, his widow married a man named Weidfeldt and then things started to change." The Baron lifted his mug and took a long draught.

"Mrs. Beitz, now Frau Weidfeldt, took over the business. They have three antique stores, one here in Cologne, one in Frankfurt, at one time headed by her son Berthold Beitz, and another in Berlin. Berthold Beitz went into the priesthood, then left the church and traveled to the Far East. He married the daughter of an executive of a pharmaceutical industrial complex. He headed an export business and the antique shop in Frankfurt but went bankrupt. The Baron shrugged, as if to say, how is this possible? "At that time his mother said that the works of art I had consigned to her for sale were being handled by her son in Frankfurt and that he had gone bankrupt, and therefore she could not return the works of art or reimburse me for them. Many people who had given works of art under consignment lost everything. I am sure it was deliberate. We lost works of art by Rembrandt, *The Witch of Harlem* by Malle Babbe, and the bust of the great Condé by Coysevox."

"How terrible! Couldn't you go after Bertholdt Beitz?"

"Our lawyers informed us that under the laws of bankruptcy we could not do a thing."

"Oh my! And what happened to your castle in East Germany?" Ann asked.

"Confiscated. By the German Democratic Republic. We hoped, yes we hoped with the fall of the wall and the reunification of Germany that we could get it back. But it's been a problem for our family. Germans have coined a phrase: '*Die mauer in kopf.*' It means, *the wall in the head*, the psychological and emotional barrier that has replaced the Berlin Wall.

"Property rights are an issue even more vexing than the wall in the head. The reunification treaty allows westerners to reclaim houses and land lost to the Communist state and, in some cases, to Nazi dictatorship. Already thousands of easterners had to give up homes they lived in for years, even decades. Others, who avoided eviction only because of unclear ownership records, feel they're on borrowed time. In the case of our castle, if we ever recapture the ownership we will convert it into a museum. And, that my dear, is my long story," the baron finished, raising his mug in the air.

Ann lifted hers. "And a fascinating one! Thank you for telling it to a perfect stranger."

"My pleasure. But it is time for me to go. If you want to see what is left of my collection and would like my humble advice on your purchase, you are welcome to visit me anytime."

"I am free tomorrow," Ann offered.

"If it is convenient, come for lunch. Here is my card. I do not live far from here." He finished his beer and offered to buy her another, but Ann rose to go.

Back at the hotel, the reception clerk handed Ann the key to her room and a note, which she read in the privacy of her room.

Sir Ronald sat in the Stube, the lacquered, wood paneled restaurant of the Excelsior Hotel and bought the *Herald Tribune*, the only English paper available. He flicked through it while he waited for Ann. The coffee made him feel a little less weary, although a real breakfast, the English breakfast with bacon and eggs and a pot of tea, would have been much better. The room was filled with German, French and Italian voices and some Yorkshire, Liverpool and London accents, too. Sipping his coffee, he glanced at the door and saw Ann's elegant figure coming toward him. He rose and gestured to her. "It is marvelous to see you, Ann."

"Good to see you, too, Sir Ronald. I have news." She described her evening at the local pub. "Through the bartender, I met a man who sold antiques to Beitz's mother. I will tell you later about him, but the important thing is that he may lead me to Beitz's whereabouts, which in turn may lead us to Robert. Today I am invited to his apartment to have lunch and get his advice on purchasing an antique, supposedly a gift for my father."

Sir Ronald looked admiringly at her.

"I think it is a great opportunity. Perhaps you may convince the Baron to help us track him."

Together, they worked out the details. The night before, it had seemed simple enough to Ann, but in the sobriety of daylight, she realized that it would not be so simple. In the end, they thought they had a good plan, allowing for dozens of snags.

Sir Ronald sipped his last drop of coffee. "Why don't I rent a car and take you to von Bülow's myself?"

They drove a BMW southward, in the direction of St. Pantaleon. As they approached Weidenback the road narrowed, and Sir Ronald had to pull onto a sidewalk to allow a truck to pass. After twenty minutes, they arrived at the address on the Baron's card, a baroque three-story house with bits of crumbling red stonework and dirty windows.

Sir Ronald parked outside the gates and let Ann out of the car. "Good luck! I'll expect you at three o'clock. If you don't come out by then, I'll knock at the door."

Weeds grew in the gravel and an old Mercedes sat in the driveway. As Ann got closer to the house, it grew more and more dilapidated. Once an imposing dwelling, it had long ago been converted into apartments. There were three entrance doors, each with a mailbox and the name of an occupant. On the right side, she read the name of Baron von Bülow. She rang the bell. The door opened.

"*Gut morgen*!" Baron von Bülow was dressed in a tweed jacket and turtleneck sweater. "Please come in. I beg your pardon for the state of my apartment."

"Don't apologize, Baron. It is good to see you." She extended her hand and the baron shook it.

He led her to the second floor.

"This is a very interesting house," Ann commented.

"It was built in the middle of the seventeenth century, when all the land around here was given to my great-great-grandfather as a reward for service in war."

"It's sort of baroque in style."

"Yes, it is. Are you interested in architecture, Miss Leigh?"

"I am interested in beauty, Baron."

He talked about the house as if retelling a familiar tale, pointing out that he'd had to convert it into three apartments in order to derive an income. "The newer aristocrats are businessmen and industrialists. Their families have no time to grow soft, living on inherited wealth. As you can see, too many repairs have been postponed."

"If you could recover the art collection, it would certainly help you."

"Well, I am already an old man and it is difficult for me to start a long and expensive legal procedure."

"May I ask how you've occupied your time since you left Heidelberg?"

"I am writing a book on the history of art, from prehistoric times. My background as a lecturer and director of the Palatine Museum has helped me with my writing."

The Baron led her to the interior of the house. The furniture was timeworn, some of the rooms smelled unused, their aroma an odd mixture of mothballs and mold. They entered a large room with Persian carpets over a highly polished floor. The walls were covered with paintings, including "St. Hugo of Grenoble in the Carthusian Refectory" by Zurburan and "Village of Becquigny" by Rousseau.

She examined a statue of Abraham in wood by Alonso Berruquete. "A masterpiece of spirituality," she murmured. Her sharp eye flitted quickly around the walls and then focused on the head of Bodhisattva, from T'ien-Lung Shan.

"Magnificent!" she exclaimed. "Is that 8th Century?"

"This is actually what is left of the collection, and some of the last treasures left from my family, which took six generations to accumulate and one generation to fritter away."

Ann expressed her sympathy and gently gave the Baron the impression that she might be willing to buy something from him. He was obviously in fairly desperate need of cash. She turned to a small sandstone relief. Probably 4th Century Byzantine, she thought, recollecting her art professor's lecture.

Before she could make an offer, the baron invited her into the dining room. The maid brought in a roasted goose with rhubarb in a cassis sauce, and the Baron's favorite wine, a Liebfraumilch; Germany's most famous wine, he told her, mild and slightly sweet. The servant hired for the occasion passed sweet potatoes and leaf spinach, and for dessert, *Pflaumenkompott,* stewed plums.

The Baron loosened his belt a notch or two, and Ann joked about having to start a diet.

After the meal they settled comfortably into the old living room chairs. All of Ann's instincts told her that here was a kind, generous, spiritual man, the sort of man one could trust absolutely. "Baron, what a wonderful lunch! And I am very impressed by your priceless collection." She hesitated and then took the plunge. "Are you familiar with the Pharma Frankfuter Company?"

"One of the older pharmaceutical companies in Germany and one of the most powerful. Their global market presence is also very large." He looked at her curiously. "Why do you ask?"

"I read a couple of weeks ago that they were being investigated on criminal charges."

Puzzlement and a trace of anticipation crossed the Baron's face.

"Baron, I must stop pretending and be frank with you. The reason I accepted your invitation was because I need your advice, and your cooperation is a matter of life and death. The past few days have been the most harrowing of my life. I came to Cologne to try to find my friend, who has been kidnapped. I do not know if he is still alive. The people who kidnapped him are merciless and very dangerous. I am sorry that I deceived you but I needed to be cautious. To be more explicit, we suspect that Berthold Beitz is instrumental in Robert's kidnapping and the disappearance of the industrialist Karl Schneider. Beitz works for Pharma Frankfuter."

Disappointment flashed briefly across the old Baron's face, but then he nodded in a gesture of understanding. He considered for a moment. "This is the first time that I've heard Berthold Beitz linked with Mr. Schneider's disappearance."

"I apologize, Baron. You must have been bewildered when I appeared out of the blue asking for advice in purchasing antiques.

But I'm not crazy — I'm desperate. I need to befriend Beitz's mother in order to find out where Beitz is staying in Cologne. At the same time I could find out if she still has some of your art collection. Will you help me? Can you give me the information you have on Bertha Weidfeldt? Everything—where she lives, her personality, and the best way to gain her confidence?"

"I appreciate your position. But tell me, Fraulein Leigh, I hope you are not acting alone in this search for such a dangerous man? Forgive me if I seem a little old-fashioned."

"No, Baron. I am not alone. The police have been alerted and a friend of my father's from England, Sir Ronald Harris, is here with me."

"I am an old man, but I think I can help you."

A buzzer sounded in the Baron's apartment. Sir Ronald entered and Ann introduced him. The Baron poured himself and Sir Ronald beer, and Ann a glass of wine. They listened as he explained Bertha's background and modus operandi. The Baron carried himself with the suave assurance of a man at ease, seasoned by years of academic life, a survivor of the war, of abundance and scarcity. His aged hands showed them photographs of the art collection swindled by Bertha. Over the next hours, the three of them slowly formed a plan.

At last, Ann and Sir Ronald bid the Baron good evening. They walked down the driveway and got into the car. The headlights sweeping around the driveway shone briefly on the Baron, still standing in the doorway, caught in that brief moment like a still life, or the photograph of a wanted man.

Early in the evening Ann had wondered, who was he? A friend or a foe? But as they sped away, she was certain that she had gained a friend.

THE next day, Ann received a package from Christoph followed by a telephone call instructing her on how to proceed. Ann was a little nervous as she walked into the antique shop. She waited in front of an open teak stairway while the sales clerk went up to fetch the proprietor. Ann thought the essential thing now was to act calm.

The proprietor came down the stairs. *"Gut morgen!"* Her platinum hair showed streaks of gray at its roots. She was healthily plump and the bones of her face indicated her prior beauty. By some standards, she might even have been elegantly dressed.

"*Gut morgen,*" Ann replied.

The proprietor switched to English. "How can I help you?"

"My name is Valerie Mercer," said Ann.

"How do you do? I am Bertha Weidfeldt."

"Very well, thank you. I represent an English art collector, Frau Weidfeldt, and we are looking for Meissen ceramics."

"We have a few of them in the back."

Ann followed her through a room full of brass, bronze, copper, iron and tin. She glanced at a teapot with an Oriental design, a Tunisian birdcage, a Spanish brass stirrup, a brass whale oil lamp, and French Empire bronze candelabra. The next section was full of Chippendale chairs, a mahogany secretary with French legs, chairs of the Jacobean period. She was gazing at a rare pair of Regency carved armchairs, when Frau Weidfeldt called her.

"Fraulein Mercer, the ceramics are in here. We have Dresden plates, vases and figurines. What is your particular interest?"

"Porcelain vases or perhaps figurines. Not Dresden, but authentic Meissen."

"The names Meissen and Dresden are synonymous with respect to ceramics, and both are similarly marked," Frau Weidfeldt said tartly.

A spasm of tension stabbed Ann between her shoulders and she tried to control the blush, which began at her throat. Then her mind clicked into gear, as she remembered the Baron's explanation of the difference,

"As you know, the original work was greatly imitated in the nineteenth century. I want to emphasize the character of the porcelains. Perhaps the English-speaking world is more familiar with Meissen, perhaps here in Germany you also call it *Dresden*, because the porcelains were sent down the Elbe River to the inland port at Dresden," Ann said smoothly. That was everything she knew about Meissen porcelain. Twenty-four hours ago she had never even heard of Meissen.

"We have two vases," Bertha Weidfeldt said grudgingly. "Both by one of the early great modelers of the Meissen works, Johann Kaendler, who worked between 1731 and 1775." She picked up one of the bases and on the bottom Ann saw the famed crossed swords of the factory mark.

"Yes. This is from the point period," Ann said.

"I can see you know more about antiques than some of the people who work for me."

Ann took this as Frau Weidfeldt's peace offering. "No doubt it's genuine," Ann said. "All I see these days are fakes. There's so much of it going on. What are you asking for it?"

"The list price is 64,000 DM. But if you are seriously interested in those two pieces, I can offer you a discount."

"I think we can make you an offer that will satisfy you, but first, I must get authorization from my client to proceed. If he agrees, I would like to look in our reference books, and then a licensed appraiser must give us his opinion. If these things go well, we may consider buying other works of art," Ann added.

"By all means," said Frau Weidfeldt gracious now. "You can use my telephone upstairs in my office."

"It is a long distance call," Ann said. "Let me use my credit card."

"No, please, call directly," Frau Weidfeldt insisted, leading the way up. Her office was paneled in walnut and her carpet was a complementary orange-brown. "Sit here." She pointed to a chair in front of the desk. "Press the red button for an outside line. I'll be downstairs. Let me know when you finish."

"Thank you so much, Frau Weidfeldt." Ann sat down in the chair and put her leather handbag in her lap. As she leaned it against the front of the desk to open it, she fished frantically for a plastic bag and took out a UHF power transmitter, a new bugging device, and connected it to the telephone socket. Suddenly, she sensed eyes on her back. She looked around the room and saw a closed-circuit camera in one of the corners, focusing on her. The footsteps trotting up the stairs echoed the thunder of her heartbeats.

With her back to the camera she lifted the receiver and called Sir Ronald. As she waited for the call to go through, she twisted the cap of the pen and put the pen adjacent to the telephone. Had she been detected? She felt the camera's presence like a pressure against her back—her hands were slippery with sweat.

Sir Ronald answered his mobile.

"Mission accomplished," whispered Ann. "Be in front of the store with the car." She hung up. As Ann opened the door and started towards the stairs, she faltered and stopped.

Frau Weidfeldt stood at the top of the stairs staring straight into Ann's eyes as if she could read what was inside of her. "Were you successful, Fraulein Mercer?"

It was all over, Ann thought. Her heart sank. "I am sure I will be."

"Then let's go into my office and see how we can proceed."

They sat down and a servant came in with coffee on a tray. Ann could feel the trickle of sweat at her temples. She prayed Frau Weidfeldt would not notice.

Ann forced the quaver out of her voice. "I called Mr. Huntington, the gentleman I work for and spoke with his secretary. She informed me that he was out of the office today, but she was expecting his telephone call, so she will ask him to call me tonight. If and when I receive his authorization to proceed with the purchase, I will immediately contact you."

Frau Weidfeldt nodded coolly.

After ten minutes of idle conversation, Ann emptied her coffee cup and stood up. "You have been most kind."

"I've enjoyed your company." Frau Weidfeldt's toneless voice conveyed nothing to Ann, nor did her expressionless demeanor, as she saw Ann to the front door.

Ann hurried across the street and got into Sir Ronald's car. "Oh, my God, we did it, Ronald!" she cried, breathing again. "I think I did it!"

Ann informed Christoph later that she had successfully implanted the bugging device. He confirmed her success, as he was now monitoring the conversations with clarity from his receiver.

By evening, Christoph had news to report. "Berthold Beitz called his mother and invited her to a gala concert at the Cologne Philharmonic on Saturday at 8 p.m. You must try to get tickets for you and Sir Ronald. Follow him after the concert, find out where he is staying, and watch him constantly. He could lead you to the victims. Keep me informed and notify the police."

At seven o'clock on Saturday the concertgoers began to arrive, a never-ending stream of music lovers, who filled every seat in the concert hall.

Ann and Sir Ronald arrived in a chauffeured Rolls, Ann in an elegant long gown and gloves, Sir Ronald in a tuxedo. They moved through the crowd in the direction of their box, scanning the concertgoers for Berthold Beitz. The lights snapped off and on. People took their places and the murmur of hundreds of voices abated.

At eight o'clock sharp, the house lights dimmed and the footlights added a warm glow to a rich velour curtain. The magic of the illuminated orchestra pulled the audience forward in their seats. At that moment Ann heard someone in the next box whisper, "They were completely sold out, they had to turn away so many people." Ann thought, *We were lucky to get tickets, but I hope Beitz was not one of those who were turned away.*

The spotlights followed the conductor to the podium while the house exploded in thunderous applause. Latecomers hurried to their seats as he bowed to the audience and lifted his baton, evoking profound silence. The baton came down.

During the intermission Ann and Sir Ronald left the orchestra to look for Beitz. The foyer was crowded, the air filled with the pungent, acrid aroma of cigarette smoke, and the gentle clicking sound of wine and champagne glasses. They walked about listening to the conversations around them. Someone was saying no two concerts are the same; the music may be the same but the conductor is different and the orchestra is different. A young girl was saying to her companion that the Symphony #2 was composed when Schubert was only seventeen. Others agreed it was quite remarkable. Ann and Sir Ronald moved slowly knowing the chances were small that the mother and son would walk through the foyer just then. That was too much to hope for. *What would we do if it happened?* wondered Ann. They stood in a strategic location, screening everybody who came from the auditorium or the balconies. Then a bell rang and the intermission was over. They walked down the corridor to their box, almost the last to return to their seats.

As soon as the curtain rose, a hush fell throughout the hall. While the "Piano Sonata in B Minor" by Franz Liszt filled the air, Ann glanced across at one of the balconies and gasped.

"There! She's there, Sir Ronald!" Ann pointed discreetly, her hand trembling, to where Bertha Weidfeldt sat with her son.

Sir Ronald lifted his opera glasses and gazed at Beitz. He was larger than he had expected, with a pale face and short gray hair.

Neither Ann nor Sir Ronald could concentrate on the performance. From time to time they glanced across the auditorium. Before the end of the sonata, Ann saw that Beitz had risen and appeared to be staring at her. She nudged Sir Ronald, but as he turned, Beitz disappeared.

Moments later, during a lull before the beginning of the second movement, the door behind them opened. A current of chill air raised the hair on the nape of Ann's neck. Ann and Ronald turned, sharply. It was only the usher. He handed an envelope to Sir Ronald, bowed, and withdrew. Sir Ronald tore it open.

Sir Ronald:

I am in the car across from the main entrance. Should you need any help. I will be waiting for you. Please be careful.

The Baron von Bülow

Sir Ronald passed the note to Ann. She read the note then returned it. It was 9:50 p.m. Her eyes instinctively went to Beitz's box, and to her relief, saw him concentrating on the orchestra.

Before the conclusion of a fairly standard rendition of Beethoven's Fifth Symphony, Ann and Sir Ronald left the auditorium. In the main foyer, Ann sat on a window seat where she could see people leaving. Sir Ronald had already spoken with the Baron, and now went upstairs where he paced the promenade. A roar of ovation indicated the end of the concert. Immediately afterwards, people converged on the main foyer. Sir Ronald spotted Beitz and Bertha. He followed, as the crowd between them shifted and surged toward the foyer. By the time he reached the foyer, they were gone. He pushed through the crowd, almost reaching the exit doors, when he saw Ann waving to him. "They're walking across the street."

The Baron shielded his face with the program as Beitz and

Bertha passed in front of his car. In his mirror, he caught a glimpse of the couple on the sidewalk hailing a taxi. A taxi pulled up in front of them. Beitz kissed his mother on the cheek and helped her inside, closed the door and the taxi swiftly pulled away. Heavy traffic prevented Ann and Sir Ronald from crossing the street. By the time did, cross they saw Beitz in the distance, as he walked under the shadow of the cathedral in the direction of the main train station.

Sir Ronald's mind clicked into gear. "Ann, get into the car and wait to hear from me. Keep the phone open."

He walked quickly after Beitz while Ann got into the car beside the Baron. Beitz descended into the S-Bahn. Sir Ronald followed at a prudent distance, but he was too prudent. When he stopped to purchase his ticket at the vending machine Beitz disappeared. Sir Ronald cursed himself for letting Beitz get away. In which direction had he gone? There were four possibilities: He took a guess and turned left, he walked a few hundred yards to the train platform. Beitz was there, but across the tracks on the other side of the platform, going south Sir Ronald was on the platform for northbound trains. He walked slowly, for he did not want to draw attention to himself. He stopped to look at a map on the wall and discreetly opened his cellular phone and called the Baron.

"I am still in the station; Beitz is taking the S-Bahn southbound express. There are only three stops left. The first station is Trimbornstrasse and then Portz. Siegburg is at the end of the line. Go to the next station. I'll try to get on the train."

"All right—"

"I have to go." The southbound train pulled in as Sir Ronald ran up the stairs onto the platform and jumped into the last car just before the doors closed. He walked casually toward the front, going through two or three cars and passing by Beitz. Averting his face, he walked into the next car and picked a strategic seat from where he could see Beitz through the door's glass window.

When the train reached the next station, he noticed that Beitz had closed his eyes. He phoned the Baron. "Baron, where are you?"

"On the Autobahn. About ten minutes from the station."

"It doesn't look as if Trimbornstrasse is his station. I'll call you again soon."

Sir Ronald worried that the heavier than expected traffic might not allow the Baron to make it to Portz in time.

Beitz stood up and entered Sir Ronald's car. He passed Sir Ronald and continued to the front of the car. Beitz closed the door. Sir Ronald followed. Beitz continued moving forward through the train. Once he glanced back in Sir Ronald's direction, and then went into the toilet and came back out again. At that moment the train chuffed, jerked, slowed with a squeal of brakes and slid into a little country station. From a distance Sir Ronald saw Beitz leave the train. Sir Ronald ran to the next exit door as people got off. Sir Ronald pushed his way through a family with two small children, a woman pushing a baby carriage, a woman with a suitcase and a tall man in tweeds; a woman screamed at him. He looked right and left for any sign of Beitz. The platform was empty. He ran to the end of the platform to the waiting room. Beitz was not there. He ran desperately to the exit door and found himself in a car park. He ran to the exit and finally saw Beitz enter a tunnel underneath the railway tracks. He followed Beitz through the tunnel and saw him get into his car. Unable to locate the Baron's car, he went to the street and flagged down a taxi.

"How much do you charge per hour?" he asked the young taxi driver.

"Thirty DM," the driver replied.

"I'll pay you three times that amount if you follow that car." He pointed to Beitz's green Mercedes coupe.

"For that money I will take you to the moon!"

Beitz drove slowly into the village. Sir Ronald saw in the dim light small, whitewashed houses, some set back behind gardens, others shoulder to shoulder at the roadside. He dialed his phone.

"Where are you, Sir Ronald?" the Baron's voice sounded in his ear. "We've just arrived at the train station. The train is still here."

"Following Beitz in a taxi. We're passing through the center of the village, heading west. Try to catch up with me."

The green Mercedes took the west road out of the village. The taxi followed. Beitz drove fast, handling the powerful car with skill. The taxi driver soon lost the flashing brake lights in the bend of the lane. He squeezed the last ounce of speed from his cab. Sir Ronald kept the phone pressed to his ear.

"A house in the southwest suburbs of Cologne, discreet and nondescript, might be a good hiding place," suggested the Baron. Driving fast, he caught up with the taxi just as the Mercedes pulled relentlessly away. It was a full kilometer ahead and still accelerating when it turned south into a narrow, two-lane country road. Both the taxi and the VW followed. As the Mercedes approached a hill, the road narrowed even further. The moon rose free of the hills. Sir Ronald saw a white sign that read: *PRIVATE ROAD * NO TRESPASSING*. They continued down a long avenue lined with cedar trees until they came to a great, stone-mounted gate, watched by the keen, half-lidded eyes of a pair of eagles perched above. Ghostly in the moonlight, with an aura of the feudal past, stood a somber, secluded, stone country house, serpentine walls enclosing the surrounding dozen acres of shadowed oak and cypress lent the whole scene an air of intrigue.

As the Mercedes slid to a stop in front of the gate, a man came out of the guardhouse and spoke with Beitz. The gates swung open and Beitz drove down the avenue of cedars.

The taxi and the Baron's car made a fast U-turn and headed back a quarter of a mile. They stopped out of sight of the house and got out. The forest around them was alive with night sounds. Sir Ronald paid the taxi driver and sent him away. Ann and the Baron stood beside their car while Sir Ronald entered the woods to get a better look at the house.

A few minutes later they heard the roar of an engine. The

noise grew louder and louder. “Let’s clear out of here!” Ann said.

They jumped into the car; the Baron started the VW and turned around. A black Porsche passed as they were pulling away. They watched the car through the rearview mirror. The Porsche came to a halt and then drove toward them in reverse. The Baron sped away out of the private road.

The only spot where Sir Ronald could conceal himself and still see what was going on was thirty feet off the straight path behind a patch of thorn bushes. He squeezed behind the bushes, thorns tearing at the back of his tuxedo pants and his hands.

Dogs were barking in the distance. For a moment silence followed, then suddenly the dogs materialized out of the shadows. They seemed to make no sound. Behind them the eyes of other dogs glinted in the darkness.

Cautiously, Sir Ronald made his way toward the gate, vaguely detecting the presence of closed-circuit cameras in the trees, as well as some black boxes, which he guessed constituted an infrared alarm system throughout the grounds. On the other side of the wall he could hear other dogs barking. He realized it would be suicidal to go closer to the house. It was too well guarded. He returned to the entrance.

THE next afternoon, Ann sat in her hotel room waiting for the telephone to ring. She had slept badly, thinking of Robert and wondering now what he was doing. Was he eating? Could he sleep? Was he bound? Imprisoned? Was he ill? Or worse? With an effort Ann dragged her thoughts back to the telephone. Her mother had called earlier, begging her to come back to England and leave the matter in the hands of the police. At least the police were now actively involved. Inspector Strenger had agreed to put the secluded stone house under surveillance.

The telephone rang and Ann picked it up. Sir Ronald's voice was taut with excitement. "Hello, Ann, Inspector Strenger is planning to apprehend Beitz tonight and interrogate him about the hostages."

Ann's knuckles whitened on the receiver. "Please, Sir Ronald, can we go with them? I want to go with them in case Robert is kept in that house."

"I'm afraid he made it very clear that under no circumstances will they permit unauthorized persons to be near the house."

"But Sir Ronald! I *must* be there when Robert comes out! I promise not to do anything foolish."

"My dear Ann, our hands are tied, but the Inspector has promised to keep us informed. But I have some news: Berolinehoff

Mansion is where the police suspect Robert is being kept. This place has a lot of history. Many well-known people have lived there throughout the years, including a Nazi general. The house has a reputation for being haunted by ghosts, it stood empty for so long. Five years ago someone bought it. The real estate agent who sold the house never met the real owner, and not even the police know who owns it now."

Twenty miles away at the police station, at exactly one o'clock in the morning, Inspector Strenger made himself think clearly and coolly as his car sped along the dark country road. What he needed was a bit of luck. If this was truly the kidnappers' lair, it might be heavily guarded. He wanted Robert Hamilton freed — alive — and he wanted the men under his command to survive the night. All he wanted was for Beitz to give himself up without offering resistance.

At 1:20 a.m., Detective Herring and his three plainclothesmen arrived at the main gate of the high-walled house, guarded by a quartet of Doberman watchdogs and four handlers. An armed guard came out from the green wooden booth and approached the police car. "Can I help you?" he asked.

"We are coming to search the house."

"I'm sorry, it's a private residence."

"Nevertheless, we have a search warrant."

The guard's face froze. "Now?" he asked stiffly. "It's late. Everybody is sleeping."

"You are not listening to me. I have a warrant to search the house."

"Please, let me call my boss and inform him." He went to his booth and made the call and returned. "My boss said you may come in."

The gate opened, allowing the police car to pass. They pulled up in the driveway and stopped outside the main door. The police detective and three plainclothes policemen jumped out of the car. At that moment, six of Beitz's guards appeared from the bushes, their rifles pointing at the policemen.

One of the policemen with a two-way-radio started to inform Inspector Strenger's office of the situation.

A man came out of the front door carrying a gun in his hand. He addressed the policemen, "Gentlemen, please drop your guns and radio and come in."

When Inspector Strenger finally reached his destination at 1:45 a.m., the scene resembled a riot more than a hostage case. Three armored vehicles, marked and unmarked patrol cars and a dozen police were deployed around the house. Inspector Strenger halted his car near the armored truck closest to the gate and prepared to take command. At that moment, he knew virtually nothing of what had happened, except that four men from his department had been taken hostage.

The negotiators divided up into three-person teams, with an intelligence gatherer, a communications expert and a primary negotiator. Detective Duisberg on the bullhorn would keep the hostage takers on the other end talking. All the while, containment officers carrying "anti-sniper" rifles surrounded the house, mapping out a quasi-military terrain—the inner perimeter, the outer perimeter, the farther reaches of the scene, and the kill zone, which was as far as the offenders could shoot. They rehearsed probes, diversions, assaults, waiting it out, but ready to go in as soon as things turned critical.

Some things were automatic. The inspector took an oversized sheet of drawing paper and taped it to his car. The field phone, the periscope, a bullhorn were ready to deploy.

All officers wore bulletproof vests. Duisberg had been one of the first at the scene, and Inspector Strenger regretted that they had decided to allow Detective Herring and three plainclothes policemen to enter first. "We thought if we used force at the beginning, we might kill innocent people but now his men have been taken hostage."

"If we make contact," the inspector told Detective Duisberg, "you man the phones."

Over a bullhorn Duisberg shouted, "Berthold Beitz! We're going to send a hand line over the serpentine wall. We want to talk to you —I repeat — we want to talk to you! Send somebody out to pick up the line and we'll run the telephone to you."

They waited for ten minutes in anticipation, then through the railing of the gate they saw a plainclothes policeman coming out, arms in the air. "Don't shoot!" he shouted. "I'm Officer Boleman!"

Duisberg tossed his line toward the door of the house. Boleman walked from the entrance, stooped slowly, picked it up and returned. A field phone was attached from behind the police encampment fifty feet away. Slowly it was pushed toward the vehicle, clothesline style.

Inside the house Beitz motioned for Detective Herring to pick up the microphone and make contact. "Tell them they've got thirty minutes to send a helicopter with only the pilot inside. It will land in the courtyard or I will kill the four of you one by one, in five-minute intervals. I'll start with you, Herring." Beitz consulted a watch he had removed from his wrist. "Starting now."

"Hello, hello," Herring stammered into the receiver, and conveyed the demand.

"You have twenty-nine minutes left," Beitz said.

Outside, Duisberg chose his words carefully. "Tell him to let him ...put him on the phone. I cannot hurt him in any way."

"He doesn't want to talk to you."

"Plead with him," Duisberg suggested.

"That won't work."

There was a pause and then Duisberg came back on the line. "Why doesn't he want to talk to us?"

"Don't worry about why," Herring pleaded. "Just do what he says."

Inspector Strenger surveyed the scene. He was not happy. There were many armed men inside the house. There was no way to sneak up on Beitz. Robert Hamilton, Müller and Schneider might be inside, and if so, Beitz could use the hostages as a bargaining chip. Therefore Beitz could refuse to speak directly to

Duisberg and it would be harder to reason with him.

"Keep trying to get him on the line," Inspector Strenger whispered. "Tell him that's the only way we can deal with him is speaking with him directly or not at all."

"We want to do everything he says," Duisberg told Herring, trying to ease the desperation he could sense through the telephone line. "We're doing everything possible for him. Tell him to understand that."

"Well," Herring replied, "he doesn't want to talk to you."

"We're trying to get everything that's available for you. Do you understand? Tell him."

A quarter of a kilometer away, on the other side of the serpentine wall, television cameramen, their tripods mounted on the roof of automobiles were ready to videotape whatever might happen.

Strenger frowned at the gathering press. A failure here would be very public, would be devastating to him, to the team and to the entire Cologne police force. He had been able to get a confession from Nick. It was possible that an indictment by the Reichsgericht of Pharma Frankfuter's top officers was imminent. But what was the point of such victories if the hostages were killed? He turned to Duisberg and spoke more sharply than he meant to. "Tell him we're getting him the helicopter. But we need more time."

Duisberg obeyed, straining to catch the conversation in the house, but he could hear no more than muffled background voices. Finally, Herring announced, "No, he doesn't want to."

"Okay," Duisberg said, starting off on another tactic. "His demands are just the helicopter, right?"

"So far."

"Well, you know, it is two o'clock in the morning, we're doing everything possible. Offices at the nearest airport are still closed. We need to get a volunteer pilot. All this makes it difficult for us. Impossible in the short time he's given. There are a thousand things to do in order to get him the helicopter."

"Can you get the helicopter?"

"That is what we are arranging now."

"I'd like to make that clear to him. But he's very stubborn. He doesn't want to cooperate in the least."

"I understand your situation. You're only an intermediary. We need to speak to Beitz directly."

"Yes." Herring sighed aloud. "I know. But he doesn't want to come to the phone. This is our only option."

Duisberg looked across at Inspector Strenger, who nodded. By now Dr. Erhard Schlieter, the police psychologist, had joined them. Nobody even knew how many men were with Beitz, or if Robert, Müller and Schneider were in the house." Listen," Duisberg finally said to Herring, "I'll get you the word as soon as we have any movement on this side."

"Yes, okay," Herring replied. He could be heard more clearly now, relaying the message to his captor and drawing an unpromising retort.

Inspector Strenger said, "Oscar, at 2:30, you have to get him talking, so when the time comes, he will ignore the deadline." Once one deadline passed, others would be easier to ignore.

The men synchronized their watches.

Herring's voice, faltering with fear, shouted over the line.

"Seven minutes," he said.

"Mr. Beitz announced seven more minutes?" Duisberg spoke calmly and slowly.

"Yes," Herring replied, with more control.

"Listen," Duisberg said, "I'm going to give you word as soon as I get it. All right? I hope in the next few minutes I can get word back to you. We're trying very hard. Does he understand that we're trying and that he's putting us at a disadvantage?"

"He doesn't believe you," Herring reported.

"Well, we're not here to lie to him," Duisberg replied. "What on earth would we gain?"

"I'll tell him."

There was a pause.

"What's taking so long?"

"Everything takes time. You think there's a line of volunteers who want to get aboard a helicopter and fly it, with Beitz and his men and the weapons he's got? Let me talk to him. I'll tell him what the problem is. Listen, if he could fly the helicopter himself, we'd give it to him now. We haven't been able to get the pilot yet. A helicopter doesn't fly by itself or by remote control. Tell him that. We're trying to get volunteers but no one wants to go."

"I told him that," Herring said nervously. "But he doesn't want to hear it."

Inspector Strenger glanced at his watch — the deadline had past.

At two-thirty they heard the crack of gunfire.

"Herring!" Duisberg blurted into the phone. "Herring! What's going on! Is anybody hurt? Herring! Herring! Do you hear me? Herring, can I talk to you?"

For the next five minutes the police could hear someone ranting in the background. Duisberg, desperate, shouted into the phone, trying to get someone.

"He's going to kill the first person in five minutes!" the voice of one of the plainclothes policeman yelled. "He's not going to give you any time! We have five minutes!"

Then Herring was back on the line. Duisberg asked whether the gunman planned to take any hostages with him in the helicopter.

"He said he will tell you when the time comes," Herring said. His voice rose. "He really doesn't believe you are going to provide him with a helicopter. He really wants to shoot us!"

Duisberg informed him that the police were able to secure a volunteer to pilot the helicopter, under the condition that he receives a personal assurance from Beitz that there would no be trouble in the air, and that he will be able to return safely in the helicopter, as soon as they arrive at Beitz's intended destination."

Herrng replied, "Yes, Beitz will talk with the pilot." Herring's voice sounded thick with relief.

"The type of helicopter that is coming is a short-range helicopter, see?" Duisberg said, trying to sound reasonable. "Now, does he intend to go out of the country very far? If he does, we may have to make other arrangements so that he has enough fuel for the trip."

"Four hundred miles," Herring responded. Duisberg continued talking, reviewing what had been said, but Herring interrupted. "There will be no more talking."

Herring's voice disappeared. All they heard was background noise.

Five minutes passed and Herring's voice returned. "Either immediately land the helicopter in the courtyard, or face a blood bath! One man will be killed every five minutes! No more excuses!"

As police forces kept a tense vigil outside the house, stories quickly spread that they had already killed one or two hostages. The spokesperson for the department told journalists at a hastily improvised press conference that nobody had been killed and that there would be no bloodshed.

At last helicopters arrived and hovered above the house. One of them landed in the courtyard. The pilot jumped out and after a quick briefing from Strenger, took the microphone.

"Mr. Beitz! I came here to rescue you!"

"Please," Herring cried, coming back onto the line. "Please! he has a gun pointing at my head. He will talk only to the pilot."

"Mr. Beitz," the pilot shouted. "I am the pilot! I have a helicopter here to take you wherever you want to go."

There was a pause, and then Herring added his own indignation to his captor's. "What the hell are those copters flying on top of the house?"

"They're here to rescue the hostages after Mr. Beitz takes off. He doesn't have to worry about it."

"He wants them out of here!" Herring cried. "Get those copters the hell out of here!"

"I'll try to negotiate that right now," the pilot said.

"He also wants all your people with guns out of here."

Now it was the detective's turn to sound incredulous. "All our what?" Duisberg asked.

"All the guys with guns," repeated the pilot. "Mr Beitz, I will take you anywhere you want to go and you can also take your people in the other helicopters, if you want. But please talk to me directly."

There was a long pause.

"Mr. Beitz will talk to you," Herring said at last.

Just then, Bertha Weidfeldt emerged from the landed helicopter and at Strenger's urging took the telephone. "Berthold, you know I love you and you are my son. Your brother is also here. He came from Werfen. Please don't do this to us. Give yourself up. Please, let me come in and talk to you."

"Mother, you'd better go home."

"It is over, Berthold. Adolf Fritz, Aren Bechen and others, are going to be indicted because Werner Bischoff betrayed them. Please Berthold, it's over. I will forgive you for whatever you have done, if you will let your people give themselves up and let me come inside."

There was a long silence, and then Herring's voice returned on the line. "He is going to let his people come out, but he will stay with us. He's going to take us together with three more people. He is very well armed."

Ten minutes later, sixteen people, hands clasped at the back of their necks, gave themselves up to the police. When they were safely in custody, Herring spoke again. "He wants to get inside the helicopter. His mother should get inside too. Otherwise he will kill us all, one by one. He is deadly serious."

"Tell him his mother is walking towards the house. Open the door for her."

"No! No! Do not send her to the house!"

At that instant a shot was heard, moments later the door opened and a limp, hooded figure was kicked out onto the entrance ground.

"Oh my God!" Herring screamed. "Officer Felten! He will kill me next!"

Bertha Weidfeldt rushed inside the house. Her steps echoed around the enclosure, then all was quiet, eerily quiet. Suddenly they heard shots and screams.

Immediately the police stormed the house and seized control of the ground floor. Men jumped from the helicopters onto the roof and dispersed throughout the house until they came upon a closed door. They surrounded the area and kicked the door open, and stopped, appalled at the gruesome spectacle before them.

A sound of gunfire reverberated in the air.

"Oh, my God!" a young officer cried. In his short year in the force he had never seen such a horrible sight. Everyone lay dead in a widening pool of blood.

ANN ordered breakfast in bed at six o'clock. She had been glued to the television for the past four hours. She ordered every daily newspaper she could. The news on the television was not encouraging, and her nerves were on edge. The hours passed, with no sign of Robert's release, hardly a mention of his name. Ann scanned the *Herald Tribune*, the *European*, and the *London Times*. But she didn't need English reporters to tell her what would be happening at home. Then she turned to the *Deutsche Morgen* and braced herself to read the headlines. "Four Pharma Frankfuter Officers Indicted for Price-Fixing."

The phone rang and Ann snatched the receiver.

"Ann, Channel NTV," Sir Ronald cried. "Quickly!"

A television announcer interrupting a program stared at her with the latest news.

Good Morning. Four officers of the Pharma Frankfuter were indicted yesterday, on charges of price fixing.

The Reichsgericht also indicted a senior executive on charges that he ordered the killing of two former employees, Paul Friedrich and Hermann Wenninger.

We will bring you more details as soon as we receive them. Now we are returning to the scheduled program.

Ann turned the TV set to another channel and was able

to watch part of a report from Bogotá, Colombia already in progress:

The indictment lays out a series of charges including: an alleged master plan to force the Colombian government to award a contract for the search and recovery of the San José's sunken treasure to Ocean Reconnaissance Fleet, a consortium of Pharma Frankfuter Group and an American company.

Also a plan to bribe Colombian officials in order to obtain the Materia Medicinal, which at present is in the hull of a galleón that was sunk off the coast of Colombia.

Those plans, if enacted, would create a world monopoly. Obtaining patents for the medicinal plants would enable them to set prices without fear of being undercut.

Ann's joy was tinged with sadness. She would be on top of the world, if only Robert could be with her. Please, God, she thought, take care of him and bring him back to me. She pressed the remote control to Channel Tele 5.

We are transmitting from Berolinahoff, a country house north of Portz Rhein, where a detective and three policemen were taken hostage, when they attempted to serve a warrant to search the house. It is believed that the men kidnapped several days ago are also imprisoned in the house. After many hours of negotiation, the Cologne police heard shots inside. An all-out assault on the house followed. A few minutes ago, sixteen people came out of the house and surrendered to police. But after six hours of siege, the authorities are still uncertain of the number of people inside, dead or alive.

The scene shifted again. *As you can see bodies are being carried out to be transported to the morgue. We have just received news that there are few survivors. One apparently was shot in the arm. He has been identified.*

Ann felt sick, utterly helpless.

She opened the *Deutsche Welle,* a Cologne daily newspaper, and read:

NEW EVIDENCE DISCOVERED IN BEROLINEHOFF MANSION

The police believe that when Beitz's mother entered the house, she found many works of art that her son had stolen from her. After a long argument, she took a rifle and shot her son. They emphasize that they will be collecting evidence. Officer Felten was fatally shot earlier inside the house, by Mr. Beitz, the police allege…"

Ann stared at the television. She pounded the bed in frustration. Where was Robert? What did they mean—everyone in the house was dead? He couldn't be one of them. Was he held captive somewhere else?

On the screen was a communications officer being interviewed.

Police have uncovered a secret corridor leading to a row of cells….

Ann sat hypnotized. The Berolinehoff Mansion appeared in the distance on the screen. The officer screamed excitedly: *We discovered more cells! We are walking in a basement with damp gray walls and old tile floors — now we are entering the cells. They are empty. Yes, we repeat: The cells are empty; they are bleak and cold with only a naked lightbulb hanging from a stone ceiling. I can see a wooden platform with filthy blankets and rotten pillows thrown on top of a bucket. Now we are showing you the graffiti scratched into the walls by past occupants. In the center of this cell is a small metal table and chair with rusty legs. In this cold temperature and with the doors open, a sour smell permeates the dungeon.*

A wave of nausea struck Ann. She reached for the telephone and dialed Sir Ronald. "I am leaving for Berolinahoff immediately! I know Robert is there. Intuition, but I am certain of it. Would you come with me?"

"All right, Ann. Stay calm. I'll come right over. Together we will determine what to do."

"Please hurry!"

Ann turned to the screen. The police found a door in the dingy corridor: *There's a door there — perhaps to a sub-basement. Here are three-steps that drop to a landing. A dim red bulb lights the place. We are going down the stairs. We can hear some kind of faint noise behind the staircase. One of our officers is crouching on the landing. Now he is going down on his stomach to investigate.*

Ann sat at the edge of her bed holding a pair of shoes in her hand—transfixed. *Officer Tuft is coming out behind the landing!*

Ann heard a knock and rushed to open the door. "Sir Ronald! Come in! Listen to the news!" She turned back to the screen.

The victims are secured with handcuffs and leg bindings. They are blindfolded and gagged with pieces of cloth. Now the first is coming out to freedom. Aided by one of our officers, he is been questioning .I repeat! The first hostage has been liberated. He has been identified as Robert Hamilton, an American. We don't know his condition. The second man that is being untied is Helmut Müller. He is asking about his son and has been informed that his son had fully recovered. The last hostage is coming now! He has been identified as Mr. Karl Schneider.

We understand that all these hostages will be rushed by ambulance to the Koln General Hospital for observation.

It was too much to take in all at once. The reality of it all did not hit her until moments later when she broke down and wept uncontrollably on their rush to the hospital.

She had not slept for almost thirty hours, thirty hours of despair and anguish but her thoughts were full of Robert.

More than a dozen reporters and photographers from radio and TV stations, newspapers, and magazines were outside the gray facade of Koln General Hospital. Ann and Sir Ronald tried to make their way to the emergency ward, but police cars and a crowd of curious passersby blocked the hill leading to it. A tall, determined police officer ordered the road closed. Ann rushed to the policeman in a moment of pure inspiration, looked at him in the eye and said in a firm voice:

"I'm Ann Leigh, Robert Hamilton's fiancée. He is one of the hostages and this gentleman is Sir Ronald Harris."

The officer knew nothing about them. He communicated with someone on a two-way radio and after ten minutes of suspense let both of them pass.

At the nurse's station, they were told, "I'm afraid you cannot see him. The doctors are with him now. Please take a seat and as soon as the doctor comes out, I will ask if he can talk to you."

They sat down in an already crowded waiting room. Minutes passed like hours, heavy, interminable.

Finally, an intern walked towards them. He was in his early twenties, but he looked old and tired. "Are you the friends of Mr. Hamilton?

Sir Ronald rose.

"I'm Doctor Colt. He's sedated now, but we have not found anything seriously wrong. We expect him to recover from his ordeal very soon."

"Wonderful news, Doctor," Ann said with a wide smile. "When can we see him?"

"I hope that by tomorrow he'll be in a condition to receive visitors. I'll let him know that you came by today."

The next day Ann trembled on her way back to the hospital.

Robert's bed was the nearest the station where two nurses in green surgical scrubs are jotted notes on clipboards, chatting in low voices.

Ann sailed past them and there he was, propped up in bed, two pillows behind his back, smiling with that wonderful smile.

"Robert—Robert!"

It was Ann's voice calling him from far off. Robert opened his eyes and slowly, his vision cleared. "Ann — Darling, is that you?"

Ann's heart skipped a beat. *My heaven, he's alive*! She moved quickly from the door to his bedside and slipped her arms around his neck. "Oh, I was so worried about you! Let me look at you," she whispered, squeezing him gently on the arm, the one with the IV.

"My darling Ann···"

Her lips were warm and loving. He whispered softly, "I love you with all my heart."

"May I come in?" Sir Ronald asked, knocking at the door. I hope I'm not interrupting a very serious conversation."

Robert told them about his abduction, beginning with the day he was to meet Müller in front of a pier and what led up to his being forced into the van. “They forced me to lie down on the floor and we drove along a smooth, paved surface for about one hour, then we bounced over rough roads for about half an hour. One of the men riding with me made senseless threats every time I tried to sit up. We went up a hill, over a dirt road.

“When we stopped, they covered my head with a black hood and made me look down when I got out, so that all I saw were my shoes. We descended several stairs and I found myself in a cell about two meters square, with a mattress on the floor and a bare lightbulb hanging from the ceiling. I was kept in this cell the entire time, up to a few a days ago. Then they put me with the others in the foul-smelling, squalid hole where the police found us. The guards wore masks, so I never saw their faces.

“The first night seemed interminable and was freezing cold. The next day, they only gave me fried meatballs and potatoes. The third day, I had coffee for breakfast, potato salad and sausage on top. The rest of the time we had only two meals a day. The plates, glasses, and sheets were used over and over again without being washed.

“The hardest things were — I didn’t know how long I was going to be held, how I’d survive the daily interrogations and the rough treatment by the guards.”

Robert looked at Ann and said: “I thought of you, day and night. That was what helped me keep my sanity. Most surprising of all was when I was moved to a cell with the others. I didn’t know there were other hostages. When we heard the roar of helicopters followed by shooting sounds, I knew the days of captivity were over.”

They talked for more than two hours until the nurse put an end to the visit.

Two days later, outside the hospital, the press waited in force. An assault of dazzling floodlights lit up the interior lobby of the hospital. Robert Hamilton, Karl Schneider, and Helmut Müller were discharged from the hospital. Ann and Robert made their way through the screaming newsmen armed with microphones.

With difficulty, they managed to reach their waiting limousine. The vehicle inched through the crowded hospital driveway, and then pulled away. The morning sun was unseasonably strong, and the wide rear glass of the car magnified its heat. Ann's head was snuggled against Robert's shoulder as close as possible.

The thirty hours of tension in the Berolinahoff siege and hostage negotiations were front page news around the country. Then scandal rocked the nation and the tabloids took full advantage.

One report alleged that Werner Bischoff had taped conversations while hidden cameras inside the walls of the Board meeting room filmed events. In a report obtained by *Deutsche Morgen* it appeared that members of the Bundestag could be linked with Pharma Frankfuter. Chancellor Gerhard Schroeder asked for a full investigation.

The case had given the team its first large taste of public acclaim. In the weeks that followed, and as details unfolded, Robert Hamilton, Helmut Müller, Karl Schneider, Ann Leigh, Sir Ronald Harris, Baron von Bülow and Christoph Beck became household names. They granted interviews, attended meetings with the investigative committee of the Bundestag, the BND, BKA and the Cologne police.

It would take many months, even a year, before the Pharma Frankfuter investigation would be closed. It appeared to gain new momentum in the weeks that followed. Reports appeared in the media of thousands of documents found at the Berolinahoff country house, implicating many executives of Pharma Frankfuter.

They also found illegally acquired art works, paintings, ancient ceramics, statues and friezes looted from the Kabul Museum, whose collection spanned more than two thousand years. In addition, works by Rembrandt, The Witch of Haarlem by Malle Babbe, and many other masterpieces were found in the house. Returning them to their rightful owners would take a long time.

Of all the special routes that crisscross Germany, none rivals the aptly named Romantiche Strasse, or Romantic Road. It is not so much the road itself that is the main attraction, for the scenery along the road is more domestic and rural than spectacular. What makes the Romantic Road so memorable are the medieval towns, villages, castles and churches, tucked away beyond low hills, their spires and towers poking up through the greenery. Robert and Ann drove slowly down the Romantic Strasse, laughing because it was so beautiful, laughing because they were alone together at last, laughing because they were happy and in love.

In Tauberbischofsheim, Robert and Ann checked into the Hotel Sonne, a charming hotel with fourteen rooms, each with its own name. Ann slept deeply, clinging to Robert as if she didn't ever want to let go.

They spent the morning making passionate love, and afterwards lingered in the town's pedestrian mall, strolled down to the sleepy Tauber River, and visited the parish church.

The Wurzburg's Mozart concert that night, the last concert of the season was magnificent. They spent a week visiting romantic places, looking at each other, living in a timeless wonder, every moment precious. Ann knew these moments were transitory and would pass, but their consuming passion would remain with them always. She enjoyed the sheer freedom of being together, minute by minute, hour upon hour, day after lingering day.

Robert looked ahead to when they could be together forever. He knew that all too soon they would be thousands of miles apart. Now it became clear to him that he had to initiate the quest for his other love, hidden deep under the ocean, the *San José*. But his love for Ann was so full in his heart, nourishing his dreams, permeating his existence so completely and intensely that he felt he, Ann, and the *San José*, were inextricably linked.

Their week of reverie ended too soon. They returned to Cologne to once again meet with Müller and to receive information concerning the presumed location of the *San José*—

the information that had cost Wenninger, Wenninger's son and Beitz their lives.

Finally, they returned to London to meet with Sir Ronald Harris and Karl Schneider for the last strategy meeting preceding the quest.

The day eventually came when Robert needed to return to the United States.

Ann accompanied him to Heathrow Airport. "You will come back to me safe and sound," she whispered. "You must promise me."

"Yes, I promise. You are my life."

"Life will be so awfully wretched without you." Ann's voice broke. She kissed him lightly and then turned away quickly.

When I see you again, Robert said to himself, *I will marry you.*

THE harsh rays of the April sun burned Jack Swanson's skin fire red. He was a stocky man of average height with brown hair that was turning gray and thinning on the crown. His rather handsome beard made him look younger than his age. He sat on the verandah of Café Bienville waiting for Robert Hamilton, looking at the massive, muddy, Mobile River that rolled through the heart of Alabama. Ocean-going vessels from distant ports of the world passed by with cargo for flourishing southern industry. In the distance he could make out the growing skyline of the thriving city. He had already spent five months of frenzied work at the Alabama Dry Docks and Shipbuilding Company on Pinto Island, trying to accomplish an almost impossible task.

Scarcely six months before, Robert Hamilton had summoned him out of the blue to come to Mobile. He had never met the man, but the voice from London convinced him to accept the assignment. By profession he was a seafaring man, a certified master mariner. But in his thirty years at sea, he had never before been asked to refit and command a submarine. Yet that was exactly what Hamilton was asking. From where he sat, he could see the dry dock where the *August Picard* lay swaddled in scaffoldings and cables, nearly at the end of her thorough overhaul.

Jack heard Robert Hamilton's step on the gravel path behind

the Café, and Jack rose to greet him. Hamilton was younger than he had expected from the authoritative voice on the phone.

They greeted each other warmly, went into the dining room and ordered lunch.

Robert told Jack he came to United States to close his house in Lewiston, Maine and to work with lawyers and financial advisers preparing a proposal to the Colombian government. He'd already traveled to Colombia.

It took weeks, but they initiated the negotiations with the Colombian authorities. Robert brought him up to speed on various agreements. "As you know, Jack, we employed you to replace the former captain of the sub, due to problems of morale. I'm told you have an excellent record. We hope the Colombian government will give us the final O.K. within the month."

Jack nodded. "We've lost some valuable time due to many problems, but we've been working overtime for five weeks and expect to finish by the end of this month. When I arrived at the end of November, almost nothing had been done. We had to dismantle her insides and rip out just about everything; we also had to remove every single item of equipment susceptible to theft or damage. It's hard to describe, the unspeakable shambles of the *Auguste Piccard* panels torn out to get at the wiring and piping, dirt everywhere, empty soda cans and sandwich wrappings stuffed into every available corner, loose screws and pieces of wire and insulation tossed unceremoniously on the floor where no one bothered to pick them up. There were even odd tools, which the workmen continually forgot and left behind at the end of the day. It was soon clear to me that the main problem was lack of leadership on the part of the chief superintendent. I managed to convince the yard management to replace him; otherwise the overhaul could never have been done in a timely manner. As for me, it's taken fourteen-hour days just to get into a routine. On top of that, I've spent a lot of time learning how to be a captain of a sub, since my experience is largely in surface vessels."

Jack mentioned the problems in obtaining material and new equipment, and having it installed correctly. "We've tested the sub three times in the water. The first test dive has been completed. Would you like to come with me and inspect her? From here you can see the dry dock across the river."

"I'd love to," Robert responded.

"Do you know that Mobile holds title to liquid treasures?" asked Jack as they drove along the river. "The treasures are in the form of enormous reserves of fresh water. In an average year the Mobile River system, which includes the Alabama, the Coosa, the Tombigbee, the Black Warrior and the Tensaw, pours fourteen trillion gallons of fresh water into Mobile—an amount greater than what the entire population of the United States consumes annually!"

They watched a freighter gliding down the river, passing some of the thirty-three cargo berths on the port's two-and-a-half-mile-long waterfront. The ship churned above Bankhead Tunnel, which carried automobile traffic between downtown Mobile and the eastern Bay Shore.

Jack parked at the Alabama Dry Dock and Shipbuilding complex, and they set out on foot to the dry dock where the *Auguste Piccard* was being overhauled. He was eager to conduct a tour.

"The submarine has a ballast system, four internal ballast tanks and external ballast with water, which have safety subtonics on top to allow flotation or purging. The main ballast tanks are used for normal surfacing and submerging. The safety tanks are held in reserve for emergencies. The auxiliary tanks serve to trim the ship to neutral buoyancy, where she weighs exactly as much as the water she displaces."

Jack pointed out the galley, berthing quarters, observation area, diving control station, and engine room. It also has what we call a 'Dart,' a remotely operated TV vehicle."

Robert asked about the operational depth.

"Six hundred seventy meters, or about 2,200 feet. The cruising range is five hundred miles. Submerged speed is a little over four knots."

"And her length?"

"Twenty-eight-and-a-half meters, or about ninety-three-and-a-half feet. Her total life support capability is ninety man-days. Crew capacity is six for a standard mission, with two observers, two overnight and four working during the daytime. We also have a very sophisticated sensor, positioning and communication system."

They agreed to depart for Colombia on the first of May.

"Tomorrow we're going to take the sub out for a brief cruise. Would you like to come along?"

"I would certainly would!" Robert gazed at the enveloping mass of steel beams, cable and men. Will she be ready?"

"Oh yes, we'll have her in the water by sunset. After the cruise, we'll load supplies into the surface support ship."

Robert nodded. "Then all we need are the import licenses from the Colombian government."

"Our ship agent is recognized by the Colombian maritime authorities. If, by the time of departure, we don't receive the license, we'll depart anyway and our agent will arrange to have all the proper papers at the port waiting for us. We can communicate by radio with him, since we're traveling on the surface support ship.

"It sounds good. If you're going to stay a few weeks, you can meet the crew. Besides me, there's the pilot, a liaison officer, the chief engineer and the maintenance engineer, an electrician, six watches, a communications officer and an oceanographer. With you, that makes fifteen," said Jack.

Robert smiled. "I can hardly wait to get aboard — I've always wanted to sail in a submarine. But I'm a little worried about her speed. Four knots isn't very fast."

"Don't worry," Jack laughed. "The support ship will tow us most of the way. She goes fifteen knots. I expect that it'll take us approximately ten days from Mobile to Cartagena."

They stood at the railing on a deck inspecting the bottom of the sub, which was being scraped and coated with red lead paint when Robert caught a movement out of the corner of his eye.

"Watch out, Jack!" Robert screamed, grabbing Jack's arm.

High above them a six-foot steel beam wildly rocked and swayed. They both jumped the rail and landed on a lower platform as the beam, freed from its restraining cable, crashed onto the space where seconds before they had been standing. Their platform rocked and swiveled dangerously. Clinging to a rope railing, they scrambled to a ladder at the end of the platform and climbed to safety.

As they looked up, white-faced, they saw two men slipping away into the shadows. The workmen, in bewilderment, shouted their dismay.

Robert and Jack pointed toward the place the men had been. "Catch them!" Robert cried, knowing it was probably already too late.

"That was a deliberate attempt to kill us," Jack said evenly.

"Who would want us dead?" asked Robert.

"I don't know. But it's not the first instance of sabotage in this place."

Late into the night, Robert wrote to Ann.

My dearest Ann:

You don't know how happy you made me with your e-mail last night. One week without news from you is torture, I miss you terribly.

I'm so glad that you had a good time with your parents in the north. I would have given anything to be with you. I'll let you know when you can come to Colombia. It would be wonderful to spend one or two weeks together.

I spent the past week at the dock with Jack Swanson overseeing the refitting of the Auguste Piccard. It is a wonderful submarine, small, but packed with sophisticated equipment. By the end of the month we expect to depart for Cartagena.

I have the feeling that I am going to get along very well with Jack. He is a veteran mariner who has devoted thirty-one years to the sea. He's easygoing and likable. So far as I can tell, his men love him. I will be e-mailing you every night if I can manage, as a sort of diary. Now that you are back at home and I'm in the US, I will try to call you, too, so I can hear your voice again. I love you with all my heart.

Robert

THE weather reports held out the promise of a bright day with moderate seas. During the early hours of May 1, the wind rippled the muddy waters of the Mobile River. The shipyard, with its numerous piers, cranes and other installations, dropped out of sight as the churning propellers of the support ship, with the sub under tow, set up a creamy wake. The delta was a vast labyrinth of marsh and bayou formed by the river's emptying into Mobile Bay. From one of his trouser pockets, the captain pulled out a watch. He looked at it and then looked again at the rising sun.

"Robert!" he said. "Today could be our lucky day. We might see half a dozen animals along the banks. Sometimes at night you can see alligators. In the spotlight their eyes glow like coals."

The spring morning was getting as hot as the inside of an oil drum, and smelled like it, too. Only the shade of a canvas awning made being in the open at all bearable. As they proceeded to open sea, the ocean glowed murky turquoise under a blue sky.

Robert and Jack entered a cabin where the chief engineer, the communications officer, the oceanographer and other men of the watch sat around a table.

"Sit down a moment, Robert." Jack introduced Robert to the watch.

Jack sat down and spoke. "To summarize our mission, we will be cruising from the Gulf of Mexico through the Yucatan channel, out to the Caribbean Sea with a stop of one day in Montego Bay, Jamaica, then towards Cartagena. At fourteen nautical miles before reaching Cartagena, we board the submarine we're towing and dive to approximately eight hundred feet. The object is to locate the *San José* before we conclude negotiations with the Colombian government. The *Sealion*, surface support ship, will wait for us in international waters. We'll work eight hours a day and in the evening return to the *Sealion*. We'll be using the deck-mounted unmanned remote vehicle, the Dart, with TV and still cameras. As you know, extensive tests give us complete assurance that the submarine is safe. Should we need to surface in Colombian waters, our newly installed sonar system will be able to detect whether there is a vessel in the proximity. The sub's active sonar will "ping" on other ships and submarines at great range. In order to prevent detection by others and interference with our own listening devices *Auguste Piccard* has been extensively soundproofed. Our underwater equipment includes two 35 mm stereoscopic cameras in separate watertight cylinders, for simultaneous focusing. And electronic flashlights. Chief engineer Terry, as you know, will coordinate the efforts of the electricians, engine men, electronic technician and sonar men.

"I want to thank all of you for helping to overhaul the sub. And I especially thank Mr. Robert Hamilton for making this all a reality. Let's not forget Mark, our great chef, who will keep us well fed, in the surface support vessel." The crew laughed.

The support ship and the sub under tow were now well out in the open sea of the Gulf of Mexico. Jack looked through his binoculars at a calm, empty sea all around them and brought the ship up to full speed. It was twelve hundred miles to Montego Bay. At this speed it would take three to four days if the weather held.

They steamed steadily southeastward. All around, the harsh rays of the sun burnished the Caribbean. The sky, until it darkened into the horizon, was a fierce white glare and cloudless. There was no wind. The seamen's bodies, long the color of mahogany, began to take on a fresh angry red. It was blistering hot, far hotter than Robert had ever known before. The crew welcomed the cool of the evening when the fire of the sun plunged in a blaze of glory below the horizon.

On the fourth day, early in the morning, having hove part of the night, land was discovered on the bow, and was reported to Captain Swanson. Moments later they could see indescribably lush vegetation laced by hundreds of cascades spilling down from the well-watered mountain heights, rushing to pure dazzling white beaches. The *Sealion* and the *Auguste Piccard* put into port at the new deepwater harbor of Montego Bay, and the crew spent twenty-four hours on the town before continuing on to their destination.

After several days at sea, the men were so filthy they could no longer stand their own body odors. They bathed with the salt-water pump used for hosing down the decks. On the eighth day, fresh water came in unexpected abundance. A torrential rain fell on the ship. The crew danced with joy. The men filled canteens and anything else that would hold water.

On the ninth day, Jack lifted his binoculars and scanned the horizon for visual identification. He noticed the dolphins that had been following them, rolling through the sea like black wheels. Otherwise, the sea appeared empty and calm, with only a moderate swell. Visibility was excellent, about ten miles; the wind blew seven knots from the north-northeast. “It’s time,” Jack announced, and ordered half the crew into the *August Piccard.*

“Prepare to dive.” He turned to the lookout and ordered Ed Molloy below. The officer moved towards the hatch. Robert Hamilton took the time for one last look at the blue sky and followed Molloy. Going on a submarine was very exciting.

“Clear the bridge.” Molloy dropped down the hatch, pulling it shut with a chain. The warrant officer shut the second hatch.

Jack made his own visual inspection. He nodded, and the warrant officer of the watch unlocked the vent controls.

“Flood the main ballast tanks. Fifteen degrees down-angle on the panes." Jack looked to see that every man did his job exactly as he should.

The *Auguste Piccard's* hull was filled with the sound of rushing air, as vents at the top of the ballast tanks opened. Water flooded the tanks at the bottom.

The *Auguste Piccard* left the *Sealion* miles behind in the safety of international waters and traveled for weeks, in dangerous Colombian waters, partially on the surface and partially submerged — mostly blind, relying heavily on charts to avoid detection. She steered various courses at various speeds and depths. They searched an area five nautical miles square and then concentrated on one nautical square mile. Using precise integrated navigation systems that employed microwave position plots, with stations located on unoccupied small Colombian islands, they set up transponders in the seabed surrounding this area without being detected by the Colombian coast guard. Just west of *Isla del Tesoro* and north of Little Baru, they tried to identify the wreck by latitude and longitude, in a circle with a radius of 3.5 nautical miles.

The ROV snapped about three thousand pictures of the wreck and debris field, allowing the assembly of a detailed photomap. On a computer screen, they zoomed in tight on specific artifacts near the wreck. After many weeks of painstaking search using extremely sensitive side-scan sonar and a sub-bottom profiler, a diver went down and couldn't believe what he saw—massive wooden beams, showing signs of having been charred, and covered by centuries of seaweed. The diver was stunned realizing what he had located: "It's a *galléon!*" He videotaped the scene, and took a sample of the wood about the size of a loaf of bread and then surfaced.

Looking at the wood, and then embracing the diver, Robert said, "This is the result of your tenacity and a hard day's work."

From the sub, the self-remote controlled vehicle was launched, connected to its co-axial umbilical cable. The Dart moved slowly along the bottom, and then passed over an area of considerable wood debris. Through the TV camera, they saw a ridge about two feet high and eight feet across. At first, the captain was afraid they might scrape the bottom of the Dart and wondered if he should order the oceanographer to raise the vehicle by its umbilical cord. He decided that they could clear the obstacle and said nothing. As the Dart skimmed over the ridge with barely three inches to spare, he could see that the ridge was really the rim of a large crater. Passing over the crater, they found the first signs of a sunken ship—petrified planks of wood, then a debris trail of wood and metal that led directly to ammunition for the cannons, split-bar shot, then a large object with some starfish clinging to it and then a cannon itself with quintal weight and date inscriptions: 24Q99L, 1698. Next they saw three pieces of what they believed was a gold chain. They reached out with the manipulator, and tried to pick up the chain, but it slipped off. The second attempt to retrieve the chain was successful.

"Really incredible!" Robert said, looking at the heavy golden links, as they were being recovered. Members of the crew crowded around him.

This meant that they had located a rich shipwreck. Robert thought that it might be one of the lost 1708 *galléons*. Or was it the *San José*?

"People have been looking for this wreck for centuries," Robert said. "Even though the general area was known, it was never enough to pinpoint the wreck. It's a big ocean, and they didn't have GPS back then."

Robert told Jack, "We need a lab to check the age of the wood."

The captain ordered the pilot to dive to the ocean bed. The constant clatter of footsteps echoed along the *Auguste Piccard's* passageway and clanged up and down the rungs of her steel ladders. Everyone was busy helping to ready the ship for descent to the sea bottom. Every spare inch was crammed with machinery of one kind or another. Robert could hardly stretch out an arm without touching some piece of equipment. No ceiling was more than a foot above his head.

"Ship is rigged for dive and ready to land, sir," reported Chief Engineer Molloy, probably the busiest man on the ship.

"Very good! Sound the diving alarm!" ordered the captain. "Make your depth eight hundred feet. Make preparation for landing!" The engineer passed the order to the control room.

"Flood auxiliary tanks,! the captain ordered. There was a gushing sound as the vents opened to admit water, which expelled the air contained in the auxiliary tanks. The *Auguste Piccard* descended to the ocean floor, landing so hard that she was buried in the sand. Around the eighth shift, they followed an artifact trail to a large mound of cannon balls. One silver ingot and many coins were found amid rich shipwreck material. Pieces of wood, thought to be a section of the *San José*'s ribs, were found and dug out, well preserved due to being buried in the sand.

The deep-sea sharks were as spectacular as any ocean floor fauna they had seen. They searched a sizable area and shot many photographs, as far as the length of the Dart's umbilical cord permitted.

As dusk began to blanket a restless sea, the captain sent out a radio message to the surface support ship, pinpointing a new rendezvous calculated to be six miles east of the original one. The time for the rendezvous was changed to 9 p.m. The message ended with "Prepare champagne aboard."

Captain Swanson gave the order to ascend to the surface. In the control room, the ballast control panel operator shoved the 'chicken switches,' blowing high-pressure air through the main ballast tank 1, to force the vessel upward. Usually, the submarine would respond at once. But as the captain and the top officer started at the depth gauge, the needle refused to budge. Only moments before, they were excited at having located the *San José*. Now, they were stuck, more than three hundred feet down.

The captain ordered the crew to start deballasting tanks 2 and 4. Nothing happened. Then, he deballasted tank 1 and 3 — and still not the slightest movement. The operator's voice betrayed anxiety: "I have been pumping from four of the main ballast tanks, but she's not lifting!"

"My God!" someone exclaimed. "I can't see through the view port!"

Despite his remoteness from the source of trouble, much farther aft and one deck below, Robert Hamilton had a pretty good idea of what was going on. The *Auguste Piccard* had sunk into the sand and refused to budge. Because of their unfamiliarity with the seabed composition, they had not realized how soft it was. Sediments could be from up to fifteen feet deep. Mud was thinner at the top and grew progressively thicker with depth.

"Blow all main ballast tanks!" the captain ordered. All the main ballast tanks were blown at once. On the upper deck, all eyes watched the gauges, which would foretell the immediate future. They waited anxiously for some kind of movement, but there was none.

The captain commanded the deballast of all auxiliary tanks. The ballast control panel operator pumped water from the auxiliary tanks into the sea, but nothing happened. Sweat formed on the captain's brow. A minor difficulty was only a hairline away from disaster. It was already three hours since they had begun trying to surface and the situation was fast growing critical. Thus far, the men maintained discipline, most of them sustained by a desperate hope that everything would turn out all right. After so many hours with the air compressors running, the temperature inside the ship began to rise. Blending into the warm stuffy air were acrid smells of human perspiration, hot lubricating oils and toilets. Under these conditions in a totally confined environment, without a break or sleep for almost twenty-four hours, any kind of irritation assumes explosive proportions.

Some members of the crew regarded the black sea as a hostile monster, voracious and implacable, waiting to envelop the sub like some giant, evil octopus. Most of the crew tried to avoid thinking of the surrounding sea at all. The captain made several attempts to communicate with the surface support ship, but to no avail. No outside help was available. The *Auguste Piccard* had to rely entirely on her own resources to regain the surface. There was now only one card to play. Jack Swanson drew a deep breath. He pulled the microphone to his mouth and ordered the entire crew to line up in the center of the ship. Then he ordered the main, auxiliary and emergency tanks to blow, and simultaneously drop the solid ballast.

Over the speakers, they heard, "This is the captain speaking. All hands secure loose gear and prepare for heavy shocks during surface at full speed."

The captain's words were scarcely out of his mouth when a tremendous hiss pervaded the whole ship. Then he ordered the members of the crew to move in unison from one side of the ship to the other, engines full ahead and the rotor pushing. The compressed air banks storing air at a pressure of four thousand pounds per square inch sent their contents ramming into the ballast tanks with a force seven times greater than the pressure of the seawater. If anything would do it, this would.

With no ballast in the sub, it lifted off like a rocket towards the surface. There was the danger of collision with any nearby ships, so the captain ordered the tanks to be filled with seawater in order to slow the sub's ascent as she neared the surface. There was a gushing sound as the vents opened to admit water, which expelled the air contained in the ballast tanks.

But the tanks filled rapidly with water and the vertical ascent slowed so that only her periscope rose above water. The ship ascended to the surface with an ease that gladdened the hearts of all aboard. But their joy was short-lived when the captain raised the periscope to scan the horizon. Two patrol cutters from the Colombian Coast Guard surrounded them.

"Damn!" growled Jack. He immediately ordered the sub to slide beneath the waves although he knew there wasn't really time to dive and escape. Shaking not with fear but with the rage of innocence accused, he ordered the sub to fully surface and face the consequences as soon as she surfaced, he opened the hatch. Jack was the first man out, followed by Robert.

A tall, slim officer of the Colombian navy screamed over a bullhorn, "You are in Colombian territorial waters! We are boarding the sub!"

The captain shouted back, "This is a registered Canadian ship, and we have all the required certificates and import papers waiting for us in Cartagena."

There was a rapid exchange of questions, answers and opinions between the armed men of the Coast Guard and the men on the submarine. Then the coast guard launched a speedboat with ten navy officers aboard. They headed towards the sub, which they boarded, carrying sub-machine guns. The lead man, Lieutenant Jaime Rodriguez, did not speak English, but with Robert translating, he notified the captain that they were entering to inspect the sub, and proceeded through the hatch. The captain looked on in somber silence. Ed Molloy, realizing what was going on, hid all the artifacts recovered from the *San José* in the engine room inside an oil barrel.

After an hour of inspection, the navy men came out on deck and informed the captain that they were under arrest and those five Colombian officers would remain aboard. The two Coast Guard cutters would escort the sub to Cartagena.

"You are under house arrest until we confirm that all your documents are in proper order."

"We have not broken any laws," protested the captain.

"You are under arrest for not having the proper import papers."

"I already told you that the import papers for the sub and for our surface support ship are waiting in Cartagena. They are with our agent, a recognized ship agent with the Colombian government."

"So what were you doing underwater?" asked the navy officer.

"We went for a test run."

"You can go for all the test runs you want, Captain! But not in Colombian territorial waters. I am telling you right now, you will come with us to Cartagena or we will sink your sub."

"Then you will start an international incident. There are Americans, Canadians and British citizens aboard, and the sub is registered in Canada, a friendly country. You piss me off, your attitude pisses me off." The captain paused to wipe sweat from his eyes.

Robert Hamilton quickly interceded. "I think we should approach the issue differently. We are very tired after a long trip. We are under negotiation with the Colombian government. We are not delinquents, so we expect you to treat us with consideration."

"What are you asking me to do, let you go free?" said the officer.

"What we are asking you is to escort the sub into port. Call our agent, verify that our papers are in order, and if they are, let us go," Robert suggested.

"Not a problem. I am just doing my job."

Then, slowly, the captain's face relaxed. He lit a cigarette and when he spoke again, his voice was soft. Without looking at Robert, he said, "Yeah. Let's follow orders."

"We'll follow you into Colombian territorial waters. You carry out Colombian policies and obey Colombian laws," said the navy officer, shouting the last words.

The captain let the pause linger. In the hot silence, the slap of the waves seemed louder than they were. Sea birds hovered, welcoming the *Auguste Piccard.* A pelican landed on the deck.

Human nature being what it is, a certain amount of confusion and chaos occurs whenever the normal order of things is disrupted. After Lieutenant Jaime Rodriquez disembarked the *Auguste Piccard* and boarded his cutter, he immediately radioed his story of the interdiction of the sub in Cartagena. It came into Radio Central at the office of the Colombian Coast Guard Commandant Alzaro Castellano. Twenty minutes later, he gave their assessment of the situation to the Ministry of Defense in Bogotá. In one hour it was passed up the line as far as the Presidential palace. A response was forthcoming within two hours, but it baffled the Coast Guard. They were ordered to confiscate the submarine and put the captain and his crew under house arrest, regardless of their nationality, and to keep it very, very quiet.

The naval base was a sprawling installation of buildings and port facilities at Boca Grande, overlooking Cartagena Bay. Most of the structures were painted white and shaded by palm trees. On the third attempt the *Auguste Piccard* was able to establish communication with the surface support ship, and ordered the ship to change course in the direction of the Cartagena Naval base. Two miles northeast of Cartagena, the Caribbean Sea was clear as cobalt glass, marbled with streaks of foam that glowed in the sunlight. They could see Cartagena on the horizon under a sky so clear it made Robert's eyes sparkle. Astern, the *Sealion* was coming towards them, even at the risk of its crew also being arrested by the Colombian navy.

The *Auguste Piccard* made the approach into Cartagena at five knots, escorted by the two navy cutters, and cut speed just as her bow passed one of the cutter's sterns, settling into the notch at a pier.

Fifteen minutes later, a group of officers were at lunch at the Navy Club, when a phone buzzed. Commandant Alzaro Castellano unhooked the receiver. When he hung up, he wiped his forehead. His arms bulged under rolled-up sleeves as he hoisted himself to his feet. "Excuse me, gentlemen," he said. "The sub has arrived." Lieutenant Arboleda followed him topside. They stood together as arriving vessels slowly pushed over the horizon, passing huge ships, sheer-walled, their empty hulls looming out of the water.

Meanwhile, the *Sealion* had moored along side the *Auguste Piccard*. Its anchor let go with a jarring rumble, charging down into the calm water of Cartagena Bay.

Lieutenant Arboleda approached the sub and looking at the captain, said, "Commandant Alzaro Castellano is coming out to see you."

"When?"

"In about five minutes."

"Molloy, please call Mark and tell him to lay out some iced tea in my cabin." Tilting his cap forward, the chief engineer made for the quarterdeck.

A few minutes later Commandant Alzaro Castellano boarded the sub. "Good evening, Captain. I am sorry to have to detain your crew and the submarine, but until things are completely cleared up, I can't let you go."

"I'm sorry, too, Commander. This is Robert Hamilton, the historian who has been negotiating with your government for permission to search for the *San José*."

"Though it is a pleasure to meet both of you, I must notify you that you are under house arrest. None of your men can leave the navy base, and the sub and the support ship are to remain in port until you are officially notified that you can leave."

"Commander, as you can understand, I would like our sub and ship to be guarded by our people," the captain said.

"Yes, of course, after both vessels are fully searched by navy personnel, you are free to man the security of your vessels. You are also free to use the navy facilities. Of course, you will have to pay for any supplies you require. Lieutenant Arboleda will show you around our base and explain which areas are off-limits. However, you two will receive a pass to the officer's mess as well as other facilities. I'd like the two of you to join me tonight for dinner at the Navy Club. Lieutenant Arboleda will come and pick you up in his car. Let's say 8 p.m.?"

"That is very kind of you. We will be delighted," Robert answered politely.

"Enjoy your stay in Colombia," said the commander with a grin.

When Castellano returned to his office, a young lieutenant waved a sheaf of messages at him. "The emergencies are on top."

"Later. Get me German Obregon."

Two minutes later, Castellano was talking to the chairman of the *San José* Negotiating Committee and director of La Direccion General Maritima Portuaria de Colombia. The Commander had known Obregon casually for a number of years.

"This is a pleasant surprise," Obregon said. "It has been a long time, Alzaro."

"Much too long. That's the trouble with the navy, German, most of the time we are in hot water. We never have time for the people we like."

"That is so true."

"I understand from the Ministry of Defense you were going to be briefed on a confidential matter related to some naval activities in Cartagena. Have you been advised already?"

"The submarine the Coast Guard intercepted in Colombian territorial waters?"

"Yes, a few hours ago I was informed by the President's office. Apparently International Thalassic chartered the sub. We've been in negotiation with them and they're offering to search for the *San José* at no cost to the government. Only if the project is successful and economically beneficial would repayment be made—as part of a percentage of the value of the salvage. "Dealing with Robert Hamilton we believe it is possible to secure the agreement."

"I met Hamilton a few hours ago, as well as the captain. It's important that the sub stays in port until we find out why it was submerged in Colombian territorial waters, and why their surface support ship was many miles away in international waters. They didn't even have their import papers in order. I hope to find out more tonight. I'm having dinner with Hamilton and the captain."

"Let me know. DAS, of course, is also inquiring into the background of Ocean Reconnaissance Fleet, since they filed suit against the government. After the lost at the Supreme Court, there were indications they might conduct a secret salvage operation. They're ruthless. You should make Hamilton aware of the people he is competing with," said Obregon.

Suddenly, the door burst open and a young lieutenant stood there, livid. "Two navy officers were found dead in the back of the supply building near Pier 10! They were found half an hour ago by another navy officer—both of them shot in the head!"

Commander Castellano, Robert Hamilton and Jack Swanson stayed until the Officers' Club closed, but their discussion became awkward. Castellano informed them that he had received all the certificates and import papers from their ship agent. They would be free to leave the base and visit Cartagena after he received authorization from Bogotá, which was expected in the next twenty-four hours. That meant Robert could travel to Bogotá and finalize the negotiations with the Colombian government.

They said good-bye, and Jack and Robert returned to the *Sealion*. As they boarded, they passed their two armed guards, Mark Salami and Benny Leeman. Salami was a forty-five-year-old high school dropout and ex-Navy man who had worked with the US Naval Combat Demolition Unit, in the Vietnam War. Tall, muscular and slightly overweight he was diamond hard, and did not confide in anyone, except for Benny Leeman.

Leeman was taller and seemed very powerful. He wore a gold bracelet on his wrist and a gold chain around his neck. His wrinkled sallow face gave the impression of emptiness.

Marine Explorations Company of California had hired them as guards for the surface support ship. Their only topics of conversation were guns and sex, depending on the hour of the day and the amount of alcohol they had consumed.

Awakened by a knock on his cabin door the next morning, Robert found Jack Swanson before him holding a piece of paper. "We've got a problem. Look at this note from Castellano."

Dear Captain Swanson, I must see you immediately. Come to my office at once and bring Hamilton. Commander Castellano.

"What on earth," Robert wondered. "I thought we had everything straightened out last night."

A digital clock read 6:15. Castellano was drinking coffee when they entered. "Please sit down," he gestured. He opened his desk drawer, and unfolded a cloth, revealing a officer's revolver. "Have you seen this before?"

"No," Robert and Jack answered simultaneously, surprise manifest on their faces.

"I would love to believe you," Castellano sighed. "But in that case, somebody is trying to implicate you in the murder of the two navy officers. They were killed two hundred meters from your sub yesterday afternoon. The gun was found by one of our guards in the galley of your sub. The serial number indicates that the gun belonged to one of the murdered navy officers. They worked on evaluating international proposals that were submitted for the search of the *San José*. Whether you know it or not, it is possible that one of your men is involved. We will make a full investigation of this case. Meantime, everybody is suspected!"

"Somebody is trying to frame us," Jack said.

Stunned, Robert crinkled up his eyes. "Who is he? and why?"

"When we know who," Castellano replied grimly, "we'll also know why."

"Obviously it's somebody who wants to delay us here, who doesn't want us to leave Cartagena," reasoned Robert. "We don't have any choice but to wait for the results of the criminal investigation. In the meantime, the government dithers among the different branches. Everyone's gotten into the act: the Ministries of Defense, DIMAR, Mines, Navy, the Attorney General, the negotiating committee and subcommittees, and even the Senate—" Robert was almost sputtering. "Each of them wants a say in to whether the contract for the *San José* salvage should be awarded to ITC."

"Bureaucracy at its best," Jack scowled.

After three days of worry that they would be more deeply implicated in the murders however improbable, Robert was summoned to Commander Castellano's office.

"Well, Mr. Hamilton, we've made progress," Castellano said.

"I hope it's good news, Commander?"

"We've received authorization from Bogotá for your release. And the government has agreed to resume negotiations with you. The sub and its support ship can remain at our base until you conclude your business there."

"Thank you, Commander. Does this mean you have found the murderer?"

"Nothing conclusive yet, except that we have determined you were not behind the killing. Why we came to that conclusion, I am not permitted to divulge."

"If Jack or I can do anything to help your investigation, just ask. We'd be happy to do anything we can."

Before Robert returned from Bogotá to Cartagena, he opened his lap top computer and wrote:

Dearest Ann:

Your two e-mails yesterday made me very happy. You have given me wonderful support during these difficult days; I wish you were here yesterday to celebrate with me the signing of the contract with the Colombian government. We are now the only group in the world authorized to search for and raise the San José.

Our agreement strikes a fair balance between the Colombian government and our consortium, as we had envisioned. The City of Cartagena will build a world-renowned museum that will be a legacy to the Colombian Spanish people and for all Ibero-American countries for generations to come. There'll be scholarships for marine archaeology, museum conservation, oceanography, marine geology, marine ecology, Colombian archeology, excavations and preservations and more.

My fingers are too tired to type all the benefits.

Just as we intended, information from the Materia Medicinal will be controlled by an international body, probably the United Nations. I've been driven by the hope that the knowledge to be gained will be readily accessible to all humanity.

Darling, I'm so happy, because concluding the agreement means we two can get together very soon.

How I wish we could be together here in Bogotá·, and perhaps climb Monserrate, the tallest mountain overlooking the city. I understand there is a lovely restaurant at the top. I think the city would charm you.

Tomorrow I will e-mail you from Cartagena as soon as I arrive.

Take good care of yourself. Remember, I need you and love you.

Robert

ONE early morning in July, off the coast of the Peninsula of Baru, Captain Jack Swanson surveyed his crew at work, pleased with their mechanical precision. There was no extraneous conversation, no distractions.

Forward, Ed Molloy watched the depth gauge go below six hundred feet. "Are we going to start leveling off soon?"

"We should wait until we get to eight hundred," responded the diving officer.

"We're at seven hundred."

"We're approaching eight hundred. Prepare for action!" ordered the captain.

As they surveyed the wreck, they mapped and recorded all the information.

"Look, I can see the bow and stern of the wreck!" exclaimed the diving officer.

"Most of the important treasure carried on old ships was in the stern castle," Robert added.

"Then that's where we begin excavating," said Jack.

With surface-supplied air, the divers worked for many hours at a time. Even in the warm waters of the shark-infested Caribbean, their neoprene suits were needed to keep them from becoming chilled after several hours in the water. The suits also protected them from coral cuts and scratches, stings from jellyfish and bites from small fish. During the excavation, large numbers of sea worms and other marine life were uncovered. The danger of attack by sharks and barracudas was always present. All divers involved in excavating the wreck knew the effects that years in the sea would have on everything. However, silver coins were sometimes mistaken for dark seashells. They pulled them aboard the salvage vessel with lines and lifting bags that raised heavy objects. The first cache of coins was lying in a tiny area that was laid open to the divers, with no pieces of hull or deck obstructing the excavation. They recovered all the visible coins, then expanded into the surrounding area.

They found amazing artifacts. The salvage vessel was rigged with heavy-lifting equipment to raise cannons. Flints from muskets with crosses etched in them dated the vessel to between 1680 and 1710. They used a plastic bag that they called the goodie bag, to send coins, musket balls and other small items to the surface. They also found anchors, but did not find the ship's bell or anything that would definitely identify the ship as the *San José*. For exploration at depths past the safe scuba range, the salvage vessel carried a two-man diving bell.

But things went terribly wrong when a bull shark about eight feet long grabbed a diver's foot and tried to pull it straight down. He pried himself free, then the blood thirsty shark circled back and bit him on his right thigh and finally devoured most of the diver's body. No one else would dive that day.

The next day, Captain Jack Swanson ordered the *Sealion* to continue with the exploration. The surface support ship deck was a blur of activity, bristling with modern technology necessary for the recovery of the sunken treasure.

A seven-ton submersible robot held precious items, its flexible arm equipped with tiny suction cups of flexible plastic. When the robot gingerly picked up its first gold coin, it fumbled, dropping it back onto the seabed instead of in the impromptu holding tank, an old chamber pot.

Among the treasures they brought to the deck were ceramic pots, a crate of three hundred-year-old iron shoes for mules, hundreds of other artifacts including portholes. The daylight slowly began to fade and the men were going to end their work for the day, when before long they were transfixed by the ship's bell. It confirmed that indeed it was the *San José*. Human skulls found on the deck of the *galléon*, were the only obvious signs of mishaps. That commanded a great celebration on the deck.

But the *Materia Medicinal* was not in sight.

The marine archaeologist and nautical historian of the team who were specialists in dating and restoring Spanish coins, and a 55-year-old diver, who had a knack for mixing caustic chemicals that could erase centuries of grime from ancients coins, started work on conserving the rescued treasures.

Conservation efforts continued around the clock to stabilize and protect fragile objects that had been immersed for almost three centuries. After cleaning, all items were measured, photographed and drawn, their images scanned and recorded onto CD's by the ship's computers. All details, including precise locations, were entered into the computerized database for the final archaeological report.

Items made of gold, silver or pewter were easy to identify and date. They found gold coins minted in Cartagena in 1697 and 1698, ten years before the *San José* went down. Gold and porcelain did not suffer from the immersion, and were recovered in a perfect state of preservation. But organic items, like wood, came under immediate attack from fungi, wood boring snails and various bacteria. Because they were exposed to salt water, some disintegrated. Organic objects they recovered were bathed in fresh water for two to four weeks. Iron and silver were corroded; but hard gemstones—sapphires, rubies, emeralds and agate—were recovered in good shape. Most glass bottles required very little cleaning.

After nine months of continuous excavation, it was evident that treasure recovered from the *San José* was the richest in history. But the whereabouts of the *Materia Medicinal* remained a mystery. Week after week they searched for it without success, even after examining every inch of the wreck.

Late in the afternoon of February 20, Al Taylor, a twenty-eight-year-old diver, dove some distance from the boat, and scanned the rocky ocean floor. Suddenly he blinked at an unbelievable sight: a cluster of big, greenish, log-like objects lay exposed at the bottom of the sea. There were three wooden barrels. He emerged from the surface with a joyful yell.

At first the crew thought sharks were attacking him; then they heard the words "*Materia Medicinal!*"

Later, two more barrels were found forty feet from the first group. For days, all other work slowed while they mapped and photographed the barrels. They used heavy lifting equipment and large metal baskets. Though some of them had disintegrated, exposing glass bottles, they were able to recover forty-nine bottles, four barrels containing ten large bottles and one only nine.

On the night that the last barrel was lifted to safety aboard the salvage vessel, Robert took a stroll on deck while most of the crew was asleep. In the night's peaceful, velvet beauty he thought of Ann. He thought of all the things that had happened to him in the past year and a half, how fortunate he was to find both — the woman he loved and the *San José*'s treasure. He didn't know what the future might hold⋯

Suddenly, he heard two planes overhead, circling around the vessel. He hurried down to the control room. "Jack, come up on deck."

"What's happening?"

"Look... See that plane? There isn't any reason for it to be there —not any *good* reason."

Jack picked up the nearest phone and dialed Commander Castellano's direct telephone line.

Lieutenant Arboleda came into Castellano's office at 6:15 p.m. "There is a telephone call from the *Auguste Piccard.* Captain Swanson says it's urgent."

“Alzaro, this is Jack. I’m sorry to disturb you, but there’s a plane overhead, circling like a bird of prey. It is one of yours?”

In the Control Room a radar specialist was examining some blips circled around his screen. He sounded the alarm, echoed a second later by the other operator. The officer of the watch hurried over to check the screen. Then he hailed the captain. “More than one aircraft, Sir.”

“Alzaro, our screens are showing blotches, lines and sparkles.”

“Give me your position. We’ll send three of our Coast Guard helicopters and three of our armed patrol cutters.”

“Roger!”

The execute order reached the *Santander* and the *Simon Bolivar* shortly thereafter. At the picket station, deckhand Jaramillo ordered a turn-in-sequence to the northwest. The *Magdalena* joined them three miles west of the hold point. Jaramillo watched her slide into line ahead, a trim and modern frigate in the lighter Colombian battle gray. The yellow, blue and red flag fluttered at her masthead. She fell astern of the *Simon Bolivar* just ahead of the *Santander*. The sea was empty. Not a blip of any kind showed on their screens as they crossed the invisible twelve-mile international line.

In Portobelo, Panama, Ernest Pohlmann, the German representative of Ocean Reconnaissance Fleet, was seated in his office with the telephone receiver to his ear. Palm trees surrounded the building property. Overhead rotating blades fanned the moist, heavy air, and an old computer hummed in the background.

“We have detected the sub and the support vessel!” a voice said through the receiver. “We’ve already informed the *Tiburón Negro* to intercept, to use artillery fire if necessary. According to Benny and Mark, there are five barrels containing bottles with the *Materia Medicinal* inside.”

“Well done, Arnold!” Ernest exclaimed. “Keep me informed. Frankfurt is very impatient.” Ernest wiped the perspiration from his forehead as he set the receiver down. He untied the collar of his white shirt and rolled up his sleeves. Opening the door of his office, he told his secretary, "I've got to go out for an hour or two."

Ernest left the white building on Calle Primavera in the heart of Portobelo, and walked a block and a half to the Tropicana bar near the Costume House. Panamanians in gleaming white shirts nipped down *cafecitos* and talked in loud, quick voices. In the back of the bar was a phone booth. Ernest entered and waited.

In Cartagena, Pedro Ramirez left La Fonda Antioqueña in San Martin Avenue, crossed the avenue to the Cartagena Real Hotel where he sat in a yellow phone booth and watched the lobby clock tick. He placed a call to a Portobelo number. "Hello. Ernest?"

"Yes, Pedro."

"I am willing to pay the Beaux Art Dealers half a million to transport five wooden barrels from Portobelo to Frankfurt," Ernest said carefully. "This will include the fee for your services for the entry of the barrels into Panama and Germany."

"These wouldn't be antiquities, would they?"

"Oh no! No, no! We do not compete! That is your territory." Ernest pressed a handkerchief nervously to his moist cheeks. "But if you want, we can pay you in underwater artifacts."

"I will ask."

Thank God, Ernest thought. He carefully detailed the movements that Pedro and his associates were to make in Panama and how the *Tiburon Negro* would link up with their BAD vessel. He repeated the instructions.

"Tomorrow, the same telephone, the same time," Pedro said, and hung up.

Ernest left the Cartagena Real Hotel, went up to his office, adjusted his glasses and hunched over his papers. He stared through the window at the tropical landscape, wiping his brow with his damp handkerchief — the harrowing days of anticipation would be over soon.

On nautical chart 408, which spans the vast sea-lanes of the Gulf of Mexico and the Caribbean, the progress of the *Auguste Piccard,* and her support vessel, appeared to be painfully slow. Yet the ship's pilot assured the captain and Robert that they were preceding at five knots toward the point of interception with the Colombian cutters. They were in the waters where the loot of plundered Spanish colonies once traversed — and where pirates plundered the plunderers three centuries ago, where Spanish *galléons* sailed eastward, laden with gold and silver, and where pirates pursued the convoy's stragglers under the skull and crossbones.

The support ship's radar indicated a vessel five thousand yards ahead. There was no vessel visible on the water, the sky was starlit and the moon was bright. The sea was calm — disturbed only by the turbulence of phosphorescence in the ship's wake. The *Tiburon Negro* closed in on her target, seven thousand yards away. Jack and Robert climbed the navigation bridge to look for the ship that the radar screen told them was there. All was dark. The support ship displayed the navigation lights of a larger vessel to conceal her true identity. Only subdued red lights in the chart house gave a sense of direction topside. The quartermasters plotted their approach from six thousand yards.

"Al, any sighting?" The sailor manning the huge binoculars on the flying bridge answered in the negative. "Anything on the night-scope?"

"Too faint, Captain. I just barely got it now. Roughly north, I think. But I need some time on that."

Robert looked at the intensity of the needle. "Yes, I can see a vessel approaching us — just where the radar found her."

"Range?"

"Three thousand yards, Sir."

"My God!" Robert whispered.

"Light plane overhead!" Al cried.

The plane disappeared as mysteriously as it had appeared.

"Getting louder! Captain! He is heading our way, I make him out to be four-five zero, more like four-five two, still real faint."

Minutes later the *Tiburon Negro* appeared clearly in the horizon.

"Full speed south. Keep the sub alongside!"

"We'll wait," ordered Jack. "The Colombian navy will be here soon. We can't escape that ship — it's too fast."

The *Tiburon Negro* hailed them at a distance of five hundred yards. "Offer no resistance, or we blow you up! We are boarding your vessel!" Its 50 mm machine guns were pointed at the deck of the support ship. A launch propelled by powerful outboard motors pulled alongside. Men swarmed up her side using ropes with grappling hooks.

Mark Salmi and Benny Leeman trained 15 mm machine guns on Jack and Robert. The captain broke his silence of incredulity with only one comment: "You bastards!"

In a few minutes the armed crew of the *Tiburon Negro* had taken up strategic positions throughout the support vessel. Jack and Robert were confined to the control room, where they were tied up with ropes. Two of the intruders entered the cabin where the *Materia Medicinal* barrels were stored and came face to face with Al Taylor and a .45 caliber pistol. The two men paused; two more men pushed into the cabin and the four of them overpowered Al. They carried away the five barrels, lowering them into the waiting launch. They left the rest of the armed crew in control of the support vessel—to loot the most valuable of the recovered artifacts.

Al Taylor was put into a rubber raft and set adrift without food or water. When the *Tiburon Negro's* crew returned to the support vessel, they conducted a search of the vessel and a body search of the vessel's crew; robbing them of all their armaments and communication devices and gaining access to the most archeological, artistic and historical artifacts. Then they returned to the *Tiburon Negro*, taking Ed Molloy with them. Without Ed and his equipment, the support ship could not communicate with the Colombian navy.

But long before the coast guard cutter appeared on the horizon, the *Tiburon Negro* had changed its registry markings and disappeared into the wide expanse of the Caribbean.

The call came in the middle of the night. Ernest Pohlmann listened. He could hardly believe his ears. *They have the Materia Medicinal and some treasure.* At last!

"All went well," Pedro said tersely. "We will transfer the cargo to our Lear jet in San Blas Islands. But Ernest, you must understand, for us to transport it to Frankfurt, we'll need one million US up front in San Blas and another million in Frankfurt, plus of course all the artifacts, which will remain in Panama for a while."

"But Pedro, we already made a deal. It was going to be half a million plus the artifacts."

"Not after we read the newspapers in Colombia, *El Tiempo, El Espectador, El Caribe.* All of them have reported on the *Materia Medicinal* and the rest of the treasures."

Ernest was trying to force himself to stay calm.

"So you understand," said Pedro. "With publicity in the media, our job becomes substantially more difficult; come with half a million to the Kuna Inn in San Blas by tomorrow morning, and you can inspect the cargo. You can take a plane from Portobelo at 9:40, and you'll be in San Blas in half an hour. Ask for Jaime Rodriguez, he will be waiting for you in Room 103. Don't be late. You have twenty-four hours to bring the other half million. In San Blas you will receive specific instructions on how your people in Frankfurt can retrieve the cargo. Have a good sleep, Ernest."

Ernest's hand shook as he replaced the receiver.

At 7 a.m. a black Ford was waiting at the curb when Ernest Pohlmann left his office. A tall man with an olive complexion sat in the back seat. The Panamanian driver got out of the car and gave Ernest a small smile. "Good morning, *Señor* Pohlmann, my boss wants to talk to you. Please get in."

"But I can't right now. I am busy."

"You are never too busy to talk to my boss."

The driver was a large hulk of a man, with a grandiose, flowing mustache and the body of a tank. Ernest's heart began to pound. "I can't, Sir. I'm late for—"

"Get in."

Ernest got into the large Ford. The man in back said to the driver, "Go around the block." Ernest was filled with sudden panic. "My name is Pablo Martinez."

Ernest took a deep breath. "Do you know me?"

Pablo was grinning. "Of course I know you, Mr. Pohlmann." He looked at Ernest with penetrating eyes. "You asked us to deliver five barrels to Frankfurt, and now the story is in every newspaper in America and Europe. Interpol, the FBI, the Colombian DAS and even the military in the Canal Zone are involved. Don't shit me, you know you caused me and my friend lot of trouble."

"I'm sorry I...Forget it. But you'd better pay the one million US dollars, or my friends will cut off your nuts and feed them to the dogs. I want you to go to San Blas this morning with the half million, and the rest is to be delivered as agreed. We deal with many delicate and unusual cargoes, but this is something else."

"Besides, you are paying us with looted artifacts."

"I never intended to get you into trouble, *Señor* Martinez," said Ernest, trembling.

"You can cut the bullshit, Ernest. Pedro wants to know what kind of games you're playing."

"Games? What are you talking about?"

"The US, Colombian, Panamanian and German governments are all involved in trying to find your five barrels. You gave us no warning."

"Besides, our business is very difficult. The looted artifacts we sold mostly in Germany with the help of Berthold Beitz and Frau Weidfeldt. We all were shocked at BAD, hearing about the dreadful things that happened to both of them. To die like that is just awful. I don't want that to happen to you," said Pablo, staring at him.

Ernest was barely able to speak. "Thank you, *Señor* Martinez."

"Let's work together and you will live a long life." He leaned forward and told the driver to stop the car. He gave Ernest a frozen smile and said: "You'd better hurry to the airport and catch your plane."

Ernest jumped out of the car and walked to his office. Pablo Martinez's words were still ringing in his ears — he had no doubt that Martinez could carry out his threat. What in God's name could have gone wrong at sea? Everything had been so carefully planned. But there was no time to speculate. The important thing now was to deliver the first million in Panama and inform his boss in Frankfurt that they must deliver another million before taking possession of the cargo.

His secretary Juanita walked into the office. "Your eight o'clock appointment is waiting. Shall I send him in?"

"No! Cancel all my appointments. I won't be back for a couple of days." He picked up the phone and minutes later he was on his way to the airport.

ANN sat on the couch of her living room, reading the headlines of *The Observer.* "Caribbean piracy, Precious Cargo Stolen, Outlaw Vessel Disappears."

The telephone rang and her mother picked up the receiver. "Ann! A call for you!" The sound of her mother's voice flowed over Ann in waves, but she was not listening to the words. She was too numbed by what she read. *Oh, my God! Where is Robert? Why haven't I heard from him?*

Vaguely, through the thunder of her pounding heart, she heard her mother's voice again. "Ann, come to the phone."

She raised her head. "Who's calling?"

"Robert!"

Ann sprang from the couch and grabbed the phone. "Robert, are you OK?"

"Yes, my love, I'm in Cartagena. The Colombian navy saved us, thank God, but the *Materia Medicinal* is gone as well as some of the treasure."

"Oh, Robert, please, I'm so worried about you. Can't you come to England now?"

"I cannot leave until we find the *Materia Medicinal,*" said Robert. "The Colombian navy and air force are trying to find the thieves. Two men from our own crew were involved. Imagine!

The US Embassy and the US Coast Guard are involved. It's critical I remain here."

"Then I will go to Cartagena!" Ann declared.

"Wonderful idea." The warmth in his voice brought tears to her eyes. "Please come. How soon can you get away?"

"Darling, I'll be there within hours."

Robert laughed. "How I miss you, Ann."

"Oh, Robert your e-mails were the only thing that kept me going. The feelings I've had inside—I never thought it was possible to love someone the way I do."

"Sweetheart, I don't know what to say first. Will you marry me when you come to Cartagena? Whether or not we find the *Materia Medicinal,* I want you to be my wife."

Tears spilled down Ann's cheeks as she clutched the receiver. "I am yours forever, Robert. The answer is Yes!"

"Then this is what I want us to do. There's a cloister on the summit of the hill. The Augustin priests built it in the seventeenth century. Near the courtyard, in front of the convent, is the church of Pedro Claver. If you like it, we will get married there. I've never been religious, but after I've seen the stars and the sun out here at sea, it's hard not to believe in God. I'm a sort of pale Christian, but I love that church. Wait until you see it."

"We can talk about this when you come. I love you, Ann."

"See you soon, darling."

Ann threw her arms around her mother, weeping and laughing at the same time.

"Why, Ann, what's wrong? Ann?"

"Nothing, Mother. I'm very, very happy. Robert asked me to marry him."

IN the middle of the night Ed Molloy was screaming in his hospital bed, drenched in sweat.

The nurse on the night watch hurried into the room. Ed was turning and tossing, his eyes tightly closed. "No!" he screamed. "Don't! Don't leave me!" The nurse put her arms around him and shook him gently. "Mr. Molloy, it's all right. It's all right, Mr. Molloy."

Ed blinked. His breath came in gasps. "They left me there in the water! They abandoned me to the sharks! Right off San Blas Island! I couldn't get to shore! The fins—the great teeth..."

"It was only a dream," the nurse crooned. "You had a bad dream."

Ed shook his head slowly. His body trembled. "No, it wasn't a dream. It was real. They tried to kill me."

The nurse frowned. "Who tried to kill you?"

"The cartel — BAD. I remember it, now. They talked of killing me. I heard them say that instead of taking me to the San Blas Island with the treasure, they would feed me to the sharks. Then they put me in the rubber raft without food or water."

"Has your memory returned? For days you haven't been able to remember how you got here."

"Yes — it just came into my mind! Call the police. I must get this information to the investigators!" But he grabbed her sleeve as she straightened. "No. No. Don't go, don't leave me alone."

"It's all right, Mr. Molloy, but I must let the doctor know your memory has returned."

"No! Please, maybe it was a dream after all." He looked nervously toward the door, toward the shaded windows.

The nurse checked her watch. "It's time for your sedative."

The doctor on night duty arrived late at the American Military Base Hospital — his first day at work after two weeks of vacation. "Good evening, Cecilia. I'm ready to take on the world again; anybody critical?"

"Molloy. His condition is stable now, and he is out of immediate danger. He was found in a rubber raft adrift the ocean. He has severe sunburn over twenty-five percent of his body, and suffered from dehydration, as well as hypothermia. He had excruciating pain in his chest and difficulty breathing. For a few days he had amnesia."

"The effect of dehydration on the human body is always unpredictable," said Dr. Baker. "Often, loss of memory and/or hallucinations occur."

"When he came to the hospital his eyes were real bad. After I cleaned them, I started on his ears and mouth. He was so weak that he couldn't swallow. But now, he is much better."

"I'll take a look at him as soon as I've caught up on the paperwork."

Later that evening, when Cecilia the night nurse took away the remains of Ed's dinner, he demanded that she call Cartagena. Over the objections of the head nurse, who didn't like her telephone to be used except for emergencies, Cecilia let Ed place a call to the offices of Alzaro Castellano. He let the phone ring and ring until a voice at the other end of the line answered.

"This is Ed Molloy, I want to talk with Commander Alzaro Castellano. I am calling from the Canal Zone Hospital."

"This is Lieutenant Arboleda, Sir. The Commander is not here, but he can call you back shortly."

"I want to talk with Commander Castellano and with Robert Hamilton."

"Just a moment, Mr. Hamilton is down the hall."

Robert hurried to the phone. "Ed, it's wonderful to hear your voice! How do you feel? We were going to try to call you tomorrow," Robert gushed. "The papers are filled with news of your miraculous rescue!"

"Robert, listen! I think I know where the *M* — where the object of our special interest is, but I don't dare tell you unless it's in person."

"Are you in danger? Isn't the hospital safe?"

"I don't know," Ed whispered furtively, "but we can't take any chances."

"I will fly down tomorrow morning then."

At the farthest tip of Old Panama City, on a finger of land extending into the deep blue bay of Panama, with Punta Patilla in the distance, stood a deserted industrial building within the shadows of its doors, where two men spoke in low voices.

"It must look like an accident," Pablo Martinez said.

"Certainly. Would you prefer an accident in the bathroom? He can break his neck falling from his bed, or he could take an overdose of medication, or he could fall asleep in bed with a lighted cigarette."

Martinez frowned. His companion stopped. Martinez's temper was well known.

"Yes, sir, I can arrange an accident. No one will ever know."

"I'll leave the method to you. All that matters is that he dies."

Later that evening, Emma, the head nurse, answered the telephone. Her body stiffened when she heard the voice at the other end of the line.

"All right, let's meet at the Café in Miraflores in an hour. Yes··· I'll come alone. Don't worry···. I'll manage!" Slowly, Emma replaced the receiver and buzzed Cecilia. When the young nurse came hurrying to the nurse's station, Emma rose and reached for her handbag. "I must go out. Will you cover for me? I'll be back in less than two hours. Don't leave Molloy alone for any reason. He mustn't speak with anyone. No visitors, no telephone calls under any circumstances." Emma leaned towards the girl. The menace in her eyes was inescapable. "I will hold you personally responsible if anything happens."

Cecilia swallowed nervously. "Yes, ma···'am."

A sedan from the Colombian Embassy picked up Robert Hamilton and Jack Swanson and drove them to the Canal Zone, in the growing heat of the morning. The forty-five minute ride to the Zone, bypassing the center of Panama City, took him along the Panama Canal. They could see the Pacific Ocean ahead, but they could not appreciate the view. Robert had only two things on his mind: Sir Ronald Harris's arrangements for Ann's trip and the *Materia Medicinal* — Ed Molloy might be a good start.

Robert had known Ed for many years, and had always admired him for his dependable sense of right and wrong. Lean, tall with a friendly smile for every one, and with a love for adventure, he was an active, outgoing, companionable man. Now he was confined to a hospital bed.

At the sight of the beautiful ocean, Robert's thoughts turned again to Ann. At times he feared his feeling for her bordered on obsession. He had never known a woman like her. He could barely control his eagerness to be reunited with her in Colombia.

After they passed Corozal, Ft. Clayton and Miraflores, the old highway was practically empty. The driver got off at the exit and slowed for the guard post at the main entrance to the American military base, at the Canal Zone. "These bases are in the process of reverting to the government of Panama," said the driver. The barrier was down.

A guard looked inside the car.

"Your names, gentlemen."

"Robert Hamilton, Jack Swanson."

"I.D., please."

Robert and Jack gave him their passports while the Embassy's driver handed over his Colombian Embassy I.D.

"Okay Antonio," the guard said to the driver. "Pull up to the main entrance. Somebody will be there to meet you."

They drove to the main entrance, through mostly empty parking lots shaded by palm trees. The armed guard who was waiting for them asked, "Who are you visiting?"

"Mr. Ed Molloy. He is a patient at the hospital."

"Please follow my car." He made a call from his mobile.

The drive was a long one, over winding roads that meandered through the lush tropical forest. They passed various military installations on the way, Gatum Lake in the distance. At the hospital, another soldier waited for them under the canopied main entrance. They were waved right through and proceeded to the elevator. As they stepped out the elevator onto the third floor, they encountered Dr. David Eaton of the Navy Medical Corps, waiting for them, with bright blue eyes and an easy manner. Eaton was a New Englander who had joined the Navy to see more of the world than was possible from an office in Gloucester, Massachusetts. Robert warmed to him at once.

"I received a fax from the American Embassy in Bogotá, informing me of your visit, Mr. Hamilton. I am afraid I don't have good news for you. Mr. Molloy is not doing well."

"May we see him?"

"Certainly." Dr. Eaton led them back down the corridor.

Half of the floor was set up for intensive care units. Unit 4 was a room thirty feet square. Of the five beds, only one was occupied. Ed was almost totally concealed by the oxygen mask covering his face. The rest of his body was fully draped, an I.V. standing next to the bed, its bottles of fluid merging in a single line that led under the cover. They could recognize him only by a thatch of brown hair.

A nurse dressed in surgical greens stood at the foot of the bed. Her dark eyes, locked on the electrocardiograph readout over the patient's head, lowered momentarily to make a notation in his chart. On the far side of the bed was a machine whose function was not immediately obvious.

"How is he?" Robert murmured.

"Critical," Dr. Eaton replied. "Yesterday he was recuperating beautifully. We thought that he might be able to leave the hospital soon but last night his condition deteriorated rapidly. It's a miracle he's still alive. He was in the water for a long time, at least for ten hours. On admission, his core temperature was 72.8° Fahrenheit. But soon he started to get better. I've read about many hypothermia cases in medical journals, but this is the first case I know where a patient recuperated and then relapsed so suddenly."

"Prognosis?" Robert asked, gazing at Ed's inert body.

Dr. Eaton shrugged. "Hard to say. From time to time he seems to understand what is happening and tries to communicate. He's in superb physical condition with a particularly strong heart. We have the hypothermia pretty much under control now. The problem is, with hypothermia, so many things can go wrong at once. We have to fight a number of separate battles against different systemic enemies."

"Dr. Eaton, is it possible to let him know that we are here?"

"You can try, but I'm afraid you can't talk to him for more than few minutes and only one at a time."

"Robert, you go ahead," Jack said.

Robert bent down close to Molloy and whispered in his ear: "Ed, it's me, Robert."

Ed's eyes fluttered open, vague and unfocused. He grabbed Robert's arm with a feeble hand. "Emma tried to kill me! Trust Cecilia, not Emma. She has a letter for you. It is very important." He stopped, exhausted, his eyes closing. Robert looked up.

Another man was pacing down the hall, younger than Dr. Eaton and shorter. He had a white lab coat over his greens. and he carried a metal chart. He entered the room and said, "We must let him rest. You must leave now."

Robert went out of the room and found Dr. Eaton in the hall. "Doctor Eaton. What is going on? Tell me what you know about what happened to him."

"A US helicopter on patrol off a frigate spotted him in the water on a rubber raft. But after some hours, the raft lost air, possibly due to a shark attack. They didn't have any rescue gear aboard, so they marked the spot with a dye marker and went back to their ship. Then some volunteer went after him. They loaded him off the Panama City coast and flew him to this base. He was in the water for over five hours."

"Who is Cecilia, may we speak with her?"

"I believe she usually works the night shift on the medical floor."

Robert walked along the corridor to a nursing station and dialed the telephone. A few minutes later Dr. Eaton said, "You are in luck, she's working today on the day's shift. Go to the fourth floor and ask for her at the nursing station."

An attractive girl with long black hair in a nurse's uniform came to the nurse's station where Robert and Jack were waiting. "My name is Cecilia. Which one of you is Mr. Hamilton?"

"I am," answered Robert.

"I'm so glad you came, Mr. Hamilton. Mr. Molloy told me so much about you before his health worsened. Come with me, please."

They entered a small office full of patient files. "I have this letter for you. Mr. Molloy told me that if anything happened to him, I was to give you this letter. Otherwise, I was to return it to him unopened. He said that it was very urgent. He looked very worried yesterday, almost as if he knew something was going to happen to him."

"Thank you very much. This letter might be invaluable." Robert put the white envelope in his breast pocket.

"I want to ask you who is Emma. Mr. Molloy is afraid of her," said Robert.

"The head nurse, a very malicious woman." Cecilia's voice was strangled whisper.

"In the ICU this morning, he told me that after the head nurse gave him some food last night, a terrible pain hit his chest and darkness overcame him. When he woke up he found himself under an oxygen tent." She stopped, and tears slid down her cheeks. "I think somebody wants to kill Mr. Molloy, but I don't have any proof. Mr. Molloy told me that I could trust you, and that's why I'm talking to you this way. Maybe it's all my imagination, and I'm sorry for how I am carrying on, but I don't have anyone else I can confide my fears to."

Suddenly the door opened and Emma walked in. "Excuse the interruption, gentlemen, but Cecilia is needed elsewhere immediately." Cecilia cast Robert a look of despair.

"Come, Cecilia, don't keep me waiting." The young nurse shook visibly as she rose.

"Sorry," she whispered to Robert. "Good-bye."

Cecilia resignedly followed Emma out of the room.

Helpless, Jack and Robert watched them go.

The De Lesseps Nursing Home was an ugly stone structure, built in the last century by the French, during their attempt to construct the Panama Canal. Now it housed elderly American and Chinese, who still remembered their fathers working on the construction of the Gatum Lock. Its walls held the overpowering stench of aging, sickness and death.

Cecilia stood on the dingy green carpet of the hall. A massive, olive-complexioned man came down the corridor. His haggard countenance was pale, and his skin hung loosely on his face. His head leaned stubbornly forward on a sturdy neck. Powerful, muscular arms hung from his wide shoulders. "What were you talking about with those two men in the file room?"

She stood looking at him, shaking. "Nothing." He grabbed her arm and pulled her down the corridor.

"Let me go! Let me go! You're hurting me!"

The man opened a metal door and pushed Cecilia inside, slamming her hard against the wall. "What the hell are you doing?"

"Nothing," she gasped, backing up. "Let me go!"

Before she could scream, the man lashed out with one hand, slamming it over her mouth and shoving her against the brick wall.

Her eyes bulged. He struck her in the temple with his other fist, a sharp hard punch that darkened her vision. She whimpered softly, her knees buckled and she dropped on to the hard stone floor. She could feel her lip going numb — the salty flow of blood in her throat. Her head snapped back, her body sagged, and she lay there unconscious until her heart almost stopped its rhythmic contractions.

Lying in darkness, she was deprived of virtually all her senses. A hot pulsing pain filled her head. The urge to escape grew overpowering, she lost the concept of time. After she tried to stand up several times without success, she dragged her body towards an imperceptible streak of light. She was able to propel herself forward, a few inches at a time. If she gathered any strength, she was not aware of it. Her stomach knotted with nausea. She drew a deep breath just as the door opened, revealing a blurred figure in the background.

The figure entered the room as Cecilia's eyes adjusted to the light.

Cecilia squeezed her eyes shut for a second, and when she opened them she saw Emma standing there. Her sight sent a shiver through her body.

Emma leaned forward. "Let me tell you something, Cecilia. I've been keeping an eye on you, I've talked with some people you work with and we don't want you to snoop on us anymore."

Cecilia tried to say something, but her throat was too dry. She was numb with fear. Finally she managed to utter "Please don't hurt me!"

"You make another sound, and you'll never see your mother again: but if you let me inject you with this marvelous drug, you will forget what has happened, and we will return you safe and sound to your mother."

Emma extracted a hypodermic syringe from her handbag, and slowly lifted Cecilia's inert arm.

Meanwhile, Robert and Jack Swanson stood uncertainly at the nurse's station as Dr. Eaton hurried up to them. "Mr. Hamilton, Mr. Swanson, please come back with me to my office." They followed him to his office. Dr. Eaton flipped on the lights, and threw his white jacket on a chair. "Please sit down, gentlemen. We're all alone now, so I can tell you what we've discovered. Somebody tried to poison Mr. Molloy. Our laboratory has detected traces of arsenic in his urine. That explains the sudden onset of his symptoms right after he ate."

"Poison? Are you sure?" Robert said.

"Our toxicology department found traces of arsenious oxide, not only in his urine but also in his feces. Arsenious oxide or white arsenic exists in the form of a white powder resembling powdered sugar. When mixed with sugar it's almost tasteless. We've removed what we could from Mr. Molloy's stomach and are administering antidotes."

"Will he recover?" asked Jack.

"Yes, I think our treatment is taking hold." Dr. Eaton flipped open the chart. "White counts are coming back. I put a unit of whole blood in him two hours ago. Temperature twenty minutes ago was 100.8. It's been fluctuating for the past hour and a half. His heartbeat sounds pretty good. When you saw him, his symptoms of rapid, feeble pulse and delirium resembled extreme hypothermia. But as soon as we detected arsenic, we immediately changed the treatment and gave him intravenous injections of calcium chloride."

A soft knock sounded at the door, and a man in a green blouse entered. "Mr. Ramirez," Dr. Eaton said, "don't leave Mr. Molloy unattended at any time. Have a corpsman come to pick up the blood samples. If you have to go to the toilet, get someone to relieve you first."

"Yes, doctor."

"No more screwing around, Mr. Ramirez. You break the rules again, and you are off the floor for good. Do you understand?"

"Yes, Doctor, Please accept my apologies."

Dr. Eaton waited until the door closed. Then he turned to Robert and Jack. "I cannot take any chances. Somebody wants to kill Mr. Molloy, and as soon as he shows enough improvement, we are going to fly him back to the States. We're already making arrangements for his return, and we have notified his family. I just notified South-Com—the US Southern command. "Their investigators will find out who is responsible."

"Can you help us get in touch with the authorities?" asked Robert. "We believe we have some information that can help the investigation."

"Certainly."

Robert rose. "I'm afraid Jack and I have to return to the city."

"Are you free this evening?" Dr. Eaton asked. "If you can meet me at the Union Club at nine o'clock, I'm having dinner with a friend, an official from the US Embassy. Perhaps he can steer you in the right direction."

"Thank you. We'd be delighted."

The shadows lengthened across the carefully manicured grass of the hospital compound, as the sedan from the Colombian Embassy drew up beside them.

"Antonio, please take us to the Continental Hotel," Robert said. He turned to Jack Swanson. "I haven't had the opportunity to show you Molloy's letter." He handed Swanson the white envelope:

Dear Robert: I hope that this letter reaches you.

The Tiburón Negro was on its way to San Blas Islands with the Materia Medicinal, when they abandoned me in the middle of the ocean.

A man by the name of Pablo Martinez from the BAD cartel arranged for air transportation of the cargo to Germany. Very dangerous people, be very careful.

You can trust Cecilia 100%.

I hope I will be still alive when you receive this, I fear for my life.

God bless you and good luck.

Ed.

They were moving slowly down the road of the Canal Zone, a strip of land five miles on either side of the waterway, where coconut trees grew amid the American houses.

Robert was concentrating on the view of the ocean as they

passed over the Bridge of the Americas that spanned the canal. Suddenly, he saw a black limousine beside them, turning toward them. Antonio had no time to react before the impact. The sedan was jolted and slid sideways towards the guard-rail, the tires slipping on the smooth steel deck of the bridge. Forty meters below, the dark blue waters of the ocean gleamed. The car hit the guardrail and slid along it for twenty or thirty feet without losing contact. To the sound of grinding-screeching-scraping of metal against metal, sprinkles of golden sparks flew up, tumbling out into the abyss.

Antonio spun the wheel, took his foot off the gas, and tried to disengage the tires from the guardrail. The black limousine pulled away and sped ahead. It took only a few seconds from the initial impact until the sedan was back on the steel road deck, but it seemed to them an agonizing lifetime. Antonio, sick to his stomach, stopped the car, shaking and dripping with sweat. He sat clutching the steering wheel, gulping for air in an attempt to keep from vomiting.

"They tried to kill us," Robert exclaimed. Jack opened his door and stepped out, feeling the full blast of the humid hot air. Robert and Antonio got out behind him; they stood looking at the damage of the doors and front fender.

"*Caramba*!" Antonio exclaimed.

A shot was heard coming from the black limousine, that was now traveling in the opposite direction. Antonio fell down on the metal deck of the bridge.

"He's been shot!" Robert cried.

Hastily, Robert and Jack lifted Antonio into the car. Robert took the wheel and they sped away toward the center of the city.

Grimacing in pain, Antonio lifted the mobile and gave it to Robert for him to call the Colombian embassy. He was directed to the emergency room of a local hospital, where officials of the embassy would be waiting.

They arrived at the business district of Panama City. At the next traffic light the black limousine appeared again from nowhere, pulling behind them. Through the rear-view mirror Robert saw the doors open, on both side of the limousine. Two men got out and hurried toward their car. Robert tightened his grip on the wheel and with a burst of acceleration made for the narrow opening in the rush hour traffic, forcing a Ford and a Mazda out of the way and shooting ahead. At the intersection, he pressed on the accelerator, ignoring the red light and the horns of a hundred cars. By a hotel on a corner, Robert hesitated, and suddenly pulled over to the curb. Jack stepped out of the car, and moving through the crowd, hailed the policeman standing in front. As Jack turned back to point at the two men, he saw them running away and then disappearing through the crowds. A few minutes later, a police car escorted them to the hospital.

At the hospital Jack and Robert slumped into their waiting room seats in exhaustion, while attendants and technicians surrounded Antonio and wheeled him away. They sat in silence, drinking coffee.

A doctor walked towards them, his gown still streaked with blood. "It's going to be all right," he said. "He will live."

"Thank God!" Robert murmured.

At nine o'clock, Robert and Jack arrived in a taxi in front of the Union Club across the bay from the old city. The club had wide tropical verandahs, a luxurious dining room, a bar with dark wood, polished glass doors and windows like portholes, and comfortable leather chairs. A man with a red jacket, golden buttons and white pants, guided them to a private dining room.

"I'm glad you could come," said Dr. Eaton. "Let me introduce you to Tom Hampton from the American Embassy."

"Please sit down. Would you like a drink? The piña coladas here at the club are exceptional."

"I could really use one, after what we're just been through," said Jack. "This afternoon on our way back from the hospital we were pushed off the bridge by a limousine and shot at by one of its passengers."

"My God!" Dr. Eaton cried. "Were you hurt?"

"Our driver was shot in the leg. But he'll be fine."

Dr. Eaton nodded gravely. "There are very dangerous people in Panama, plenty of them. Some years ago, Panama was credited with freezing fifty-two suspected money laundering accounts in eighteen Panamanian banks."

"We would like to get in touch with the right person at the DEA," said Robert. "The Dealers Enforcement Association ought to be central to this case."

"I'm working for a branch of the secret service attached to the US embassy," said Tom, "but I suggest you talk with Doug Young. He is a high-ranking DEA officer also attached to the US Embassy. If you'd like, I can ask him to join us here. He lives nearby."

"If it is not too late for him, we'd appreciate his help."

Hampton rose and went to make the call.

"By the way," Eaton said, "Ed Molloy sends you his regards. He is getting better by the minute and we are planning to fly him home in the next three days." Dr. Eaton stuffed tobacco into the bowl of a battered old pipe. "He asked if you'd received his letter about Cecilia, the nurse. I tried to contact her and was told she'd left the hospital. I called her at home an hour ago, but her mother told me that she had not arrived. I will try again later."

"Please give her our regards when you talk to her," said Robert.

A few minutes later Hampton returned to the table. "Doug Young is on his way." He sat back in his chair and beckoned the waiter for another drink.

Within ten minutes a disheveled, white-haired man in his early sixties, who dressed like a professor, flung open the door of the private room.

Hampton rose. "Thanks for coming, Doug, I believe you have already met Dr. Eaton? Let me introduce Robert Hamilton and Jack Swanson."

"Mr. Young, is the DEA involved in any official capacity in the *San José*'s case?" asked Robert.

Hampton nodded "Yes, as an enforcing agency, this case falls under our jurisdiction. Ed Molloy's near assassination prompted the DEA to investigate the piracy and hijacking of your support vessel. The U.S. Coast Guard will board and seize the *Tiburón Negro* when it is found."

"As I mentioned to Mr. Hampton, we have information that leads us to believe that art traffickers were involved in the hijacking," said Robert.

"May I ask what makes you believe that?" Young said, folding his wrinkled hands.

"This letter from Ed Molloy." Robert handed a white envelope to Young.

Young scanned the white paper for few minutes, his bushy eyebrows furled in concern. "Mr. Hamilton, if indeed BAD is a cartel of art dealers and is involved, you must let us handle the case without getting involved yourselves. We are dealing with very unscrupulous people—they could be connected to the richest and most powerful men in Panama."

"Mr. Young, we appreciate your efforts and your concern for our safety. But we can't promise that we're going to abandon our own investigation. We will keep you informed of our findings and we hope you do the same. We need your support to find the *Materia Medicinal*. In other words, we could work as a partnership in this investigation," said Robert.

"I wish I could convince you not to risk your lives. Do keep us informed and we will do likewise. If you need protection, please call me at this number," said Young.

"Mr. Young, where do you think they will sell the treasure?" Robert asked.

Young said, "We still have a few minutes to dinner. Because looting and smuggling are illegal in most source countries, there is no incentive to dig up antiquities without a commercial motive. The demand comes from collectors who, through the dealers, are willing to pay for the product.

The looters respond to the demand by creating a supply."

"How the market does operate? Dr. Eaton asked.

"The antiquities market is a fascinating case of a quasi-black market, or a 'double market.' Once the material gets to a market country usually in the West, such as the United States, United Kingdom, Germany, but also Japan, it is often legally traded; in other words, most market countries do not enforce the antiquities legislation of the source countries. Thus the loot starts out illegal and ends up legal.

"Who profits most? Robert asked.

"The looters, who take most of the risks, earn the least. The dealers, who arrange the trade and often the looting, too, make the most. Everyone agrees that looting is bad. Yet, in many art-importing countries, collecting looted material is a matter of pride and even honor. Collectors are praised for their enthusiasm and passion, and museums are treated as secular churches of culture.

"Tom and I have to go, I'm afraid, but please remember that we are ready to help you in any way we can," said Young as both stood up to leave.

"Let's move into the dining room," suggested Dr. Eaton.

Candlelight diffused through crystal lanterns flowed delicately over the flagstone patio. In one corner a pianist mourned nostalgically a Spanish bolero. Under the wicker chairs, spirals of incense smoldered, keeping the mosquitoes at bay and mixing with the pervasive aroma of the ocean.

After an excellent dinner a uniformed doorman escorted them to Dr. Eaton's Mercedes.

Dr. Eaton dropped his passengers off at the Panama Hotel. "We will be in touch."

THE charter company of Pablo Martinez and Jaime Rodriguez, Aviones Panameños—operated out of a large hangar at Paitilla Airport, on the bay in Panama City. Looted works of art and antiquities flowed in, overlapping and duplicating a clandestine network. Only ten minutes from the banking district on a straight shot up 50th Avenue, was the airport of choice for the private flights of Panamanian and foreign businessmen.

DE Havilland DASH 7 Beechcrafts capable of making trips to Florida in six hours flew regular passenger service every hour on the hour from Panama City to the San Blas Islands. The service included a stay at Kora Inn with water skiing, surfboarding, skin-diving, big game hunting, and the Cuna Indians thrown in. It was on one of those tourist flights that Robert and Jack arrived in San Blas the next morning.

For Martinez, transporting loot from the high seas to San Blas and then to Germany was a profitable sideline. But international coverage of the hijacking on the high seas forced him to take more interest in this operation — it was also an opportunity. It gave him and Pharma Frankfuter a chance to get to know one another.

Crates of treasure were stored in a building until they could be shipped to an air strip near Warsaw, Poland, taken from there by train to Berlin, then by truck to their ultimate destination,

Frankfurt. The route was a familiar one. The plane would carry looted art in one direction and would return with AK-47 automatic rifles produced in Russia. For the first leg, Pablo recruited two young Panamanian pilots he had known from the day he started Aviones Panameños. Armando Azuero and Cesar Chavez were hustlers who hung around airports, always available for odd jobs. They had a reputation as bushwhacker pilots who could land and take off anywhere. Fearless. They had met Mark Salmi and Benny Leeman before the latter entered the service of Pharma Frankfuter. The four had trained together at an American base in the Canal Zone, where they had taken courses with a naval demolition unit. All liked the dangerous work and good money.

"You must leave tomorrow morning with the cargo. Nothing can delay your mission to Poland," Pablo Martinez told his men.

At the airstrip, BAD cartel people were in a hurry to load the plane. When Ernest Pohlmann paid Jaime Rodriguez his one million dollars, Pablo Martinez sent Armando to the San Blas islands in his own plane to collect the *Materia Medicinal*. While the BAD's men were loading it, Robert and Jack came through the entrance of the Kora Inn, an entrance decorated with a profusion of tropical plants and flowers. At one of the corners was a finely appointed aviary, with parrots, macaws and other tropical birds.

"Jack, see that man standing at the entrance?" asked Robert, grabbing his sleeve. Robert recognized him as the one who drove the limousine that tried to kill them.

"Let's get out of here!" Jack said, also recognizing him.

They walked briskly toward a mezzanine where they could observe him without being seen.

A large clock chimed nine.

"We must find out if he is staying in this hotel," Robert said.

"I am going to find out who is he and where he's staying. I'll be back."

"Be careful," Robert called after him.

Jack descended the wooden stairs. At the information desk,

Jack waited impatiently for a uniformed Indian-looking man to finish giving directions to a young female tourist. Extracting a fifty-dollar bill from his wallet he said, "This is yours if you find out for me who that man is at the door and if he is staying here."

"That's easy. For another I'll introduce you. His name is Pablo Martinez, he is my boss and the owner of the hotel."

"I'll give you another fifty if you don't introduce me to him and another fifty if you don't tell him that I asked about him. If you work with me, you could have a little fortune. So will you cooperate with me?" Jack asked.

"Yes, sir," the man responded. "I will work with you for a while."

"His room number?"

"Suite 400, the best room in the hotel."

"How long is he staying here?"

"He leaves tomorrow night for Panama City."

"That's all I want to know for now." Jack pulled out an additional $100. "A deal is a deal."

"Yes, sir. *A sus ordenes.*"

Jack returned to Robert. "I think we have what we need. His name is Pablo Martinez and he's the owner of the hotel."

Just then, Martinez got into a green Cadillac and his driver sped away. The morning sun hung low, a metallic disk beyond the haze. Water stood in placid pools in the street after the tropical storm the night before. Jack and Robert entered the post office and placed a call to Doug Young.

"Good morning, Doug, this is Robert Hamilton calling from San Blas Island. I think we have the man we were looking for."

"Robert I am very glad you called. I was talking with James Rothman, the chief Art Dealers enforcement agent in charge of the case, I'll put him on."

Rothman assured Robert that DEA would provide them full assistance.

Robert and Jack rented an old Toyota pick-up truck with a mobile telephone, and bought two *campesino* straw hats, white

T-shirts and blue jeans, drove to the hotel and parked near the entrance, and waited until Pablo Martinez came out and got into the green Cadillac.

They followed the green Cadillac through the streets of the small Indian town, and twenty minutes later were driving on an open road surrounded on one side by the blue waters of the Caribbean and on the other by the Las Cercanias coastal ridge. The Cadillac turned into a deserted unpaved road where the shadows of huge trees created a dusk-like dimness.

Robert stopped the car and they waited for ten minutes before continuing down the road. Then, through the trees, they could see the green Cadillac parked in front of a path.

"Let's go back a quarter of a mile and park the truck, then walk back here," Jack suggested.

Soon they were following a path that had been heavily traveled. After a few dozen yards, the path became a raised walkway constructed of sheets of marine plywood, two-by-fours and hefty posts. A dozen fuel barrels were hidden just beyond the ravine. The builders had taken advantage of the natural setting to achieve almost total concealment.

From the air, nothing of the landing strip was visible until the plane was directly overhead. Even then, it could easily have been taken for a field cleared by an Indian farmer.

Robert and Jack approached cautiously. They could see men with rifles slung over their shoulders loading a plane.

"Robert, we must inform Rothman." When they were several hundred yards away Robert pulled out his mobile and called the DEA office at the US Embassy. "Mr. Rothman, we need your help immediately! We found the air strip and they are loading the plane."

"Our men are already their way to San Blas. Can you describe the location of the airstrip? It is important for one of you to stay near the airstrip with your mobile open, and the other one to come back to town and guide the PDF."

"I'll stay here and Jack will return to town," Robert decided.

He waited impatiently at the airstrip. Three hours passed but it felt more like three years.

At both sides of the barely visible landing strip, the upper canopy of broadleaf evergreens stood like giant walls; shorter trees formed a second canopy fifty feet above the ground. Between the two layers was an incredibly luxuriant rain forest with ferns, bromeliads and mosses whose roots never touched the ground, but drew moisture and nutrients from the air and from the contact with the trees. Most of the fauna—snakes, monkeys and birds of a thousand varieties—lived a high-rise existence in the trees, indifferent to intruders. Animal screams, clacks and thumps mingled with insects and human voices in the background.

Robert felt helpless irritation as the men, finished loading and secured the cargo doors. He looked frantically down the road; no truck, no cars, no sirens. His hands bunched into fists, impotent fury burning in his gut. All his instincts told him the *Material Medicinal* might be on that plane, and he was about to lose it, after all they had done, all the work, the hopes, Ann's kidnapping, his abduction, all of it would be in vain if that plane took off. But there was nothing he could do to stop it. All he could do was pray.

With tears in his eyes, Robert bowed his head and prayed.

Armando Azuero climbed into the cockpit of a Merlin III 8-seat, twin-turboprop executive aircraft and buckled his seat belt, nodded down at the men on the wheel chocks. He saw them yank at the ropes, and felt the wheels go free as he pulled the throttle. The plane began to taxi towards the other end of the airstrip, but the ground was so soggy that he was hardly moving.

"I think we are overloaded," grunted Azuero.

"It feels more like a truck than a plane," Mark Salmi agreed.

"Should we unload some of the boxes?" Chavez asked nervously.

"And you will explain it to Pablo? Forget it," Armando snickered.

"We'll be flying quite low; we should expect a lot of turbulence and ground effect until we hit the Caribbean. But the weather system should pass by mid-day."

"We're increasing speed. It's too late to abort."

Chaves, Salmi and Leeman exchanged apprehensive glances. No one spoke.

Plowing through the mud, concentrating on the runway, holding the wheels down hard until the right moment for taking off, Armando bumped along the muddy dirt runway, pulled the stick back and waited — while the heavy plane lifted up in the air. Finally, the wheels became light and the tail came up, and they took off.

Now Armando pulled up sharply in a familiar maneuver to retract the landing gear; but the wheels failed to close into their wells against the pressure of the air.

Armando saw a tall tree coming ever so near. He had no time to think, almost no time to act. The wheels and the wingtip hit the tree, spewing wood fragments. The aileron and lower panel crumpled, as did the N strut. The propeller split and shattered in a thousand different directions.

"You clipped the tree!" Chavez screamed.

The plane lurched sideways. Armando fought the controls, and they began to lose altitude.

"I am going to land on a main road, get ready!" he cried.

They felt the tail go up and the wheels left the ground, but seconds later they were touching again. The plane splashed through a puddle of water, but skimmed the next one.

"The control wheel is not operating," Azuero cried. "The tree must have damaged the aileron. I can't steer it, I have no lateral control!"

"Look! Watch out! Military trucks!" Leeman screamed.

Azuero swerved abruptly to avoid a collision.

"We are going to hit that tree! Watch out! Watch out!"

The plane swerved wildly, missing the trucks but crashing into the forest. Armandos's chest belts broke, his head hit the instrument panel and broke through it. After the jarring sound of crumbled metal, the hissing of hot fuel, everything went silent.

Military men quickly got to the plane. They tried to free the four men from the wreck. Mark Salmi and Benny Leeman were dead. Armando Azuero had been badly hurt but was still alive and moaned as the military men dragged him through the window. Chavez, the copilot, was in good condition but in shock. The soldiers radioed for ambulances.

Jack Swanson swung out of the truck and ran toward the plane. "You must unload the cargo very carefully, as if it was dynamite," he said to a young officer.

"Yes, sir, we have instructions to take it to the American Embassy in Panama City," the officer responded.

"We must inspect at least one of the boxes here," Jack demanded.

The soldiers crouched at the cargo door. In less than half an hour the entire cargo was unloaded from the wreck and into armored trucks. They waited for instructions to inspect the cargo, before putting it into a military plane for transport to Panama.

Back in the middle of the forest, Robert looked at his watch, it was three o'clock and he had not received yet any communication from Jack or James Rothman He was about to walk out of the forest, when two men armed with rifles approached him.

"Who are you? What are you doing here?" asked one in Spanish.

I'm an American tourist, I got lost in the jungle. Can you help me find the way to my hotel?" Robert answered.

"Oh, sure. Gringo, you must be a CIA agent. Come with us, and don't make any wrong moves or today is going to be your last day in Panama. For that matter, the last day of your life."

Both men starting laughing.

"Do you understand what I'm saying, Gringo?"

There was a long pause, then Robert said: "Yes, Sir."

"Good. You go in front of us."

The three men walked in silence towards the camp. Robert walked in front of the two men across a courtyard.

Inside the main building, a young guard opened the door and they entered a narrow passage. On the right were two offices. On the left was a window overlooking the courtyard. They came to another door, this one made of thick steel. The guard unlocked it and ushered Robert through and locked the door.

The first thing Robert saw was four of the *Material Medicinal* barrels.

He heard the whirring helicopters and men began running out of the building.

The helicopters flew in an open V formation over the only hole in the otherwise unbroken canopy, a shaft three hundred feet deep where giant trees had been previously cut down by the Cartel to clear a landing strip on the jungle floor. Four Hueys dropped swiftly into the clearing. The soldiers, carrying M-16 assault rifles, ten in each chopper, leaped into the blowing debris and scrambled to establish a protective perimeter among the stumps lining the landing field. This was what their trainers had called a "hot LZ approach." However, this was not a training exercise; in sixty seconds they expected to be in a real firefight. The swift and abrupt attack took everyone by surprise.

Robert rushed to inspect the barrels but they were empty. He looked around in desperation. As he went around the storage room, one Panamanian soldier with an assault rifle cried, "Don't move or I shoot."

"I'm Robert Hamilton, I was waiting for you to rescue me."

"You follow me!" cried the soldier.

As they walked into the open, there was no sign of resistance or gunfire. Twenty-four men were taken into custody, including Ernest Pohlmann, Jaime Rodriguez and Pablo Martinez. Just past five o'clock, another helicopter landed in the now-crowded clearing. Several men in PDF officers' uniforms got out. With them was a civilian with an athletic stride and open manner. The chief art sleuth for the United States in Panama, James Rothman, the Dealer Enforcement Administration's agent-in-charge, ran an international anti-looted or smuggled art operation out of the US Embassy.

Robert walked towards the helicopter. "Sir, are you Mr. Rothman?" After Rothman nodded, Robert thanked him.

"We have good news for you. The treasure has been recovered. Your friend Jack Swanson is with us."

Just then, Swanson stepped out of the helicopter. "Robert, are you all right?"

"You almost came too late."

The PDF's special art crime unit and the DEA explored the camp. There were several buildings with roofs covered with corrugated zinc sheets. Wires strung on poles carried electricity to buildings, including a kitchen and mess hall and three sleeping cabins with hammocks. In the buildings were many cells containing sculptures, antiquities, the royal Tombs of Ur, gold jewelry, Persian, Greek, Roman, Incan, Chipcha and Aztecan art.

Robert and Jack were transported by helicopter to inspect the site where the plane crashed, and where the precious cargo had been found. They waited nervously until some of the wooden boxes were opened. Some of the bottles containing *Materia Medicinal* had been put into new boxes, but apparently were in good condition.

Robert and Jack agreed to let the cargo be flown to the American Embassy in Panama City—thankful and satisfied that they had recovered their precious treasure. Then they traveled by land in a military truck to Kora Inn for an overnight stay. The next morning they would fly to Panama City.

THE next morning, Doug Young, the high-ranking DEA officer, entered Robert's room, and tossed the day's newspapers on the bed. Robert saw his name in headlines on the front page.

Cargo plane with the Materia Medicinal, Recovered! Robert Hamilton and Jack Swanson guided the rescue operation.

The principal article gave a vivid description of the rescue operation. A sidebar detailed the scientific and medical significance of the discovery of the *Materia Medicinal.* It also speculated as to what country or organization should control this wealth of information for the benefit of all humanity.

"Mr. Hamilton, congratulations, you are now a celebrity," said Young with a broad smile.

Landing at Paitilla Airport late the same morning, Robert discovered what it was like to be an international celebrity. Newsmen mobbed the plane, all converging on the door of the craft. Cameras held overhead, strobes flashing, microphones thrust forward, the media crowded and jostled Robert and Jack, shouting questions and blinding them with their flashes. The American Ambassador shook Robert's hand and thanked him for his heroic efforts. Then he turned to Jack in appreciation. Embassy personnel guided him towards a bank of microphones. With Jack Swanson at his side, Robert held an impromptu press conference in the small passenger terminal.

"What does the discovery of the *San José* treasure mean to the world? Ladies and gentlemen of the press," Robert said, "first, I want to thank you for your interest." He explained the intent of the agreement with the Colombian government and the significance of the recovery of the *San José*'s treasure. "All artifacts of archaeological and historical value will remain in Colombia in a museum to be constructed in Cartagena.

"The Colombian government agrees with our desire to create an autonomous international organization, Earth Health Resources. HER will work closely with the World Health Organization to control and ensure the safety of the *Materia Medicinal*. In this way, all nations, including industrialized and developing countries, can benefit from the wealth of information, and can be sure that no one will monopolize it."

The crowd moved towards him, hands in the air; they waved and called his name. "Hamilton! Hamilton!" The flashes blinded him. How he longed to be back in the privacy of his hotel — or better yet, in Ann's arms.

A fax was waiting for him back at his hotel.

My Dearest Robert:

Sorry I missed your call. I was away in London and I was making last arrangements for my trip. Mother told me about your last adventure. I am so happy to know that you recovered the treasure and you are safe. I was not able to sleep last night thinking about you and how at last we will be together.

To my greatest surprise this morning, I found that the TV and radio here in England were carrying continuous bulletins about the rescuing of the Materia Medicinal. Your picture was in major newspapers. You are famous now, my dear. Like it or not. Am I not the luckiest girl in the world to be yours? Take care of yourself. I need you. Love and kisses,

Ann

Robert folded the fax and put it into his pocket. "Here," Jack said, handing him a paper. "Look at this Robert, opened the international edition of the Herald Tribune."

Colombia Seizes Ship with Millions of Dollars of Antiquities

BOGOTA, Colombia, July 20 (Reuters)

The Colombian Navy seized the Tiburón Negro, the ship accused of piracy for having stolen the Material Medicinal. The Tiburón Negro sailed off the Caribbean coast carrying more than a hundred million dollars' worth of antiquities, authorities reported today.

Navy officers boarded the vessel during heavy seas on Saturday and forced it to dock in Cartagena, where it was searched, a spokesman for the navy's Atlantic command in Cartagena told the radio network Radionet. "There is a significant quantity of art, I think the largest finding of stolen art in a century."

All the crewmembers were detained, three Germans, one Polish, seven Panamanians, two Ecuadorians, four Italians, three Lebanese, and one Croat.

The ship's registry was not clear, but the spokesman said the ship had been bound for Trinidad.

ANN looked out the window as the aircraft approached Cartagena Bay. The veil of clouds broke for a moment to reveal the walled city of Cartagena and the blue water of the Caribbean. Ann raised her handkerchief to her eyes and pressed it hard against her lids. The middle-aged woman seated next to her looked at her in concern. "Is anything wrong, Miss?"

"No, on the contrary, I am so happy."

"This is the captain speaking. We are approaching Rafael Nuñez International Airport. Welcome to Cartagena of the Indies. We wish you a pleasant stay in the city of castles, walls, balconies, sun and sea."

The plane landed smoothly. The roaring of the jet engines was mixed with the roaring in Ann's head. *Robert, please be here, please be here, please be here.* She crossed her fingers, opened a purse and extracted a small mirror. She looked at herself. "God, if Robert sees me in this condition!" She began to work hurriedly on her make-up. She put on a wide-brimmed hat. Around her, people rose and jostled one another as they gathered up their belongings.

A soft female voice with a Spanish accent said, "Good afternoon, Miss Leigh. Do you have your passport?"

"Yes, here it is." She handed it over.

"Please wait here."

Ann pressed her hands together to keep them from trembling. A few minutes later the uniformed attendant returned with Ann's passport. "Everything has been taken care of. Your suitcases will be sent directly to your hotel. Can you give me your baggage claim tickets so that you do not have to wait?"

"Oh yes. Here they are."

"Please follow me," the attendant said. "A Mr. Hamilton is waiting for you upstairs."

They saw each other at a distance. They ran toward each other with open arms, their embrace lasted minutes but was not long enough. Robert kissed Ann holding her tightly to him.

"Robert, promise me you won't ever leave me again."

"I promise, darling. You are the reason for my existence." She lay her head against his chest. A feeling of joy filled her. *No longer will my future await me. It is here.* They walked out of the airport hand in hand, too full for words.

On a bright sunny day, Robert and Ann stood in the bow of a thirty-foot boat, steaming down the Amazon River, marveling at the swamps and jungle on either bank. That night, listening to the weird noises in the blackness, Robert and Ann planned every detail of their wedding. In the safety of their hotel room, Ann poured out her enthusiasm and delight in a hastily scrawled letter to her parents.

Dear Mom and Dad,

Robert and I were floating down the most beautiful Amazon River. We spent the last two days visiting the jungle. The trees are full of monkeys and birds, big and small of all descriptions and colors. There are alligators on the banks. Every once in a while we saw a big turtle fast asleep on top of the water. But most interesting of all are the Indians. Today we also discussed our wedding. We set the date for August 29th. This will give us time to be ready and for you to come here. I am very much in love.

Please take care.

Love, Ann

When Robert and Ann returned to Cartagena, they wandered slowly through the old part of the city, going where they wished and taking in the balconies full of flowers, the huge grilled windows and tantalizing glimpses of inside courtyards. They discovered Bolivar Park with its fountains, old dungeons, and great stone walls.

One early afternoon, Jack Swanson was waiting for them at their hotel. He rubbed his hands together and said, "I was getting very worried, Robert. I've been waiting for you for a long time."

"Why? What for?"

Jack's eyes twinkled. "Today we are bringing up the hull of the *San José* and I didn't want you to miss it. This is the last rescue mission. Why don't you go to La Popa? From this hill, there is an exquisite view over almost all the city. To the north lies the Rafael Nuñez Airport, the hamlet called 'La Boquilla' and on the horizon, the peninsula of Punta Canoa and immediately below the hill lies Cartagena itself."

"Yes, we know the hill well; we have been there a few times, to talk with the Augustin priest at the convent. That is where we are getting married," said Ann.

"Excellent. From there, you can see far into the distance the lifting of the *San José*," said Jack.

"After they bring the *San José* ashore, we can have dinner together with the crew of the *Auguste Piccard* at the Club of Pescadores," Robert suggested.

"I look forward to that."

Late that afternoon Robert and Ann sat on a rock high above the Popa Hill. They watched the blazing sun set over the blue waters of the Caribbean.

"There is a theory that nothing in nature is ever lost," Robert told her. "Soon we will see the *San José*'s hull come to the surface. Cartagena is a city rich of legends and history. "From this rock, Isabel waited for Don Francisco almost three hundred years ago. Maybe every sound ever made, every word ever spoken, still exists somewhere in time and space and may one day be recalled. Perhaps one day we'll be able to travel back in time and listen to the voices of Don Francisco and Isabel."

"Look, far out to the horizon. I think the hull of the *San José* is finally coming home," said Ann.

In a cloud of piety and incense, amid a cacophony of bells from the parish churches, the *San José*'s hull was welcomed into Cartagena's harbor. The Archbishop of Cartagena raised his hands to bless the rescue. The welcome ceremonies came to a climax as the harbor resounded with the fire of three guns — a lucky number.

At nine o'clock, they entered the Club de Pescadores. All the crew of the *Auguste Piccard* submarine and its support vessel were on hand. So were Alzaro Castellano, the Governor of Cartagena, and many others. They celebrated long into the night. Ann and Robert left the club hand in hand and walked toward their hotel.

"I used to think every night before I fell asleep about what it would be like to be with you in Cartagena. I made so many plans. When I'm with you, Robert, I don't think of that at all. It doesn't matter, I don't have to do or plan anything, I just am." She raised her eyes anxiously to his face. "Do you understand that? That just being is enough?"

"I feel the same," Robert said quietly. "It's more than enough."

"It's beautiful here, Cartagena is beautiful. I love you, Robert," and with the quick shy gestures he loved, she turned her face and buried it against his shoulder. Robert held her gently and pressed his lips against her hair.

"My darling, with you at my side I don't need anything else."

ON a sunny tropical windy morning, Karl Schneider finished climbing the last steps leading to the convent, on top of Popa Hill. He could hear the sounds of Pedro Claver Church's bells, as he approached the convent. Church ushers appeared at the doorway. Quickly the guests entered one by one and proceeded down the aisle to their pews. When all were seated, the wedding march began, and Mr. Leigh, recuperating from nine hours jet lag, went to collect his jubilant daughter. Ann, magnificent in white satin and trailed by many yards of tulle, walked down the aisle on her father's arm. From time to time she would stop to pull up her train with her gloved hands. Under the eyes of fifty guests, Mr. Leigh delivered his daughter over to her tall handsome historian-adventurer, while Ann's mother wept softly in the background.

At the altar, among the grandeur of the three-hundred-year-old Spanish church, the Franciscan Father Pedro from Seville bid welcome in English, German and Spanish to the international congregation. A traditional *misa de matrimonio* was celebrated among candelabra and beautiful tropical flowers.

"Dear Friends, we are gathered here today to witness and to celebrate the bringing together of two separate lives. We have come from many parts of the world to witness Robert and Ann joining together in the sacrament of matrimony. It is not to be entered lightly, but with certainty, mutual respect, and a sense of reverence, which does not preclude beauty, humor and joy.

"Love can be the highest experience that comes to humankind. At its best, it reduces our selfishness, deepens our personalities and makes life far more meaningful."

"Will you now please clasp your right hands?" Father Pedro turned to Robert. "Do you, Robert Edward Hamilton, take Ann Vanessa Leigh to be your lawful wife, to love and to cherish, to honor and to comfort, in sorrow or in joy, in sickness and in health, to have and to hold from this day forth?"

Robert responded, "I do."

Then Father Pedro turned to the bride. "Do you, Ann Vanessa Leigh, take Robert Edward Hamilton to be your lawful husband, to love and to cherish, to honor and comfort, in sorrow or in joy, in sickness and in health, to have and to hold from this day forth?"

"I do," Ann replied.

Accompanied during the signing of the registry by Bach's "Magnificat" and then Verdi' s "Ave Maria," Father Pedro's formalities concluded with, *"Por favor abracense . . ."* which received a spontaneous round of applause.

Outside, the crowd renewed their affectionate cheers. A few minutes before noon, Robert and Ann walked down the aisle, man and wife.

"She looks so radiant," said Sir Ronald Harris's wife.

"I think Robert is a very lucky man to have gotten such a lovely and charming wife," Ed Molloy said to his wife and to Jack Sanger, who had just arrived from the South Pacific.

"I must say, I never saw two people more in love or happier than they are," commented Karl Schneider to Christoph Beck.

At four o'clock the Leigh's family greeted the last of the guests on the receiving line. Mr. and Mrs. Mustafa Koprulu from Berlin. Then everyone gathered at the plaza overlooking Cartagena Bay, for a portrait session with the photographer.

Baron Von Bülow approached Jack Swanson, who was talking with Commandant Alzaro Castellano "This is a beautiful setting for a wedding."

"The Augustine priests built this cloister here on the summit of the hill at the beginning of the seventeenth century, and called it, 'The Convent of Our Lady of the Candelaria.' Afterwards it became the site of many battles and was used both as a barracks and as a fort. The building was then abandoned for a long time, to be restored by the same order of Augustine monks."

As the candelabras were lit in the darkening dining rooms, casting their arc lights on the array of wineglasses on the tables, and up through their flowery vases to create magic on the ceiling, another more intimate drama began. Gypsy violinists from Ronda, Andalucia played from the back, as the wedding party swept down to dinner, two by two in formality, to set in motion a long, noisy feast. The violinists then circulated between rooms of the old convent, playing Manuel De Falla's melodies. An unabashed romanticism spilled out through the cloisters.

Near the baptistry were bottles of wine, Champagne, canters of brandy. Sweet bottled cider frothed around the tables, and all the glasses had been filled to the brim. Beforehand, Guillermo Olano's sister had been entrusted with the tarts, sweets and a cream cake that trembled with the least shake of the table. On their smooth surface was a representation of the *galléon San José* and the initials of the newly wedded pair in old Spanish characters, with Cupid balancing himself in a chocolate swing, whose two uprights ended in real roses.

They partied well into the night. When some of them were too tired of sitting, they went out for a stroll on the terrace overlooking the Bay of Cartagena. But with Colombian coffee, everyone woke up and began singing. The guests seemed reluctant for the evening to end. Mr. Leigh danced many times with his wife and daughter. Robert danced many times with Ann. Hans Vogel, Otto Bar, Michael Harley, Anthony Hunt and John Reed settled on cushions against the stairs to watch the show, drinking wine.

Guillermo Olano commented to Padre Pedro: "It was so wonderful of Mr. Hamilton to cover all the traveling expenses for some of his guests."

"My son, he is very generous indeed. He is going to donate some money to our convent. As you know he is now a very wealthy man."

Late in the day, Christoph Beck returned from his rented car armed with an array of videos and photographic cameras to record the event, until everybody left.

As the sun went down, light rays projected dramatically against the buildings, and when the crescent moon rose in the sky, it found a place directly above the convent entrance, making a magical scene high above the Popa Hill.

The next morning, while Robert was still asleep, Ann left a note on the breakfast table and went to the market to buy fresh fruits.

My Dearest,

Never did I believe there could be such utter happiness in this world, such a feeling of togetherness and wholeness between two human beings.

What I mean by wholeness is being completely integrated, without any sense of being separated, fragmented, or limited. It means experiencing, like last night, real joy together.

When we both closed our eyes, I felt the perfect silence. Without silence, there cannot be any real appreciation of life, which is as delicate in its inner fabric as a closed rosebud.

When I tell you "I love you," you may catch the feeling, but the pure essence cannot be spoken.

Love is more than an emotion. It is a force of nature and therefore must contain truth.

It was indeed thrilling to wake up this morning and realize that what happened last night was not a dream but the reality of a lucky girl.

I will return shortly.

I love you.

Ann

As he finished reading the note, Robert saw Ann coming back with a bunch of roses in her hand. He walked towards her and took her in his arms and kissed her for a long time.

"You are my happiness, my love! You are my everything."

A few minutes later he looked at her with an expectant expression. "I just received a fax from the United Nations. They are inviting me to head up the new agency in Geneva. Would you like to come with me to Geneva after our honeymoon?"

"With you, Robert, I will go to the end of the world."

"I am afraid that if I accept the position in Geneva, we will never go to the end of the world," said Robert.

She turned to him. "Well, then, this is our plan, our first son will circle the globe: Robert, Junior, who will continue your dream of making dozens of expeditions to the remotest regions of the upper Amazons, befriend the local Indians and slowly learn the secrets of their vast medical lore."

She laughed, delighted.

Luis T. Castillo was born in Colombia from a family of politicians, journalists and writers. After graduating from McGill University with an engineering degree he moved to the United States, where he made his permanent home.

He is the president and founder of International Technologies Corporation, and was responsible for the engineering of many prestigious projects such as the Lincoln Center in New York, Pompidou Center in Paris, Lloyds Headquarters in London, L' Enfant Plaza in Washington.

The novel Echoes of Time was inspired while he was doing research at the Archive of Indies in Seville, Spain, on the San José, a Spanish galleon that was sunk by British warships in 1708. It was part of his effort to assemble a team with a unique combination of expertise in both the historical and technical aspects of underwater salvage, for the actual sub-sea recovery of galleons.

He has traveled and worked in four continents. He lives with his family in Seattle Washington and New York where he works and writes.

www.echoesoftimebook.com